D0955496

ALL THE WESTERN STARS

PHILIP LEE WILLIAMS

PEACHTREE PUBLISHERS, LTD.

Published by
Peachtree Publishers, Ltd.
494 Armour Circle, NE
Atlanta, Georgia 30324

Manufactured in the United States of America

10 9 8 7 6 5 4 3 2 1

Design and illustration by Paulette L. Lambert

Library of Congress Catalog Card Number 88-60001

ISBN 0-934601-47-X

This book is for

Ruth and Marshall W. Williams

The best

Old age hath yet his honor and his toil.
Death closes all; but something ere the end,
Some work of noble note, may yet be done,
Not unbecoming men that strove with Gods.
The lights begin to twinkle from the rocks;
The long day wanes; the slow moon climbs; the deep
Moans round with many voices. Come, my friends.
'T is not too late to seek a newer world.
Push off, and sitting well in order smite
The sounding furrows; for my purpose holds
To sail beyond the sunset, and the baths
Of all the western stars, until I die.

— "Ulysses," Alfred, Lord Tennyson

PART I

I DON'T RECKON LUCAS will mind me telling about us, at least he never told me not to. Sometimes now when I wake up early and look out of the house and see that prairie stretching out brown and blowing, I can't believe how I managed to end up here. But it's a peaceful satisfaction. I'll walk down to the creek there where Lucas used to come to hide and I can almost see him coming up through the morning fog.

Lucas would talk all the time about how we're in this ruined world for no reason. I never did believe that, but then I never did much thinking before I met Lucas and by then I was seventy-three years old. I never met a man who could go from plumb giddy to sulky as a child in such a short time. But I've had my own faults pointed out to me a few times, and I've always tried to reserve judging others as long as I wasn't a pearl either. So far, I'm not getting to be much better of a person, but you can always hope.

That was two years ago now I first met Lucas Kraft. Of course, I'd never heard of him and never read any of his books. I think the only poem I'd ever read then was something about a girl from Nantucket, but you picked up that sort of thing when you wandered around much as I did.

I didn't think I was getting feeble, but by comparison with what I used to be, I reckon it seemed that way to my niece, Belle. She's a nice girl but doesn't have a lick of feeling for anybody that might cost her and that boy husband of hers any money. My house was getting a spell run down and we were standing on the back porch looking out over the woods and the meadow when she told me she'd got a place for me in Fieldstone.

"It's a really good place for you, Uncle Jake," she said. "And I had to pay good money to get you a place. They had an old lady from Eatonton ahead of you and I bribed the director into letting me get you in first."

"I ain't going," I said, with what I thought was enough spit to end it right there, but it turned out she was more stubborn than I was. And I was sick. I knew I was sick but that cross-eyed doctor I always went to kept telling me it was only my nerves, and I said, hell, my nerves never failed me yet. I started telling him about the time I worked steel and stood up on top of the Allied Consolidated building in Chicago, but he needed that fifteen bucks from his next patient too bad to listen to me. I hear he wound up an alcoholic at home babbling and shaking, and I'm sorry for his family, but I can't summon up much pity for him.

Anyway, in the middle of arguing with my niece, I passed out. Just slap fell out on the porch like I was going to sleep, and that was just what she needed to convince me she was right. A few days later, in a moment of weak-

4

ness, I allowed her to shove some paper in front of me and I signed it and didn't find out till later I'd given her power of attorney. Not one month later she sold my house to a developer who wanted to build retirement condominiums. Lucas later explained to me the meaning of that word "irony," and I had to admit this situation seemed full of it.

Like I say, I was sick, and the day they came to take me away, Belle and her husband, I had been up since dawn looking out over the pasture and wondering if I'd ever see it again. I'd built the house with my own hands thirty years before, back when I could work any man into the ground, back when Betty and me had just got married and spent all night huddled up beneath the sheets giggling like children and touching one another in all the good-feeling places God put on a body.

Well, she'd left me about six years after that and run off with a taxidermist from Monroe who had made a lot of money after deer season. I followed them around for a while, since I once spent two years working for an insurance company in New Jersey doing the same kind of work, but when I caught up with them, the taxidermist was scared I was going to kill him and Betty was clinging to him like she'd been sewed to his body, and I felt sick inside and went off by myself like a wounded old bear and got stupid drunk for a couple of days and found I was over her.

But that day Belle came for me, I still loved that house and I remembered what Betty looked like the day I'd finished it. The wind was blowing and her hair kept coming up in her face, and when she'd push it back there was a smile on her face that wouldn't go away. I don't reckon I've ever made anybody as happy as I did that one day, and it was worth every busted finger and cuss word I gave the place while it was going up. It wasn't much of a house, but ever since Betty had left, I'd come to fit it like a foot fits an old boot. I figured Belle and her boy husband would store all my gear, but damn if they didn't sell it off, too, just like I was already dead and that stuff didn't mean much to me.

It meant more to me than I want to remember now. I told Lucas one time about an old hand mirror that I'd inherited from my mama that I'd lost there, and he wrote a poem about it. I didn't understand it until he explained it, but then it made me feel like weeping a little, though I didn't do it.

Anyway, I was standing there when I heard their car come up, this ugly little foreign car that looked like a rolling outhouse turned on end. I knew I might never see the place again and as I was standing there, a hawk came swooping down from somewhere and went flying across the field, claws down like a plane about to make a landing, but then it just touched the ground, like it was making sure it was still there, then it went up into the rising sun and flew off. When Lucas and I met up with Old Buffalo out in Texas, the Indian told me that it was what's called an omen, and now I can see that, but then it just struck me as being something right pretty.

"You ready, Uncle Jake?" Belle asked. I'll have to admit that even though she was my sister's girl, Belle looked like a bored horse, with a jaw long as a sack of grain. I was still sick then (they didn't find out what was wrong with me until later), so I just nodded and got my grip, in which I'd snuck a quart of liquor and went on out the door. Her husband drove like he couldn't figure out which pedals made the car stop and go, and more than once I thought I was going to meet my maker on the way over to Fieldstone. Belle yelled at him the whole time, and he looked so miserable I guessed it was best not to make him feel any worse than he already did by telling him he couldn't drive worth a shit. Anyway, I reckon he knew it.

The town I lived in was called Branton, a nice little stop in the road in north central Georgia, which reminded me so much of my home town in Mississippi that I'd just stopped the car and settled down there years before. My being there was the reason Belle and her husband had moved to the country, them being hippies in the early seventies and me being agreeable about letting them live on a piece of the land I'd been buying. In those days, they lived in a tent and ate nuts and berries and I didn't mind if they did, though some of my neighbors told me they were Reds, but I don't think either one of them had ever read past Classic Comics.

Branton was a clean little town with wide streets and plenty of dogwoods and old water oaks, the kind of things that make you say this is a place that will last. That was what I was looking for when I came off the road, I reckon, a place that would last since hardly anything in my life had lasted for more than a few months. I picked up work here and there.

That day, though, as Belle's husband drove me through Branton, it looked like any of those places I'd passed through for a day or two when I was a boy, nothing special anymore, and I was amazed that I'd thought anything could last even as long as I had.

Fieldstone wasn't a new place. It was a long, flat brick building on the outskirts of town that looked out over a pasture that reminded me of a cemetery without any gravestones. Belle parked in front on a circular driveway and a big colored fellow came pushing a wheelchair out. I got out and looked real mean at him and ambled up to the doors, and damned if they didn't flap out like the wings of a vulture and nearly knock me on my ass.

"Is this your idea of a joke?" I shouted. I realized by the way the colored man reacted that I was acting like a crazy old man, which was what they figured I was anyway. Well, to hell with it, I thought. I went on inside with Belle on my arm while her husband was trying to park the car without destroying anything. There was a small check-in station and the place smelled like alcohol and school cafeteria food. While Belle was filling something out, I shuffled into a big room to the left and it was full of folks with at least one foot in the grave, some of them all but laid out with daisies in their hands.

I stood there for a minute trying to figure it all out. Four or five men and women were watching television, some game show, but their mouths were hanging open and I wondered if they ever caught flies that way, horrible as it sounds now. It seemed funny to me at the time. I was thinking about dead people and the smell of the place when I realized a tiny little fellow was standing at my left elbow.

"Who are you?" he asked. I'm six-two, least I was when I was a man, and he looked like something from *The Wizard of Oz*.

"Jake Baker," I said. "Who are you?"

He said, "Comer Bird, Jr."

"Comer Bird, Jr.?" I said somewhat sourly. "Is your paw here, too?" He did something I didn't think he'd do: he cackled like a hen, and his laughter going across the room was about as useful as hubcaps on a tractor.

"Don't eat any of the food," he said, whispering like it was some kind of secret. His put his knobby fingers around my arm and sort of pulled me off to one side. His fingers felt like they had scales and I had the awful feel-

8

ing he was really a lizard. Women in white uniforms came wandering through, heading down the tiled halls, but I didn't see a one that appeared to enjoy being there any more than I did.

"How come?" I asked.

He said, "They put dog food and poison in it. They will try to kill you first thing. Don't eat anything but seeds. My daughter can bring you seeds." I never ate many seeds, but I figured if things ever got that bad, Belle and her husband, being former hippies, could advise me on which ones were good.

"Seeds," I said, trying to think of something to say.

"And don't let them give you a shot of any kind," he said. "They're drawing your blood out and putting it in the ones who die and making them come back to life." I've been around my share of fruitcakes and this guy, Comer, Jr., seemed like he came right out of the box. I gave him my "don't screw with me" look and got away from him.

I backed up a couple of steps and turned around, and a woman who looked about two hundred years old was standing there holding on to a walker and growling at me like a dog.

"How are you this morning?" I said. My daddy always made me be polite to people and often times now I'll do it without thinking, which surely must be making him happy wherever he is.

She growled at me again and bared her teeth, which were too ugly to be store-bought. Belle came and got me then, along with a tall man in a suit. His name was Mr. Denny, and he was the manager. He looked remarkable like a gravedigger I'd once known in Ohio, which was funny to me, so I laughed a little and they looked at me that way. The woman was still growling.

"That one got off her leash," I said.

"Let's not be unkind about others' infirmities," Mr. Denny said. His voice sounded like it was being poured out of an oil can and he worked his fingers together like he was trying to weave a rug out of them.

"Uncle Jake, please," said Belle. About that time, her husband came through the front doors, looking like a sheep heading for the slaughterhouse. "The people here will look after you and you will love it so much. All the people here are so happy they've come and it's a blessing for them all." I wanted to ask her about who was supposed to bless me, since she'd once tried to convince me somebody named Krishna was running things, but I just kept my mouth shut. Comer, Jr., stood up and started waltzing by himself and singing something I couldn't catch.

Being sick, I didn't want to do anything but lay down, so I just shrugged and one of those women wearing white clothes and squeaky shoes came and took me down the hall until we got to a room on the right, and there was my name beside the door on a little piece of paper, and when I saw it, I felt really defeated and down about everything.

Belle and her husband came and said a few things, but to this day I don't recollect what they were. There was another bed in the room and there was a man in it who looked like he'd died some time before. Belle finally left and I sat and looked out the window at the pasture, snuck out the bottle, had a few drinks and figured it was only a matter of time before I got the hell out of there.

I made the mistake of hiding my bottle under the mattress, which was the first place they looked for it when they changed the bed the next morning. I got a tongue-lashing by this hippo-faced nurse, and I just took it like a dumb beast in a storm.

10

Fieldstone is all one floor, which was mighty decent of them since half the people who lived there could barely walk anyway. I made my way down to the cafeteria for breakfast, and I was late on account of the tongue-lashing, and when I sat down, a tall skinny woman with a big nose was thanking the Lord for our food. It went on and on, so I said the hell with that and started eating the eggs, which tasted like they'd been beat up with alum before they were cooked.

The lady finally finished with the blessing and when the man next to me opened his eyes and saw I was already eating, he told me I was going to hell for eating during the blessing.

"The food'll probably be better in hell," I said. He made this little face with his lips, pursed them like a girl and started yelling for an orderly. I tried to shush him, but it wasn't any good. Once somebody's wounded, you can't stop the pain by asking them to remember their manners.

A colored man the size of a Volkswagen came over and stood over us and I felt small and stupid. The bacon wasn't much better.

"He's new and he started eating during the blessing," the man said. He was mad as hell and I couldn't figure out why.

"It's all right," the orderly said. He talked soothingly and said it again, "It's all right." The old man nodded as if he'd won some victory and I just shrugged. Then the orderly went away.

"I'm going to heaven when I die," the man said, looking up into the ceiling somewhere. I looked up there but I didn't see anything.

"Congratulations," I said. He didn't seem too pleased with that, so I just finished up and went into the recreation area where some old women were playing cards and Comer, Jr., was waltzing with himself. I sat down and looked at the magazines, which were old and all for women. The sun had come up good and the recreation room had a picture window that looked out over that pasture. I looked out there for a time while I listened to the women talk about how old they were. I didn't take a lick of comfort from being in the recreation room, so I went back to my bed to watch a little television.

My roommate, whose name was Robert Welsh, had not said word one to me, and when I got back to the room, I was reasonably sure he never would. He was laying on his back staring at the ceiling and I couldn't see his chest rising and falling at all. I figured I wasn't much of a doctor, so I turned on the TV and some stupid game show was on that I knew all the answers to.

After a while, I got up and walked over to Mr. Welsh's bed and looked at him up close. He was dead, no doubt about it, so I went back to my bed and rang the little buzzer attached to my bed and waited for the nurse to come. Nothing happened. I watched a woman on TV win a car because she knew the word "persimmon," which didn't strike me as much of a reason to give somebody a car. I rang again and waited ten minutes and nobody came. I did it one more time just to make sure they were ignoring me, and when they didn't come this time, I walked down toward the admitting station where the director, Mr. Denny, was talking to some rich man about putting his daddy in Fieldstone.

"You got a stiff down here in 4B," I said as loud as I could to make sure they heard me. Everything stopped, and I mean in the whole place. Mr. Denny looked at me like he wanted to strangle me, but I figured I'd given them fair warning with the buzzer and all.

12

"Would you return to your room?" Mr. Denny said about as happy as a stuck pig. "You should have rung for the nurse."

"I did that for about an hour," I said. "I guess the nurse is asleep or something." He looked so hurt that I just turned around and went back to the room, and damned if it still wasn't nearly twenty minutes before a nurse came in with a stethoscope dangling from her neck. Not that Mr. Robert Welsh cared a whole hell of a lot, being dead as he was.

"He's dead," I said. "Been dead for a good long while."

"I'll make the medical analysis," she said. She leaned down and put the stethoscope on Mr. Welsh's chest and listened for a few seconds and then pulled the sheet up over his face. She went away and I sat there for nearly forty minutes with a dead man and I wasn't sure but that I envied him.

It was later that day, after they finally took Mr. Welsh away, that I passed out again and landed on the floor so hard I busted my head.

It's funny, but I never once thought I was dying. The only time I remember thinking I was dying was when I got this scar on my stomach, but that was when I was just a kid and barely stronger than the guy who gave me the scar. I remember them carrying me out of Fieldstone, taking me to the hospital, but it was like I saw it through gauze. I remember the trees blowing with their bright green leaves and the sky high overhead, and I thought it might be a good day for fishing.

But then they put me in the ambulance. They seemed to be talking about something, but not in much of a hurry. Something was hissing. Then I went to sleep, and when I woke back up I was lying in a bed with a hose sticking in the back of my hand, which wasn't a thing to give you much confidence.

I looked to my left and the first thing I saw was the rear end of a nurse who was bending over to pick up a piece of paper she'd dropped, and for a minute I wondered if I'd died and gone to heaven. The room was almost suffocating hot, and so I stirred and pushed the covers back. She turned around, and I felt my heart flop over a couple of times in shock: she looked an awful lot like a girl I'd lived with for a year in New York City years ago.

"Son of a bitch," I said, which seemed like the right thing for me to say, but it struck her right odd.

"I beg your pardon?" she said.

"You look just like a woman I used to know," I said. It was then I realized my voice was something of a froggy croak. She smiled, but not like she wanted to jump in bed with me or anything, which was probably just as well since I'd not been to bed with a woman in years and wasn't sure I remembered what to do first.

"My goodness," she said. She smiled and I felt better about the fact that I was suddenly sleepy. She turned and went out of the room, and the last thing I saw before I went under was her rear end again, and I went to sleep and had me this wicked dream that made it unpleasant when I finally woke up later on.

What I had wrong with me was a vitamin deficiency and a couple of other minor things, nothing big. Belle and her husband came to see me once; well, Belle did, as her husband was trying to find a place to park the car. If he didn't park any better than he drove, he was probably inside a dumpster or something.

The nurse's name was Jessica and the day they released me to go back to Fieldstone, I reached up and grabbed her tit, figuring nobody was going to yell rape from a sick old man. She just took my hand off and gave me an indulgent look, like you do a kid, and I was mighty glad I'd had the thought to touch her.

A van from Fieldstone came and got me and brought me back over there after I'd declined an offer from Belle to have her husband pick me up. Already, the change I felt was amazing. I knew all along I wasn't feeble, just sick, and on the way back to Fieldstone, I had me this idea that I didn't belong there.

I was in the hospital three days, but when I got back, Mr. Robert Welsh's bed was still empty. A nurse came in once while I was watching that movie *Pork Chop Hill*, about Korea, which wasn't my war, but it was okay anyway. The nurses at Fieldstone all looked like they were finalists in the Miss Ugly Nursing Home Contest, and this one, Miss Fincher, was uglier than most. And mean to nearly everybody.

"Y'all usually let stiffs hang around as long as y'all did Mr. Robert Welsh?" I asked. She was putting fresh linen on the other bed, and she stood up and glared at me like she wanted to fight. "Oh . . . my heart . . ." Well, it was a lie. I felt fine, but when she came over close to me, ugly as she was, I reached up and grabbed her tit and she reacted a little different from the nurse at the hospital.

She slapped the everloving shit out of me. Before you could say a word, I had been hauled down to Mr. Denny's office, where he paced around with his hands behind his back. I know I was supposed to be sorry for what I did, but to be honest, I had this shit-eating grin on my face that I just couldn't get off.

"Jake, if you think you can do this kind of thing and stay here, you're wrong," he said. I started laughing. "I'm serious."

"All I done was grab her ugly old titty," I said, which sounded funny coming from an old man.

"Now look here," Mr. Denny said, but then damned if he didn't start laughing, too, and in a minute we were both laughing so hard we couldn't stop, and it felt so good I made up my mind to be as crazy as I could. He let me go after trying to warn me.

When I got back to my room, a man was sitting on Mr. Robert Welsh's bed. It was Lucas, of course, the first time I'd ever set eyes on him, and he was a sight. He looked sort of like a troll, all round and hairy, bald on top, but with hair sticking out all over the sides of his head. He had this big hard belly and little legs, and he was sitting like an Indian on the bed sipping a Diet Coke through a straw. He had already set up his bedside table with several books, and he seemed to be awful unhappy about being at Fieldstone.

"Good morning," I said. "You must be the new boy."

"Go to hell," he said, which I thought was not all that inappropriate. I started laughing again. "What in the hell are you laughing about? My God in heaven, I have been stuck with a senile maniac."

For a good while, things went downhill from there.

A WOMAN NAMED Miss Louise Adler lived there at Fieldstone like the rest of us, but she tried to run things. I just ignored her when she fussed about my table manners, but Lucas wouldn't put up with it. That first day, we were eating lunch, which was something like spaghetti, but it was cold and starchy as a new shirt. I tried not to let it bother me much because I had definitely decided I was getting the hell out of there sometime soon.

But I guess Lucas Kraft felt trapped, and I could sure understand that. You could see it in the eyes of them who felt like rats in a maze. Some were so old and sick they wouldn't of known if they'd been in the bomb bay of a B-17, but most of us were just slow from age and at the point where nobody wanted to fool with us any more, which wasn't a happy thought if you dwelled on it too often. Lots of them did.

Anyway, Miss Louise Adler was tall and tried to look like the daughter of a king, always wearing fake jewels

17

and a look of pure disgust for those of us below her, which included everybody but one other lady who also kept her nose in the air.

So we were eating our spaghetti that day at lunch and it was quiet like, except for the man, Comer Bird, Jr., the one who waltzed by himself all the time. Fred Astaire had nothing on Mr. Bird. He wasn't eating, just dancing by himself. And in the corner was this enormous colored woman named Bessie who was recounting her whole life out loud, something they told me she'd been doing for two years.

"This food tastes like shit!" Lucas yelled. He threw his fork down on the plate and curled his lip. The place fell into a powerful uproar. I hadn't said much to him since he'd told me to go to hell, and this sure didn't encourage me about being his roommate. The staff, which couldn't bear to watch us slobber and choke down the grub, wasn't in there, but Miss Louise Adler was, and she got up, all trembling with rage from her place at the end of the table, and trotted up to Lucas, who was sitting there scowling.

Lucas had one of the most remarkable faces I've ever seen, and I've seen my share, traveling around. His face was round, but not really fat, and he had these bushy eyebrows that looked like caterpillars stopped just above his eyes, which were of a bright blue, the kind you don't see all that often. His mouth seemed always to be working, and I learned later that he never stopped thinking. I didn't have any idea he was a writer or had published all kinds of things.

Miss Louise Adler stood over him, shaking like she was in the middle of an electrocution. I reckon that was the first time I felt a twinge of feeling for Lucas, though it didn't amount to much.

18

"We do not speak that way at Fieldstone," she said with a voice that dripped poison. "This is a community and we respect others here." Lucas looked up at her and I'll admit she was imposing, and I had the feeling she'd run things all her life. She was a widow and I had this picture in my head of her dead husband smiling in his coffin because he didn't have to put up with her any more. Lucas nodded a bit.

"Go to hell," he said.

She gasped like somebody had squeezed the breath out of her and I could have sworn I heard somebody giggle but I didn't see who it was. This time, all heads turned to see Mr. Denny standing in the doorway. I guess one of the kitchen help had heard and fetched him.

"Mr. Kraft, would you come with me, please?" he said. Miss Louise Adler got this look of triumph on her face that really got under my skin, and when Lucas sighed and got up and walked with Mr. Denny, I followed at a distance. Nobody said anything to me and I sort of lolled in the hall next to the office while Mr. Denny gave it to Lucas, who sat there like a dumb beast in a storm and took it. I found out later that Lucas had this strange idea about authority, something like fear and admiration all mixed up. I never could understand that because I always hated the guy in charge like it was part of my religion.

When Mr. Denny got through, Lucas came out looking like a lizard trying to slide under a rock, and I walked with him back toward our room.

"You were right about the food," I said after a spell.

"Oh, go to hell," he said. I was a foot taller than him and it would've been disgraceful to smack him, and besides he already had enough trouble. I remembered a time in my life when I'd of loved to get in a tumble with

19

somebody who told me to go to hell, but that was long ago and in another state.

We got to the room and he opened a bag and took out a book and read for a long time while I watched a soap opera, from which I got hardly any pleasure, but I didn't know what to do next.

It went like that for two, maybe three weeks. Lucas would insult somebody and get hauled to Mr. Denny's office so regular they could have written it in the schedule they hung on the bulletin board every Monday morning.

We argued, too. I remember one night he started screaming about being old, but hell, we were all old.

"There is no dignity in dying in this cattle market," he said, sitting on his bed and looking more sad than angry. "We should be able to die where we please, even if we need to lie down under a blanket of stars and stare God in the face while we leave. This place is fit only for death, and no place fit only for death should exist in this world."

"Then how come you're here?" I asked. Before that, he'd told me nothing about himself. He exhaled like a furnace and I was afraid he wouldn't inhale again, but he did.

"I've been exiled by my nephew who does not wish to be responsible for my actions," he said. "On a couple of occasions, I wandered afield from my house in Atlanta, where he also lives, and on that basis he is able, by the laws of this godforsaken land, to push me into this stable. It is demeaning and I will not have it."

"I feel that way," I said, and I told him about Belle and her boy husband for a good long time, and he seemed interested in me, not fighting or trying to goad me into yelling back. In three weeks, he had made enemies with about everyone there.

"Tell me about yourself," he said.

"Well, I was born out in Mississippi," I said. "My daddy was a machinist and Mama spent most of her time raising us kids. He was killed in a car wreck.

"After he died I was raised up by my mama, who made us read all the time, told us about the value of an education, wanted us all to go to college, and the others did, but I just sort of left on my own after high school. I traveled around. Went up to Iowa for a couple of years and worked in mills, having grown up in 'em, but it was too cold so I moved to Montgomery, Alabama, but I didn't like it there, either, so I went to New York City and New Jersey for seven years, I think it was, and then I went to Chicago. I liked it there and stayed right up until the War come."

"You were in the service?" he asked.

"Yeah, I joined the Army," I said. "I was with Patton's Third Army. Got me a little nick on the leg in the Bulge. That was one hell of a thing. Only place I never been I really wanted to go was out West. I've done all kind of odd jobs over the years, carpenter work, textile plants, pulpwood, whatever happened to come up. I been spending the last few years getting my Social Security and wasting it on liquor."

His eyes lit up and he sat in the chair that was between our beds.

"Could you get us a bottle?" he asked, excited as a kid at Christmas.

"I could try to bribe one of them colored orderlies," I said. "Belle's been giving me a little pocket money."

That's exactly what we did. That night this man, whose name was Odum, slipped me a quart of Old Grand Dad, which I thought was pretty funny and Lucas even chuckled, and I gave him twenty dollars, which was too much, but what the hell. Lucas hopped around and took the chair from between our beds and jammed it under the door handle so nobody could come in.

"Let's crack it," he said. One thing about a place like Fieldstone, everything's plastic. I got us these two plastic cups and poured the liquor out and we drank the first one without saying much. But on the second one, we both had these jackal grins on our faces so that if we'd died, our families would have thought we'd loved Fieldstone, which wasn't too happy of a thought.

"You tell me about yourself," I said. He nodded and laughed, but he didn't seem altogether pleased about it.

"I am a writer," he said grandly. "I have published seven books of poetry, five novels and more than seventy essays. I was born in Atlanta and I suppose I shall die here. I made more than half a million dollars and lost most of it gambling and hanging around with lewd women. For some years I was a professor of literature at Chapel Hill and now, in the twilight of my years, I have been exiled to this dump against my will."

"You writing a book now?" I asked. "I don't see how you wrote all them books in the first place."

"Oh, it was easy," he said. He finished the second drink and poured a third and I joined him, feeling better all the time. "I had a lot to say back then, years ago. I thought the world was a good place, that man could survive and overcome all the horrors he had heaped upon himself because, more than anything, he had the capacity to love. Now I see that I was hopelessly wrong. The world is a desperate ball of ashes and dust and soon we will obliterate the whole thing, and all evidence that we were once civilized will be gone with it."

"That don't sound too good," I said stupidly, not really knowing how to react.

"Anyway, I woke up one day and said, No more writing," he said. "And I have stuck to that resolve."

"Ever been married?" I asked.

"Jesus Christ," he said. "Why did you have to bring that up. Yeah, I was married once, many years ago, to Sally Crandall."

"The movie actress?"

"Yeah."

"I'll be damn. I bet that was something. What was she like?"

"I don't want to talk about it." He was looking down into his drink and I knew I'd hit a nerve, and I sure understood that, because some of my worst problems came from women, although being old I missed them right smart.

"It's okay," I said.

"You don't have any idea."

"I reckon I don't," I said.

After that, we went silent for a while, so we kept drinking and I turned on the TV and we watched *Stagecoach* with John Wayne, which is one of my favorite movies. Turned out old Lucas was a fan of Westerns, too.

"Look at the land there," Lucas said dreamily. I'd turned the lights out, which was the way I liked to watch TV. I don't know how, but my eyesight had stayed fine all these years. I know it wasn't from clean living so I figured it must have been luck. I believe in luck, always have, and up until Belle had put me in Fieldstone I'd had my share of the good times. "It's like the inside of your dreams. It's the place where John Wayne and Tom Mix and William S. Hart all live, and they all still live there on the screen. I bet there's a place out there on the Plains where you can come over a hill and the sun is setting and they're all in camp, all those great cowboys. And they'll ask you to sit down and have a drink at the campfire. And they'll all be alive again."

"Sounds like you been out West," I said.

"Never have," he said.

"It's funny, but I never have, either." I had to fly to the West Coast one time to get a friend out of jail, but other than that, I never been in cowboy country.

Lucas said, "Now neither one of us will ever find out what it's like."

I had a powerful urge to sleep and Lucas went on talking for a time, but I don't remember about what, and when I roused myself again, some talk show was on and Lucas wasn't in his bed. I sat up and saw that the bottle was tipped over on the floor, but none was spilled and I had to figure most of the Old Grand Dad had gone into poor old Lucas.

I was thinking about going to look for him when I heard a scream from down the hall, a scream like something from an old scary movie, so I came out into the hall, none too steady from the liquor, and there was the scream again. Suddenly the hall was full of people; residents and a colored orderly came alongside me. We went into the room where the scream came from, me and the orderly, and Lucas was standing on the end of the bed of Miss Louise Adler, his hands up by his hips, yelling, "Draw!" over and over. She was huddled under the covers, jerking around and sort of whimpering, and Lucas had his head turned, one eye trying to stare her down. The lady in the other bed, a woman named Mary, had this stupid sort of grin on her face. I always thought the sight of a woman in bed was a good thing, but these two looked like something left over for display in a taxidermy shop.

24

"Draw!" screamed Lucas. He drew a couple of times, yelled "Bang! Bang!" at Miss Louise Adler and was just starting his routine again when the orderly grabbed him by the legs and he fell over, passed out, like a sack of feed. Miss Louise screamed once more for effect. The other lady was sort of chuckling low.

"Where does he go?" the orderly asked. He was new to the job, I reckon. I realized then that I was right drunk, too, but I managed to get us back to the room and the orderly laid Lucas out like a corpse, took off his clothes, and folded his hands on his stomach. He snored like an old hog.

"You all know better than this," the orderly said, picking up the bottle and looking at the label. I didn't have the heart to tell him another orderly had brought it to me.

"It was my birthday," I said suddenly. Well, that was a lie they could figure out easy enough, since they had all my records. At that time, it was April, and my birthday was in September, but it was good enough to get him out of the room for the night, and it wasn't until the next morning that Mr. Denny hauled us into his office.

I remember it was raining that day, dark and mean looking outside, and that was how I felt, my head hurting, but it was comforting somehow to have a hangover, since it meant I was still a man. If I had a big head, Lucas was in desperate bad trouble. He looked green and had felt so bad he didn't shave, and he had a heavy beard, so he looked like shit, to be honest.

"What am I going to do with you two?" Mr. Denny asked. His office was bigger than our room and the carpet was so deep if you dropped a quarter you'd never find it again. On one wall was a huge picture of a woman I'd been told was his mother, who owned the place and came by occasionally to show him who was still in charge. I'd never seen her yet. On his desk was a little plaque that said "Have a nice day," but I knew he didn't mean it that morning.

"Why don't you make us stay after school and bang the chalk dust out of the erasers," Lucas said sourly. Mr. Denny shook his head.

"Mr. Kraft, when we found out you were coming here," he said, "it was a red-letter day for me. I have read all your novels and think you are one of the finest writers in America."

"Hah," said Lucas. "You got any Valiums?"

Mr. Denny rolled his eyes up like he was trying to be patient with a feisty child, and I reckon I understood that. "Mr. Kraft, you frightened Miss Louise Adler half to death. Fortunately she doesn't have any relatives who can demand that you be thrown out."

"Shit," said Lucas, snapping his fingers.

"He don't mean it," I said.

"Go to hell," he said, which wasn't the first time I'd heard it.

"Please, please," said Mr. Denny. "I don't know how that bottle got in here, but if there is a repeat of this incident, you may face the most severe consequences. Fieldstone has a reputation to uphold."

"Fieldstone is a brothel," said Lucas grandly, "and the whore is death." I thought that was a pretty good statement, but Mr. Denny went absolutely crazy and started screaming and waving his arms, and that's when the awe of those in power finally came out in Lucas and he crumbled like an old cracker, apologized and went out of the office with small round shoulders. We went on to breakfast.

Lucas and I ate by ourselves at the end of one table in the dining room. That wasn't too hard since everybody got out of our way like the parting of the Red Sea. Miss Louise Adler sat all the way on the other end of the room with a couple of other old biddies who sometimes glanced down at us and looked like they'd just as soon strangle us.

The food was cold and awful. Lucas pushed his from one side of the plate to another and looked out the big window at the cold rain.

"John Wayne wouldn't put up with this crap," he said sadly.

"He's dead," I reminded him, but he looked at me real mean so I didn't push it.

"You know what I mean," he said. "He wouldn't get trapped in here with a bunch of crazy old ladies." He was talking kind of loud and I tried to shush him, but it didn't do much good. He was like a little boy who was used to having his way, used to having somebody take care of him while he pretended to be in charge. "I don't care who hears me. I'm tired of living here in the midst of this pestilence with the WHORE OF DEATH LINGER- ING . . ."

He was yelling and the women and a few of the men were starting to get up, making angry motions toward Lucas, so I grabbed him up by his chubby arm and dragged him back to the room before they lynched him.

"You've got to learn how to act right," I yelled at him. "You can't come in here and start treating everybody like shit. They don't like being old no more than you do."

He laid down on his bed and said, "I'm so miserable."

I don't know whether he meant from being old or from the hangover, and before I could ask him, he was snoring, dead asleep.

27

A few days later, we watched *Jeremiah Johnson*, one hell of a fine movie about a mountain man and how he came to live on his own terms with the wilderness. When it was over, Lucas, who'd hardly been out of the room, was crying like a baby and I sat next to his bed for a spell until he calmed down.

"It's awful," he said. "How terrible never to be able to live that way anymore. Even you traveled around during your life. I was always inside some cocoon, never able to feel anything outside of it but myself. I have never been able to leave my own mind in this armpit of a country."

"Hell, let's just leave," I suggested. He smiled real bitterly and stared at the wall. "I'm serious." And for the first time, I guess I was. I'd been feeling better and better, almost like my old self, and Lucas looked okay.

"We can't just leave," he said. I thought he was going to cry again. "You can't just disappear that way. There must be some connection."

"Shit," I said. "Let's us go out West and be cowboys." He laughed like a crazy man and I laughed too, so I reckon I knew what that made me. We didn't talk about it the rest of that day or the next, but three days later, Lucas and I were sitting outside on the patio when he brought it up again.

The sun was shining and it was warm and we could see down across the field behind the home that construction was going on. The world was creeping closer.

"If we just left, where would we go?" he asked.

"I got a car and some money," I said. "We'll go get my car and then just light out for Texas. I'd rather do that than hang around here."

"And I'd rather die unwept on the wind-swept plains than rot in this hot house of darkness," he said with some feeling. I don't know what it was, but that sentence made

28

the hair rise up along my arms and for the first time I thought I really liked Lucas.

"Let's get the hell out of here, then," I said.

"When?"

"Why don't we get a few things from here and then go in a couple of days?"

"What do you mean get a few things?"

"You know, vitamins, medicine, some things like that."

"Steal them?"

"Yeah.

"Okay." He grinned and clapped his hands and we set about becoming conspirators. That night, after everybody else was asleep, we stuffed a towel under the door and drew up a plan.

The next night, I went down to the nurses' station where the orderly was hanging out with the night duty nurse and proceeded to talk to them about baseball, lying that I had once played for the New York Yankees and batted behind Lou Gehrig for two years, and they believed it, the fools. When I got back, Lucas had performed like a cat burglar, rounding up twelve bottles of pills, penicillin tablets, vitamins and such.

I knew a way to cut across a field to a road and then to another one to get to my house, and I drew out the route we would take the following night. Lucas slept like a corpse that evening and I did, too.

The next day we were eating lunch when Miss Louise Adler sat down in her usual place.

"Watch this," said Lucas, nodding toward her. She was wearing her hair up in a beehive and looked even meaner than usual. She picked up a salt shaker, turned it over and the top came off and the whole contents went on her food. Her jaw fell open like a trap door and she immediately looked at Lucas who was, I swear to God, winking at her and carrying on like you would with a girl in grade school.

She narrowed her eyes, then picked up the pepper and damned if the same thing didn't happen. She was talking out loud, mad as hell, when the leg on her chair gave out and she went splat on her big rear end on the floor. Lucas and I laughed so hard I nearly got sick, but by the time Miss Louise Adler got up, she was screaming mad.

"I will have you thrown out for this!" she yelled, pointing at Lucas.

"I'm innocent, ma'am," Lucas said, trying not to giggle. "You've suffered a misfortune, that's all."

"I'll have these bottles fingerprinted!" she screamed.

"I protest my innocence," said Lucas.

She said, "You are a bastard," and threw the salt shaker clear across the room toward us, but she was an awful shot and instead it broke out a window. She looked up to see Mr. Denny standing there with his hand on his forehead, shaking his head.

He said, "Miss Louise, come with me," and he got her by the arm and took her away while Lucas and I tried not to laugh. Comer Bird, Jr., got up from his chair and waltzed around the room a while.

There were a lot of mumblings, and about half an hour later Mr. Denny came and got Lucas, but they couldn't prove he'd done anything, and he denied it all. I never did find out how he got in the dining room to set that poor lady up. It seems childish to think on it now, but she was such a self-righteous old biddy I don't doubt the experience was instructive to her.

We waited until after midnight to leave. Fieldstone wasn't really like a prison, but the old folks couldn't just walk out the front door. They'd figure you'd gone senile and they'd grab you, lock you in your room and keep a close eye. But anybody agile enough could climb out the window and get away.

I'd filched a flashlight from the storage room, and I opened the window and punched out the screen as softly as I could manage. Turned out the evening was warm, a full moon bathing Branton, so we could see almost without the flashlight.

"I'll get out first," I whispered. I'll have to admit it was exciting, breaking out. It was like war movies, only I'd been to war and I didn't think it was fun at all, so I thought it was like the cowboys, two cowboys escaping from the Indians, and in Miss Louise Adler's case, you could compare her to a bloodthirsty savage without stretching the truth much. I got through the window okay.

"Here," said Lucas, and he handed me a heavy laundry bag, which had the medicine and stuff he'd got. Then he slung his leg up, took it down, slung the other up and then backed up completely. "I can't get out."

"Aw hell," I said. "It's not hardly a drop at all. Come on." He tried it again, but he was afraid he was going to fall, and heavy as he was, I reckon he might have broke something, so I got him to lean out the window head first and I grabbed him like a big baby and hauled him out with barely a groan.

"Thanks," he said, but he said it like he was talking to a servant.

"You be of some help to yourself or you can go your own way," I said. He chewed on the thought for a time and then nodded. We crawled to the end of the building because we didn't want to pass any of the windows. Some of the folks in Fieldstone hardly ever slept. But we didn't wake anybody up and we made it to the woods and the road that cut back toward my house.

31

"Freedom!" Lucas said over and over, like it was a magic word that would change us to being young again. The night, as I said, was warm, and it was full of cricket and tree frog sounds, the barking of a dog sometimes, a distant truck. After a spell, I noticed Lucas had fallen way back, even though I was carrying the bag with our stuff in it. I went back to him.

"You got to keep up, fella," I said. We were standing at the edge of the highway, not forty yards from Mr. Ed Rushton's place. He raised turkeys and the smell came over us like a blanket.

"I shall set the pace on this expedition," Lucas said. "I am the partner with the intelligence, and in this desiccated ruin of a globe I shall be the one to summon the human heart whenever I can, and that must be done at my own pace." I didn't really know what in the hell he was talking about.

"Bullshit," I said. "Goodbye." I turned and crossed the road, thinking I didn't need Lucas or his bag, since my house was less than a mile away. I walked down an old dirt road past a few colored folks' houses, and in a couple the light was still glowing like yellow eyes. The more I walked, the stronger I felt, and I was in a dark shady spot, knowing each step, when I heard my name being called way back. I turned and the flashlight beam was wavering all over the road behind me like it was bobbing on a string. I stopped for a minute and shook my head.

"Jake!" Lucas shouted, and I shushed him real loud until he noticed and finally caught back up with me. Even in the moonlight I could see his face sparkling with sweat and he was breathing like he'd run a mile. "Wait." He wheezed a while, grabbed my shoulder and then got his breath back in little ragged pieces. "You're in charge. Don't leave me. I'm just a smart mouth."

"You sure are that," I said. We walked on for a while up the road. I felt better than I had in weeks. Just smelling the dirt road and the woods that ran on either side made me feel more alive.

"Jake, you will have to take care of me," Lucas said. I laughed.

"You're not no big baby," I said. "I didn't sign up to take care of you. You don't look all that sick to me anyway."

"I'm not sick," he said, unhappy as I'd ever seen him. "I'm just like an old fighter. I need a manager. I've always needed a manager."

"I fought prize fights for a while in Chicago in the thirties," I said. "I reckon I understand."

"You're lying."

"About what?" We were almost to my house. I could lock him out until he went away.

"About being a fighter. Aren't you?" He really hoped I was.

"No. I really did that." He sighed heavily. "I've never done anything in my whole life," he said.

"You've written all them books," I said.

"Balls," he said. "Fame is like a candle that flickers once and is gone."

"That's pretty," I said.

"Jesus Christ," said Lucas, and I didn't know why he would be sore. We got to the end of the road, where it dead ends into another one, and my house was down the hill in a little cove. I loved this land and just being on it made my heart swell up a little. But when we walked down the driveway, I could see the For Sale sign out front. Lucas thought I was mad at him when I said, "Son of a bitch," right out loud.

BECAUSE BELLE WAS MY own flesh and blood, I didn't go over to her house and give her a tongue-lashing. Them being ex-hippies, they'd come to cuddling up with money late, and I figured I'd never be able to reason with them.

"Let's go break her knuckles," Lucas said helpfully while I stormed around yelling. We walked on down to the house and went behind it. Nobody had cut the grass in the weeks I'd been gone, and it was knee deep and wet as a river in the darkness.

"She's my niece," I sighed.

"Let's break his knuckles!" Lucas yelled. I knew what he was thinking. With my car gone, we were in pretty miserable shape for getting out to the Great Plains. "They have fouled their own nest."

"Aw hell," I managed to say. I broke out the back window next to the door and reached in and opened the door. The inside of my house was quiet as a tomb as we followed the flashlight beam around. Belle had had the electricity cut off, too.

"There's not a speck of stuff left," I said stupidly. "She just up and got rid of everything I owned."

"Let's break her thumbs," Lucas suggested, but he was starting to sound the way I felt, sad and disgusted rather than angry.

I stood there in the quiet for a right smart time. Lucas wandered into another room. From the light of the moon, you could see to walk. I just stood there, and I remembered Betty and how we'd get up in the middle of the night sometimes and make love on the couch because it was a different place, and the moon would come in on us and I could see her smiling under me. Lord, that was a thing. I just couldn't stand being there any more with the remembrances.

"Come on," I said, my voice hard and sort of cold. "We're getting the hell out of this dump." Lucas came back out, his heavy body creaking on the floorboards.

"Sue the bastards," he said like he was a king. "I think you should enter litigation, Jake. This is an abomination against your good name. Why, once I was sued by this jackleg son of a bitch who said I'd copied his novel and . . ."

"Would you shut up?" I said, turning to walk back out, and he could tell by my tone not to fool with me, so he just waddled after me. Lord, we must have been a sight.

I didn't really know what to do. The night didn't seem particular friendly any more, just damp and warm, and even the crickets and tree frogs sort of got under my skin. We walked back out to Highway 78, heading west. Lucas was breathing like he'd just finished the marathon, and once he tripped over an empty can of Budweiser and fell flat on his big rear end, cussing a blue streak. I grabbed his arm and helped him up.

"This enterprise has started like a herd of turtles," he said, and I started laughing and so did he, and we both felt better for a time. We walked down the highway, past the Purina Store, past Branton Memorial Hospital, past Mr. Colfax's hardware store where I bought most of the materials when I built my house for Betty. I had a powerful sense of leaving what had come to be my home, leaving it for the last time, and for no account I felt as blue as I had in ages.

We went on past the furniture plant. They'd had a strike there four years ago and the management had just shut the damn plant down, and now it looked like a monument, floodlights on it at night. There was always rumors they'd open it back up, but they hadn't yet. When I was a boy I belonged to a labor union in Chicago, but I've come around to believe now they're just about the worst thing ever happened to this country. We passed a fertilizer plant, and then a gas station that was closed down for the night, and then we came to the intersection with Highway 96, and the last spot with any light before you got out of Branton completely.

"I think we should go back to Fieldstone," said Lucas, whining like a child. Well, it had crossed my mind, too, but I knew I was gone from this land now, a feeling like I hadn't had in years, that feeling of leaving everything, making a break and going on the road.

"I'm heading on out," I said. A few cars came by. Nobody paid us much attention. "I'm going to Texas. If you hear they've found me dead along the road, drink one for me." I put my thumb out.

"You can't leave me!" he yelled. He put his hands in his pockets and started circling me. "I don't have anything to do now. I am in pain, goddamnit! Living here in this land is a pitiful thing, let me tell you. I had just as soon be on a commune somewhere in the wilds of Siberia."

"Nobody's holding you," I said.

He said, "Go to hell, Jake!" I knew what he needed, but I'd kept from it for a while. He was hopping around now, just wild from being cut loose of his bonds and afraid of it all. So I just stepped up to him and slapped the holy shit out of him. He didn't even make to hit me back, just started shaking and then he cried a bit and then quit.

"You okay?"

"Yeah," he said. "I suppose we are out on our own now, just living by our wits."

I said, "I reckon we are."

While that didn't seem to cheer Lucas up a whole hell of a lot, I felt better. The road. Well, I knew the damn road all right. I was restless as a coon when I was a boy, and it seemed like every time I'd light somewhere I'd be looking for some excuse to get back again. I liked to talk to the hoboes back in the thirties, not the kinds of trash you have roaming the country these days, but real honest-to-God hoboes who were on the road because they couldn't light anywhere, either.

Lucas and I had walked about a mile on the side of the road west toward Bobbin, a small town named after part of a textile mill, I reckon. He stayed behind me and was grumbling powerful strong until a man driving a beat-up Oldsmobile pulled off ahead of me when I stuck out my thumb.

"We are rescued!" shouted Lucas. "Home is the sailor, home from the sea, and the hunter home from the hill!" He started to run toward the car and knocked me flat on my ass. I wasn't hurt, but I knew then this wasn't a part-

38

nership made in heaven and if we ever did get out West, some cowboy would likely shoot Lucas on the first day.

I caught up to Lucas just as the door of the car opened and this huge colored man, who looked to weigh three, four hundred, got out and stood there. The smoke from the car was thick and Lucas just stopped dead when he saw the man; the smoke seemed to hang all over him like mist in a scary movie.

"We need a lift," I said.

"It's Othello," Lucas gasped. "I need a drink."

"Where to?" the man said. His voice was as deep as God's. He was wearing low-slung work pants and his shirt was open three or four buttons at the bottom where his belly hung out. He was holding a can of Budweiser.

"We're headed out West," I said.

"We're going to become cowboys," Lucas said, and I wished he hadn't of said that because the colored man laughed.

"You boys look a little old to be out thumbing," he said. "Get in the back if you can find a place. I ain't going out West but I'll carry you to Atlanta."

"Awright," I said. Lucas looked doubtful about getting in, so I shoved him, I climbed in right after him and the low-slung car jerked a couple of times and we were off.

"My name's Holloway," the colored man said. We introduced ourselves. "You boys want a beer?" I thought Lucas was going to climb over the seat and kiss him.

"That'd be right nice," I said. He handed two beers back, turning all the way around, not even pretending to look at the road. Lucas didn't seem to notice. In fact, I do believe I was the only one who did, and it was only then I realized Holloway was polluted as a skunk. The car headed toward a ditch, a deep one.

39

"Jesus Christ, the road!" I yelled, and Holloway chuckled and turned around in time to jerk the car back on the road and slam the pedal to the floorboard. The back floorboard was full of junk and on the seat was, unless I was wrong, a carburetor and the pressure plate from a clutch. The floor was a jumbled mess of jumper cables, screws, old beer cans, and mail order catalogs.

"Don't pay any attention to my colleague, Mr. Holloway," Lucas said, after he'd drank most of his beer in two gulps. "He's been incarcerated for some time and has lost his sense of gratitude."

"Haw," said Holloway. "Let me tell you boys a goddamn thing. I used to be a headliner in wrasslin, I mean making money like I never heard of. Maybe you heard of me; my wrasslin name was Big Red."

"An admirable profession, wrestling," Lucas said.

"They fucked me over, boy," Holloway said, his voice heavy with anger.

"Of course they did," said Lucas. We passed on out of Branton County and I felt a little twinge of regret at leaving Belle without any explanation, but I figured I'd get over it when I thought back on what she'd done with my house, and I was sure right about that.

"They decided I couldn't work no more, and they just damn told Big Red he couldn't wrassle no more," he said. "I been poor as a son of a bitch now for two years, and I'm going to Atlanta and kill the goddamn promoter."

"Capital idea!" said Lucas, finishing his beer and throwing the can on the floor with the others.

"You mean really kill somebody?" I asked.

Holloway said, "I mean really goddamn kill the son of a bitch dead." He fumbled on the front seat and Lucas thought he was getting another beer, but instead he raised up a Beretta. I know a lot about guns, sort of a hobby of mine.

"Holy shit," I whispered.

"Dead as a doornail," Holloway said, and he started laughing and then shot out the window on the passenger side of the front seat. He shot about three times, and it all happened so quick I didn't realize until a few seconds later that Lucas was all but under me on the seat.

"Oh my God," Lucas said, weak as a baby.

"Bang, bang, bang," yelled Holloway, then he went quiet and drove in a stew all the way to Atlanta. I'd seen my share of crazy folks on the road, but Lucas had never seen a living soul like Holloway, and I kept patting him on the back like you would a dog to keep it calm, and finally he calmed down a bit and we drank another beer.

Holloway turned the radio on to something that sounded like a cat being poked with a hot iron. He turned it up loud as the radio would go, and Lucas clapped his hands over his ears. Holloway yelled something.

"What's that?" I shouted, leaning over.

"Where you boys want out?" he was asking.

"Oh, anywhere," I said. Holloway took me literal and hit the brakes and slid about two, three hundred feet, mostly sideways, and Lucas took another dive into the floorboards with the jumper cables. We finally came to a stop just before going over a steep bank.

I had the door open, and Lucas was mumbling something about death and transfiguration. I thanked Holloway and jerked Lucas out by his shirt collar, grabbing the laundry bag full of our stuff on the way.

"Tell 'em Big Red is coming back!" Holloway screamed. We were standing by the side of the freeway, the tall buildings of downtown Atlanta all lit up ahead of us.

41

Holloway stomped it, slid sideways again and lit out like a dove from a covey.

"That man is a psychopath and shouldn't be allowed to roam the streets freely," Lucas muttered.

"He did give us a ride," I said, trying to calm him down.

"He is a pestilence," Lucas said. We stood and looked around us. Cars were coming by steadily but I didn't put my thumb out, and I knew from experience that soon a cop car would come by with lots of questions.

"Do you know any place we can stay tonight?" I asked.

Lucas said, "I sure as hell do. Katrina's." We walked down the freeway and up an off-ramp and called a cab from a pay phone at a service station. We had about that much money left. We stood around for a right smart time waiting.

"Who's Katrina?" I asked to break the quietness.

"When we get to Texas," Lucas said, ignoring me, "I'm going to get me a cowboy gun and holster, and if anybody screws with me I'm going to shoot them dead."

"Who's Katrina?"

"Then I'll blow the escaping wisps of smoke from the end of my barrel and hack a notch in the handle." He grabbed my arm. "We have to get guns with wooden handles. Can you still get those?"

"I guess so."

"Damn right. And a ten-gallon hat. And black chaps and pointy-toed cowboy boots. And a horse. A golden palomino with a mane like silk flowing in the wind."

"That's pretty."

"Oh great," said Lucas Kraft.

It wasn't until we were in the taxi that he told me who Katrina was.

"She is somebody who can be relied upon for discretion," Lucas said. "An old friend who will undoubtedly not be pleased to see me but will not, shall we say, rat on us, either." Lucas gave the cabbie the address and we finally stopped in a ritzy suburb of the city where all the lawns looked like they'd been spray-painted. Lucas paid the driver. The ride was downright peaceful after the trip over with Holloway, and I was recollecting that boredom's not so bad when you see what excitement can be like.

The house was long and low and we couldn't see a light in front, so Lucas led me around back, creeping like an Indian. A dog not too far away barked like somebody'd stepped on its nose. Lucas went up onto a wide flagstone patio, which we could see right well in the moonlight, not wanting to get the flashlight out of the bag. He walked up to a broad sliding glass door and tapped on it softly. I looked around, feeling like a cat burglar and wishing we were somewhere else, anywhere but Fieldstone. By now, they'd probably found us gone and gotten all put out.

Nobody came to the door from Lucas's tapping, so he started knocking regular like, and when that didn't work, he started slamming his small palm on the glass so hard I thought he'd break it.

"Good God," I whispered, "you're going to wake up the whole neighborhood."

"They should be awake," he said too loud. "Society should care for its artists as it once did. Now we are pariahs, condemned to roam the earth without reward."

Nothing happened inside the house.

"I don't think anybody's home," I said.

"Katrina! Goddamnit, come to the door!" Lucas screamed. I got under a big bush. He started landing blows on the glass like a drunk boxer and I expected the cops to come any minute and throw us both in jail, or at least the neighbors to sic their dobermans on us. As it turned out, neither of them happened.

A light over the patio came on and a woman in her fifties holding a shotgun up high was standing at the glass doors, looking like she'd kill the first thing that moved. Lucas smiled this sick smile, seeming smaller than I'd seen him in a while, and then he waved, his fat fingers folding over into his palm three times.

"Son of a bitch!" the woman yelled, and she put down the gun and unlocked the door. Since she seemed friendly, I got out from under the big bush and stood up and I thought she was going for the gun again when she saw me.

"He's with me," Lucas said. She looked like I was probably a poison snake, but she let us both inside. We came into a little dining area that had a table, and chairs and a huge painting of Lucas hanging on one wall, at least Lucas the way he looked some years before. A bar separated the dining room from the kitchen. The place smelled good, like something rich had been cooked there that evening.

"Hey, that's you," I said, pointing to the painting.

"Oh great," said Lucas. Katrina was standing there staring at Lucas.

"How are you going to explain this?" she asked.

"Get us a bottle, wench," Lucas said.

"You should lay off the sauce, honey," she said. "You're looking porkish."

"You are a wonderful judge of human character," Lucas said. "Oh. This is my friend Jake. We are going west to become cowboys."

"Ma'am," I said. She looked at me and I tried to smile, but we were tired, a little beery and I reckon I looked like death's best buddy.

"Cowboys?" she said, and then she started laughing as she walked out of the room.

"The bottle, wench," Lucas repeated. "She'll let us spend the night and perhaps help me obtain a few dollars."

"You talk funny," I said.

Katrina came back with a full bottle of bourbon and three glasses. We sat down at the little table with the painting of Lucas scowling down on us.

"Now, what in the hell are you doing here?" Katrina asked. The whiskey tasted about as wonderful as nectar.

"I am serious," said Lucas.

"I can vouch for that," I said.

"Watch it," Lucas said, and I just shrugged. Lucas could get after you, but it was like getting mad at a gnat on a summer evening. He buzzed around but he never really lit and did any damage.

"You can't just wander out West," Katrina said. She might have once been a pretty woman, but now her face had fallen and she looked sad. But all of us get that way. I knew I had. You probably won't believe this but one time, long before I met Betty, I was considered a right fetching man and I had my share of ladies.

"Oh hell," said Lucas. "We can do anything we wish. Age has taken us in its warm arms and now we no longer know fear."

"Cut the goddamn fairy talk with me," she said, and Lucas wilted like a dead flower.

"Sorry," he squeaked.

"You happen to be a genius, which is nothing new," said Katrina. "*Destiny* went out of print ten years ago and that was the last one. Have you written anything Lucas? Is there one more book in your miserable little claws?"

45

"I am not a writer anymore," he said. "I am going to be a cowboy and die in front of a fire with my boots and six-gun on." He made it sound awful foolish and I wondered if I ought to be doing this after all.

"Good luck," she said. We finished our drinks and I was powerful sleepy, and Katrina said we could spend the night but we had to be gone in the morning.

"You have to give us money," said Lucas.

"Not much," Katrina said. She pulled her houserobe tight around her and looked at Lucas with something like regret and lost affection. It was right touching and I didn't know what to say.

We went to bed in a double bed, Lucas and me, and when he turned the lights out, and the room was dark, I asked him, "How come she's got a painting of you in the dining room?"

"Huh?" He was already nearly asleep.

"That painting," I said. "Who is she?"

"Oh, that," he said, the words full of sleep. "We used to be married for a couple of years." I was going to ask him about when and where but he was all of a sudden snoring and then I drifted off myself.

In the morning, we showered and Katrina washed our clothes while we sat around in a couple of her house-robes, which made me feel stupid as hell, but I didn't want to make Lucas mad. The clothes got dry, she cooked us bacon and eggs and when we left, she slipped a roll of bills to Lucas and he took her in his arms. I slipped on outdoors and left them alone.

I was feeling awful fine that morning. The road was out in front of us, and I didn't know what we'd do. I reckoned we could take a bus or something, but I wanted to hitchhike. The day was sunny and warm and the neighborhood where Katrina lived was full of dogwoods and rock gardens and such, not a place for millions of dollars, but folks comfortable off anyway, though I doubted any had built their house with their own hands like I did mine for Betty.

Lucas came out in a hurry and his face was wet with tears.

"You okay?" I asked.

"Go to hell," he said. For somebody who'd wrote books and supposed to have deep feelings, Lucas had a hard time dealing with how he felt about things. I tried to ignore him, and I was realizing that wasn't too hard because everything he'd felt, I'd felt, too, which didn't qualify me to be a writer but it was a small comfort anyway.

We walked out of her neighborhood, Lucas keeping to himself, looking around like he was seeing the outdoors for the first time. I wouldn't have been surprised; he was pale and his skin didn't look too good, and his hands were soft and fat. We walked for a time. A few dogs came charging out at us but didn't leave their lawns.

"How should we proceed?" Lucas asked, stopping and staring at me. I was still carrying that durned laundry bag and I felt like Santy Claus looking down on him.

"I'd say let's us hitchhike," I said. "I done it half my life. It's an interesting way to travel on." He thought about it, his mouth working over the idea like a piece of tough steak.

"I suppose we may be assaulted by brigands," he sighed. I told him I'd never been assaulted by anybody, unless you counted that time in Atlantic City when I got the scar on my stomach. "Oh great."

"Look, how much money you got?" I asked.

"That's for something else," he said. "For when we get to the vast flatlands of Texas."

"Then that settles it," I said.

We came out of the neighborhood and onto a road called North Druid Hills Road. As we got to travelling more, I found out that Lucas was superstitious as an old lady about names and such, and when he saw the word "Druid," his eyes lit up and he got down on his knees and started making this low chanting sound in his throat.

"Get up, Lucas," I pleaded. He was salaaming, like you used to see in Ali Baba movies, his pudgy round face coming down to the damp grass and back up. A woman in a cherry red sports car drove by us and nearly wrecked when she saw Lucas.

"I'm praying, you fascist," he growled. He continued to make those low growling noises. I sort of kept lookout while Lucas was praying to the street sign, and I just stood there until I thought he'd done about as much as he could and then I jerked him up by his collar. "Ghosts of Sigismondo Malatesta! Dictator of the heart!"

He was sort of spluttering, so I smacked him across the mouth and he stopped and seemed to be all right after that.

"Sorry I had to hit you," I said as we walked off with the sun at our backs.

"You had to," he said quietly, which sure made me think more of Lucas Kraft. We came to an intersection that had a church on one corner, a gas station across from it, and on the third corner was a home for retarded folks. On the fourth corner was a liquor store, and without saying anything, we both headed for that.

"What's your poison?" I asked as we went inside.

"I seem to prefer Scotch," he said.

"I can't drink it," I said. "Let's get us one of Scotch and one of bourbon." Lucas thought that was a good idea, so he got two fifths with the money rolled up with the rubber band and we were on our way again.

By then it was getting really hot, and we were sweating by the time we got to the freeway. I led down the on-ramp dodging a blue Cadillac, the driver of which didn't have any respect for his elders. We got down onto the freeway and I stuck my thumb out right under a sign that said "No Hitchhiking."

"A good omen," said Lucas, noticing the sign. We stood there, me with my old beat-up thumb out for only a few minutes when this van slowed down and pulled over about ten yards ahead of us. This little bitty fella who looked like some kind of overgrown insect hopped out grinning as we hustled on up to the ride.

"Look here, Lord have mercy," the insect said, his voice full of grinning. "You old fellas just pull a bank job or something?"

"Don't be an asshole," Lucas said, and I elbowed him in the shoulder, but the insect didn't seem to mind. I had the feeling news of Pearl Harbor being bombed again wouldn't have bothered him all that much.

"Miles Carpenter," he said, reaching out to me with his bony hand. "Glad as hell to meet you."

"The protagonist in *Deep Waters* was named Miles," Lucas said, trying to look important.

"What's that?" the insect asked.

"A novel I wrote when I was a man," Lucas said, but the young man obviously didn't believe him for nothing.

"Where you fellas heading?"

I was starting to say Mississippi, me having family still there and thinking it would sound good, when Lucas said, "We are going to Texas to become cowboys." Well, I was shaking my head thinking, there goes the ride, when the insect's eyes lit up and he took my laundry bag and made a sound that meant, I figured, he liked the idea.

Inside this van there was a big seat up front that swiveled and a bench behind it, and Lucas never asked, just got up in the front seat, his short legs dangling over the edge. I sat in back and opened the bottle of bourbon as we sped off and took a gulp, and it made me think I felt better than I probably did.

"What's your name?" Miles asked. He drove slow as Christmas and at that rate, we'd be hours getting out of Atlanta. Lucas cleared his throat.

"Saul Bellow," he said, "Nobel Laureate in literature, winner of the Pulitzer Prize."

"Nice to meet you, Mr. Bellow," Miles said. "What's your name?" He looked at me in the rearview mirror.

"Jake," I said.

"Jake who?"

"Jake Wayne," I lied.

"He's John Wayne's brother," Lucas said. Miles looked at me again in the mirror.

"I be dog," he said.

That was two lies in thirty seconds, but we were on our way.

MILES WAS GOING to his brother's house, about forty miles west, and so I sat in the back seat and sipped my bourbon while Lucas sat up front babbling about the failures of mankind and such, all things I don't think Miles knew much about, him appearing to be simpler than me.

He was turning south after a time, and he let us out still on I-20.

"My good man, I hope we haven't been too much of a burden," Lucas said.

"Aw hell, I enjoyed it," Miles said as we got out. I didn't have a way on God's green earth of knowing it then, but that ride was nearly the last sane one we'd have all the way to Texas. As Miles drove off after shaking our hands and wishing us well, Lucas pulled himself up and said, "That man is living with one foot in the grave."

I didn't ask him what he meant, but Lucas, like I said, was real deep sometimes, and about all I'd ever written was bad checks while he'd written books and such. I figured we'd get some rides right off, just for the novelty of two old boys hitching if nothing else, because between us we should have had some damn good stories. But we walked all day and by then we'd nearly been run over a good half dozen times and I was downright discouraged. Lucas was so tired I thought he was going to fall out.

I said we got some strange rides later on, and that was true, but somehow luck was always following one of us, though I never knew which of us it was. So it was that first sunny day that we found ourselves at an intersection on the highway where there was a small service station.

"If I die on this road, stretch me out for the predators and vermin," Lucas said.

"Aw hell, they wouldn't touch you," I said.

"Jake, you're the Torquemada of the Highway," Lucas said with great resignation.

I didn't know who that was, but I got tired of asking Lucas to explain himself. We took the off-ramp and nearly got run over again by an old woman driving a station wagon blowing blue smoke all over God's creation.

"Get a ring job!" I yelled, and Lucas thought that was funny. The store was called McGuffin's Country Store, and it was a nice spot, so we went in and bought us some Van Camp's pork and beans, bread, peanut butter, sardines, a couple of big Cokes, candy bars and such, plus three, four cans of canned heat and some matches.

"You fellas out on the road?" the man behind the counter asked. It was a cheerful place, cluttered with all manner of old and new stuff, the kind of place a man could stop off for a couple of years while wandering around.

"Just hitchhiking to Mississippi to see my family," I said before Lucas could tell him we were going to be cowboys.

"I wish y'all a lot of luck," he said. He was a big fat man with a stub of a toothpick that kept moving around in his mouth. "Not meaning disrespect, but you guys look a mite old to be out wandering around."

"Sir, this is America!" Lucas boomed. He had already paid, taking a couple of bills from his wad. "This great land was molded by those not afraid to strike out into the wilderness. From one great ocean to another, man has never . . ." I grabbed his arm and started easing him out the door. I never in my life saw a man who liked to give speeches more than Lucas, and I wondered why he never had run for office.

"Let's head up that way," I said, pointing to the road that was crossing the interstate near McGuffin's Country Store. "We want to be off the interstate. Too noisy."

"My God, are we to sleep with the beasts of the field?" he said.

"Come on," I said. He commenced to grumbling, but I didn't pay him much mind, and we walked half a mile north on that road and then cut across a pasture and settled down in a nice shady grove of trees just as the sun was setting. Lucas sat down against a pine tree and opened his bottle of Scotch and started declaiming while I built a fire.

> I am become a name;
> For always roaming with a hungry heart
> Much have I seen and known — cities of men
> And manners, climates, councils, governments,
> Myself not least, but honor'd of them all, —
> And drunk delight of battle with my peers,
> Far on the ringing plains of windy Troy.

"What's that?" I asked.

"A bad poem about an old man," Lucas said. "By Alfred Lord His Worship Tennyson."

"I've heard of him," I said. "You ever meet him?" Lucas busted out laughing like a maniac.

"He had shuffled off his mortal coil before either you or I was hatched," he said.

The night came on, cool and sweet, and all the good feelings I'd ever had about evenings came back. There were Holsteins in the pasture we'd crossed and you could hear them lowing as they headed in a line somewhere we could not see. A few lightning bugs early for the summer were hanging around. It made me a little sad, too, because Betty and I used to sit around on evenings like this just holding hands and watching the sun go down, but after she'd run off with that taxidermist from Monroe, I'd felt sour toward everything we'd loved for a long time. Now, I felt better.

I found plenty of wood for a fine fire, which I started by using strips of bark I pulled off a cedar tree. The heat from the fire felt good as the evening got cool and the stars came out. I lit one can of the sterno and set the pork and beans on it and made us some peanut butter sandwiches. Lucas didn't seem able to help at all.

"I forgot to get some of them plastic forks," I said. "We'll have to eat these here beans with our fingers when they cool."

"My God, barbarity," he shuddered, but he did it anyway, and I don't reckon a thing I've ever eaten tasted better. I rumbled around in the laundry bag after we ate and got us each a couple of vitamins, which we washed down with Coke. I showed Lucas how to make a pillow by wrapping his pants around his shoes, but he wouldn't take his pants off in front of me. I made my pillow, but for a while I stared into the fire and had me a drink.

54

We sat that way for a right long spell, listening to the crackle of the fire and the singing of the crickets and tree frogs. I could of died right there and gone to wherever I'm going happy as anything.

"I want to become involved in a range war," Lucas said out of the blue. Our beards had started to come out, and though mine was all white, Lucas's was still sort of blue-black, and with his eyes looking a bit hollow and the beard starting to cover his face, he was a sight.

"You want to do what?"

He said, "I want to find a small town in Texas where a hated gang of villains is blackmailing the honest and hardworking ranchers. Did you ever read about Billy the Kid?"

"I heard about him, sure."

"He was fighting in a range war against such slime."

"I thought he was a crazy little-boy killer."

"Aaaaagh," Lucas said, like he was tasting something bad. "You and everybody else. Billy the Kid was a noble outlaw and he died like a man."

"I want to die like a man," I agreed.

"Then you wish to be gunned down just as I do," Lucas said, his eyes getting bright. He took a swig from his bottle and I matched him. He was getting a little wild-eyed. A car went past out on the road across the pasture, but it didn't even scratch the quietness and the crackling of the fire.

"Naw, I don't want to get shot," I said. "What kind of stupid talk is that?"

"Oh, you'd rather die curled up in your orthopedic hose at Fieldstone, is that it?" he said.

"You got no cause to talk to me that way."

He looked into the fire, and for the first time since I'd met Lucas Kraft, he seemed almost like a normal person, with feelings like I had sometimes if I let them through. He said, "I know. I just want to die better than I've lived."

"Well, that's just horseshit," I said. "Everybody dies, that's all. My daddy died in a car wreck. What did your daddy die of?"

Lucas said, "My father was killed by a man named Josiah Reece because Daddy was fooling around with his wife." Lucas grinned. "But it was of no satisfaction for Mr. Reece because when they found him, he still had Daddy's knife stuck up to the hilt in his stomach where they'd fought. He died the next day. Happened in Atlanta, too."

"How old were you?"

"Twelve."

"Lord have mercy."

"My mother, rest her soul, lapsed into childhood again, losing her husband and being disgraced, and she took me to the shore country in Maryland, little town named Camden. She changed her named to Kraft, just pulled it out of the air. My real last name was Lewiston."

"I be dog," I said.

"Josiah Reece's wife ran off with her children, too, I heard, so my father managed to screw up a number of lives. I grew up quietly. My mother's sister Anna came to live with us when I was fourteen and the two of them raised me in this gloomy mansion there in Camden, reading to me from the classics, listening to opera on the gramophone. Anna always believed she could have been the next Nellie Melba except for her looks. She did have a lovely voice but was a cross-eye." I didn't know who Nellie Melba was, but he was in the middle of a speech so I didn't stop him. "Incredible. Now, with modern medicine, there are no more people cross-eyed. What a loss for fancy, that all the cross-eyes are gone. Anyway, they raised me to forget who my father was, my dear demented mother even trying to get me to believe my father had been killed in Europe and that the man I knew to be dear old Dad was actually my father's brother. She never did explain why she slept with him all those years."

He took another sip. The fire was starting to die down and I was feeling awful sleepy, the good kind of sleepy you feel when you've worked hard all day long.

"How'd you come to be a writer?"

"It was Aunt Anna's ambition for me," he said slowly. "She knew all of the fine arts, having grown up so ugly that she sought out all beauty inside herself. She wrote a fair poem and even had several published under a pen name. She wanted me to be a writer, a painter, a composer, everything. She wanted me to be the most famous artist of the twentieth century. When she read my first novel, she wrote me an eighteen-page letter forgiving me for having birthed, as she said, 'one of the most monstrous works of fiction ever hatched in the current century.' I never saw her again after that. Mother had already died and Anna shriveled up and died there in Camden. I went to her funeral and found she had written a letter for me, to be read after her death, urging me to follow holy art and turn my back on commercialism." He laughed. "So that was when I wrote *The Edge of Camden*, the book of stories that won the National Book Award. Shortly after that, I wrote another novel, got rich and the critics spent their spleen hating every word I wrote after that."

"You've had an interesting life," I said.

"I have been," he said, his voice sounding too loud there in the woods, "a water strider on the surface of humanity. I want to be killed by a gunfighter in a range war!"

"Okay," I said, trying to calm him down. "If we can't find one, I'll have you shot myself."

He lay back and put his head on his shoes and sleep came over him before me, and he slept deep and heavy. I let the fire die down. Lucas was like a boy in a lot of ways, I thought, but I knew what he meant by wanting to be gunned down, silly as it was. I was thinking about cowboys when I finally eased off under a blanket of crickets and stars.

When I woke up the next morning, I saw Lucas standing out at the edge of the field.

"Morning," I said as I stood, feeling the bones trying to fall back into place but not doing too terrible good of a job at it.

"I could write a poem about this place," he said without looking back at me.

"I thought you didn't write anymore," I said.

"I don't," he said, his voice suddenly not happy. He turned and came back toward me. The morning was cool and gray, sort of threatening to drizzle, and I started the fire back and made us some peanut butter sandwiches. They tasted fine, and within an hour of waking we had hiked back down the road to I-20. Lucas spent a lot of time on that trip talking about the names of places, and he almost talked me into hitching north to see a town named Muscadine.

We had to stand down on I-20 nearly an hour before a pulpwood truck without a load, belching diesel and gargling, stopped not far in front of us.

"We got us a ride," I said, walking fast to catch up. It had started to drizzle.

"Oh, great," Lucas said as he looked at the truck. We caught up and I nearly had to push Lucas into the cab because it was so high and he was so short. I got in after him and slammed the door, which sounded like it was made out of cardboard.

"Where you all heading?" the driver asked. He was a big fat feller, wearing dirty overalls and three days of beard. His eyes were bloodshot and poked out over his cheeks. I noticed his hands, short and hard, all cracked from work and dirty for whatever was left of his life. He wore a baseball cap with "Red Man" on it. He took a Tampa Nugget cigar from a pack off the dash and lit it as we rumbled back on to the road. I could tell Lucas wasn't liking it none at all.

"West, young man," said Lucas.

"Mississippi, thereabouts," I said. "I got me some family out there, and that's where we're going." I could have told him we were going to San Francisco to become hair dressers and he would of believed me as much.

"Well, shit," he said, "you all got a good piece of a ride left. Name's Reuben Murlock. You all want a cigar?"

"Don't be absurd," Lucas said before I put my elbow in his side.

"I'd be taking one," I said, and Reuben reached up, hard as it was, him being so fat, and pulled one out and gave it to me along with a pack of matches from his shirt pocket.

"Gonna be having us some rain today," Reuben said. "Course, we need it bad as hell, don't you know. But I got a load to get down at Ashland, and I'm about goddamn sick and tired of mud." He licked his lips and then spit out the window. Lucas turned to me and mouthed the word "no" with something scared in his eyes.

59

"Would you like a swallow of liquor?" I asked. Reuben grinned and you could see he didn't have much of his teeth. I was just trying to be neighborly, I reckon, but it turned out to be a mistake.

"I pure-T would like that," Reuben said, so I dug down in the laundry bag and got my bottle and handed it to him and he drank about half of what was left. He let it go down for a second. "Son of a bitch!" He shook his head like a dog trying to get water off his back.

We drove like that, down the interstate for a while with nobody saying much. Before long, we came to the state line and Lucas said, "Oh wonderful, Alabama," with a powerful lot of disgust, which wasn't lost on Reuben.

"You a goddamn Yankee?" he asked. His voice was getting thick and he seemed to be driving a little faster.

"He didn't mean nothing by that," I said, trying to be helpful. Reuben fumed for a time and his eyes were looking a little glazed. He slammed the truck through three or four gears and I knew we were in trouble.

"You fellas ever killed a queer?" he asked. I choked on the smoke from my cigar and rolled the window down even though it was raining in.

"What did you say?" Lucas asked, waving the smoke from in front of his face. He looked even stranger with the beard growing, like a troll. A mean troll. Reuben laughed and coughed. He was weaving and bobbing around the cab of the truck and we were going hell bent for leather down the interstate, passing everything in sight.

"You all are fags, ain't you?" he laughed. He looked over at us and didn't look back at the road for nearly ten seconds. Lucas was sitting next to him and was pointing at the road and yelling about the traffic.

"Shit no," I said. "Would you watch the road?"

"I never seen queers old as you," Reuben said.

"You are insulting me, and I shall not abide it," Lucas said. Reuben was fat but he was big, and he looked down at Lucas and busted out laughing.

"How about I killed you, then?" he asked.

"We'll be getting out about now," I said.

Reuben said, "Because I always kills queers when I pick 'em up. You all want to kiss one another before I kill you?"

"You're the fag," Lucas said, to my surprise, and Reuben reached over and got my bottle and drank the rest of it, which was bad news for sure.

We drove that way for a spell, with Reuben staring like a dead fish through the windshield of that pulpwood truck at the Alabama countryside unrolling before us. Lucas muttered under his breath about how awful it all was, and though I was too smart to open my mouth, I have to admit I agreed with him.

"Yeah, I kill queers," Reuben said. "And niggers. I kill all the niggers I pick up." His words were getting thick with the liquor, something I knew more than my fair share about. "I bet both of you old fags have nigger blood, don't you?"

"I'd rather be black than you," Lucas said, and I could have hugged him, except for the wrong impression it would have given under the circumstances. Rather than get screaming mad, Reuben just smiled funny like and nodded, then his face went flat and he pulled off the side of the road.

"Would you boys be wanting any sex this morning?" he asked, sort of sad, whiny like. I opened the door and jumped out, dragging the laundry bag after me, and Lucas came out, too quick, and I realized when I looked up that Reuben had shoved him out the door.

"You, sir, are no gentleman!" Lucas yelled, and I was surprised as hell when Reuben looked down, put the truck in gear and said real soft, "I know that." Then he pulled out, weaving off down the road, going across both lanes and nearly cutting off a BMW that was trying to pass. I was watching the truck disappear over a hill and turned to Lucas to tell him I was proud of him when I noticed that he had flat passed out.

I put the laundry bag in my lap and under his big old head and was fanning him when a Cadillac pulled over so close it damn near ran over my right foot. I stood up to yell at the thoughtless bastard when I realized I'd dropped Lucas's head like a canteloupe on the pavement, which didn't seem too kind. I picked it back up in my lap and was fanning his face when the door of the Cadillac opened and a woman wearing a dress that looked like it had been painted on came toward us.

"Oh, dear," she said, which was pretty mild considering how we looked.

"You nearly run over my right foot," I said, but she didn't have the kind of look that would make you mad for long. She was maybe forty, but her body hadn't heard that and was just out of high school. I remembered when I'd graduated from high school because that night I got my first experience with a woman's flesh, an experience I admit I've never quite got over.

"I'm terribly sorry," she said. She came close to us and she put her palm upside her nose, which reminded me we hadn't bathed in a few days. "Is your friend sick?"

"Oh, he's all right," I said. "We was riding with a pulp-wooder who was threatening to do something unnatural to us and my friend is still trying to recover."

"Oh, dear," she said. She was trying to think of something to say, and I could tell just from looking at her that

62

she was a woman with compassion, maybe too much, since we could have been two neck-slicing maniacs. "Did your car break down?"

"Ain't got none," I said. I had this habit of talking a little stupider than I was that had hung on with me from all my years hanging around dummies because it got you through some scrapes with folks who hated you if you knew more than they did. "Me and him's going to Mississippi where I got family. I want to go home to die." I don't know why I said that. I hadn't thought much about dying, not ever, thinking that when it came on you that was it and not even God Almighty could do much about it. Anyway, it touched her so deep that she started to cry a little, and just about that time Lucas came out of his faint and sat up and stared at the lady.

"Beatrice, I am come on thy holy mission," he said, which didn't mean a damn thing to me and I thought his brains were scrambled from the excitement. Later he told me it was only an allusion, of which I got to know a lot about later on.

"Are you okay?" she asked.

"We are in the need of the succor of thy human kindness," he said, and I thought he was proposing something indecent for a minute until he repeated it. She nodded.

"I live over in Heflin," she said. "You come on and I'll make you some breakfast and we'll talk about your getting to Mississippi."

"Mississippi?" said Lucas. He stood up, snorting and coughing. "My God, woman, we are going to Texas to become . . ." I jerked his arm hard enough to make him shut up, though he gave me a hard look.

"We'll be proud for a little hospitality," I said, and we all three went to the Cadillac. It was dark blue and looked like it cost ten million dollars.

63

Lucas said, "This is more like it," when we got into the car, me in the back, him in the front with the lady. The countryside was pretty in that way that you can't know unless you've lived around, pine trees and rolling hills and the endless ribbon of I-20 that went dead ahead all the way to west Texas.

"My name is Nell Marino," she said. "My husband and I own a cattle farm. Tell me about yourselves." That was a mistake. Lucas started telling her all about himself, about his books, about winning that prize, and she nearly about dropped her uppers she was so impressed. For twenty minutes Lucas kept up, babbling about himself like a preacher talking about the Lord. "And what about you?" she asked, looking in the rearview mirror.

"Name's Jake," I said. "I reckon the only worthwhile thing I ever done in my life was build a house for me and my wife, Betty."

"Has she passed away?" Mrs. Marino asked.

"She run off with a taxidermist from Monroe," I said.

"What did you do before that?" she asked. Her voice was deeper than it should have been, and I realized she was trying to be kind, glancing at me in the mirror. We got off I-20 and took a small road north heading toward Heflin.

"Worked lots of different jobs," I said. "You wouldn't happen to have any country fried steak at your house, would you? I got an awful hankering for some country fried steak."

"Oh, great," said Lucas.

"Believe we do," she said. I couldn't think of a thing else to say, so I shut up. Having nothing to say never stopped Lucas as I could see, so he talked right up until we turned into a dirt road with these big pillars at the front, and over them, hanging over the road, was this big sign that said "N Bar O Ranch."

"Have you had a range war lately?" Lucas asked excitedly. He was jumping around in the seat like it was a skillet and he was a seed of popcorn. "If so, I'd like to offer to gun down the scum that's trying to take your land." Mrs. Marino grinned and tried not to laugh, but I didn't have any sense of restraint, as they say, so I busted out laughing, which didn't please Lucas at all. "You shut up, smart guy."

"What does the 'N Bar O' stand for?" I asked, trying to change the conversation.

"Death means nothing to me," said Lucas, trying to make himself taller on the seat. "I would sooner die in a righteous fight than on some set of white sheets they'll starch and give some other dying bastard the next day."

"Uh . . . well," said Mrs. Marino. "Yes, well, the 'N Bar O' stands for the first and last letters of my name. My husband gave it that name."

"That's good," I said.

"You may call me Kid," Lucas said out of the blue, looking out the window.

It didn't look much like Texas. The pastures were fringed with pine woods and I didn't see but a few cows, and the hills rolled gently under us as we came down this curling gravel road and then up a hill. The house was huge, a long, low sort of thing, with a front yard maybe half an acre across and cut close as a golf course. Two spreading oak trees held on to the dirt in front of the house.

"God, Kid," I said, "look at this spread."

"Not you, asshole," he said, turning and looking awful disgusted with me. "Her. I don't want you to call me Kid."

"Whatever you say, Kid," I answered, not very happy with him.

Lucas said, "Jake is senile, so you forgive him. I helped him escape from an asylum for the elderly in the wilds of Georgia."

"You're some talker, Kid," I said. We stopped under one of the oak trees and got out. The place smelled like a home, though I can't rightly put my finger on what that might be; maybe something of folks having been there for a good spell and planning to stay.

"Why don't you fellas come on and I'll set out some of my husband's clothes. You can shower while I wash those and cook you something to eat," Nell Marino said. If she'd a been a widow lady, I'd have proposed. My life's not found many folks who'd give such kindness to strangers.

"We'd be much obliged," I said. We went on inside. There was a long hallway with a deer head on one wall and an antique hatrack on another. Nell told us where the bathroom was, the guest bathroom (there must have been five or six of them), and Lucas went first. She set us out some overalls, and I had the idea, just holding up a pair, that her husband was a big man.

I went with her out to the kitchen while Lucas showered. The kitchen was big as a saloon. She started cooking country fried steak and put on a pot of water to boil.

"Where's your husband?" I asked.

"He's around," she said, working fast as a short-order cook.

"Around here?"

"Yes."

"Oh."

I'd took off my boots and was padding around the kitchen looking at all her knick-knacks and such. I wanted to ask her what her husband would think when he came in here, but I kept my mouth shut. Presently Lucas came out wearing a pair of overalls about six sizes too big and I busted out laughing, and he came over and punched me in the stomach but it was like being hit by a gnat wearing a marshmallow on his fist.

I went on back and stood in the shower for a long time. I felt pretty good, not too tired. I got out and dried off and dressed. The clothes were too big for me, too. Back when I was a man, they'd of fit better, but you shrink as you go along.

I was standing there in the guest bedroom when I got this awful urge to wander through the house. It was a long way to the kitchen, and I figured Lucas would be keeping Nell busy. There was a hall that went through the middle of the house, so I took that. There was a large den off to the right, a bedroom to the left. I went into the bedroom feeling like a pervert, but I didn't seem to be able to help myself.

The room was neat as anything I ever saw. There were lots of pictures of Nell when she was younger with her husband, who was plain looking and big. I stood there, thinking about Nell, wondering what color underwear she wore when I saw something in the bed, up on the pillow, something looking like a note. I used to leave Betty notes on her pillow suggesting all manner of dirty things I was going to do to her. She would get it and giggle and tell me how awful I was. Maybe Mr. Marino had left a dirty note for Nell. I'd just read it and get back to the kitchen before he wandered in.

I leaned over the bed and looked at it and felt my heart break into a funny gallop. It was one of those funeral home plaques, the kind they put in the ground before you buy a stone. It said Wilson Marino and gave the

67

dates, saying, unless I misunderstood, that he'd died a couple of weeks before. I hoped it was her brother-in-law or somebody, but it was weird to the point of being sick.

I got the hell out of the bedroom. I went into the kitchen where Lucas was trying to get Nell to feel his muscle. I got to feeling hot while we ate. The food was good as I ever ate, but my heart wasn't in it.

I had to ask, so I said, "What's your husband's name?"

Nell said, "Why do you ask?" I didn't know what to say so I just smiled while Lucas made these awful slurping sounds as he ate. I never in my life saw a sloppier eater than Lucas Kraft.

I said, "Just curious. I knowed some Marinos in New Jersey one time."

"Wilson," she said. I felt my skin go clammy. I looked down in my plate and tried not to let her see me, but I reckon I blanched. Lucas was babbling about range wars, happy as a hog in warm mud. I looked up at Nell and she was standing up slow, her eyes gone hard and cold. I wanted to say something like "shit," but nothing would come. "Have you been in my bedroom?"

Lucas stopped eating. I looked at him. She looked at him.

"What in the hell is going on?" Lucas asked. That's when Nell started to grin. I never saw a grin like that before. She turned and walked out of the room.

"Lucas," I said, jumping up, "we got to get the hell out of here. She's crazy as a loon."

"I wouldn't leave this abode for the paps of all the college girls in America," he said. I tugged on his arm.

"I'm telling you to get up, Kid," I said.

"I don't want you to call me Kid," he said. We both looked up right then and saw Nell Marino standing in the doorway holding a shotgun with both barrels pointing right at us.

I STOOD SLOWLY and got Lucas by the arm. He was staring at the gun and grinning like a jack-o-lantern, but Nell was staring hard at us and I felt real bad about it all.

"Thou murderess," Lucas said low and full of hissing. It sounded dramatic, but it's not the kind of thing you say to somebody holding a tight choke double-barrel shotgun on you.

"We'll be going now," I said. I pushed Lucas, but he felt like he was stuck to the floor.

"Foul and dark is thy deed," said Lucas.

"Jesus Christ, Lucas," I said, "the lady don't want us here."

"I'm gone have to shoot both of you," she said, but it didn't sound like the same voice, this one full of something that hurt awful bad.

"Lady, I don't care if your old man is propped up in the basement," I said. "We'd be right glad to get the hell out of here." Lucas pulled away from me and was just about to make another speech when she cocked both hammers of the gun and lifted it heavily to her shoulder. I grabbed Lucas's arm and pulled him strong as I could out into the hall. His eyes were big and round and I reckoned mine probably didn't look all that different.

She didn't follow us and when we got to the front door, I could hear her starting to cry like the end of the world was at hand, and maybe it was for her. It was the middle of the day by then, but we were stuck on a farm near Heflin, Alabama, without our laundry bag, which I'd left trying to keep from being shot.

"That woman is not right," said Lucas. I was walking real fast, looking back over my shoulder, and he was keeping up. We went through a barb-wire fence and across a pasture and finally got back to the main road. Half a mile down the road there was a crossroads, and on one side was a small, cramped-looking diner.

"Let's get something to eat just to calm us down," I said. "And rest."

"Indeed," Lucas said. By the time we got to the place, which was called Clell's, we were both skunk tired and nervous hungry. It was made out of knotty pine and, being the middle of the day, had right many people inside eating. I was aware, going up the steps, that I was not a young man any more.

I ordered a hamburger and a big Coke and Lucas got him a ham and cheese sandwich and three bags of Lay's barbecue potato chips.

"Look," I said, after we'd eaten enough to calm down, "maybe we're just too old for this kind of thing. You ever think about that?" He looked out the windows that were lined along the front of Clell's, staring at the highway.

72

"It's all I ever think about," he said. "It's the first thing I think of in the morning and the last thing I think of at night. It follows me like another skin. Death is nothing I fear. Maybe dying like a dog on the road is."

"You want to go back?" I'd grown right fond of old Lucas by that time over in Heflin. It had been kind of exciting and we hadn't been shot yet, but we were both old men.

Lucas said, "No."

I said, "I don't either." Then he grinned, not much, but he grinned and I did too. We finished and stood up, not really knowing what to do next, though I was going to suggest getting a lift on into Heflin and taking the bus for a spell. Lucas patted his pockets in front and back, and all of a sudden I had a real bad feeling something was wrong again.

"I left the money in Miss Nell's bathroom," he said. "You'll have to pay."

"I don't have any money," I said.

"You mean we're broke?" he said, his voice getting so high nobody but a dog could of heard it. He rolled his eyes. At least we'd showered and shaved so we didn't look quite so much like bums. The room was still full.

"You just go on outside," I said. I knew a trick I'd learned years before, and maybe it would work again. Lucas just shrugged like a man on his way to the chair and slid through the door. I made a big show of taking out my billfold and looking in it while walking into the bathroom. I then locked the door and climbed out through the window, landing hard on an old axle. My foot felt like it had about two hundred extra bones in it. As I stood up, I realized a stranger was helping me. I thanked him before I realized it didn't look all that good, me having just fell out of the bathroom window of Clell's place.

"That looked like it would of hurt," the man said. He was a young guy with greasy black hair, buck teeth and skinny as a finger.

"I'm practicing for the Olympics," I said, and he laughed down in his throat like uchnnn, uchnnn, real fast.

"I'm Marvin Peabody," he said. I stood on the hurt foot and it wasn't too bad. He had his hand stuck out, so I shook it, and he pumped my arm twice like he was trying to get water out of a well. "You need some help, old feller?" I started creeping around the building and Marvin followed me. Lucas was standing out front acting like he was conducting an orchestra, which didn't make it any easier to escape from Clell's.

"Psssst," I said, and Lucas saw me and straightened up and came walking over like he was Clell himself.

"Let's get the hell out of here," I said when he got close.

"Did you successfully avoid making remuneration?" Lucas asked. Marvin looked at him with awe, I reckon it was, his eyes bright as they probably ever got. "Who is this character?"

"Marvin Peabody," Marvin said, and he pumped Lucas's arm twice just like he'd done mine. "You fellers on the road?"

"My God, terminology from the Dust Bowl era still has currency in Alabama," Lucas said.

"Yeah," I said, sorry Lucas wasn't terrible polite. Marvin Peabody grinned and told us to wait and ran back to Clell's, got a bag with a fishing rod hanging out both ends and caught back up.

"You fellers mind if we go along together for a spell?" asked Marvin.

"Are you adept at confiscating provisions?" Lucas asked as Marvin fell into step with us. Marvin Peabody had this funny look on his face like he was just pleased to be alive, not worrying about things like death and starvation, and it made one inclined to like him right off.

"Is he talking English?" Marvin said to me.

"No," I said. "Sometimes he don't talk English for hours at a time."

"Oh, great," said Lucas. "How are you at getting us something to eat and drink? Can you get us some wheels?"

"You asking him to steal?" I asked.

"I prefer borrow," said Lucas as we headed off down the side of the road toward Heflin. I kept looking back up to Clell's, but nobody came after us with a gun for skipping out on our bill. They were busy, as I said, and they'd probably remember it later when it didn't make any difference.

"You fellers don't have a red cent?" Marvin Peabody asked.

"Not one between us," I admitted.

"Then we's in the same boat," he said.

He said he was from the tobacco country in North Carolina, that he was thirty-eight years old, that he'd once had a wife and a gal baby, but his wife had left him and now he'd got stuck for not paying child support, thrown in jail, from which he'd broken out two months before. He was trying to hitchhike to California, but he hadn't been getting very far these days.

"I hope you fellers don't mind me being an excapee and all," Marvin said. "Either one of you excaped from anything?"

"The Kid there is," I said, pointing at Lucas.

"Why do they call him the Kid?" Marvin asked. Lucas was scowling something awful at me, but he liked a good story, being a writer, and I think he wanted to see how I'd do before he told me to go to hell.

"It happened years and years ago," I said. I don't know why I'd lie to Marvin, but it seemed like a way to get along. "Lucas there was eighteen years old. He lived on a farm in Maryland. A crazy man was running loose up there, had kilt near about eight folks, and he come to Lucas's ranch. Lucas was at school and when he come home, he could tell by, uh, a sense none of us has like him, that something was wrong. He creeped around the house and looked in the window and there was the crazy man holding his mama by the hair, fixing to cut her throat."

"Holy shit," said Marvin Peabody.

"Anyway, Lucas got the old gun from the well house and creeped back up to the house," I said, "and just as the crazy man was about to kill his ma, he busted into the house and without touching a hair on his old ma's head, he shot the crazy man between the eyes."

"Lordy mercy!" said Marvin. Lucas's eyebrows went up and he nodded lightly as we walked, approving the story, which I took as quite an honor, considering.

"Yeah, the sheriff come out there," I said, "and when he asked who'd been brave enough to kill the crazy man face to face, Lucas's ma just said, 'The Kid did it,' and from that day on, everybody called him Kid. And from that day on, he's gone about looking for mad-dog killers to shoot. Don't make him mad, Marvin." Lucas laughed, his big old stomach heaving up and down.

We didn't get any rides and had to hoof the three miles on into Heflin, which isn't much of a town, but most

76

towns aren't. We stood around on a corner. I didn't really know what to do next, not having any money at all.

"We need a car," Lucas sighed. Marvin Peabody's eyes got bright and he set his bag down and said he'd be right back and he went around a corner.

"This traveller is a cretin," said Lucas. "Proves my theory that mankind is not worth saving. It has evolved from Michelangelo to Marvin and your putrid stories about my name."

"I thought you liked it," I said.

"I did, but I, myself, have evolved from a writer of some note to just another bubble in the slime of mankind," he said, which sounds right awful now but didn't sound quite so bad then. We were standing there looking around when a policeman was all of a sudden walking down the sidewalk in front of us, then stopping. We looked like somebody who ought to be in jail.

"Where you men from?" he asked. He had a deep voice like an actor.

We spoke at the same time. Lucas said New York and I said Atlanta. The cop narrowed his eyes and cocked his head a bit and nodded and walked off, but I could tell he didn't believe us any more than he still believed in Santy Claus. I was staring at the cop, feeling Lucas at my elbow, when Marvin Peabody came flying around the corner in a beat-up old pickup truck. He stopped right in front of us, grinning through his buck teeth, his eyes still dull as old marbles.

"My God, the hayseed is involved in larceny," said Lucas.

"Get in fellers," Marvin Peabody said. Lucas didn't move, but I did. I threw Marvin's pack in the back and grabbed Lucas's arm and we climbed up into the cab and rumbled off. I don't think the truck had a muffler, and we went straight through Heflin sounding like something from that last book in the Bible, whose name I disremember but which my mother used to read out loud to keep me from acting up when I was a kid. I don't ever remember it having any effect on me at all. "It's slap full of gas. We can go a long ways."

"We'll go straight to perdition," sighed Lucas, but he had to admit Marvin had got us wheels and it had been his idea. We got out of town without much trouble and headed west on I-20 again. I opened the glove box and it was then I knew somebody was looking out after us. After we finally got to Texas and things calmed down, I often told Lucas, looking back, that when Marvin Peabody stole that truck in Heflin, Alabama, it was a sign that God approved of us. Lucas, who didn't believe in God, would just snort. But I believed it and still think it's so. Inside was a pint bottle of Jack Daniel's and an envelope. They were so excited about the bottle, grabbing and fussing, that I had time to open the envelope. Inside was a neat little pile of fifteen one-hundred-dollar bills.

"We rich," I said, taking the money out. Well, Marvin grinned, sort of, but Lucas went absolutely apeshit and started giving speeches again, something about Spartans and Greeks and battles and such. As usual, I couldn't make much of all of it, and Marvin Peabody didn't act like he even heard Lucas, which was just as well.

We drove as far as Tuscaloosa, where we got a room because Marvin wanted to see where Bear Bryant had coached, him being a big football fan. We parked the truck in a long full lot by a grocery store before we walked to the motel. It was the first good sleep I'd had in days, and I slept for two hours before I woke up and Lucas and I got something to eat, Marvin Peabody being gone out looking for Bear Bryant's footsteps.

We wandered around Tuscaloosa as the evening came on, a nice enough town even though it was Bear Bryant's place, and me being a Georgia Bulldog fan not in awe at all. We stopped by a bookstore that was just about closing and Lucas chewed them out for not carrying any of his books. It was just about then that I realized I'd never seen one of his books and wondered if maybe he was just crazy and had never written a line.

I went back to the motel while Lucas went out for a few drinks. I was feeling tired again, maybe something hanging on from the sickness I had. I waited for a long time for Lucas or Marvin to come back to the room, but finally I fell asleep. When I woke up, there was a banging on the door. I didn't know what time it was, but I figured it for late.

"Just a minute," I said. I got off the bed feeling like a broke tree limb, stiff and weak, and opened the door. It was Lucas, covered with blood and panting like a dog.

"God in heaven," I said. I brought him into the room. He sat on the edge of the bed, looking blank for a time and then he started to cry. "Lucas, what happened?" I sat down beside him and put my arm around his shoulder. He put his face on my shoulder, getting blood all over me and making me feel kind of hot and embarrassed. He was sobbing so loud I couldn't make anything of what he was babbling about.

"They took me," he finally said. I understood that, and I also understood he'd had most of the money. I'd took a hundred, Marvin had took two hundred and Lucas had the rest. I pushed him off of me and looked at his face, which was bloody from a cut on his forehead. I had me the idea he'd let it run down all over his face on purpose, but that was probably a passing mean thought, which I'm apt to have from time to time.

"They took you?"

"They took me." He nodded.

I said, "Who took you?" Lucas sighed real heavy and I could smell the whiskey on his breath. Him sitting next to me was like being brother to a hairy bowling ball, but I felt bad for him, for all of us.

He said, "I got into a card game and . . ."

"A card game?" I said. "Here?"

"Unh huh," he said. "Oh, I knew I never should have done it. I was brought whole cloth into this den of iniquity by a young woman I'd chanced upon at a nearby tavern. I would have followed her to the clapping rocks of Scylla and Charybdis, so lovely was she." I was still half asleep and thought Lucas had said he had the clap, which made me push him away.

"How in the hell did you get the clap so quick?" I said.

"Oh Lord," he said. "Not the clap." He repeated what he said about the clapping rocks. "I never touched her, for God's sake. She took me upstairs over the tavern and got me to playing five-card draw, and before you know it . . . oh God, you're going to hate me, Jake."

I was getting mad, which made me feel better. I got a drink from the bottle, what was left of it. He sat on the bed, his lower lip poked out like a kid you'd just fussed at.

"How much is left?"

"Just a little bit," he said. "What if I'd come back with double?"

"What if frogs had wings?" I said. "How much?"

"Twelve dollars and some odd change," he said. He flinched and he should have, because I thought for a minute I was going to kill him.

"You stupid son of a bitch!" I yelled. Lucas started crying again, I sat down on the edge of the other bed. Now we couldn't pay for the room, we couldn't get

80

clothes or bus tickets, and we were stuck with Marvin
Peabody, who'd already stole a car for us. Jail wasn't
where I wanted to spend my last days. "How in the hell
could you be so stupid?"

"I need you to be my . . . uh . . . manager," he said. "I
seem incapable of the life lived independent of a help-
mate."

"You are one stupid son of a bitch," I said. I'd left the
door open a crack, and just as I'd called Lucas a son of a
bitch for the second time in a minute, Marvin Peabody
came into the room looking like he'd been saved in a tent
meeting and was waiting to be dunked in the river.

"I saw where he coached," Marvin said. "Bar Bryant
coached where I seen. They call the stadium after him. I
stared at it and stared at it. Lord, it was pretty." He
looked at Lucas. "What in the hell hit you?" I was curious
myself since Lucas hadn't told me yet.

"I demanded that they return our capital," he said.

"He's not talking English again," said Marvin.

"You don't want to hear it in English," I said. We all
stared at one another for a good minute. "Lucas lost all
our money in a card game." Marvin's face was unmoving
at first, then it began to crumble like a biscuit, his lips
quivering, eyes getting narrowed up.

"A card game?" he finally said.

"That is correct," said Lucas, seeming to defend himself.

"Oh no," said Marvin and he sat down on the bed and
put his face in his hands. His voice came up muffled: "I
was going to buy us a whore." The very idea made me
mad at Lucas again, since I'd been thinking more often
about women lately. I'd never been a damn monk and
didn't intend to start, even though when Betty'd left me
I'd took it pretty hard.

81

"A woman of the night?" asked Lucas. "That was not a bad idea."

"You stupid shit," Marvin said, and he jumped across the bed and grabbed Lucas around the throat and started choking him. I jumped on top of Marvin, which squashed Lucas flat. Lucas's eyes were bugging out and his face was turning red. I learned a trick one time in a bar in New Jersey, so I did it to Marvin, clapping my palms real hard on his ears. Somebody did it to me, and it hurts like hell and makes you think for a time that you've gone stone deaf. Marvin jumped up howling, and I kicked him hard as I could in the balls. His mouth went open, he quit holding his ears and grabbed the family jewels and went down in a heap on the carpet.

I said, "You all right?" as I picked Lucas up and held him in my arms. He wheezed and nodded. It was just about then I saw the patrol cars. Our door was still open, and across the parking lot two cars, lights revolving, had stopped by the truck Marvin Peabody'd stolen, and cops were out kicking around it, writing stuff down.

"Come on," I said soft as I could. "We got to get the hell out of here." He stood. Marvin was still lying there, and I led Lucas outside and we crept along the breezeway. Lucas saw the cops and knew right off it was trouble so I didn't have to urge him to get going. We got to the end of the breezeway, walked across another parking lot and found ourselves back on the street, broke again.

"This has evolved surely into a savage journey," said Lucas, which was right well put, if you asked me. "What are we going to do?"

"Get a ride," I said. We walked and walked until we came back to I-20, which headed southwest toward Meridian, Mississippi. By this time, it was almost midnight and I was so tired I wanted to die. By now Marvin

82

Peabody was probably locked up in jail babbling all about me and Lucas, even though he didn't know my last name, I didn't believe, and he might not have remembered Lucas's. I didn't feel bad about getting out of Tuscaloosa and to this day I still pull for whoever the University of Alabama is playing.

I put my thumb out. We stood there until it started to rain, nobody even thinking about stopping. I wished I still had my cans of sterno, but they were back in Nell's house. I was feeling low that night, low as I'd felt in a long time. I've always been a hopeful sort of man, believing that if you keep heading straight sooner or later things will work out for you. But that night I was feeling like Lucas said he felt. Being a human being wasn't all that hot and I didn't see it getting better anytime soon.

We went under an overpass. The rain was coming down steady by then and the traffic on I-20 splashed along beside us. You'd think people would be more helpful when they see you standing in the rain, but there's too many baby rapers wandering around now. I wouldn't have picked us up, neither.

"I'm cold," Lucas said miserably. "We have neither the comfort of a bottle nor of women. I used to wonder what I would do with my few remaining days. Now I know. I shall spend them trying to get out of Alabama." He was shivering, the blood had caked on his face and in general the miseries had got both of us down.

"Let's try to sleep," I said. "Things can't be no worse than this in the morning." I took off my wet shoes to put my head on and Lucas did the same, and we huddled up next to each other. Lucas had lost some weight, but he was still heavy and gave off heat like a winter fire. I remember that night I dreamed about Betty for the longest time, about how excited she'd been about the house I built for her, about how we would get drunk and then light candles in the bedroom and spend half the night loving one another, even though she was sort of fat and not very pretty and I was not too bright. It was a good dream, one to keep the cold away.

But it didn't last all night because most dreams don't, and I woke up before dawn and saw it was still raining and I still felt blue. My daddy never would have believed I got myself into this mess. He was a self-made man and expected me to be the same, able to make anything I needed, track and hunt food, live off the land. Instead, when I was a boy back then in the Depression, I got started getting on trains, riding with people up and down the East coast. Hell, people'd pick a fella up back then, but nowadays I didn't blame them.

Morning finally broke over Tuscaloosa, and Lucas, who snored the night away, woke in fine fettle, stretching and wondering where we could get some food.

"First off we got to get a ride out of here," I said. "I wonder if Marvin Peabody's in jail. He might of told on us."

"Fie," said Lucas Kraft.

"Huh?"

"A pox on the Tuscaloosa police," said Lucas.

I put my shoes on and we went down to the roadside, where we stood for a while. It was getting light but the cars still had their lights on. We stood for a long time like that.

"Are you afraid of dying?" Lucas asked. A transfer truck came rumbling past, scattering up mud from the roadway. I thought about it.

"I'm afraid of starving to death," I said.

Lucas said, "Nicely avoided."

"I'd just as lief live now, Kid." He stuck his right index finger in my side and cocked his thumb like a gun and went "Bam!" and then blew over the end of his finger like he'd shot me.

"We are both outrageous liars," he said, and that was when a green Pontiac came off on the shoulder and we got another ride. The license plate said the car was from Mississippi. We hustled up to the car, but Lucas had left his shoelaces untied and tripped and fell flat on the concrete. I had to help him up while he was cussing a blue streak.

"We shouldn't be riding in a Pontiac," Lucas said mysteriously. "They're named after a dead Indian. We're cowboys. We have to believe in signs."

An old feller wearing a black suit was driving the Pontiac and seemed happy to see us, though I couldn't tell you why, since we were both still wearing the overalls that belonged to Nell Marino's dead husband and we'd both spent the night under a bridge.

"Morning, men," he said cheerily. I got in the back and Lucas got in the front, which he always did as a sign of him being superior. "Where you all heading?"

"Mississippi," I said, meaning it for the first time. "Up toward Greenville. Quacaretchee." That was my town, and I hadn't been there in nearly twenty years.

"Well good gravy, I'm heading up 92 toward Greenville," he said, his false teeth slipping and clacking all the time. "I'd be proud to have you ride with me." We rolled off, and Lucas looked over the old guy like he was a leper.

"My travelling companion back there is Jake Baker," Lucas said. "And I am Kid Kraft. Perhaps you have heard of me. I was Lightweight Champion of the World from 1938 to 1941."

"Good gravy," the man said, grinning. "I'm Reverend Otha Calhoun. I've been a circuit rider hereabouts for fifty-six years now. I'm preaching a prayer meeting service up in Indianola tonight. I know how tiring it can be out on the road. You boys down on your luck or what?"

"I told you about Pontiacs," Lucas said, shaking his head as he turned his squat little body toward me. He turned back toward Reverend Calhoun. "Actually, we are living the life of men of free will. We intend henceforth to live dissolute and fascinating lives about which men will write for years. I am going to be killed in a range war."

Reverend Calhoun looked sideways at Lucas, trying to make sure, I reckon, that he didn't bite. I didn't know how tired I was, because one minute I was watching Lucas and the Reverend staring at each other and the next the car was stopping in front of the first place in my life I ever ate store-bought ice cream.

I WAS BORN IN Quacaretchee in 1912 and left the place when I was eighteen, heading out with the Depression bums on the road, traveling all up and down the East. That was one hell of a mistake. I don't know if home is where the heart is. I've heard that an awful lot over the years. Like I said, I never lit anywhere long enough for it to be home again, except for Branton, and it meant something because of Betty.

Quacaretchee was a bump in the road off state 442 not far from Doddsville in Flower County. The roads were all dirt when I was a boy, and it was more like the countryside with a few buildings thrown about. We lived right up snug to the town where my daddy worked at the livery stable, horses still being important in those parts until, I guess, the start of the second big war. My mama was a big woman with a face like a horse, but it was always said Belle Baker never hurt a soul and was honest as the day is long. You could get a worse sentence for your stone. My niece Belle was named after my mama, named by my sister, Lassie. I always thought Lassie was a pretty name, Daddy being descended from Highlanders as many folks hereabouts were, but they ruined it with that TV show about the dog.

"Jake, Jake," Lucas was saying, looking around disgusted. "Is this your patrimony? My God, it looks more like the edge of this sorry world, the place after which there is no place."

"That sounds right nice, Kid," said Reverend Otha Calhoun. I was still groggy from being asleep, and my overalls had gone stiff on me, so I was having trouble moving around. "Jake, isn't this it? I drove up here just for you."

"This is it, Reverend," I said. "We'll be getting out here."

"Of course we won't," snorted Lucas. "Drive on, good man. We must needs be getting on toward Texas." I opened the door and got out and slammed it.

"I'm getting out here," I said, looking around. "You can go on, Kid. Been nice knowing you."

"You can't taunt a former professional boxer like that," he said. I wanted to remind him that I was really the one who had fought for money one time, but I didn't bother. I was standing there looking at the spot where the bank used to be when the Pontiac drove off. I stared at the back of the car. I don't know what I felt for Lucas, except it was a sad kind of feeling thinking he was gone. He wasn't a prize, but hell, neither was I, and when you're out on the road the only thing you can count on is a friend. You make good friends when you are lost.

The car went one block, stopped, and Lucas got out and just stood there looking at me while the Reverend drove away. Lucas and I stared at one another for a time

88

and then we started walking toward each other, down the sidewalks of Quacaretchee, under the shade of some old water oaks.

I could tell it was the same town, but in the twenty years since I'd been there, it seemed like they'd torn down everything about it I liked. The town was laid out in a small square, and when I was a boy, there was the newspaper, the livery stable, the Chautauqua House, Mr. McCandless's dry goods, the butcher, John Henry Bayless, and some other stores I disremembered at the time. Now, there was a fried chicken place, a garage where two grease monkeys were arguing over a timing chain and a boutique called Brides 'n' Things. It was enough to make you feel real bad.

When we got close enough to talk, Lucas said, "Now that I have made the worst decision in my life, perhaps you can show me to the City Hall where they have the statue of Jake surmounted by an eternal flame."

"Come on," I said. "I want to go visit some of my relatives."

"Oh, great," said Lucas Kraft. We walked down the main drag, and I felt like people were staring at us. When I was a boy there was an old man named Jefferson who had fought the Yankees at Shiloh, and he just wandered around town telling his story over and over. A tramp we called them back then, except he'd lit in Quacaretchee and never left. He would see us boys walking down to the drug store for a soda pop and come at us like a dragonfly at a mosquito. He'd say, "Boys, did you ever hear about me and the Battle of Shiloh?" and the boys would make merciless fun of him. I always felt sorry for him myself, but I couldn't let on or the other boys would have picked at me forever. He came to mind because I saw a reflection of me and Lucas in the broad front window of the new drugstore and I thought I looked an awful lot like Jefferson. I wasn't too happy about that, but at least I was alive. Maybe I could wander about and tell some of my stories.

"Where in the name of Hades are you taking me?" Lucas asked. "I am not properly attired for calling on someone."

"These folks won't mind," I said, and that was the truth because I was taking him to the Faith Baptist Church Cemetery. Quacaretchee is only about thirty miles from the Mississippi River and Arkansas, so the soil is kind of soft and sandy, dark and good for farming, which was good for my family, my daddy being in the livery stable business, as was his daddy before him. I mention the soil because to get to the cemetery, you had to turn off the main drag and walk down a dusty side street.

"Are you taking me to a cemetery?" Lucas asked, as he spotted the rows of tombstones at the end of the street. "I'm getting hungry and we're still broke."

"We can go to my cousin's house," I said.

"Let's go there first," Lucas said.

"No," I said as firm as I could.

"You're right," he said softly. "We have to pay homage first. You're right." He reached up and patted me on the shoulder and it comforted me, though I wondered what anybody would of thought had they seen it. Comfort is hard to come by and I've often thought that being touched by another human being is about the best way to come by it, even if it was from somebody like Lucas.

We walked down the dirt road and came to the gates of the cemetery where the stones — marble, granite, and fieldstones — held out against the sun and the rain. The sun had come out hot and heavy and we were both sweating, but it felt good. Straight ahead, the cemetery looked like it always had, but down on the left in what had once been a field, there was a new part to the cemetery I hadn't seen. Toward the front part there was a funeral home tent up.

"You have family in here?" asked Lucas.

"Yeah," I said. He followed me down toward the back. The cedar tree they were under had grown enormous big, but it looked pretty much the same. We came up beside one another and looked at the stones of my mama and daddy and the baby girl mama'd had stillborn in 1910. To one side, daddy's kid brother Hector was buried, him having been killed by a tree limb falling on him on Christmas Day in 1888.

"Your parents?" Lucas asked. I looked at their names, Belle and Thomas, thinking, Lord, I'd give anything to see them again, to hold my mama's hand the way we used to walk downtown to Mr. McCandless's dry goods store. I could almost see my daddy's big arms forging barrel hoops. I was just a boy when he died. I was just going to take a look, head on out to my cousin's house and get some food, but there's no accounting for sentiment or age, so I busted out crying instead.

"Kid, I miss them so bad it hurts," I said. He nodded and sniffed a few times, too, probably thinking about his own mama and how she'd raised him after his father had been killed. "They was just plain hard-working country folks. But my daddy'd take his shirt off his back to help any man who needed it and my ma was a saint."

"That's what Nixon said about his mother," said Lucas. I gave him a hard look and he didn't look like he was trying to be ugly about it, so I let it pass.

"Anyway, if I die, I want you to get me back here and plant me next to them," I said. I started crying again and realized I couldn't take standing there, being an old man now and thinking about them, dead and all, so I turned and me and Lucas put our arms around one another and left the dead folks for my cousin's house.

His name was Lester Buckley, him being the son of my mother's sister Mary and her husband Francis Buckley. Everybody gave Francis a hard time about his name, so he had changed it to Frank when he was not even twenty, but it didn't matter because Francis had stuck. Lester lived in our old family house. Lucas and I let our arms go from one another after it got to feeling silly, and we got to the house after about ten minutes of walking.

"I'll be durned," I said. "It ain't hardly changed one bit." I was standing there marvelling at how much it was the same when this big black dog that looked like a wolf came bristling out toward us, barking to raise the dead.

"That hound is from hell!" yelled Lucas, who was the most superstitious man I ever knew. He got behind me and I stood there, trying to talk the dog down. That was when Lester Buckley came out of the house.

"Morgan!" he yelled. The dog stopped barking and came over to the house.

"Lester," I said, "I'm shore glad you came out and called off that dog." He narrowed his eyes and peered at me, and then his eyes got big.

"Jake?" he said, stretching the word out so long it was a wonder he ever got it finished. "You're dead, ain't you?" I grinned. I couldn't help it. The house was made of creosoted wood and the old wisteria vine mama'd planted was still there, run wild. She'd planted it and other stuff when daddy'd died to keep herself busy.

"Naw, I'm alive," I said. "This here's my friend, Kid Kraft. We need something to eat mighty bad. We've been on the road a good spell. Can we come in?"

"Lord have mercy," Lester said, and then we went inside. I almost fainted since it was so much like it used to be, the parlor with mama's rocking chair, the piano, which nobody could play for the past thirty years, the clock on the mantel still ticking like it did when I was a boy. You get to believing that nothing is ever the same, but that's not true.

We went on into the den, which did look a little different, Lester having put in a color TV and a video recorder and such.

"Where's Miss Molly?" I asked. That was his wife, a woman who looked to me like a rat would look if it over-eat itself nearly into the grave. We went on into the kitchen and sat down at the table. Lester put on some water for coffee and got out a frying pan.

"She's gone," he said.

"Oh," I said.

"Do you have any country sausage, eggs, toast, grits, such as that?" Lucas asked.

"Sure do," said Lester.

"Oh boy," said Lucas, his eyes lighting up. "By the way, they call me Kid because I was the youngest man in history to fly solo across the Atlantic."

"Well what do you know," Lester said. He looked at Lucas, admiring. "What year was that?"

"That would have been 1930," Lucas said. "I was seventeen years old. They said I was the bravest boy who ever flew up into the clouds."

Lester said, "Well, was that true?"

"Modesty," said Lucas Kraft, "prevents me."

Lester got out some slab bacon and put it in the frying pan, and after the water had boiled, he made us some coffee. I had memories of this place, Lord help, and though I was trying to keep them down, they kept coming back. Old home places are pleasing and awful sad at the same time because they remind you of everything you loved and lost. The food was not bad, though the bacon was a bit burned and the grits watery, Lester never having been much of a cook, as I recalled.

"How in the world did you all get out here?" Lester asked.

"Mostly hitchhiked," I said. "Neither one of us has much of any money."

"We're going to Texas," said Lucas. "We're retiring there for health reasons." After we ate we went out on the front porch. The day had clouded over and it was raining real slow. We sat in the chairs on the porch and leaned back. I wish I had a nickel for every time I saw my daddy do that. Every day he'd come home for dinner and then go on the porch and smoke a cigar and lean back with his hat down over his eyes and nap for a spell.

"Catch me up on what's going on with the family," I said. "Is Miss Molly . . ."

"She didn't die," he said, looking at the rain. "Been gone a year in July, next month."

"I'm sorry," said Lucas, and I don't think he even knew he'd said it. Between the three of us, we'd lost more women than made good sense.

"What about Diz and Lou?" I asked. They were cousins. He sighed and shook his head.

"You ain't heard nothing in so long," he drawled, "that I don't hardly know how to catch you up. Let me see. Okay. Diz got cancer in 1980, no . . .'81, and when it got real bad he drank a bottle of mineral spirits."

"Lord," I said.

"That animal should be restrained," Lucas said, pointing to the black dog, Morgan, who was standing wet in the yard glaring at Lucas.

Lester said, "After they buried Diz, Lou got remarried to a feller named Holton from Winona who runs a fertil-

94

izer business, but he dropped dead of a heart attack a few months later. Let's see. Felton and Mae and the kids are all fine, except for Bucky. You remember little Bucky? He was a kid last time you were in these parts."

"I remember."

"They caught him stealing from a Co-Cola machine up in Oxford," said Lester. "Put him away for a time. Missy won a scholarship to some Bible College in Little Rock, but she come home pregnant the first year."

"Are you related to the Snopeses?" asked Lucas, leaning forward.

"Not that I've heard of," said Lester. "Bud's got hisself rich selling land. I quit at the station six months ago on account of my back. I don't do too much."

"That animal is considering an attack upon my person," said Lucas, who drew his short legs up into the chair. The rain was coming harder and I wanted to take a nap.

"Naw, he never hurt nobody in his mangy life," said Lester. "All mouth."

"You and him might be related, Kid," I said, and Lucas, in spite of wanting to be mad, let his eyes smile before he could control it. All the talk about family started me to feeling awful guilty about Belle. I wondered if I should call her.

"Can I make a collect call on your phone?" I asked. Lester nodded and Lucas said something else about the dog. I went on inside and dialed the number at the house Belle and that boy husband of hers had built on what used to be my land. She answered it on the first ring. I let her say hello a couple of times before I said anything.

"Howdy, Belle." There was this silence and then a yell.

"Uncle Jake? My God, is this you? Where are you? I've

been worried half sick." She said it with all the sincerity of John Dillinger.

"I've been fine," I said. "I ain't telling you where I am. I just wanted you to know I'm all right. I just couldn't take that place and when I found out about the house . . ."

". . . oh Jesus Mary," said Belle. She started to sniffle. "My poor husband had a wreck."

"He all right?"

"He broke his leg in three places."

"I can't say I'm surprised. He land inside a dumpster?"

"That was a mean thing to say."

"Selling my house was a mean thing to do."

"After all we did for you, scaring us to death thinking you were dead."

"I ain't dead." That was about all I could take. I heard her talking on, but I just hung up and lay down on the bed in the front room, the one that had been mine. I don't think anybody'd slept there for years. The room was musty and dark with the rain, and I almost felt like I did when I was a boy. I could hear Lucas and Lester talking softly on the front porch and the sound of an occasional car sloshing past. It was a mighty peaceful feeling, but I knew I wanted to get on.

We spent the night with Lester, eating our fill, and the next morning he drove us down to Greenville to catch the bus. He also gave us fifty dollars apiece, which I thought was nice of him, though Lucas kept mumbling we should have looted the house. The rain was still coming down as I shook hands with Lester and I thought to myself he wouldn't live very long because he was giving up. Modern medicine hasn't found a way to save somebody who is tired of this life. I guess Lucas and I were tired of the life we had led, but so far I hadn't been bored.

The bus headed down toward Vicksburg on U.S. 61. It was half full, mostly of working folks, old colored ladies and a few smart-mouth looking kids. I sat on the window and Lucas on the aisle right across from a pretty young girl who was reading a novel by Norman Mailer. I saw Lucas getting agitated.

"What's the matter?" I asked. We'd got tickets that would take us far as Dallas.

"That book is a false picture of war in the Pacific," he said. I glanced up at the woman who had cut her eyes at Lucas and then back down at the book, looking a little scared. "That man has denigrated my writing." He fumed for a couple of minutes. Finally, he couldn't keep his mouth shut any longer, which was something that would get us into trouble several times later on.

"You are melting your brain reading that drivel," Lucas said, reaching out and grabbing the book and snatching it away from the woman. He closed it, looked at the cover with the title and groaned a little. The woman got up and stood over Lucas. She was right handsome, but she had that look you see often enough.

"He's a writer who's had hisself some bad luck," I said, but she started yelling anyway.

"Who in the hell do you think you are?" she shouted. She reached down to take the book back, but Lucas hugged it to him and she had to slap the shit out of him before he'd let go. There wasn't another word being spoke in the bus, everybody staring at us like we had something bad they might catch. She got the book and then walked down the aisle and sat muttering near the driver. I could see her leaning over telling him something and then the driver looked up in his mirror. I looked away like I didn't know Lucas.

"You gone get us throwed off the bus, Kid," I whispered.

"Go to hell," he said. He got up and tottered back to the little bathroom they got in back and closed the door. I watched the towns unroll in front of us, Hollandale, Panther Burn, Rolling Fork, all names from my boyhood, places I never thought I'd see again, going down Highway 61. I was starting to feel a mite melancholy. Lucas came back and finally calmed down, though he called Norman Mailer a few names just for good measure. He was going through Mr. Mailer's books one by one, saying they were all this and that when, about Vicksburg, he finally fell into a dead sleep.

That was too bad for Lucas, because that was where we crossed the Mississippi, and a sight that brought more tears to my eyes, I've never seen. He was snoring peaceful-like next to me. My daddy used to take me over to the river up near Greenville when I was a boy, and we'd take these long cane poles and fish for catfish, and lord, they were monsters in those days. My daddy'd always start to laughing when he got a big one, something I never seen another man do. He'd hook into one and start shaking just a little bit laughing, and then as he got it closer to the bank, he'd be laughing so hard the tears would make his face wet. I never thought a catfish was funny that way, but I reckon that's the only way daddy could show how he felt, not being one to cry and all.

Lucas slept right into Louisiana, through Thomastown and Tallulah and Quebec. I used to have me a honey in Quebec, a pretty redheaded gal with green eyes, but she wanted me to marry her after we sat in the back seat of my car and I got spooked and never even saw her again, even though she wrote me six or seven times. I've always felt bad about it. When the bus went through, I felt something, but I'm not sure what it was. The bus turned after we got through Quebec and went back down to I-20, and then I went to sleep, too.

Lucas and I nodded on and off all the way across Louisiana. We were both tired, I guess, and sometimes we'd wake up when we'd get off the interstate and wander off to a small town, and Lucas would say something unpleasant about the town. I tried to get him to calm down, but he didn't seem to be able to. I reckon he was doing the best he could. The girl with the book finally got off in Shreveport, and it wasn't until then I noticed she had red hair.

JUST PAST GREENWOOD, Louisiana, we finally went over the state line into Texas, and Lucas, who was sitting on the window and saw the sign first, got up and started walking up and down the aisle practicing his quick draw and yelling, "Howdy, podner!" until the bus driver'd had enough and said he was going to throw Lucas off if he didn't shut up. Lucas sat back down, grinning like a dog in a garbage can.

"We must needs find money," he said, "so we can purchase our chaps and spurs and boots. And I want a set of six guns. And a horse, just like Tom Mix's Tony. Jake, my boy, we have finally reached the promised land."

"Well, that's a miracle, Kid," I said. "You got any idea where we can get any dough?"

"Two ways," he said. "Honestly or dishonestly. One way involves days of sweat and toil and the good-feeling, muscle-stretching labor of the men of the fields. The other involves deception, lies, and some kind of larceny, for which we may spend the rest of our natural-born days in the slam, fending off advances by gigantic fags with tattoos of daggers on their forearms."

"We going to get jobs?"

"I was thinking of knocking over a liquor store," said Lucas Kraft. Our tickets went only as far as Dallas, and as we saw the towns pass by, Longview, Tyler, then little ones like Canton and Myrtle Springs, I realized that once we got to Dallas, we didn't have much of nothing to do. It was a right dismal prospect, but Lucas was bouncing around like a child. He even told a guy across the aisle reading a book by Hemingway that it wasn't half bad.

We pulled into Dallas, the bus hissing and squeaking to a stop and the driver didn't look at all sad to see us go, even though we'd been with him since Mississippi and spent several nights there, eating crackers and Cokes at all the little knothole towns where we stopped. Now, we didn't have hardly a penny to our names, but Lucas was still excited.

The heat was awful. The overalls felt like they weighed a thousand pounds, and I wondered what Nell Marino had done with our other clothes, the ones that were really comfortable. Almost as soon as we got there, Lucas started babbling about President Kennedy.

He said, "My boy, we are going to do some primary research at Dealey Plaza."

"What's that?"

"What's that?" he said, exasperated with me, and not for the first time. "It's where the dastardly act took place. We shall go there, I shall assume the position of the second assassin on the famed grassy knoll and you shall walk down the street along the route our beloved president took."

"Ain't you getting hungry, Kid?" I asked.

"Later, later," Lucas said. We walked for a long time along the steaming sidewalk, Lucas grabbing strangers asking for directions, and finally, after maybe an hour, we were at a place I recognized. It felt real funny, and I wanted to leave, but Lucas was beside himself.

"Here it is!" he yelled. A man walking past us looked at Lucas like a lot of folks looked at Lucas. "I'm going up there behind that wall. You go up to the corner and walk down the sidewalk like a president."

"Like a president? How's that, Kid?"

"My God," said Lucas, shoulders sagging. "With dignity, Jake. Do you know what dignity is?"

"Yeah." I wasn't completely sure, but I thought it was a quality the Kid was lacking altogether.

"Then go to it," he said. "It might help if you hum 'Hail to the Chief.' Do you know that venerable tune?" I didn't, but he waved it off and scrambled up the hill, at least as fast as his short legs would carry his body. I shrugged, walked up to the corner, turned around and waited for him to yell. I wanted to please Lucas. I don't know why I always wanted to please him, but others did, too; awe, I reckon, in dealing with somebody who'd wrote a whole book. I didn't know that song he said, so I hummed "Home on the Range," which seemed more appropriate anyway.

He yelled something and I started walking. He had climbed up on this low brick wall and was aiming at me like he was holding a rifle. I kept humming and walking and it felt odd, as if he might really have a rifle. It must have been a hundred degrees, and I was sweating like a mule, and I thought if he didn't shoot me soon I'd be slathering at the mouth.

Well, he shot me all right. I heard him scream "Bang!" at the top of his lungs, and then he fell head first off the wall and rolled nearly down to the street. A few cars went by, but nobody seemed to notice. I ran down to him, which left me feeling lightheaded and sick. He was lying completely still and staring up at the sky.

"Kid!" I yelled. "You all right? You all right?" He didn't say a word. I got to him and leaned down, a stream of sweat falling down my face on to his fat chest. "Kid, you dead?" He looked at me.

"Lee Harvey Oswald was framed," said Lucas. He sat up and brushed himself off.

"You hurt?"

"Of course not," said Lucas, but I had to help him up and he acted like something hurt somewhere. The run down to him had left me feeling like I was going to faint. "We must needs find some shade and succor."

"Now wait a minute . . ." I said.

"Forget it," he said.

We walked for a long time until we came to a rundown five-story brick building with a sign out front saying it was the Cowboy Arms. Lucas started saying it was an omen, but I said it looked like a flophouse, which didn't make him none too happy. I was so wore out and needing a flat bed so bad I didn't give a good damn what it was, so we went in with what little money we had left, got a room and rattled up to the fourth floor in an old elevator. We got out and found ourselves facing a long dark hall. The first door on the right was open and some woman was screaming at the top of her lungs about somebody being stupid drunk. No matter what I did back in Branton, Betty never yelled at me about drinking, thinking instead it was like being sick, and she'd help me off with my

clothes and put me to bed. That may be the nicest thing
one person can do for another in this life anyway.

We stood there, and Lucas looked in the room with the
open door and stared at the woman, who was short and
fat and mean looking. She said, "What do you want,
fuckhead?" so I grabbed Lucas and went on down to our
room. It was so hot I could hardly stand it — one little
window, a double bed and a chair. It also had a mirror
and I was so surprised at how I looked I could hardly
take my eyes off it. I had pretty much of a white beard,
wore out overalls and a look on my face like I was going
to die some time soon.

And it's a fact, I think, that if we'd spent more than one
night in that cowboy hotel we'd of never got out at all.
Without saying a word, we both got out of the overalls
and laid down on the bed, which bowed down in the
middle. But stretching out felt so good I didn't even
mind.

"What are we doing here?" muttered Lucas, looking at
the ceiling. "What in God's name has become of us, Jake?"

"We're going to be cowboys, Kid," I said, and he smiled
just a little, but he looked sad, which was how I felt.

"What on earth will become of us?" he asked again. I
had to admit that was the one thing I wanted to know,
too. "Jake, old friend, I think I'm starting to have some
feelings again that are vaguely human. I think it starts
with pity. The first thing you feel for this world is pity, for
yourself, for all the poor dumb creatures who wind up
sweating in a dark room in a strange town. You realize
you have long lost the comforts of home, of love, or
another's touch. And then pity gives way to fear and then
to sorrow, finally sorrow, always sorrow." It made me feel
bad to hear the Kid talk that way, but I knew what he was
talking about anyway.

"You talk like we're going to die here," I said. Despite the heat, I was starting to get sleepy and it felt real good.

"We aren't going to die here," said Lucas. "I am going to be gunned down in a range war, falling in slow motion, my gun out and shining in the sun, hair tousled by the desert wind. And I will become part of legend, and they will write songs about me, how I rode in from the East and became one of them so fast, how I helped rid them of the evil robber barons from town."

"You sure about that, Kid?" I asked, too sleepy to think much anymore.

"Go to hell," he said, but he was sleepy as I was, and when we woke up, we'd slept plumb through the afternoon and all night, too. I woke up first, and it was cool and the light was just coming in the window. I realized I was starving. I crawled off the end of the bed, feeling my age but happy to be alive, ready to get going again. I woke Lucas up, and he wasn't talking philosophy anymore, just grumbling because he felt like shit and so on. We did both get a good shower, and I felt a whole lot better.

We had about eight dollars left, so we went to a McDonald's and ate right, and when we got through it was still early morning, so we walked back down to the interstate and I stuck my thumb out while Lucas stood there with his hands in his pockets, not saying much, which spooked me a little.

"All towns look alike when you are on the road," Lucas said.

"That ain't true at all," I said.

"So what?" Lucas said.

We were standing there when a truck slowed down, an old beat-up pickup truck. It stopped a few yards ahead and Lucas and I walked up to it, and the man driving, a tall, leathery man, told us we could come on and ride with him.

"I'm Bo Kersh," he said. "Where you all heading?"

"West," I said. "We're looking for work." I reckon it did sound funny, but he didn't have to bust out laughing. Something in it struck Lucas as funny, and he was laughing, too, so I just shrugged as we pulled on to I-20 and headed West away from the rising sun.

"I'm going to over Abilene," he said. "What kind of work you looking for?"

"Ranch work or something," I said. "Handy work, like that."

"Do you know how much a set of six guns costs these days, podner?" asked Lucas. Bo said he didn't know and tried to act serious, but Lucas could seem powerful ridiculous at times.

"I might be able to help you fellers a bit," said Bo. "Friend of mine named Chuck Owens owns a big cattle ranch in Harkin County, up north of Abilene. He might be able to pay you a little, board you or something."

"The promised land," whispered Lucas, and I imagine I felt the same way.

Once we got past Dallas and Fort Worth, we could see the land unrolling all around us, some mountains down to the south, land straight out of a movie, and I was feeling like maybe we'd make it after all. Bo Kersh wasn't a cowboy, but he could of passed for one. Back when I was a man, I might have looked like a cowboy one time, but now I looked like an old hillbilly.

I thought back to looking at the TV at Fieldstone with Lucas and talking about breaking out, and well, here we were just like we'd planned. It made me feel good to know Lucas would still be standing on the road in Branton without me. Not that he'd ever admit it.

107

With a full stomach, I dozed off, and when I woke up, Lucas was saying in a loud voice that we were in Abilene, Texas, which was a right smart drive from Fort Worth on I-20.

Abilene, what I saw of it that first day, is a pretty town, but I didn't want to see towns any more, just wanted to see pastures and cattle and some cottonwood trees along some gulleys, maybe an Indian or two. We stopped at a nice store, which had the name Kersh's across the front in letters ten feet tall. Turned out it was a hardware store, and that Bo's daddy owned it. We got out and followed him inside.

"You all just make yourselves at home for a spell and I'll call Chuck," said Bo. The inside of the store was bigger than a football field, shelves and shelves of wire and lumber and pipes and such, and Lucas looked around like a lost bear, his beard shining in the lights.

"I'll wager they have never even read a book here, much less one of mine," said Lucas. "Nobody much knows who I am any more."

"Nobody's never known who I am," I said.

"Oh, great," said Lucas. I was looking at the price tag on a door with a little glass window when I heard something that sounded like a ripsaw on a pine knot. I turned around and saw Lucas laid out in a recliner they had for sale, snoring. I was going to wake him up when Bo came walking toward us. He took one look at Lucas, but instead of being mad at him for sleeping in a for-sale chair, he looked at him with pity. I guessed sorrow would come next if Lucas was right.

"He's not had much good rest lately," I said. When I said that, the snoring stopped and Lucas opened one eye.

"Horseshit, sir," he said, and he sprang up from the chair like a young man, which gave me a feeling I can't hardly describe, like something good and electric running through me, making me strong, feeling young even. Bo laughed and I liked him. I liked him even more when he said he'd called Chuck Owens up in Harkin County, and he'd agreed to let us have a go, for a few bucks a week each and room and board.

My old eyes filled up with tears, not so much because we'd done what we set out to do, but because this stranger had spent his day doing something nice for us.

"Kid, you can't be thinking bad thoughts about the world no more," I said.

"Glory," Lucas said, walking toward the front display window like he was in a state of some sort. "Glory, glory."

"His name really Kid?" asked Bo.

"He got that name when he was a movie actor," I said. Lucas turned to look at me and raised one eyebrow but didn't say anything. "He was a silent movie actor. Yep, made all kinds of movies. Once him and Francis X. Bushman was roommates. Old Francis X. was the one give him that Kid name because he was the youngest star in Hollywood. Then he married Sally Crandall."

"Oh sweet Jesus," said Lucas.

"Who was Francis X. Bushman?" asked Bo.

"A dead Catholic," said Lucas. "When do we hit the trail?"

Well, we hit the trail right then, driving north out of Abilene on U.S. 277. We went north through Jones County and then came into the town of Harkin, turned west and drove to a little old town on 380 called Rule, then we swung north for about five miles. By then Lucas was so excited I had to keep hitting him in the ribs with my elbow to calm him down. From far off we could see this gate rising out of the prairie grass like a pair of wings. I almost thought we'd all start to fly.

There was this big gate just like at Nell Marino's, but this time it said "Owensville," like it was a town, and Bo said we'd really like it there, that his old pal Chuck was fair, a good man to work for.

"I'm mighty grateful for what you done for us," I said.

Lucas said, "Indeed." The road wound slowly through some pretty land, prairie grasslands that cows had cropped down real close, and they were all about in little clumps, beef cattle as I reckoned. I didn't seem to find much to say, but Lucas was babbling all the while about cowboys and William S. Hart, and all I could do was grin and shrug at Bo, who seemed right amused by Lucas. We came between two tall hills and then it opened up into a wide flat valley. Right in the middle was a huge house, like a mansion, I reckon, two stories with cottonwoods up close all around it, a yard, two or three cars, and a ways from it, sitting up on a little rise, was another house, this one long and low with a flat top.

"Kid, would you look at that, " I said.

"It's just like I thought it would be," said Lucas. His eyes got all wet and his voice was thick. "It looks just like it should. I want a horse. A gun. Two guns and a ten-gallon hat. A quart of liquor and a squaw. I want a squaw!"

"Aw, come on," I said, sort of embarrassed.

"I want a squaw! I want her to stand by silently and wait on me and talk in sign language! I want to have an entire teepee full of bastard children by her!" Bo was laughing so hard I thought he'd have a wreck before we got to the house, but he didn't, which was a blessing.

We pulled up in front of it, and I could see it had a long porch on the first floor with hanging baskets of ferns and trailing green things, rocking chairs, a trellis covered in yellow roses. Bo stopped and a cloud of dust we'd kicked up drifted past us as the front door opened and a lady who was maybe forty, smiling and wiping her hands on an apron, came out. Me and Lucas got on out and stood there like kids at summer camp. I won't say it looked like home, but it looked like a place to lie down and rest, stay for a time.

Bo was talking to the lady when the front screen door of the house flew open and a tall, thin, weather-worn man came out. Bo motioned for us to come over. The man looked over us, up and down, and I smiled and tried to look strong, puffing out my chest. Bo introduced us to Chuck Owens.

"What can you boys do?" he asked. The woman, now I could see her, had the most beautiful eyes I ever saw on a woman in my life, and it was at that moment I decided to find me a little romance, something I'd thought I'd never want again.

"I can cook," I said. "And I'm still strong enough to do anything around here, cut grass, do anything, wash cars. I'll make you proud."

"I'm sure," said Chuck. "Mr. Kraft, are you the Lucas Kraft, the writer?"

"Oh my God," said Lucas, putting his hands on his face.

"I was on Iwo Jima during the war, and when I read *Deep Waters* I cried like a baby. You were there, too," he said.

"I was there," said Lucas. "You didn't ask me what I can do." Lucas puffed himself up, tugged at his overalls and walked around in a small circle.

"What can you do besides writing?" Chuck asked.

"I want to fight for justice in a range war," said Lucas, grand as a king. "I want to find the men who are trying to cheat you out of your spread and mercilessly hunt them down. And I want a set of pearl-handled six guns, chaps, and liquor and a squaw." Well, I figured he'd done it now, that after all his blowing he'd finally done it once too many times, but Chuck was laughing, and his lady was laughing, and Bo was shaking his head and shrugging.

"You haven't had a book in a while," said Chuck, still giggling a bit.

"I am no longer a writer," said Lucas.

"Well, that'll be your job here," said Chuck, "to write another book." Lucas stopped walking around in circles and stared at Chuck. I thought he was going to tell Chuck to go to hell. We weren't quite under the shade of one of the cottonwoods, and it was hot as I always thought Texas would be.

"What about the range war?" asked Lucas.

"If we have one, I'll call on you," said Chuck.

"Well, all right," said Lucas, looking down. "But only if you'll get me a set of revolvers and a horse."

"You'll both have horses to use," said Chuck. "We got about ten other fellers live up there in the Long House. Come on and I'll get you settled. You got any bags or anything?"

"Just what's on our backs," I admitted, feeling a little ashamed about it. "I'd sure be grateful for a razor and some clothes. Could you advance us a little for that?"

"Sure," said Chuck. "Y'all come on and follow me." I looked at Lucas and smiled and he rolled his eyes. Chuck said he'd pay us forty bucks a week plus room and board, which sounded like a lot to me, though I 'spect it didn't to Lucas, who'd been rich one time, after all.

We left the lady with the blue eyes, said goodbye to Bo Kersh and watched his truck as it headed back toward Abilene, which was where he'd been headed in the first

112

place. I was mighty grateful to him, and it hurt awful bad when I found out a couple of months later he'd got himself killed in a wreck down near Laredo.

As we walked up toward the Long House, I thought about a lot of things. I couldn't help it. I thought about Branton, back in Georgia, how it seemed so far away, about Fieldstone and how us two old buzzards didn't belong there, had made it all the way to Texas without croaking, how folks had helped and hindered us along the way. I thought about seeing my home town and the first place I ever got me an ice cream. I don't know why I thought on those things while we walked up to the Long House. I thought about Betty, too, about my house, the one I'd built for her with my own hands, and I thought about the Kid, too, him up there ahead of us now, walking like a king. Lucas said there were patterns to life, but I didn't see none of them. I only thought we might still have a lot of living left here in Texas, and I was sure right about that. I damn sure was.

PART II

ON ONE END OF THE Long House you could see down this pretty slope to a creek where there were rocks and cottonwood trees and a cow trail. Me and some of the boys had put chairs out there to watch the sun come up and see the color in the trees, now that it was fall. I was sitting there as Lucas came waddling up the hill.

Lucas and me had settled on the ranch like it had always been home, like we'd been reared in Texas, though I always felt some kind of pain when I thought about the house I built for Betty. But you always feel one sort of pain or another anytime you think on it, for folks who've passed away, things you lost and can never get back. I tried not to think on what I'd lost, but sometimes I couldn't help it.

I say we fit in like it was home. Well, I reckon it was true I did, anyway. I helped Wool, the colored cook who was the most foul-mouthed man I ever heard in my life, and that's saying something. I'd told Chuck I could cook and that was true, but I'd never cooked for twelve hungry men, and let me tell you, it's a thing. I thought Wool wasn't all that nice a name for a man who was colored, him with this gray fuzzy hair, but he didn't seem to mind. At dinner when everybody said the grub was good, Wool wouldn't show much emotion, but after we'd cleaned up, he'd sit back in the kitchen smoking his corncob pipe, nodding like somebody was talking to him, heaping praise on him. Wool must have been twenty years younger than me, but he sort of adopted me.

Wool and Lucas didn't get along at all, and at first, Lucas didn't get along with anybody. I've told you what Lucas was like, so it's not much of a surprise folks didn't understand him. Only thing was, nobody could do a thing about it because Mr. Owens liked Lucas's books so much. None of the rest of us was ever invited to the big house where Mr. Owens and his blue-eyed wife, who was named Missy, lived. But Lucas went up there at least once a week all summer, and they would talk about the war in the Pacific, about how everybody believed in the same things during the war, how after that everybody believed in different things, and now nobody believed in anything.

That was still true of Lucas, I guess. We'd only been there a couple of weeks when he told everybody at the table he didn't believe in God, Mom, apple pie or the flag of any country that could do what America did to the Indians. A trail hand named Whizzer Pippin threw his whole glass of iced tea in Lucas's face, and if I hadn't dragged Lucas back to our bunks they'd of probably beat the shit out of him.

After that, he would only pop off to me, which I was at least used to. We all lived in this open bunkhouse, just like an old cowboy movie, with a pot-bellied stove in the

118

middle. We'd used it a couple of times, now that it was early October, and I was in charge of keeping it filled with coal. Mr. Owens had given Lucas this small room on one end of the Long House, given him an electric type-writer and some paper. Lucas was filling up pages, but he hadn't showed any of them to Mr. Owens, which was good because Lucas said he was just typing things that popped into his head from his books and other things.

Anyway, I was sitting there late in the afternoon at the end of the Long House. Not everybody had come in yet, so there was time before Wool called me to come and help him. Whizzer Pippin was on the plains to the north working on a fence. I could see him up there moving back and forth. I liked to watch people working all about the ranch, the ones I could see from the house. Lucas and I both had horses we could use, and I'd been out once or twice, but Lucas wouldn't get near his after one black horse up and bit him on top of the head.

"What you been doing down there?" I asked when Lucas got close enough to hear me. The slope down to the creek isn't too steep, but Lucas was puffing and red faced.

"Thinking of fair Ophelia," he said in little gasps. I didn't know what he was talking about, but I'd gotten to where I didn't ask him to explain because it upset him that people weren't as smart as him, and he was my best friend.

"You going with us to Hector's tonight?" I asked. That was a country bar down in Stamford, and I'd been a couple of times, but Lucas never had. It was a Friday night, and every Friday night a bunch of the boys would go in there and listen to a band and get stupid drunk. I'd outgrown lots of things, but drinking didn't seem to be one of them.

"I believe I must needs imbibe some spirits this evening," he said, sitting next to me. A little breeze came up and you could feel winter in it. That was one thing I learned about Texas — you live with the land, letting it control you and not the other way around.

"I was hoping you might come and drink with me," I said.

"Jake," he said sadly, "Jake what in the world will I do with you? My aged companion, *mon semblable, mon frère.*" I smiled, not wanting to believe he'd say anything mean to me in Spanish or whatever that was.

"Does that mean you're coming?"

"Indeed it does," he said.

The Long House had a door on the end that went into Lucas's little office where he typed, and we went in there. The light was getting thin, but I could see all the naked women pictures he'd put up on the walls, and some of them women was doing things I'd only heard about in the service.

"How's the book coming, Kid?" I asked.

"Oh, great," he said.

There was another door from his study into the bunk area, and while we were standing there, it flew open and there was Wool, scowling, arms folded across the white apron he always wore.

"Let's go, Jake," Wool said, his voice deep as God's. "Leave this asshole to write on his machine." He glared right hard at Lucas, whose jaw dropped, then he rolled his eyes.

"Chapter Seven," said Lucas, sitting down and rolling paper into his typewriter. "The Death of the Nigger Cook."

"Shit," said Wool, and I pushed him out the door into

120

the bunk room before they had a chance to get into it again.

We ate that night, all of us — me and Lucas, Whizzer Pippin and Tom Ivey, Jack Ransom, John Smith, Tree Jefferson and J.T. Knox and the others. I knew their names, the others, but those I just named hung around together in a bunch and they were the ones I knew best. Whizzer was really all right, and Tom was as smart a man as I ever knew. He'd read one of Lucas's books when he was in college in Ohio, but he'd wanted to get away from the world and this was good a place as any. He was handsome, with blond hair and blue eyes, and all the guys used to get him to tell stories about his girls in town, even all the way down to Abilene.

Jack Ransom and John Smith were just good old boys, hard and tall, good workers who knew how to work and drink but didn't have much to say. Tree Jefferson had one time been a pro wrestler, and he was the only colored man in the Long House besides Wool, and nobody fooled with him because he was damn near seven foot tall. I reckon J.T. was my favorite. He was quiet, shy sort of, and small as a boy, not more than twenty-five. Everybody there liked J.T. because he didn't seem like a person who could hurt another on purpose. He was born kind, and there's only a few of them in a town.

Anyway, we cooked, me and Wool, him mumbling about Lucas the whole time and how he was a smartass honkey that deserved to get his butt whipped, and I just kept nodding like one of those dogs you put in the back window of the car. I won't say I was born kind, but I was born to get by, and sometimes the only way you get by is to turn away from a hard word.

Wool cleaned up after the meal and we all got ready to go into town, everybody but a guy named Scout who sat

121

every night outside looking up at the stars and drinking. Scout had been hurt real bad by a woman, at least that's what Tom Ivey told me. I felt bad for Scout and wanted to talk to him about losing your woman, but so far, I hadn't done it.

Me and Lucas, Tom and Tree Jefferson went down to Stamford in an old Jeep. A few of the others were coming there, but most were heading down to Abilene to hear some cowboy singer whose name I've forgot. I liked Hector's. They had a house band, and the crowd never got too rowdy, just a place where a hard-working man could have a few drinks.

The parking lot was crowded. We got out and went on in, Lucas babbling the whole time about gathering local color from the rubes, saying that sentence over and over until Tree looked hard at Lucas and he shut up. Inside, there was a big horseshoe-shaped room with tables and chairs and a stage up front where the band was playing. The lights were low and folks were talking. We took a table near the back, the four of us. When I was a young man, some folks would kill you for sitting with a colored man, but nobody noticed anymore, though everybody noticed Tree. He stood out.

"I'm going to get me a talking part," said Tree after our drinks came. I had a whiskey, and Tree and J.T. had beers. Lucas drank something green and foamy, for which he got some stares. He drank it in one gulp and grabbed the waitress before she had a chance to leave.

"I'll have another of these," said Lucas. "My compliments to the bartendress." She leaned over to get the empty glass and Lucas looked down the front of her dress. "I'm a famous writer. Would you like to come see my drafts?" She smiled real flat, like you smile when you want somebody to take a hike, and J.T. laughed low in his throat and she went away. "That woman is the concubine of some dustbowl turkey. What a waste."

"How you going to get a talking part?" I asked. "I just heard about it today."

"Go up and ask real nice," said Tree. I laughed and Lucas was staring at the waitress, who was bringing his new green drink. She set it down in front of him and he drank it in one more gulp and asked for another. The waitress wasn't too happy about it, but she got the glass and went off for another.

"Of what are you gentlemen speaking?" asked Lucas. "A talking part? Are you becoming thespians here in the wilds of Texas?"

"You lucky I got a sense of humor," said Tree. "And you an old man. I be beating the shit out of you if you ain't."

"It means actors," said Lucas, trying real hard to be buddy-buddy. "Just a word means actors. You going to be in a play hereabouts?"

"The movie," I said. "They're making a movie right here in Harkin County." Hector's was almost full, and already the noise was a little much for me, and I liked it better weeknights, but I was glad I could still drink and that I was still alive.

"A movie?" said Lucas, sitting up. The waitress came with his third green drink. She set it on the table in front of him and he picked it up and drank it in one gulp again. "Can you get me a blue drink?"

"Blue?" she said. "How about a pitcher of beer? And a tip."

"Wonderful suggestion," said Lucas. He got out a five-dollar bill and gave it to her, and she put it in her apron pocket and went off for beer. Lucas could be reasonable, though most people didn't believe it.

123

"Everybody says they pay a lot," said J.T. "I could use me some money with Christmas coming up, but they're not starting until January, ain't that right?"

"Heard they're waiting for snow," said Tree.

"What kind of movie?" asked Lucas.

"A Western," said J.T. "I only heard of one who's in it. Sally Crandall. You ever heard of her?" Lord, I thought, here it comes. I didn't want to say anything until Lucas did and I figured he would start yelling and they'd throw us out. Instead he nodded a couple of times and got kind of quiet and stared sort of blank-like. "I said you ever heard of her?"

"Oh yeah," said Lucas. By then, Lucas was weaving a mite like an old boxer, drunk in his chair, and when the waitress came back, he leaned over and bit her on the titty and she poured the pitcher of beer on his head. He licked at the suds dripping off his nose and nodded while Tree leaned back laughing so hard he could barely get his breath. I was trying to wipe the beer off his fat face when I noticed the waitress was smiling, too.

"He ain't been himself lately," I said. "He's had a spell of bad luck." I reckon it was the right thing to say because the waitress looked down on poor old Lucas with what seemed like pity and went off for another pitcher of beer. It was good luck that we were sitting toward the back and nobody saw it happen. J.T. was sipping his drink and Tree finally stopped laughing.

"Sally," Lucas whispered, looking at me.

"Yeah," I said. He was quiet for a time and J.T. and Tree talked about the cattle and fences, about how Mrs. Owens, the blue-eyed lady, had been sick lately and Chuck wouldn't let her go down to Abilene to the doctor, even though he should have. The waitress came back with the beer and I'll be goddamn if Lucas didn't lean over

124

and bite her on the titty again, but this time she just backed off and said, "Shit," real soft and looked up at the ceiling like God was up there and might give her some advice. But that was the problem with Lucas. Advice didn't help much because he always acted just the way he wanted.

"Kid, what if she's got a big boyfriend?" I asked.

"Fuck him if he can't take a joke," said Lucas. He drank a mug of beer, and that was all it took to open him up. I was drunk myself, though as I've said before, it didn't take as much as it did once. He got this wild look on his face and started muttering about movies.

"What's that?" asked J.T. "Our writer pissed off about something?" Lucas stood, put his right hand over his heart and licked his lips.

"Sally Crandall," he boomed, "is a shameless whore!" The band was between sets and everybody stopped and stared at Lucas, who looked like he would fall over any minute. I grabbed him and pulled him into his seat, but not before he could say it again. This big fella got up out of his chair down near the front and came back toward us.

"Why'd you have to do that?" asked Tree groaning. He could hold himself in a fight, but fighting for Lucas was like fighting a tree for dropping its leaves in fall. It didn't change anything and it never would. "You're just one stupid old son of a bitch."

"Indeed," said Lucas. The man got to our table and I was trying to think of something funny to say when he sat down beside Lucas. He had a look of real hatred in his eye, but then something happened and he squinted at Lucas and his mouth fell open. The man was maybe sixty, but he looked like he was made of a tree stripped of all its bark, lean and hard.

"Jesus H. Christ," the man said. "Lucas? What in God's name are you doing out here? This is incredible." Lucas's eyes would hardly focus on anything by then, but he looked at the man hard and then he looked disgusted, tried to sip his beer and poured half of it in his lap. I took the beer out of his hand and set it on the table.

"Howdy, Hugh," said Lucas.

"My God," said Hugh, his face spreading into a smile. "I thought you were dead."

"Oh that," said Lucas. "I am. Died years ago. Unfortunately" — he had trouble with the word and had to say it three times before he got it right — "my body keeps thumping along."

"Who are you?" I asked.

"I'm Sally Crandall's agent," Hugh said.

"And you know this clown?" J.T. asked, pointing at Lucas.

"I reckon," said Hugh, chuckling. "Didn't he ever tell you about him and Sally?" Tree and J.T. looked at each other, and I'll have to admit I wasn't sure I'd ever believed it when he said he'd been married to Sally Crandall.

"Unh uhn," said Tree. "What?'

"I've got to pee pee," said Lucas, trying to stand.

"They used to be married," laughed Hugh. "And look at him now. Just look at that." Lucas looked down at Hugh, weaving, mouth open like he'd run a race. I heard Tree say, "No shit," just as Lucas took a big looping swing at Hugh and went crashing down to the floor over a chair. He laid there, flat out, snoring softly. I got down and shook him.

"Kid," I said. "Come on, Kid." I turned him over and a bump was coming up over his right eye, but he didn't seem to be hurt any other way. "Help me get him outside." Hugh, Tree and J.T. helped me pick him up and head for the door. I saw a couple of the boys from the Long House who were there laughing and pointing at Lucas, and if I'd been younger, I'd have busted them. We took Lucas out and laid him across the back seat of the Jeep under the roll bar. It was cool but not real cold that night and you could see millions of stars all over heaven.

Hugh followed us outside and stood there with his hands in his hip pockets, looking down at Lucas.

"To think he'd come to this," Hugh said. Lucas lifted his head and looked at Hugh and said something that sounded like "Go to hell," which is what it was, I imagine, but it was so thick and slurred nobody but me knew it. Then Lucas went back down into his drunk. "He used to be one of the most gifted writers in this country."

"Is that a fact?" said J.T. "We seen him writing there and Mr. Owens said he was a famous writer but didn't none of us hardly believe him. And he was really married to Sally Crandall?"

"He was indeed," said Hugh. "Lord, that's been years ago, back when all of us were young or almost. We felt young, anyway. Now don't anybody feel all that young any more. Oh, he was something. Back there in the early sixties, there were men thought Lucas Kraft would win the Nobel Prize before he was through, and him and Sally made a cute couple. But then things started going wrong for both of them. He wrote that book about women, and Sally up and left him and the critics just killed him."

"What book about women?" I asked.

"You'd just as well not know," said Hugh. Lucas was snoring peacefully in the back seat of the Jeep. "Anyway, that's all water over the dam now. He never was the same after that. We hadn't heard from him in years."

127

"Is she hereabouts?" asked Tree.

"No," said Hugh. "She's still in L.A. I just came down here to look around for her. She's got this quirk, always wanting me to look around where she's going to work before she gets there. Hell, I do it, even though it's going to be weeks before they get here."

"I be dog," said J.T.

"You all take care of him," said Hugh, pointing down at Lucas. Hugh had a southern accent, but I couldn't place it. I didn't sound at all like Tree and J.T. and none of us sounded like Lucas, but it seemed Hugh fit in between us somewhere.

"I'm his friend," I said.

We drove on back out to Owensville, J.T. driving and me and Tree crammed into the front seat with Lucas snoring in the back. For some reason I felt awful low hearing Hugh talk about how Lucas had once been. When folks talk like that, it makes me think of what I used to be and what I am now, an old man.

The next morning, Wool woke me up cussing like a wounded sailor, shit this, fuck that, throwing things around in the kitchen, which was on the back side of the Long House. It was still dark and my head hurt from the liquor the night before, but I knew it was time to go cook, so I put on my pants and stumbled into the kitchen.

"What's the matter, Wool?" I asked, yawning.

"My head hurts like a son of a bitch," he said, "and now I got to cook for these assholes." He picked up a big black frying pan and threw it on the stove. "Go get me some fresh eggs." I yawned again and nodded and went down through the Long House, through Lucas's study and out the end door. There was a chicken house up to the left, and sometimes I'd have to go get fresh eggs when Wool'd

128

forgotten to get them the night before when he was in his cups.

Scout was still sitting in his chair there looking at the stars, and the faintest hint of sunlight was coming up due east, right where he was looking.

"Morning, Scout," I said. He was sitting there with his cowboy hat tilted back on his head. He'd have to work soon, and it looked like he'd been awake all night, so whatever he was thinking on must have hurt pretty bad.

"Jake, you going for eggs?" he asked. I was standing there in my kitchen apron, looking awful silly, I knew. I usually carried back a couple of dozen at a time in the apron, though it made no sense. He came on up to the chicken house with me and he put as many as he could carry in his hat and went back down to the kitchen. By then, bacon was frying, and Wool was boiling water for our coffee. You could hear men starting to stir, and Scout went on back to the showers.

I was thinking about women while I set the table, trying to remember how long it had been since I'd bedded one, and I was half happy at the thought of doing it, half scared I couldn't anymore.

We ate and the men went to work, and Wool and I cleaned up, him cussing all the time about how nobody appreciated a damn thing he did. Lucas didn't get up after we'd got everything cleaned away, so I went to his bunk and he was lying there awake, looking at the ceiling. Sunlight was coming in through the windows of the Long House. It was going to be a pretty day. I pulled a chair up to Lucas's bed and sat a spell before either of us said a thing.

"How's your head, Kid?" I asked finally. He stared straight up into the ceiling for a long time. "You threw back a few last night." He started to say something and then stopped. I waited.

"I have wasted my life," he said finally, not looking at me, and then one tear came up in his right eye and rolled down his plump cheek.

FROM THEN ON, all Lucas could think about was that movie they were going to make, and all I could think about was finding a girlfriend. It's nice to have something to live for. People think Texas is hot as an oven in hell, and that's true in season, but when winter came it was so cold it made my teeth hurt, and by the middle of December it had snowed twice.

Lucas kept being invited to the Big House with Chuck and his blue-eyed wife, and I was sort of jealous, I reckon, since among us all, Lucas had done the least to deserve it. One night a couple of weeks before Christmas I felt it strong.

It had snowed a week before, but it was all gone now, though it was still cold. It got cold back home in Branton, but the difference here was the wind, which blew straight south out of Oklahoma, across the plains, a fingernail-freezing wind. The wind that night was rattling the windows of the Long House. I haven't mentioned that the Long House had like a den, on the other end from Lucas's office, with a stone fireplace, sofas and chairs, a TV and magazines and such. I was sitting in there watching a Christmas special about some cartoon chipmunks when I thought, Lord, there's got to be more than this.

Lucas was down at Chuck and Missy's. Nobody minded it from Lucas because they were mostly happy when he was gone from us, him still being cranky and tending to be foul-mouthed, though not as bad as Wool. I started thinking they probably had up a Christmas tree and were having nice drinks and such and I just wanted to see it.

Well, it was stupid, but I thought I could just slip into the back door and wander around until I got a peek of what they were doing, then leave. I say it was stupid because all the hands were given strict orders to stay away from the house unless invited in. It was something to get fired for. For some reason, I don't recall that ever having gone through my mind.

I took a shower and shaved. It was maybe 9 P.M. and Wool and I had already cleaned up and he was sitting in the kitchen smoking his pipe by the chimney when I came back through.

"You smell like a whore," he said in that deep voice of his.

"Oh go to hell," I said. He grinned.

"You and Tree got a date in town?" he asked. He was always needling me about something, but he did it with some affection. I think he liked me, but you couldn't always tell. He didn't like humanity in general. "You two make a cute couple."

"You funny, Wool," I said. I went on out and got my coat and went into Lucas's study. I went out that way mostly by habit rather than either the front door, which entered in a hall area near the bunks, or on the end with the den. The moon was near full that night and it swept through the broad open window over Lucas's desk and I could see a stack of typed papers. I didn't turn on the light, but I picked up the top sheet and turned it to the moonlight and read it. He said he was still doing nothing, but this was part of a story about a small boy being alone in the dark, sitting there listening to his aunt call his name from another room, thinking about his daddy, who was dead. I've admitted I was never much of a reader before I met Lucas, but something about it put chills along my arms, and I knew it wasn't the cold.

I went on out. Scout's chair was right where it always was, but he was inside. He seemed a little more happy lately, and J.T. said it was because he had a honey in town. I hoped it was true. The cold felt good and I let my weight carry me down the hill toward Chuck's house. The sky was full of stars and the moon glowed over the ranch, and I stopped halfway to the house and said to myself that I knew why they made movies in Texas: it's so pretty sometimes it makes your eyes ache.

I walked like an Indian around toward the back door of the house. I'd taken to telling everybody I had Indian blood in me, and had told it so much I believed it, though I'd just made it up like you do things. Anyway, I crept on to the back porch, which was long and open like a balcony, and then I tried the back door and it was open and I went on inside, hanging my coat on a hat tree inside the hall.

There were good smells coming from somewhere, cinnamon and apples and roast beef and coffee, enough to make me realize me and Wool weren't much at cheffing. It was the first time I'd ever been in there, and I felt scared all of a sudden, like a burglar, and I'll admit that I did wonder where the silver was. When you live on the road, you think these things, even though you're not always a bad person.

I stood there for a minute and I heard voices from straight ahead and to the right. I was standing in a hallway that split in half just ahead, a narrow corridor on the right and the back of the stairs on the left. From some clanking around I heard, I figured the kitchen to be on the left in a room just before you got to the stairs. On the right there were two rooms, the first one, which was dark, and the second from where the talking was coming.

I realized those two rooms on the right were probably connected, so I started to Indian walk into the first room, and that was when I found out the floor squeaked like crazy, and I was just standing there wondering what to do when a woman stuck her head out of the kitchen. She jumped for a second and put her hand on her chest, and then her eyes narrowed and I guess she recognized me as being a hand, though I didn't ever remember seeing her.

"I'll just be goddamned," she said. I was wondering if maybe she and Wool went to the same cooking school when she came out, grabbed me by the arm and pulled me into the kitchen, which was where all the good smells were coming from.

"I just wanted to see the Christmas tree," I said like a fool. She pushed me over into a corner next to a big walk-in pantry and looked mean at me while waving a big wooden spoon that was dripping something on the black-and-white tile floor.

"Mr. Owens'll fire your ass quick as a flea," she said. She poked me in the chest with the spoon. "Even if you are Lucas's friend." She was breathing hard. I looked at her for the first time, and she was maybe fifty or so, about medium build, hair flecked with gray. The thing I couldn't stop looking at, though, was her eyes, which were a pale, smoky gray. She wasn't within three blocks of pretty, but standing there in the kitchen, she seemed mighty attractive to me, so I smiled. "What in God's holy name are you grinning like a possum for?"

"Am I in time for supper?" I asked.

"Sweet Jesus," she said, shaking her head.

"How do you know I'm a friend of Lucas?" I asked. She turned and looked into the hall like she expected Adolf Hitler to come stomping through the door any minute, then she lowered the spoon that she was using to keep me in the corner.

"Ain't you Jake Baker?"

"Yeah."

"I know everything about everybody who works here," she said. "I reckon you could call it a hobby." She went and stirred something that was simmering on the stove. The kitchen was half as big as our bunk area, with a high ceiling, and up there in it a fan that was slowly turning.

"A hobby?" I said. "What's your name?"

"Betty Silver," she said, "if it's any of your business."

"It's just a hobby of mine," I said. I thought she sort of smiled, but I wasn't sure. Betty. Lord, this was strange. Lucas was always talking to me about signs. "I'm a cook, too, you know."

"You and that crazy nigger," she said.

"He ain't crazy," I said. "He's just got a bad attitude about humankind." I heard a man laugh from the front of the house, a long, loud laugh, and I knew it must have been Chuck because Lucas's laugh was kind of high and irritating.

"He's crazy." She looked in the oven and swore at whatever was cooking in there and then set three plates out on top of the stove and got a bottle of white wine out of the refrigerator and went out of the kitchen to refill their glasses. I moseyed over to the stove and lifted the top on a saucepan where some green beans were slowly cooking. I got the cooking spoon and was tasting one of the beans when Betty came back in.

"You stupid cracker, get away from them beans!" she hissed.

"They need salt," I said, not thinking at all about being insulting. For somebody who'd worked high steel and boxed professional, cooking was a real strange career to be setting out on.

"I know they need salt, damnit," she said, swiping the spoon from my hand. "Mrs. Owens's got blood pressure problems, so they can't eat no salt. Need salt. Hell." There was a tall stool, so I sat on it and watched her cook for a while. "You better be getting on back before somebody finds you in here."

"Are you married?" I was real surprised I asked that, but I felt awful reckless being in there illegal.

"None of your beeswax," she said.

"How'd you know I was a cracker?" I asked.

She smiled and said, "I told you, it's a hobby knowing about people who work here."

"Then you tell me what the tattoo on my muscle says," I whispered. She turned and looked at me and narrowed her eyes.

"I never saw a tattoo on you."

"I never even saw you at all," I said. "How could you of seen me?"

"Windows," she said. "I stay inside mostly. I got too much work to be hanging out at that bar in town, even though I do take a nip now and then if I do say so." She got three forks, three knives and three spoons out of a drawer. "What does it say?"

I wasn't too proud of my tattoo, having got it done as a birthday present for my ex-wife, but I wanted her to see it. I rolled up my shirt sleeve and it was still there, though faded a little bit, in nice blue script: "Betty." She leaned over and looked at it and read it a couple of time like she couldn't believe it.

"It's an omen," I said. "Get Lucas to tell you about omens." Just as I said his name, I heard a noise in the hall, looked up and there was Lucas with an empty wine glass, mouth open.

"Oh, great," he said when he saw me.

"Evening, Kid," I said.

"Get out of here," Lucas said. "Only special people can come in here and I'm special and you're not." Betty's shoulders rose up a little and she turned and glared at Lucas like she wanted to belt him one. "What in God's name is that on your arm?" I wasn't in the habit of showing my tattoo off and it was almost always covered by my shirtsleeve. He got the wine bottle out of the refrigerator and filled his glass and then handed me the bottle while he looked at my tattoo.

"Thanks, Kid," I said. I took a big swig from the wine, which was cold as a creek and tasted a little bland, but it was alcohol. Betty swiped the bottle from me and called me a name I won't even write down.

"Your bicep has been defaced," he said a little drunkenly. "You should leave this house before my benefactor, Duke Charles de Medici, has you exiled to the hinterlands."

"What in the hell are you talking about?" asked Betty.

I said, "Don't pay him no attention. Sometimes he speaks a different language. He can't help it, he was raised that way." Lucas grabbed me by the arm and

137

dragged me into the pantry while Betty took the silver-
ware and went to set the table.

"Jake, my good man," he said excitedly, "I have interesting intelligence to part unto you. They will be starting
to film the movie on January 15. And they will shoot for
six weeks, and then come back in June for the entire
summer. I am debating an illicit liaison with my former
bride."

"Come again?"

"I have decided to win back the hand of Sally Crandall," he said.

"I thought you said she was a whore."

"Don't tell me what I said," he clucked.

"Okay."

"This cinematic perturbation will be called *Shadow of the
Wind* and is the story of a woman and her daughter kidnapped by Comanches, where they become members of
the tribe until they are rescued by a dashing young cavalry lieutenant, who just happens to be the lady's husband. Is that drivel or what?"

"Kid, the wind don't cast a shadow," I said. I looked up
on the pantry wall and there was a bottle of Jose Cuervo
tequila, so I got it down and took a swallow.

"Absolutely," said Lucas. "They have many cowboys in
the movie." He was snickering and laughing. "Sally is the
mother, she who has the maternal instincts of Lady Mac-
beth."

"Who's she?"

"Never mind," he said. Betty was cussing, coming back
and forth from setting the table. "They had Robert Red-
ford all lined up to play the cavalry lieutenant but then he
had to go make a documentary about people shooting
wolves or something equally officious. So they got a new-
comer named Thad Wheatley. Nobody named Thad ever

did a single thing worthwhile." Lucas was in fine fettle, and it made me feel good to see him doing so well, and I started thinking about the movie myself, wondering if I'd get to see them make any of it.

I was just fixing to tell Lucas I didn't want to hear any more about his sex life with Sally Crandall when I heard Missy Owens's voice not more than ten feet away, and I backed up and squatted down beside two rows of canned tomatoes while Lucas turned and closed the pantry door.

"There you are," she said. Lucas said something, but I couldn't make it out as they were walking away back toward the dining room. It sounds stupid now, but I felt happy sitting there in the dark of the pantry, smelling all the good smells of Betty's cooking, knowing Lucas was happy and with his friends. I sat there a long time until I realized I was still holding the bottle of Jose Cuervo, so I took another swallow, and I felt fatheaded and smart as Albert Einstein.

It was about ten minutes later when the door opened a crack and I saw Betty standing there, and I thought, what the hell, so I grabbed her by the waist and pulled her inside and shut the door back.

"Are you crazy, Jake?" she said, trying not to giggle. I growled like an old bear and nibbled on her neck. She slapped the shit out of me, and I stepped backward into a shelf, and a can of tomatoes fell square on top of my head. I groaned and went down and suddenly a light was on in the pantry and she was kneeling beside me, touching me on the cheek, saying every cussword I'd ever heard except for a few dozen Wool had invented. "You are a crazy old man."

"I'm sorry," I said. "You were just there in the light looking so pretty."

139

"Oh, go on," she said. "You better get out of here before somebody sees you." She helped me to my feet and held on to my arm while looking out of the pantry, and it had been so long since a woman had touched me that way I thought for a minute I might either cry or do something against the law to her. Fortunate for me, she went out, looked both ways and then dragged me to the back door. I got my coat on with some help, since I was starting to get swim-headed with the liquor. She buttoned it up for me and I tried to kiss her, but she pushed me away.

"You ain't seen the last of Jake Baker," I said.

"You goddamn stupid cracker," she said, which wasn't exactly love words, but I wasn't being picky. I went on down the steps. The night was bright as the inside of the house with the moon full and cold. Maybe it was the booze, but I think it was having been touched that way. I felt like I would live forever and be happy all the while, which is a special kind of feeling because if you think about it you know you will die and feel all sorts of terrors and fears if you live long enough.

I wandered down toward the creek where the cotton-wood trees grew, thinking about cowboys and Indians and the cavalry, about men who lived right on the face of the land like I'd always wanted to, even though it would kill you. I sat down on the bank of the creek. It was nice and wide and bubbled over rocks, and after my eyes got used to the light, I could see it, and I leaned down to wash my face and I saw my reflection, and something about the light made me look like I had as a boy, young and good-looking. I laid back on the creekbank, even though it was cold, and I howled at the moon like a wolf and laughed until I was almost too sleepy to get up the

140

slope, past Scout's empty chair and inside the warm bunkhouse.

I woke up before dawn the next morning, Wool shaking my shoulder like he always did, saying my name real
soft, "Jake, Jake, come on buddy, let's go." Wool could be
awful tough, but I was getting to where I was fond of
him, and when he cussed at me I usually deserved it.

I got dressed and went into the kitchen and started
getting out the coffee mugs and making the coffee, which
was the first thing I did every day. Wool had the bacon
sizzling in the big black skillets and he stood over them,
his corncob pipe dangling from his lips.

We didn't say much to each other, just listened to the
radio. Wool liked heavy rock and roll, so we listened to
that, though I thought it was pretty bad. He would always
turn it up when songs by a group named Twisted Sister
came on, and dance around the stove, turning and
scrambling and stirring in rhythm, which is a thing, if
you've never seen it.

I had filled the four big urns and was listening to the
coffee gurgle when I thought I heard something coming
from Lucas's study. I sort of unofficially kept an eye on it
because anybody could go through it.

"I'll be back in a minute," I said.

"You better, you son of a bitch," said Wool without
much emotion. I walked out, down the hall and stopped
outside the door to Lucas's study. It was typing I heard. I
opened the door and Lucas was sitting there wearing a
big cowboy hat I'd never seen before, fingers working
along the keys so fast I thought the thing might catch
on fire.

"Get away from me," Lucas growled. "I am in bed with
the muse." He went on typing and I backed up, but left
the door cracked and he talked to himself, moaned and

laughed, and somebody who didn't know him would have thought he was half crazy, and maybe he was. All I knew was something had changed in him.

The other men finally got up, and as I set the table I could hear the showers humming and the sweet sounds of birds through the cool open windows of the kitchen. It had been cold, but this morning it was only cool, the promise of a beautiful early late-winter day. J.T. came into the kitchen and got himself a cup of coffee and patted me on the back.

"Morning, Jake," he said cheerily. "You hear about the storm? Said on the radio it'll be here by this afternoon late."

"I heard it," said Wool. "Lots of work for you fellers."

"A snowstorm?" I asked. "Here?"

"Say what?" It was Tree, who came in stretching and looking twenty feet tall.

"Blizzard," said J.T.

"Aw shit," said Tree. "We got to get them that's down at the Half Mile." He was talking about cattle in a big field called the Half Mile, which was a long ways away from the ranch house.

"I reckon so," said J.T. The other men trickled in, even Scout who still looked happy in a sort of dreamy way, and they ate, talking all the time about the storm. The sun came up, bright and cool, and I was inclined to believe the weather people were crazy. Lucas didn't come to breakfast and after we'd cleaned the dishes away, I walked quiet as an Indian down to his study and listened and he was still typing, cussing, laughing, that silly old cowboy hat up on his head.

With nothing particular to do, I decided to walk down around the main house and see if I could scare up Betty. I wasn't stupid enough to go back inside, but maybe I could hang around the remains of the vegetable garden out back and get a peek at her.

I got down there and was hanging around in the dead cornstalks when I realized that she might be married to some cowboy who was seven feet tall and killed people like me for fun. That's what it was. She was married and her old man would kill me if he knew I was looking at her. I should have been Kid Kraft, getting mowed down by her husband, not quite as good as a range war, but something.

I was starting to head back to the Long House when the back door opened a crack and Betty was there, setting a big orange cat outside and telling him he was a stupid son of a bitch if he thought he could sleep on the stove. She looked up and saw me looking at her and stopped, wiped her hands and smiled, which I took as a good sign.

"Morning," I said, waving at her.

"Morning to yourself," she said. I wish I could describe her voice. It was kind of deep but feminine anyway, throaty I think they call it, and she looked strong and full of life. "What are you doing down here?"

"Checking the corn," I said. Well, that was stupid, but she didn't have to bust out laughing, and I felt myself blush, God help me, but she wasn't trying to be mean, even I could tell that.

"Why don't you take a break and come get a cup of coffee?" she said. "That goddamn corn's dead as it'll ever get."

"Come inside?" I asked, looking around. All the men had scattered to their jobs, all of them worrying about weather and cattle.

"It's okay," she said. "They're gone to town for the morning."

"You sure it's okay?" She smiled and nodded like she wanted me up there and I felt like doing a flip. When I was a young man I one time did a flip on a steel beam forty-six stories in the sky in New York, and the workers all loved it, but the man I worked for went redfaced, just crazy, and fired me on the spot. I went on up the steps. She kept squinting, even though the light was not too sharp, and I followed her inside. "You hear about the storm?"

"Yes, ma'am," I said. "The men are all worried about the cattle." She turned and poked me in the chest. I was a head taller than her.

"Don't call me ma'am," she said.

"Betty," I said.

"Jake," she said. We went into the kitchen and I sat on a stool and she put water on to boil. I didn't tell her I'd already had me two cups this morning and a third would probably make me jumpy. I was already jumpy just being around her. "Missy had to go to the doctor." She made a face and shook her head.

"What's wrong with her?" I asked.

"I don't know," she said, but she did, and it made me feel bad. "You sleep good last night?"

"Sure," I said. "Do you live here in the house? I don't know hardly a thing about you." I have to admit I was looking at her chest and trying to figure out how big it was without her dress, and I reckoned it was passing large.

"Here? Jesus H. Christ," she said. "Not for love nor money. I live in Harkin. I just come down here five days a week and cook." I looked at her finger and there was some kind of ring with a blue stone but it didn't look like a wedding ring. But you could be wrong. My niece Belle's wedding ring was made out of woven hair, something she

144

and her hippie husband thought was real cute and it
made me gag, but I never said so to them.

"You married?"

"Do you care?" She folded her arms over her chest.
The water was starting to heat up, hissing in the yellow
tea kettle.

"Just curious," I said.

"I ain't married," she laughed. "Was one time, but I'm
not no more." She poured us a cup of coffee and pulled
up another stool and we sat there in the kitchen.

"Oh."

"You ever married, Jake?"

"One time," I said.

"To that Betty on your muscle?"

"I didn't think you noticed. You were yelling at me
something awful last night." She grinned like a girl and
sipped her coffee.

"I get that way when it's supper time," she said. "It's my
job." I told her I knew what she meant. "Well, was it her?"

"Yeah," I said. "What happened to your husband?"

"Oh my Lord," she said, shaking her head. "It's been
fifteen years, he took my baby and just left. I've never
seen neither one of them since." She took a Kleenex out
of her apron pocket and dabbed at her eyes. "A little girl,
with eyes blue as the sky. I didn't have no money to go
look much. The welfare put out a paper about it, but it
didn't do any good." I was sitting close enough to reach
out and touch her hand, and she took my hand in hers
and held it in her lap.

"Do you think they're around here?" I asked.

"Could be," she said. "I probably wouldn't know
Loretta if I seen her."

"Your last name's Silver?"

"I don't know what he'd call her," she sniffed. "Silver's my old name. His name was Buddy Buckley, the son of a bitch. I named her Loretta Michelle, but I don't know no more. They might be living in London, England, for all I know." It was then I said something that would change things for me, though I didn't know it then.

"You want me to see if I can find her?" As soon as the words were out of my mouth, I knew I'd done something dumb. I didn't have a car, no driver's license anyway, and I didn't even know where to look.

"Oh, Jake," she said, squeezing my hand. "Would you look? Would you look?" I started to say no, but that would have made me look crazy and I had decided I wanted to see Betty without her apron or anything else on. You can call it a bad motive or anything you want, but there it was.

"I can't promise nothing, but I'll try," I said. Tears were coming down her cheeks and she stood and came over and hugged me and I hugged her back. We talked for half an hour until she looked at the clock and told me I had to go, and I did, but not before she kissed me on the cheek.

"I once did a flip on a steel beam forty-six stories in the air," I said, proud as a peacock.

"Why in hell'd you do a stupid fool thing like that?" she asked, so I let it drop. I was halfway up to the Long House before I noticed it had gone cloudy and a cold wind had come up. Late that afternoon, just like they said, we had a stem-winding snowstorm, but the cattle were okay thanks to the boys, and the last thing I did before helping Wool start supper was peek into Lucas's study. He was still there, but he was lying on his typing table, his cowboy hat over his snoring face, and on his feet were the most pointy-toed cowboy boots I'd ever seen.

146

SNOW HAD NOT FALLEN again by the middle of January, but the movie people came anyway, and the first day we heard they'd set up for a shoot, Lucas talked me into borrowing a Jeep.

"My God, man, no coward ever changed this world," he said.

"I don't want to change the world, Kid," I said.

"Just drive, private!" he shouted, and Lord help me, I did it. Christmas had come and gone, and I'd got a little low a few days before Christmas but I snapped out of it when we got our tree up in the Long House, and even Scout sang along when we did "White Christmas." Sometimes it seems like my string has run out and I can see myself dead and laid out, and it's not such a bad feeling, rest from this world they say.

Betty Silver and me'd got along famously since I'd met her in Chuck and Missy's kitchen, and I'd see her a little every day, which caused Lucas to give me his lecture on wenches and venereal diseases. I'd not done much yet about looking for Betty's daughter, but I kept telling her I would, so much that I'd begun to believe myself I could find her. The one thing I needed was to drive, and as we drove along that day, the old familiar feel of the wheel and road came back right quick.

"Yes, sir, General Kraft," I said. "You know how in the hell to get where we going, sir?"

"Cursing at an officer will get you hanged," he fumed. "God, what is this man's army coming to?"

"I thought you was a cowboy," I said.

"Oh go to hell," he said. "Chuck told me. Go up like we're going to town, hang a right and go down about five miles to a crossroads where you'll see Coker's Country Store. Take a left there and go on out the Charles Bridge Road for six miles and there you have it."

"There you have it," I said. The day was clear and cold, but I had on a heavy sheepskin coat I'd bought with money I'd saved and Lucas was wearing a bright blue camping coat, lace-up cavalry boots and mirror-reflecting aviator glasses. We drove for a while and I asked Lucas how his book was coming. It was sort of an unspoken rule that I didn't ask, but I was just trying to make conversation so he wouldn't watch my driving so close.

"It has become absolutely incomprehensible," he said.

"That's good," I said, stupid as to the meaning.

"Jake, Jake," he said, looking away out the window. I looked over at him and he was shaking his head and I could see the land of Texas going back and forth on the front of his glasses, and that was when I ran over the mailbox. I'd forgot how easy it is to slip off the road just a bit, and I lost it about five feet and plowed down this mailbox like it wasn't there, except it had a little eagle on

148

top of it and when I smacked it, this eagle flew up on the hood of the Jeep and stuck on the windshield for a couple of seconds while I was trying to get back on the road.

"Vultures!" Lucas yelled. "We are being attacked by vultures!" Then the eagle went up over the cab and away, and my hands were shaking so bad I could barely keep it on the road after that. Lucas rattled on about my driving for a couple of miles until I pulled over next to a fence where some Brahma bulls were gnawing at a big roll of hay that'd been put there.

"You drive," I said. I got out and walked around and opened Lucas's door and stood there, shaking mad. "If you are such a good driver, you drive us." He pushed his lips out like a little kid and said, "By God, I will!" And then he jumped out of the cab and fell flat on his face into a ditch. I helped him up and his aviator glasses were twisted sideways on his face and he had dirt on his cheeks and I felt one heartbeat of pity for him there.

"You okay, Kid?" I asked.

"Don't call me that again, you rube," he muttered. He tried to looked important walking around to drive the Jeep, but he slipped and banged his poor old head on the fender and I was fixing to pick him up again when he scrambled up and called me a name and went around and got in. I got in, too, and he began to drive.

Lucas drove like he expected the Jeep to go flying apart any minute and he was trying to hold it all together with his hands and elbows. I didn't want to look. We went from one side of the road to another and once, when he saw a car coming from a long distance off, Lucas slowed down to maybe ten miles an hour. He looked to his left to make sure the car had passed us and then mashed the accelerator and drove us across a ditch, through a barbed wire fence and into a field where some birds exploded up into the sunshine. He managed to get it stopped, but by then I had my arms over my face and was down in the floorboard.

"Oh Lordy," Lucas said, breathing hard as a runner. "Something's wrong with the steering mechanism on this vehicle, Jake." I took back over after that, and though I drove like a boy, I still drove better than Lucas.

"But you don't drive as bad as my niece Belle's husband," I said.

"The scurvy rats who dispatched your patrimony," said Lucas. I just drove on, and it took us about twenty minutes. As soon as I saw the trailers all along the road and cars, I knew we were there.

But that wasn't all I saw. I parked and got out and looked up a slope to my left and there, looking real as you could imagine, was a fort, just like the kind from the Westerns, walls made of long cottonwood logs, with little houses on the corners and holes cut through for people to shoot. And it had soldiers milling about in uniform.

"Would you look at that, Lucas?" I said. "Would you just look at that?"

He said, "Jake, don't admire these people, for they are all gypsies. They wander over the earth trying to show off in front of an orb of ground glass. It's a demeaning profession." He hiked up his pants and walked across a ditch and up toward a rope where a few people had gathered to watch. They were letting folks come out, but they were kept a long way from the cameras, watched over by two men who looked like wrestlers. I had me big muscles back when I worked steel. Up near the fort, over which a blue flag was snapping there in the rising breeze, somebody came out with some horses and eight or ten of the soldiers mounted up and just sat around while a man was yelling something at them I couldn't catch.

Lucas wormed his way to the front of the crowd watching the spectacle, me right behind him. It was cooler than I thought it would be, but my coat felt good and I kept it up to my face. I had told Lucas folks our age might not ought to be hanging around outside in weather like this, but he called me a name, and so did Wool, who happened to be standing around that morning when we'd talked. Between Lucas, Wool and Betty, I was learning a lot of new cuss words.

"Boy, that's something," I said, real excited because I'd never seen a movie being made. There were two cameras, and people everywhere, mostly soldiers, but I heard a walkie-talkie squeal, saw a man barking into it, and damned if the trailers out along the road didn't open and about thirty or forty men dressed up like Indians came out, heading slowly for the fort. They had on buckskin clothes, but they were muttering about how cold it was and such. One of the Indians reached in his pocket and took out a box of Skoal and took a dip.

"Behold, the noble savage," Lucas said, and a couple of people gave him a hard look. The Indians went on toward the fort where two men came suddenly from somewhere leading pinto ponies by their bridles. A voice that sounded like God yelled "Quiet!" though I wasn't saying anything and neither was anyone else.

"Mount up," a man with a bullhorn said two or three times.

"You see her?" I whispered, leaning down to Lucas.

"I think that's her," he said, pointing to a horse that was relieving itself.

"That's awful crude," I said.

"I excel at crudity in all its forms," said Lucas. The soldiers and Indians were suddenly all up on their horses, milling about, and the director barked another command

and the Indians rode off to our right, out in a field and huddled up there. The soldiers went off to the left on the other side of the fort, and then men started popping up above the wall of the fort.

"I be dog," I said. "Look at all that."

"Come on, private," said Lucas. He moved through the silent crowd and walked slowly back toward the trailers and then started moving down the ditch along the road.

"What in the heck are we doing, General?" I asked.

"We are reconnoitering," he said. "We shall circle them and help defend from the rear. I have been trained in all forms of gunplay. I was once a soldier and soldiers never forget tactics." I had been a soldier, too, and I'd forgot it all, and anyway I'd never had to fight Indians.

"But this is a movie," I reminded him, "and besides, they told us to stay behind the rope."

He turned and stared at me hard and stomped his foot one time and said, "Stay behind the rope? Private, are you going to spend what's left of your miserable life staying behind the rope? Are you going to let some tinhorn peckerwood stand between you and glory? Where is your vision?"

"Would you mind repeating that?" I asked. He spit and motioned for me to follow him, and of course I did it, not because he was the leader but because I was worried about him getting hurt or falling in a ditch. We made a huge circle, walking far down the road past the Indians, whose ponies were snorting and stamping, ready to run. Then we cut back in the field and down toward the rear of the fort.

"I shall kill seven of the foul bastards," he said, getting hard of breathing. We slowed down so he could inhale easier.

"You talking about the Indians, sir?" I asked.

"My God, of course," he said.

"I have Indian blood," I said, not looking at Lucas. "I'm one-eighth Cherokee."

"I shall spare you on account of your driving skills," Lucas said like it wasn't a joke or anything. We kept moving slowly and I was looking at the fort when the Indians suddenly bolted toward it and gunfire broke out all over the place. You could see puffs of smoke coming from the soldiers' guns in the fort and then cannons fired and great clods of dirt exploded. I'd seen how they did that before, little charges in the dirt they set off, and in fact I'd been a demolitions man during the war in Europe, so it was just interesting to me. But Lucas acted so excited I had to grab his arm.

"They are in desperate need of help!" he yelled over the gunfire. The Indians were shooting back with guns and arrows, circling the fort, and then there was suddenly a big cloud of black smoke coming up from somewhere inside the fort. "Why does the cavalry not attack? Can they be saved?"

There was a lot of whooping and hollering from the Indians and the guns sure sounded real, and I felt my blood pounding as we kept moving toward the rear of the fort. The field was frozen under foot and crunched as we went along. Lucas got to crouching down as he walked and I started doing it, too, though I felt kind of foolish. Finally we got to where we could see the back of the fort, except there wasn't any back of the fort; it was all open and it had a couple of Airstream trailers inside and three men standing beside a smoke machine.

"It don't look very well defended from this angle, General," I said.

"You're heading for a court martial," Lucas said, breathing hard. "Follow me." It was just about that time that the cavalry suddenly came into view and both them and the Indians were circling the fort, fighting and shooting at one another. I say they were fighting, but when they got to the back of the fort they were just riding, since it was out of camera view, and then they circled back around where all the shooting was going on.

I followed Lucas, heaven help me, straight for the battle and once an Indian looked up and saw us and motioned for us to get away, but Lucas kept on coming and I followed him to make sure he wasn't trampled or something. We were only about forty yards from the fort and right in the middle of the circling Indians and soldiers.

"Get out of here!" a bluecoat yelled as he came by us, and then an Indian on a pinto pony yelled, "Piss off!"

"Can you translate that, General?" I asked.

Without turning, Lucas said, "That's it, private. You'll have to get your neck stretched for that one."

"For what?" I felt like laughing because this was so ridiculous.

"Violation of the heavy-handed sarcasm rule," he said, and I kept after him until we were inside the open back end of the fort. There were the three men in there making the smoke machine go, another holding a microphone on the end of a long pole and one with a headset on, talking like crazy. He touched the earphone lightly one time and then turned sharply and saw us. I suspected somebody'd tattled.

"Get in here!" he screamed. Lucas ignored him and ran for a ladder that went up to the parapet along the wall. It wasn't until then I noticed it had gone cloudy and a few snowflakes were floating in the smoke. I thought about it. I could obey the man or take out after Lucas. My being good at obeying the man had been a recent thing in my life, so I went with the General. "Hey! Get away from that ladder!"

The gunfire seemed to get louder. A cannon boomed from one of the bastions up front and then a cannon went off in the other one. I felt like Errol Flynn, and I don't know who Lucas felt like, but for a couple of old bastards who'd been given up for dead, we weren't doing all that bad.

"Follow me, lad!" Lucas yelled, turning toward me. We got to the top of the ladder and on the parapet, which went around the inside of the wall on a wide ledge that had a balcony and everything.

"Right here, General!" I yelled back. The man with the earphones was coming toward the ladder, yelling and cussing at us now. "We've got company, sir!" He turned and saw the man coming after us up the ladder and went scuttling down the parapet, me right behind. We came to two grizzled-looking bluecoats who were looking down and firing their guns.

"We're from the relief unit," Lucas said. "Give us the pieces." We were both breathing hard and I thought one of us might croak, but we held our own. The men stopped firing and stared at us like we'd popped right up from hell.

"Are you second unit?" one asked. "Are they still rolling or what?"

"Property!" Lucas yelled over the racket. "Stand and deliver!" Lucas opened his hands for the gun and the man, completely surprised, gave it to him, and the other man gave me his gun. The first man turned to the other and said, "This is some shit," and they moved past us in time to hear the man with the headset screaming and yelling at all of us.

"What now, sir?" I asked.

"Follow me!" Lucas screamed, holding his gun over his head and pumping it three times. We took our guns and had gotten to the front of the fort when the gunfire slowly stopped, and over the wall I could see the Indians and soldiers slowing their horses and ponies down to a walk. Some words were crackling over a bullhorn, though I couldn't make them out.

We were right over the front gate, in the middle of a bunch of bluecoats. They all needed shaves and really looked like bedraggled soldiers. They just stared at us while the headset man and the two soldiers whose guns we'd got came on after us.

"We're outnumbered, corporal," I said slowly, sensing there wasn't much sense in going farther.

"I'm a general," he said low and hard, turning to glare at me.

"Not any more," I said, and he started to laugh, a little giggle at first, and then I was laughing and we just sat down laughing, and I didn't care when they got us under the arms and took us back down, took our guns, didn't care at all where they took us. They escorted us back down to where the smoke machine was now turned off, and the front gate was open and four or five men were coming toward us, including a man I recognized as Hugh, Sally Crandall's manager, though I'd not seen anybody who looked like her. She wasn't my favorite actress but I liked *Horizon* and *Midnight Blues* and my favorite of hers was *Ever After Rose*.

"Okay, who in the hell are you?" asked a man who didn't seem pleased to see us at all. Two huge men with open coats over blue T-shirts were standing there ready to beat the shit out of us if we goofed up.

"Don't tell 'em nothing, private," I said to Lucas.

"Oh, go to hell," said Lucas Kraft.

"Jesus H. Christ," said Hugh when he got close to us.

"You know these clowns?" asked one of the men in the blue T-shirts. Another man said, "Mr. Roberts says the shot's okay."

"Yeah, I know 'em," Hugh said. "Lucas, what in the hell's wrong with you? You know you can't come on to a set and fuck up like this."

"You want cops, Hugh?" asked one of the men. "Does Mr. Roberts want cops?"

Hugh said, "Let me get 'em out of here. They won't be a bother any more." He grabbed Lucas by the sleeve and took us back through the front gate toward the crowd of gawking onlookers. A few soldiers and Indians were hanging around on their ponies.

"God, they're more desperate in the fort than we thought," said one Indian with war paint all over his face. "Maybe we should finish them off now." Another Indian laughed and spit chewing tobacco.

"We should never have sold you heathens firewater," said Lucas. The Indians laughed and so did a cavalryman who was sitting on his big horse drinking a caffeine-free Diet Pepsi. "You're a disgrace to the uniform," Lucas said to him.

"Whatever you say, captain," the man grinned. Lucas, as I have said, was short and round and hairy as a bear and he looked more than passing strange to them, I'm sure.

"He's a private," I said.

"He's going to be shot for disrespecting an officer," Lucas said, sticking his thumb out at me. "You want to join him, soldier?" Hugh took us past the citizens of Harkin County, nice folks all, who couldn't decide if we were a threat or just dumb old boys who'd screwed up. We followed him to a Cadillac with an Airstream trailer behind it that was parked on the other side of the road in a field with other cars and trailers. Hugh went inside and so did we. It was cramped up, sort of, not the kind of place I'd care to live, but it had all manner of homey touches, a guitar, stereo, sofa and TV, all the kinds of things that mark a room as one man's. It made me think on my house back home in Branton, at least before Belle sold all my stuff. We sat down and Hugh asked us if we wanted a beer, and we did. Me and Lucas took off our coats. Hugh got us each a Coors.

"Lucas, you can't just come in here and pull this kind of shit," Hugh said. "You're damn lucky they didn't have you thrown in the slam."

"Where is my darling bride?" asked Lucas, sipping his beer. I opened mine and after running around and fighting Indians, it was like a reward or something. I felt like I could drink two or four maybe.

"Be careful with the firewater, Kid," I said.

"Up yours, private," Lucas said. "So where is she, Hugh?"

"Beverly Hills," he said. He had a way of speaking flat and through his nose and I found out later he was not from California at all but from Texas, from San Angelo, which was one of the reasons he was there.

"My God," Lucas said, and you could see his shoulders sag like a tire with all the air going out. "I came to rescue her from the clutches of the infidels." Hugh just stared at him, shaking his head slowly from one side to another and sipping his Coors.

"Let me tell you something," Hugh said, quiet, patient like a forgiving father to a kid who'd messed up. "You are nothing to her, old history. When you went down, she wrote you off and buried you. In fact, and I don't mean this to be spiteful, everybody's wrote you off, Lucas. I

158

mean, look at you. Out here playing like a boy where they've got millions at stake. That's not the way a man behaves. Sally's not here for the winter filming. She won't be here till late spring. "I'm down visiting some kin and she wanted me to watch for her so I'm doing that. But when she does come down, you're going to stay away from her. She's had a tough time the past few years, and though this may be just a Western, the part means a lot to her and she's planning on it being special. You understand what I'm saying, Lucas?" Hugh had these light blue eyes and I immediately liked him, felt like he could be trusted. His big mustache was wet with beer he sipped.

Lucas looked down into his can and his lips twitched once or twice. I'd seen it before, Lucas all of a sudden feeling dressed down proper and not able to fight back, but this time it was worse, humiliating, and I felt worse for him than I ever had since first I'd met him back at Fieldstone.

"I'm trying to recreate my life," Lucas whispered. "I don't know what I'm doing sometimes. I'm like a clock that keeps on running after everybody in the house has died. I know what I'm like, Hugh." He looked up at Hugh, who looked like he felt bad for Lucas without much he could do about it. "I know that once I could say things of beauty, and that by saying them I, too, became beautiful because I've always looked like nothing, not like those people out there in California. And when I stopped saying beautiful things, people realized I was ugly. I realized it, too."

"Come on, General," I said, feeling my throat getting tight.

"While you got breath left, it's not too late," Hugh said.

Lucas ignored me. He said, "Death closes all; but something ere the end, Some work of noble note may yet be done."

"Now that sounds more hopeful," said Hugh.

"The deluded rantings of an old poet writing about an old man," said Lucas so soft I had to lean to hear him. "Is she still wonderfully lovely?"

"Let's go home, Lucas," I said.

"Don't do this to yourself," said Hugh. "Yes, she is, Lucas. She's fifty-three years old now, but she looks fifteen years younger. She's not married but she's living with Antonio Strinetti, the race car driver." Lucas acted like he didn't hear.

He said, "My, but that was the best time I ever had." He got up and put his coat on and so did I, and Hugh and I looked at each other, and you could tell it hurt Hugh to see Lucas like this, and it hurt me, too. I'd rather see my friend crazy and charging ahead, not like this, not thinking things were over for him. It made me feel real bad.

"If you behave, you can see her when she comes," Hugh said. "It'll be the middle of May."

"Thanks," said Lucas. We went on out and I shook hands with Hugh and thanked him for helping us out back at the fort. Snow was falling steadily now, smoke was billowing back out of the fort and the Indians and cavalry were fighting again.

"Would you look at that," I said to Lucas. "They're back on the warpath." Lucas looked up at them as we walked to the Jeep and smiled, but just a little.

"We showed them, didn't we, Jake?" he said. "Me and you showed them."

11

LORETTA MICHELLE WOULD BE fifteen by now, and all I had to look at were three pictures taken when she was two. They were all taken the same day, a cute girl with blonde pigtails and a big grin. She was playing in the bright sun in a little inflated swimming pool. "That was when me and Buddy was living over in Jacksboro," said Betty.

It was early March and the sky was high and thin, a fresh breeze pouring down from the north. Whizzer Pippin had broken his leg falling off his horse a couple of days before and was laid up in the Long House now, thinking he'd as soon be dead, and from time to time I'd tell him stories and cheer him up.

We'd lost Scout. Everybody felt real bad about it and we'd called the police, but nothing had turned up. We were sitting around one night in January, late in the month as I recollect, and it wasn't snowing but it felt like it. Lucas and I were sitting there with seven or eight of the others watching a TV show about a man whose wife turns into a frog and he was either trying to be a frog himself or turn her back. It was supposed to be funny because people on the TV you couldn't see kept laughing, but I didn't laugh and Lucas kept up talking about them, saying nasty things that made the others chuckle. They'd all got to where they at least understood Lucas a little and were willing to give him a little slack, mainly, I reckon, because they trusted me and I was Lucas's manager.

Anyway, we were sitting there when the front door opened. You could hear it in the room where the TV was, but you could feel the draft, too, and into the room, staggering and covered with blood, comes Scout. He was blowing blood out of his mouth.

"My God," said Tree, who got up to go help. But Scout held up his hands.

"Get away from me," he whispered. "Just get away!" J.T. Knox and Tom Ivey tried to help him again, but Scout just drawed back to strike and then turned, went and got a bag full of stuff and went flying out the front door, leaving it open, and we all went for a look. Scout owned his own truck. Maybe half of the boys owned a vehicle of one kind or another, and Mr. Owens had five or six Jeeps we all used from time to time. I'd even gone right after Christmas and got myself a driver's license. Lucas had tried to get one, but he'd run over six or eight of them red hats on the test course and then backed into the car of somebody who worked there, so they wouldn't give him one.

That was the last thing we heard from Scout, that "Get away," and I thought on it for a right smart spell. I missed seeing him out there sitting in his chair, though he couldn't do it much in winter anyway. And now that spring was coming on, his chair was still there, and that's where me and Betty were sitting.

All kinds of stuff went on there that the men talked about that I don't really know so much about. They bought and sold cattle, fed them, moved them around, worked on fences, all the stuff you do on a ranch. Since I'd got my license I'd started driving around the ranch some, and it was huge, crossed with dirt roads, and now it seemed like home. Since Lucas couldn't get a driving license, he had taken to riding this little sway-backed pony named Butter, though he always called it Sally.

"Where's Jacksboro?" I asked. Betty leaned back and stared east, her eyes getting clouded a little.

"It's over between Fort Worth and Wichita Falls," she said. "Buddy had hisself a job on this goddamn chicken farm, and he'd come home stinking like the mouth of hell. I'd tell him he smelled like chickenshit but he couldn't smell it, working there all day, and he would take a shower and I'd give him hell, and Loretta would start crying and then he'd up and go out and drink and come home all slobbery and want to lie with me and I wouldn't let him, make him sleep out on the back porch on a pallet." She put the pictures down and turned in her chair and put her hands on my arm. "Where can you look first?"

Where could I look first? I'd been stringing her along for weeks. We'd grown to like each other enormous and for the past couple of weeks we'd started to hold hands and smooch a little when we could get away with it. Except for her foul mouth, she was pretty as morning to me. Lucas called her the drill sergeant, but he didn't mean anything by it. He was blue because one morning I'd found him down by the creek burning everything he'd written so far at the Long House, and since then he'd not hit a key far as I could tell.

"I got me some ideas," I said, and that was the truth. As I've said before, I once worked a couple or three years, I forget, for an insurance company in New Jersey, finding folks who'd inherited money but didn't know about it. I learned a lot about finding folks, but I'd got an offer to work steel about that time and so had never become a lifetime investigator, though it was work I liked.

But that was nearly fifty years ago, and you'd be surprised how much you can forget in fifty years. For truth's sake, I wanted to go to bed with Betty, and I think she did, too, but you have to do these things right, get her beholden so much to you that you can make her feel bad if she doesn't come through.

"Can you bring her back to me if you find her?" she asked.

"I can't," I said. "But maybe the authorities could if her daddy stole her away from you."

"The son of a bitch sure done that," she said.

"So maybe on Sunday I'll drive me over to Jacksboro and talk to some folks," I said.

"Well, it weren't really Jacksboro," she said. "It was this little piece of shit town called Ideal, which is out in the country in Jack County. Can I come?" I thought about it.

"Be better if you didn't," I said. "These things can get rough." Truth was I didn't want her to see me drive because I was afraid she'd cuss the whole time and make me nervous.

"Oh," she said. She leaned over and kissed me on the cheek, even though it was morning and we'd usually smooch a little just at dark after she'd finished supper. Chuck had seen me hanging out back talking to her and so had Missy but neither of them said a thing about it.

164

Missy had been sickly and Lucas had not been spending so many evenings there. Hell, I thought. I turned and kissed Betty on the mouth and then reached out and touched her breast real light like, and she took my hand off but she wasn't mad.

Lucas was watching *The Price is Right* when I got back into the TV room. All the other men were out working but Wool, who was sitting there smoking his corncob pipe.

"That asshole is so far over they ought to shoot him," Wool said out of the side of his mouth, pointing at a grinning man who thought a refrigerator cost $2,200. I sat down beside Lucas, who didn't seem too pleased about sitting there watching TV.

"How's it going, Kid?" I asked.

"Oh go to hell," he said sourly.

"How about taking a ride over to Jack County Sunday with me to look for Betty's daughter?" I asked.

He said, "Are you still deluding yourself that you can find your way past your own nose, Jake?" He turned and looked at me, turning that huge body in the chair. "What you are telling her you can do, you can't. You can't find that girl. She might live anywhere in the whole world. Shall you become the Flying Dutchman, harnessed to the wind, skating over stormy seas in search of something you can never possess?"

"It's better than not having nothing at all to look for," I said, a little testy. He tried to smile, but it was a phony and he knew it. I think he was going to tell me to go to hell again when he stopped and his shoulders went down and he seemed to shrink in the chair.

"You're right," he said. "I have wasted my life."

"You've said that before," I said, "and it wasn't true

then and it's not true now. You're just getting to be a pro at feeling bad for yourself when you've got no call to."

"See, you stupid son of a bitch, I told you," said Wool, when they showed that the refrigerator cost $1,175.

"You want to go take a ride?" Lucas asked.

And so we did, getting Jimbo, who worked in the horse barns, to saddle the horses so we could be on our way. We walked the horses slow for a long time, down to the creek and up along it for a long way, the trees just coming into their leaves, everything starting to become all green and new.

"Why do you keep saying you've wasted your life?" I asked. The only sound was the jingling of the saddles, the slow clop of the horse hooves and the wind in the new green trees.

"Because I have lost the ability to love," he said.

"That's a damn fool thing," I said.

"But it's true," he sighed. We didn't talk much after that, but he did say he would go with me over to Jack County, and early Sunday morning, he and I were sitting in the Jeep, Betty handing me a big bag of lunch and a plastic cooler full of lemonade to take along with us.

"See if you can find a man named Ottis Osborne," said Betty, wiping her hands on a blue apron. "He lived near us then. And a woman named Louise Bellmon, I think. Buddy might have run off with her. I don't know. She looked like a picture from a magazine. I'd of liked to kick her goddamn teeth in."

"Swearing, madam, is evidence of indifferent vocabulary," said Lucas, who seemed in fine fettle again, wearing a light jacket and an Australian bush hat he'd picked up somewhere, one side snapped up and the strap dangling low under his chin.

166

"Look, you little shit, I don't care if you did write . . ." she began, but I cut her off.

". . . so we'll look for Ottis or Louise," I said. "In Ideal, in Jack County. We'll get our first leads for sure." She scowled at Lucas and then leaned into the Jeep and kissed me, and she smelled like breakfast, like bacon and butter and eggs and coffee, and I wanted her to cook for me, but with only $40 a week, I couldn't support her worth anything.

"Be careful," she said.

"Be reckless," said Lucas like God. "Point this chariot east, my good man. Not since I was the youngest man to cross the Atlantic by plane have I felt this edge of adventure." Betty stared at him while I started the Jeep.

"You did that?" she asked, eyes narrowing.

"I landed at Le Bourget, and when I came back to my homeland, my feet firmly on good old terra cotta," said Lucas, "they gave me a ticker tape parade in Manhattan to end them all. I was young and foolish, but bravery is often the realm of the young men. All the sad and dying young men."

"Did he do that?" Betty asked me. I looked at Lucas, hat high, eyes straight ahead, looking like a man I'd actually known for a good spell, General Patton, with that same eyes-ahead look, like go ahead and try to believe in anything but me. It made me feel good and strong.

"Lord, did he ever," I said. "He was as brave a man as ever went into the sky." Betty looked like she wasn't quite sure, but what she looked at him with was admiration, and Lucas saw it and he smiled at her grand as a king, and we were off.

"We should have knocked over a liquor store when we first gained this fabled land," said Lucas as we headed east. "We are a fine team, Jake."

"We ought to tell the truth once in a while," I said.

"Bah!" he yelled. "Nothing is less real than the truth. The only real things are fable and legend and men who loved the land and lived on it, fought it. Men who saved the ranchers from the preying scum, who died in range wars with their boots on! I want to die in a range war! I want guns and chaps and . . ." Well, he went on with the speech I've told before, and he told it good, and I knew then he'd be back writing again soon, and about that I was right.

Ideal, Texas, was a flat, burnt-out little square of houses and stores in a crossroads. It couldn't have had more than three, four hundred people scattered out in houses that started spreading out from the center of town and went out north and east toward Wichita Falls. I parked the Jeep in front of a store called Hardeman Mercantile. The town reminded me a bit of my old home town, but it hadn't caught up with the times like mine had. It seemed to have stopped in the thirties, the sidewalks cracked, and stores full of dust and spooks from earlier years. I was tired from the drive and so was Lucas, but I wanted to get on with it, so I figured Hardeman Mercantile was as good a place as any to start.

Lucas said, "But who's Ideal, fair Helen?" I didn't ask him, but I had no idea what he was talking on. The front door of the store was open and it was cool outside but not cold, and inside a stove was sitting near the back and some men were on ladderback chairs talking soft and laughing ever once in a while. After we'd stood just inside the door for maybe thirty seconds, one old feller got up slowly and came walking up toward us.

The store, once you got in, had the worn-in look of an old boot — canned goods, bags of feed here, toggle bolts and alarm clocks there, and in one corner near the front

168

a postal window with the words Ideal, Texas, faded out but readable on a ledge of dark wood.

"What can we help you fellers with?" he asked. He stuck out his hand and I took it, and it felt like old harness leather. He was probably my age but the wind and sun had taken the juice out of him. "I'm D.Q. Rawson."

"D.Q.?" asked Lucas, suddenly interested.

"Just like Dairy Queen," he said like he'd said it a million times and I'm sure he had. "It stands for Dystrell Quentin, so you know why I go by D.Q."

"Well, Mr. Rawson, I'm Jake Baker and this here's Kid Kraft," I said. He shook with us and the men in the back stopped and stared. "They call him Kid because that was his name when he was boxing back in the forties. He once fought Billy Conn, but the Kid's career was all but over by then."

"Dang," said D.Q. "You all come on back and set down a spell." I figured it was the thing to do, so we went on back, and Lucas was saying "yup" under his breath and walking like he was bowlegged, hands on his hips, sighing and snorting. He'd wore his hat and it was pushed back from his face, and I do believe he thought he was walking into a saloon in Dodge City. We sat down around the old coal stove, whose flue went straight up into the ceiling, glowing red at the bottom. Three others were back there, all about our age, except for one old guy who looked to be ninety. D.Q. told us their names but they went out of my head like water through a sieve, and by the time the last one had a name, all three were still strangers to me.

"You all want a cold drink?" one man said. He wore overalls and his face looked like something heavy had dropped on it from some height, his eyes squashed down to near his mouth, everything slightly out of plumb. I'd done my share of carpentering, and this guy looked put

169

together poorly. "D.Q., get them boys a cold drink." He got up and got us a Coke. Lucas stared at the bottle for a second, took a big swig, wiped his mouth, made a sound of pleasure and then nodded.

"Good stuff," Lucas said. "Sasparilly."

"That's a Coke," the ancient one said, real deep down and serious.

"Well, I appreciate that," I said. "I'm trying to locate somebody who used to live here years ago, maybe fifteen years ago, fella named Buddy Buckley." D.Q. nodded and one of the other guys started talking like he was in the middle of a sentence.

". . . because he was deep-down sorry, Buddy Buckley was. He worked for Duck Fontana over to the garage and one day Duck says, 'That Buddy Buckley's just deep-down sorry.' And I said that was true because he never learned how a man should act. Duck put up with him a long time."

"Duck Fontana?" said Lucas, eyes bright, happy as a boy at Christmas. "My God, is that moniker accurate, boys? Is this person still in residence hereabouts?" I elbowed Lucas, and thank God they treated him like you do a bug on your pants leg, just brush it off and keep on going.

"Yeah, I remember Buddy," said D.Q. "Married to this woman who'd as lief cuss you out as look at you."

"That's Betty," I said. "I'm looking for her daughter for her. Buddy stole their girl baby fifteen years ago and run off with her, and Betty's trying to find out where she is." One of the men spit into a rusty pork-and-bean can and cackled like he was crazy.

"You got about as much chance of finding that girl as finding God," he said, talking through his nose.

"I remember that," said D.Q. "I remember when he up and left, cause my ex-wife used to work for the welfare and she'd come home telling me how awful it was about him stealing that baby. I'd not thought about it in years. I guess that baby'd be . . ."

"Sixteen," I said.

"Oh boy," said Lucas about nothing I could figure.

"You go talk to John Charles Gregory," the oldest man said. He stood and turned, taking about half a minute and pointed up the road. "Out there in Carver." I looked where he was pointing, and it was directly at a bag of 10-10-10 fertilizer, so I looked at D.Q. for a translation.

"He might know something," D.Q. nodded. "He was their closest neighbor. Didn't they live out on the old Rogers place?" The old man was still pointing at the fertilizer and he made a sound that meant, I reckon, that he agreed. I think he knew more than he let on.

"Dang good sasparilly," said Lucas, finishing his Coke. He set it down, leaned back and propped his feet up on the stove. The men looked at him with wonder and Lucas grinned for about fifteen seconds until the heat came through his shoes and he jumped up yelling "Shit!" and such, hopping around like he was doing some secret dance.

"You shouldn't orta put yore feet up on the stove," one of the men said, and Lucas was just fixing to say something when I interrupted.

"Whereabouts is this old Rogers place?" I asked, and D.Q. told me, and I hustled Lucas out, him still hopping and cussing. I got him in the Jeep and he whipped off his boots and rubbed his feet.

"That furnace is in violation of every safety standard known to civilization," yowled Lucas Kraft. "I fully intend to report that disgrace to the proper authorities."

171

"Oh shut up," I said with some firmness. He looked at me while I put the Jeep into gear and then nodded and kept rubbing his feet. We drove smack through the middle of Ideal, which took about twelve seconds, and then on up the road to Carver, which wasn't anything but a few farm houses and an old brick building that had a gas station downstairs. We came to the crossroads D.Q. had described, took a left and went a mile, then right at a sign for a fishing lake. We went down that dirt road for half a mile. There were two houses not far apart. The one on the left sitting in a grove of cottonwood trees was John Charles Gregory's. The other one, across a small gully, was hardly more than a shack, and when I saw it, I could send myself back and see Loretta as a baby and Betty a younger woman and no more than the shadow of Buddy Buckley, him not a real person, and I felt something then I couldn't name, that I somehow belonged with that family.

"Oh, great," said Lucas when he saw the houses. "We have inherited the white trash of the earth."

"You look down on folks too much, Kid," I said.

"I told you not to call me that," he said. "If you wish to append a moniker, you may call me General or Commandant."

"You one of the Ten Commandants?" I knew what he meant, but I was poking fun.

"Get thee behind me, Jake," he said, shaking his head like he couldn't believe me. I drove down a long dusty road between two fields of new grass to the nicer house, the Gregory place, I reckoned they would call it. Everything was turning green again and I don't know what it was but I felt young, and I think Lucas felt it too, sitting there in his Australian bush hat and pretending. Lucas was always pretending something else was happening in

172

his life, which mystified me, since his life had been exciting enough. I stopped in front of the house and our dust drifted past us, rose on a fresh wind and went up over the house.

It wasn't much of a house, but it was comfortable, and I wondered if John Charles Gregory had built it with his own hands. It would mean more to him, I knew. We were getting out of the Jeep when a dog the size of a pony came loping out from under the house, mouth open, lips up in a snarl, not making a noise.

"Yea," said Lucas, hopping up on the hood as best he could, "though I walk through the valley of the shadow of death I will fear no evil." The dog veered toward me, and I could almost feel this strength come over me and I just held up my hand and talked soothing to the dog, and it sat down and began to swish its tail in the dusty yard, then lifted one paw to shake hands.

"Looky here, General," I said. "He's a shaking my hand."

"That's about as worthless a dog as ever lived in Texas," a man drawled coming down the steps. He was tall and lean as a snap bean, wearing overalls and a greasy old hat. "Come on down. He won't hurt you." Lucas slid off the hood and fell flat on his face, but he scrambled up cussing and for a minute I thought the dog might bite him just for the hell of it. "Jessie, get under that house." The dog turned and loped back under the house and sat down, tongue out. "You fellers got business here?"

"You John Charles Gregory?" I asked.

"That's right," he said. "Come on up on the porch. You boys want some sweet tea or something?"

"I'd like a pitcher of margaritas," said Lucas. "That animal has elevated my blood pressure."

173

"Well, I ain't got no margaritas," Gregory said thoughtfully, "but I got me some of the best moonshine whiskey made in Texas. Kind of early, but you all wanting a sip?"

"Too early for medicine?" asked Lucas. "They'd never let you in the AMA."

"What's that?" asked Gregory.

"Never you mind," said Lucas, pointing toward the front door. "The whiskey, sir!" Gregory went inside while we sat in rocking chairs and I told Lucas to cool it, and he nodded but he wasn't listening to me. "Jake, I have decided to get married again."

"Okay, but I won't wash your socks," I said. He turned and looked at me with right smart disgust.

"Not you, you ninny," he said. "Sally. I am going to prove to her that I am all the man I once was and she will melt and find that I was all she ever wanted, and it will be glorious and all will be as it was."

"Uh huh," I said. "By the way, Hugh said you and Sally broke up after you wrote some books about women. What was that all about?"

"That scum," said Lucas. Gregory came back out with three glasses and a plastic milk jug half full of a clear liquid.

"This'll clear out yore head," he said. We all poured and drank and he was right, but it also tasted like it was made in God's personal liquor still, a nice charcoal taste that went down like honey liquor. "Ain't that something?"

"I would like to purchase some of this ere we depart," said Lucas. The man nodded.

"I'm a friend of a woman named Betty Silver," I said. He looked at me like he was trying to remember something. "I understand she and her husband Buddy Buckley and their daughter Loretta Michelle used to live over there." I pointed next door.

"Lord have mercy upon my soul," he said. "I knowed them. I wondered what happened to Betty. She would of been pretty if she hadn't of cussed all day long."

"That is the lady," said Lucas, toasting Gregory's words.

"Betty's trying to find her daughter," I said. "Buddy up and run off with her fourteen, fifteen year ago. Betty's not seen her since then and wants to know where she's at."

"Yessir," said Gregory, rubbing his chin. "I don't have an idea where that girl might be. Pretty thing she was, hair almost white as the sun. Now Buddy, I know about." I got so excited I could hardly stay in my rocker. If I could talk to him, maybe he'd let Loretta see her mama and I'd get Betty.

"I'd like to talk to him, if you know how to get wherever he is," I said.

"He's up yonder in the Corinth Baptist Church cemetery," said Gregory, pointing up the dirt road.

"Shit," I said. "What happened to him?"

"He was shot through the temple in a poker game's what I heard, but you hear things," said Gregory. "He was gone a couple years and him and the baby come back up the road, stayed in a place owned by Mr. Jasper Calhoun. But that was years ago."

"Could I talk to this Mr. Calhoun?" I asked.

"He's up there to Corinth, too," said Gregory. "He bled to death from hemorrhoids. You ever hear of such a thing in your life?"

"I can see the epitaph," said Lucas writing on the air. "Sitting Now With His God."

"So who'd of got the girl?" I asked.

"You know, now that I think on it, I think Buddy had hisself a sister who might of taken that girl," said Gregory. "I seem to recollect somebody saying that." He didn't know more than that, and after one drink, my head was buzzing, so I sat there talking about weather, dogs, trucks and such until my head cleared and we left. Unfortunately, Lucas had not stopped drinking and his head was not clear at all.

By the time we got home, Wool was cussing because I was late helping with supper, Lucas was so drunk four of us had to unload him from the Jeep and put him in bed, and I felt, for the first time in a spell, like I was doing something worthwhile.

ME AND LUCAS DROVE all over north central Texas that spring, following all sorts of ridiculous leads, hoping Loretta Michelle would turn up somewhere. It sounds awful strange now, but we'd taken to making up stories about her, and she'd started to mean something to Lucas, too, though he and Betty still got along as well as oil and water.

We were down near Brownwood one day, on 183 past Zephyr in Mills County. It was early May and since we'd visited Ideal, Texas, over in Jack County, we'd been steered by all kinds of relatives and welfare folks, and it appeared that we'd finally found a place she might be, at a cousin of Buddy Buckley's.

Betty hadn't been too broke up when she found out Buddy'd died, maybe a little sad, but more sad because she couldn't get Loretta through him.

"What would have happened to her?" she asked. "Why didn't they bring her to me?"

"Now, you know how things happen," I said. "They didn't know where you were, didn't know where to send her, so one thing happened and then another."

"And she is a lovely child," said Lucas. "She has developed an interest in reading great literature and her hair is golden, like golden dust, fine and lovely. And she rides a stallion into the countryside and sits to listen to all manner of birds, to the wind and its kin."

"How do you know that?" sniffed Betty, holding an old handkerchief to her nose.

"Intuition," said Lucas. "Ah, the insights of the heart."

Well, that was weeks ago, and since then we'd all begun to make up things about Loretta Michelle. Lucas had started writing again, but he wouldn't let me know about what. Missy Owens had taken to her bed and Betty whispered that she was very sick, and we all felt real bad about that. Chuck looked half dead himself from worry and Lucas never went down to the big house any more.

Whizzer Pippin's leg had healed and we'd still not heard a word from Scout, even though we'd called the sheriff and he'd done all he could to find him. Tree and J.T. and Tom had stayed friends with me, better than most of the other boys. Of late, Wool had taken to throwing frying pans and yelling a lot, but nobody paid that much attention.

The only thing anybody in Haskell County was talking about was *Shadow of the Wind*. By this time, of course, everybody knew Lucas and Sally Crandall had been married. They wanted to see her, but all the women in the county were slathering because some man from a TV show I'd never seen was now going to be the man star, a fella named Mack Taylor. I never found out what happened to that other guy. Wool had seen Mack Taylor on TV and said he was a son of a bitch, but most all the

world was a son of a bitch to Wool. One time he said the
Pope was a son of a bitch because he was from Poland.

They were all supposed to get there in a couple of
weeks, and Lucas had taken to wearing lots of after shave,
trying to diet, though it didn't do much good, and he had
bought some real Western clothes, which made him look
silly, but I didn't tell him. Late at night, long after the
bunkroom was filled with good sounds of soft snoring,
Lucas and I would talk.

"She is lovely, so beautiful," he would drone.

"Loretta Michelle?" I asked.

"No, you stupid cook," he said, "Sally. Oh God, she was
a tiger in bed. I ever tell you about that?" Well, he'd told
me about it and I didn't really believe him, how she'd
worshipped him, would go at it with him for hours and
hours. Lately, me and Betty'd been talking about going to
a motel, one over in Breckenridge, but she kept putting it
off, and I was about ready to spend my evenings howling
at the moon.

"Yeah."

"But, of course, there is Loretta, too," he whispered.
"She is, of course, a virgin. Face scrubbed clean as the
prairie by the wind, perhaps freckles." That made me
think on my redheaded gal back home in Mississippi, and
I felt sad for a time, but mostly I felt good.

"I want to see her," I said. "She probably looks like a
young Betty."

"More's the pity," said Lucas, but I let it go, being
drowsy and not wanting to fight. "Jake, have you ever
regretted not having children?" I wasn't expecting that
question, not from Lucas, and it was suddenly like a knife
in my heart.

"All the time," I said. "I always wished I'd had me a
boy, though I wouldn't of minded a girl. You feel like

179

something has stayed inside of you that should have come out, some part of yourself."

"It hurts, doesn't it?" he said, gone into sleep. "That surely hurts."

Now, with a solid idea where she might be, the three of us, Lucas, Betty and me, were driving south to Mills County. We passed through Zephyr, me driving and Lucas holding up a map that kept flopping in front of Betty's face.

"Would you keep that goddamn thing off me?" she said. "You can't read maps no how."

"Madam," said Lucas, covering her up even more, "I once moved across the whole of the south Pacific using maps. You are not to speak to me in that manner."

"Bullshit," she said, stretching the word out about three seconds. Lucas started trying to fold the map back up, and he was doing a bad job of it, fumbling, refolding, and I could see Betty glancing at him, getting more and more upset. Finally she couldn't take it and she just grabbed the map, wadded it into a little ball and threw it out the window.

"Destruction of personal property is a felony in the great state of Texas," boomed Lucas. She turned in the seat and was about to lay into him good when I saw the road with the big sign where the welfare woman over in Jack County had said we should look. It said "Jesus Saves," though somebody had spray painted under it, "Roger sucks."

"Here's our turn off," I said, and Lucas and Betty quit fighting. It was a dirt road, straight and dusty, as it hadn't rained. Everybody kept telling me about storms, but we'd not had one to amount to much that spring.

180

"She will be on a slope hanging out wash," said Lucas. "Hair shining and blowing in the breeze, and when she sees fair Betty she will know and run into her arms." Betty stared at Lucas.

"You really think so?" she asked. Her voice had suddenly gone soft, pretty sounding. I'm not sure I was in love with her yet, but I felt awful warm about her and she liked me, too.

"Of course," said Lucas.

"Oh my," said Betty.

"Thanks, Kid," I said, but he was staring out the window thinking deep thoughts, which he often did. The road passed all manner of poor farmhouses, most of them tired, not minding if somebody kicked the slats out and they fell into a heap of boards. Some days I knew that feeling and when I got it, dying didn't seem too bad, a rest, a sleep, a good thing.

I believed I would come around the corner in the Jeep and see some fine house sitting up on a hill. My heart was beating fast. The lady who'd told me where Buddy Buckley's cousin lived said it was the first house on the left past the Antioch Baptist Church. We came to the church and the first house on the left past it was the most pitiful thing you've ever seen in your life, frame with the boards gone brown and a few stringy chickens wandering around in the dust.

"Is that it?" said Betty. "What a piece of shit."

"Perhaps we have made a slight miscalculation in this matter," mumbled Lucas, looking around. I parked under a big chinaberry tree and the front door opened and a woman big as the Jeep came out, hair falling down around her face and a long just-lit cigarette dangling from her lips. Betty and Lucas stared at me, so I cleared my throat and went walking toward her. She didn't

181

change that expression, just stared with the smoke curling around her head. A chicken raced past me and disappeared somewhere under the house. I don't care what anybody says, it's low-rent to allow chickens under your house.

"Are you Buddy Buckley's cousin?" I asked.

"What if I am?" she said in a deep voice. She squinted when she saw Betty and then her eyes opened up big and she took the cigarette out of her mouth with her fat fingers and blew smoke up over her head. "Oh Jesus."

"She recognizes me," said Betty. "I met you one time at the reunion up in Abilene."

"Sure took you long enough to get here," the woman said. She sat down on the porch steps and smoked as we got near. You could smell her, a kind of disgusting sweet-sour smell, and there were lines of dirt in the folds of her neck.

"Where is my child?" Betty asked, her voice shaky. The woman kept staring straight ahead, saying nothing.

"How'd you get here?" she asked, not all that unpleasant. "My name's Rita. You know Buddy's dead up there in Jack County."

"I know," said Betty. "A lady welfare worker up there heard it from somebody, she wouldn't tell me who, that you got Loretta Michelle after Buddy died."

"She told you right," Rita said. Betty was breathing hard and looking around and I thought she might pull the door off its hinges and go looking through the house.

"We'd like to see her," I said.

"I would, too," said Rita. "If you run into her, tell her I said howdy."

"Woman, where is our darling Loretta?" said Lucas. Rita looked at him like everybody else looked at him.

182

"Don't have no idea," Rita said. "Two years ago September she up and left, gave me a note saying she weren't coming back, said she was going away with this girl she knew to live with her. I've not heard word one since that day." Betty sat down on the steps and started to cry and I put my arms around her, but she didn't want to be happy.

"Was she . . . happy when she lived here?" Betty asked. She thought about it for a second, but before Rita could say anything, Betty popped up and slapped the everloving shit out of her, sending the cigarette flying across the yard where a chicken picked it up and went off in the bushes.

"Don't you goddamn touch me again," said Rita, yelling at the top of the lungs. I was glad they weren't having church next door. Betty turned slightly, like she was going to walk away, and then she hit Rita in the mouth so hard she fell sideways off the porch and into the dirt. I thought with Rita being so fat and all she wouldn't get up, but up she came, blood coming from her mouth, her eyes big as dollars, charging into Betty, and then both of them went down in the dusty yard. Chickens were yelling. Betty landed hard. Lucas was shadow boxing, hopping up on his tiptoes yelling "Left! Right!" and such.

"You stupid bitch!" screamed Betty, pounding on Rita's back. "You kidnapped my baby!" Rita rolled over on Betty and hit her in the face once time but Betty roared sort of, I don't know what else to call it, and threw Rita off and was kicking her in the ribs when I finally pulled her away. Rita didn't move. One side of her cheap old brown dress was torn away and her big old breast was just laying there like it didn't know what it was for any more.

"I'll call the sheriff," said Rita. When she said that, Betty broke away from me again and went over and jumped on Rita and was clawing at her face and kneeing her in the stomach before I got her off this time. Rita was a mess of blood and sweat and dirt. A chicken came out and stood near Rita, who sat up as I pushed Betty back toward the Jeep. The other side of her dress was down and both her breasts hung down, and a sorrier sight you never saw in your life, and I felt a little pity for a human being to look like that, man or woman. It was just a shame.

Rita started laughing through the blood, laughing real low, and she said, "You'll never find her. Buddy was right about you. You are a whore. You'll never see that girl again."

I thought the police had come because this high, whining sound just started, sharp as a siren, but it was Betty, starting to cry and saying "Noooooo!" with the worst sort of agony you could imagine. Lucas helped me get her in the Jeep, and she was crying and dirty and her face was streaked with dust and tears. Lucas held her hand as I backed up and put the Jeep in gear. Rita had a whole row of pottery animals along the edge of her driveway, and I flattened the little sons of bitches and I could hear her screaming as I headed past the church, going north toward Harkin County and home.

Betty sobbed for a long time, so we stopped in Brownwood and got a six pack and opened it. I didn't drink, being as I was driving, but Lucas and Betty did. Two or three times Betty tried to say something, but she'd get all choked up and it wouldn't come out. Lucas had his hairy arm around her shoulder, and she let him, which said a whole lot for both of them.

"Seems like," said Betty, finally getting her voice, "you spend half your life losing things you never can find again." Well, right there out of the blue, Lucas started to cry, big gasping sobs, tears running down his cheeks.

184

"Honey, what's wrong with you? Did I say something to hurt you?"

"It's all right," said Lucas. I knew what he was thinking about, but I didn't want to say it. Betty took a Kleenex out of her bag and wiped away his tears like you do a child. Her face was a mess and under one eye there was a swelling where Rita had smacked her. "It's really all right." I felt like crying, too, but for some reason I didn't, and then Betty put her head on my shoulder and nuzzled close to me and said, real soft, "Thank you," and I'll be durned if I didn't start bawling, and then all three of us were driving up 183 with enough tears to raise the ark. I took me a beer and by the time we'd all stopped crying, I felt as good as I had in my entire life, a peaceful, strong feeling.

"I ain't never losing nothing again," I said, and Betty leaned up and kissed me on the cheek.

When we got home Wool was cussing at me because I was half an hour late getting there to help with supper.

"I'm not gonna sit here and do all this goddamn work myself," he fumed as I set the long table for the men. He had the radio on and they said we might have bad thunderstorms that night. I didn't know it then, but Wool was awful scared of thunder and wind, and so he was more foul-mouthed than usual. He had his heavy rock station so loud it made my teeth hurt.

"Them people sound like they're being stomped on," I said.

"What do you know?" he said, stirring a big vat of beans in time to the music. "Did you and Lucas find that bitch's gal? Yeah, you're smart, Jake."

"Don't talk about her that way," I said. He stopped and stared at me, holding the spoon out and dripping bean juice on to the bricks that made up the kitchen floor. He grinned mean.

"You got the hots for that old bitch, huh, Jake?" he said. I felt my neck muscles get tight. He was twenty years younger than me, but he was talking about my girl, and you don't take such a thing, no matter how old you are. He was talking about Betty.

"Nigger," I said, "you better get back to stirring your beans. You such a man, you got the job for it." He threw the spoon down hard and it skittered across the floor. The music changed, something sort of slow, but still loud and ugly.

"What did you call me, asshole?"

"Just nigger," I said. "But don't think it's because you're colored. Tree's just a man. But you're a nigger, Wool. You'll never be nothing but a nigger." He came at me. Wool was a big man and I realized I might get my head mashed, but when I was a young man, I'd been in more fights than I could count, in bars, in parking lots, even for a few years in Chicago in the ring. I was slower, but I still remembered.

He came for my neck with both hands and I gave him a straight right that set him down on his butt and brought blood. J.T. and Whizzer Pippin happened to be walking past the kitchen and they saw it and yelled, "Fight in the kitchen!" and soon the place was half filled, Wool up and circling me. I stood in my boxing crouch.

"Fisticuffs! Fisticuffs!" yelled someone in the rear. I knew it was Lucas before I saw him. "Let's do this properly."

Wool dropped his fists and stared at me, his eyes mean. "Let's go outside," he said, and he went past me to hooting and hollering for the others and Lucas was behind me trying to rub on my shoulders like a boxing manager.

186

"Let go a me," I said, but Lucas kept rubbing and then there was a big circle and me and Wool were in the middle of it. He came rushing at me. Once I could have just stepped to one side, but I was a step too slow now and he knocked me down. It wasn't more than forty minutes until dark, and we could hear thunder up to the north, and the air was heavy and wet and hot.

"Get up!" screamed Lucas. "Kill the bastard, Jake!" Wool turned and glared at Lucas while we lay wrestling on the ground. "I mean your fellow pugilist."

"Say what?" said Wool, and as he started to go for Lucas, I kicked him in the balls, which is dirty pool, but anybody's who's ever fought professional will tell you it's not a business for people with ideals. Well, Wool went down like a pole-axed steer, and I hit him with a little looping right on the jaw. That was a big mistake. Instead of making him yell uncle, it just gave him the fight to hit me in the side of my head with his forearm, which is how you really hit a man if you don't want to break your knuckles. I saw stars. I went flat down on my back and didn't move because I couldn't.

But instead of hitting me again, Wool collapsed beside me. A wind was coming up and I tried to sit up and the wind felt good on my face, but I was dizzy and fell back down. Me and Wool were face to face. Lucas had gone absolutely crazy, yelling about range wars and squaws, and I was glad he was so excited, but it wasn't much of a fight, and when I heard this deep sound I thought it was somebody clearing their throat, but it was Wool laughing real low.

We both finally sat up and looked at one another, and he grinned at me and I grinned back at him and we helped each other up, and Lucas acted like it was the worst thing he'd ever seen.

"This is no time for civilities!" he yelled. But Wool and me walked back toward the kitchen, ignoring Lucas.

"You got a good punch for a nigger," I said, rubbing the side of my head.

"You not bad for some old honkey, neither," he said.

We finished cooking, still laughing a little, and by then the lightning was down right on us, and it was windy, but I liked it. Wool sat in front of the fireplace in the kitchen smoking his corncob pipe, looking worried, but I decided I'd go down and see if Betty was still at Mr. Owens's house. It was only just spitting rain. I went out through the end door, through the study where Lucas was pounding on his typewriter and cussing a blue streak at somebody. He didn't even notice me. My head was throbbing even though I'd taken some aspirins and had me a drink.

I got to the back door, and like in a dream, Betty was standing there, smiling at me and looking pretty.

"Where's Chuck and Missy?" I whispered. I'd often come down and we'd sit on the back steps, but I wasn't supposed to go in the house.

"They're gone to spend a few days at her mother's, her feeling poorly and all," Betty said. The rain started to fall hard and when I came on to the porch she could see where Wool had slammed me. "Was that you in that fight? My God in heaven. I saw them fighting from upstairs. Who . . ."

"It was me and Wool," I said. "I'm okay. What are you doing here if nobody's in the house?" She touched where my head hurt and I could smell perfume on her, and I recognized it as Missy's and it made my heart run like wind.

"Why were you and Wool fighting?" she asked. "That black son of a bitch."

"It was nothing, and don't call him that," I said. "He's a friend of mine."

"Okay," she said in a little voice. "Mr. Owens asked me to stay here and keep an eye on the house." The rain was falling steadily now and the air was cool and fresh, and the ground smelled like it does when it rains and the dirt is hard and dry.

"Yeah?" Sometimes I'm awful dumb, but I realized at that minute what it meant and I felt my heart beating hard as a boy's.

"Come on," she said. She took my hand and we went down the hall and turned and headed up the stairs. There was a light on somewhere upstairs but it was dark in the stairwell, and she took my hand and walked close to me.

The light was on at one end of the hall and it was weak, but enough to make everything look weird, and I felt like something was watching us hand in hand in there. The hall was straight through from the front to the back of the house and windows were open, curtains flapping gently on both ends. I looked at Betty and she looked at me and then we both looked down as she turned away from the light and went toward the front of the house. There were rooms on either side of the hall, and we went into the one on the left and Betty closed the door.

There was a light Chuck had had put on a pole outside and its glow let you see everything in the room in outline. He'd had the light put in when Missy had become afraid of the dark for some reason nobody understood.

"Is this their room?" I asked.

"No," Betty whispered. A few chairs and tables were about, a mantel with a clock ticking slowly on it, but the bed took up most of the room, an old-fashioned four-poster canopy bed, with winding posts that in the dark looked mighty like snakes to me. The room was warm and dusty.

189

"Let's open up the windows," I said. I opened the two on the front, which looked out over the front driveway where I'd first laid eyes on the place back when poor old Bo Kersh brought us. Betty opened the two on the other side and the room was filled with fresh rain air and wind. The canopy on the bed rose and fell quietly like a sail in a breeze.

"I love the rain," Betty said. I was going to say something sort of poetic, something maybe I'd picked up from Lucas, but before I could, she said, "Let's get naked," which sort of made romance talk unnecessary. Well, I was happy and scared as I'd been in a long time. I hadn't made love to a woman in probably fifteen years, though I sure as hell hadn't forgotten how. But the old equipment didn't work well as it used to, and I was afraid I'd humiliate myself.

"Okay," I choked, but I felt like my big old feet had been nailed to the floor and all I could do was stand there looking at Betty's outlines while she took off her dress, then her slip and shoes and climbed up into the big bed.

"Come on, Jake," she said, holding open the covers. I could see her face all right, and I had to admit it was nothing special, but neither was I, and I was a good bit older than her. While I was standing there fumbling with my shirt buttons, which somehow seemed to be sewed onto my chest, she reached behind her and took off her bra and her bosoms fell down and I realized then that things were going to work. "Come on, honey. Let's love on one another."

I'm by nature modest about some things, and I won't tell the details of how things went between me and Betty that night, but if there's a Texas Hall of Fame for lovemaking, me and Betty should have been put in it for the

190

sheer variety, powerfulness and persistence, long after I knew I was through for the night.

We were breathing hard and the clock on the mantel had this soft little chime on the hour and half hour, and it had just chimed three times. The rain had not stopped and had become steady, the kind of rain farmers love. We lay there tangled up in one another's arms.

"You make me feel so good," she whispered, her face on my neck. "There's nothing wrong with it, is there, with a person not wanting to be lonely and touch another person?"

"Of course there ain't nothing wrong with it," I said.

"I'm all mixed up sometimes," she said. "Making love with Buddy wasn't about love, it was about hurting and then not hurting. It made him not hurt for a spell. I always thought God took Loretta Michelle away from me because of that. You shouldn't screw somebody if you don't love them. Isn't that right?"

"Mmmmmm," I said, sleepy and not wanting to talk about her ex-husband, rest his soul.

"And now I reckon I'll never see my little girl again," she said, sad, but not hurting too bad about it. "You really think she's all those things you say, that she's pretty and fine and good and all those things?"

"I believe it," I said. "She has become a fine young woman."

"I wish she could be here," said Betty. "It's a good place to be, here in Harkin County. This ranch and now the movie folks coming. Everybody's fit to be tied about that movie." She shifted and sat up, breasts hanging in front of me, the cool wind pouring over us. I reached up and fiddled with one breast and she held my hand to it and closed her eyes for a second. "I won't never forget all us sitting there in that Jeep today and all us old farts crying.

I thought a lot of bad things about your buddy before, but it'll be hard for me to do nothing but love him now."

"It's hard for me to do anything but love him," I said. "It's a wonder. He can act like an awful jerk, but he's been the best friend I ever had in my life."

"You told him that?" she asked. A little roll of thunder came from far off, but it didn't last long.

"Naw," I said. "One man don't tell another things like that."

"What horseshit," she said. She held my hand to her breast and the nipple was all hard, and I realized to my surprise I was ready again and we went at it until we both fell asleep with the clock giving back one soft chime at 3:30.

I woke up with Betty pushing on my shoulder and the day was not yet breaking, but I knew I was late for helping Wool and he was probably already throwing things. We helped one another get dressed and she went downstairs for a shower and I headed back to the Long House after we kissed a long time and made plans to sleep together again that night. I looked at myself in the plate glass of the back door on my way out. I needed a shave and my hair was up all over, but I felt like Clark Gable, so I grinned at myself.

When I got back up to the Long House, Whizzer Pippin was out hitting golf balls across the creek in the new light, with the rain gone, and Lucas was asleep in his study with a piece of paper in the typewriter and the last word being "asshole." When I got into the kitchen, the bacon was already frying and Wool looked up at me.

"I'm awful sorry," I said. "I overslept."

"You one sorry white boy," he said, but he was grinning from ear to ear and his laugh echoed through the kitchen for the longest time.

BETTY WOULD PACK PICNIC lunches, and on weekends she, Lucas and I would drive around looking for Loretta Michelle, but without much of a plan and without much hope. We'd stop in every cowtown and look in the phone books that dangled from the chains of phone booths, not find her name and then eat, drink and laugh. We knew we weren't going to find her, but that didn't seem as important as the search.

By the middle of May, we knew two things — that the movie company would be arriving for *Shadow of the Wind* in a week, and that Missy Owens was dying. I realize I haven't said all that much about Chuck, but God's truth is I didn't see him much. He didn't run the ranch day to day and he was sort of a mystery figure, though folks in the Long House said he hadn't always been that way, only in the past year since Missy'd been sick.

The last time any of us had seen her had been about three weeks before when she came out of the house, wearing a long dress, even though it was warm. I, by happenstance, was down near the house using a Weedeater Wool had bought and wanted me to try out. She came out on Chuck's arm, wobbly, and I took off my cowboy hat when she passed me, her blue eyes looking big as china plates, straight ahead. He helped her into the car and she looked back at the house, and I waved and I know she saw me but she acted like I wasn't there. She was so skinny there didn't seem to be much under the dress and Chuck's face was blind terror and agony. They drove off and I felt something awful. I went right up the front steps, opened the door, and walked inside, the first time I'd ever done that since we'd come there.

Betty was sitting in the living room holding a cup of coffee that had a small ring of bright red lipstick on the rim. When she saw me, her eyes filled with tears, but the tears didn't fall.

"She'll never see this place again," she said.

"What is wrong with her?" I asked. "I thought it was her blood pressure." She busied around, picking up a napkin, and I realized it was Missy's cup and napkin and a cold chill feeling ran all along my arms. I realized I was still holding the Weedeater.

"Put that thing outside," Betty said. "You'll get shit all over the carpets." I set it on the front porch and went back into the kitchen.

"What's wrong with Missy?"

"She's got cancer," Betty said, but the sentence was more like a sigh. I felt a shudder go through my bones; I was sort of afraid of cancer, always had been.

"Cancer of what?"

"Cancer of everything. Mr. Owens told me she only had a few weeks. It's God's pity, a young woman like that going home like that, it's God's pity."

194

I felt numb and couldn't hardly believe it. And as you'll be selfish thinking about such things, I wondered if Chuck would keep the ranch together or maybe sell it to somebody who watched his money a mite closer and would have no use for old writers and white-haired cooks.

I went back out the front door and would have thought on it and got all glum if I hadn't seen Lucas come flying down the hill toward me, wearing his cowboy hat, boots and a nice leather vest he'd bought in town. He was yelling my name and waving his arm over his head, and something about it made all the bad feelings pass out of me like a bird out of a tree. There was a long slope from the Long House down to the Big House, and halfway down, Lucas sort of slid on his big old bottom and rolled a couple of times, and I headed up to meet him.

"Are you all right?" I asked.

He said, "Jake, Jake, appropriate a vehicle this moment and hie us hither to the set. They are here, all of them, including my beloved! The paper says they've built an entire town up there where the fort was last winter." I wanted to tell him about Missy, but his face was bright as sun and I was afraid it was bad luck.

"Kid, you remember what Hugh said," I reminded him. "She's living with that race car driver and probly don't want nothing to do with you. He got up and dusted himself off, full of energy like he could be, so full it rubbed off all over me like glory.

"Ah, the hell with regrets and failed passions," he said in his deep rolling voice. "I shall pursue, she shall resist and ultimately we shall lie on victory's bed, tangled with the passion of Tristan and Isolde."

"Who are they?"

"Never mind, my friend," he laughed. "Never mind. Appropriate a Jeep." I didn't have much to do, so I did, and as we were driving down the long road to the edge of the ranch, he noticed my feelings, which I couldn't keep inside me and asked what was wrong and I told him. He was quiet for a minute. "That's rotten luck for him. Just rotten luck."

"What about for her?"

"No bad luck in dying," he said. "Just in watching someone you love die." I thought about his father getting killed, about his mother up there in Maryland, and decided he knew what he was talking about. After I told him, I felt better and more than anything wanted to meet Sally Crandall.

I had thought about dying more often lately, though not in such a bad way. I wondered if those folks back in Fieldstone had died yet. Maybe one or two, but I'd bet most were still there, Miss Louise Adler still running things and Mr. Denny still wandering around trying to figure things out.

I drove up toward the movie town, and a mile down the road, you knew something strange was happening. There were signs telling all visitors to come to the visitors' center, that trespassers on the sets would be prosecuted. Lucas said the paper told of them all staying at the Holiday Inn in Abilene, all except a few who lived in trailers and such near the site of the fort.

"Listen to this," Lucas said, taking a clipping out of his pocket and hitting the rear-view mirror with his head. "Why in the hell do they even make these things? Useless." I fixed the mirror. "Listen to this. 'The movie's main star, Miss Sally Crandall, is the one most everybody in Harkin is talking about. This is her first film part in some years, and she's already been seen at Bardell's House of Barbecue.'" Lucas laid the clipping on his lap. "She wouldn't eat barbecue if it was her last meal before the electric chair. She eats pate and sturgeon eggs and ambrosia. What do you think she drinks?" He didn't wait for me to answer. "Grasshoppers. Does that make you gag or what?"

"Is that those green things?" I asked.

"Every inch the lady," he continued, ignoring me. "She is in the tradition of the grand dame."

"Great dane?" That's what I thought he said at first, and he giggled and stomped his boots on the floor like he was dancing. I pulled into the parking lot of the visitors' center and already it was nearly full, and we could see, down the way in the field where only the fort stood in the winter, a whole group of sets, a small group of houses in one place, the fort, of course, and across the road, over where Hugh's trailer had been, was an Indian village with teepees. But we were still a hundred yards away and there wasn't much chance of getting closer since it was all roped off. There was a booth where they were selling *Shadow of the Wind* T-shirts and pictures of the stars, including Sally Crandall. Lucas picked one up off a stack on a ledge in front of the booth.

"That's her," I said, recognizing her face. It still seemed impossible Lucas could once have been married to her, but I knew it was true.

"She looks older than this in person," Lucas said.

"I thought you hadn't seen her in years."

"Don't question me, you ignorant cracker," he said. "There are things a man knows through dint of insight, instinct, intellect. Besides, we used to live next door to a plastic surgeon who tinkered with her from time to time. Ah, the salad days of Lucas Kraft." We wandered around for a while, and people looked at Lucas like he worked for the movie.

"With that outfit, you could walk right on to the movie," I laughed. He turned and looked at me and raised his eyebrows and smiled just a little bit. "You can't be serious. We nearly got throwed in the slam for trying to help the cavalry last time."

"We shall have parts in this wretched picture as extras," said Lucas. "Come forth, Jake. I happen to be on good terms with the assistant director." To this day, I still don't know how he found out his old buddy Will McKelsey was working the film, but by using his name with a couple of guards, we were suddenly in front of another Airstream trailer. There was a piece of masking tape on the door with the word "McKelsey" written on it with a ballpoint pen. Lucas hit the door a couple of times with his palm. It was still kind of early, I guess, for movie people and there was a muffled voice from inside. Lucas assaulted the door again.

"Go away!" somebody inside yelled, unhappy as could be.

"He must know it's you," I said.

"Go to hell," Lucas said, and he started slamming into the door again. It opened so fast that Lucas nearly fell inside. It was a woman, a tall woman who might have looked nice after an hour in front of a mirror, but we'd rousted her from bed and her hair was up all over like snakes. She was wearing a long shirt that just barely covered her panties and didn't at all cover her long legs.

"Oh boy," I said out loud.

"What's that, asshole?" she said, and I realized what I'd done. What was it with the women around this place? Whatever happened to women who never swore?

"I was, uh, just admiring your legs," I said, figuring the truth wouldn't harm me none. She got her eyes focused

198

and she looked at me and then busted out laughing, which made me feel bad.

"Who the hell is it?" a voice somewhere behind her said. "This is our last goddamn day and somebody's messing with me."

"It's a dwarf cowboy and his keeper," the woman said. She stretched and the shirt came way up over her panties, which were black bikinis and were twisted like she'd just put them on. I wondered if I was drooling, but I was too excited to care.

"Dwarf cowboy?" boomed Lucas. "Dwarf cowboy? I will have you know I am five feet six inches tall, and more man than you'll ever be." The woman looked at him like she was having a dream. A man appeared at her shoulder, a fella who needed a shave and whose eyes were watery and red. That was the first time I think I realized this movie might not be another *Gone With the Wind*.

"Lucas?" the man said. "Holy Mother of God. You've come to see Sally, right?" He yawned and lifted a lit cigarette from behind the woman's back. "Come on in." She peeled back and Will McKelsey was standing there, letting us in. The inside of the trailer looked like a pig pen. Will cleaned papers and beer cans off the couch and we sat down, Lucas grinning like a cat with a fish.

"Still living in the lap of luxury," said Lucas. Will stared at him for a few seconds.

"Babe, get us a beer," he said. "You boys want a beer?" I didn't, but Lucas said sure before I could open my mouth. Will was wearing an old-fashioned sleeveless undershirt and striped boxer shorts that weren't together very good, and he kept standing there fooling with his balls like he'd just realized they were hanging there. The woman came in with four beers hanging from the plastic loops. She had put on some shorts and a halter top. Damn.

"You know this dwarf cowboy?" she asked Will.

"I predict for you an early death from whatever disease you have been carrying lo these many years," said Lucas. We all opened our beers and she sat next to Will, who'd sat in this spindly looking chair.

"You're kind of cute," she said, grinning at Lucas. "I have a weakness for ugly things." Lucas looked around the inside of the trailer and sipped his beer.

"I'd say it was more of a genius than a weakness," he said. Just then there was a sound from the back somewhere, and a little yappy dog came tipping out, growling deep in its throat like wool tearing.

"Kill, Scooter," she said, pointing at Lucas. The dog stopped in front of Lucas, who'd pulled his feet up on the couch.

"Scooter?" Lucas said. "It looks like an asthmatic rat."

"Hah," she said.

"This is Lucas Kraft," Will sighed, lighting a Winston. "Danielle Sarbane. I don't know your friend, Lucas."

"This is old Jack Cody," Lucas said, pointing to me with his thumb. "Direct descendant of Buffalo Bill himself." They seemed impressed so I didn't relieve them of the notion.

"Jack," Will said, reaching out, and we shook hands. "What in God's holy name finds you out here in this piece of shit land?"

"Well, hell, boy," said Lucas, leaning back and pushing his cowboy hat back on his head, "me and Cody live right here in Harkin County on a ranch. Yeah, got us five hundred head of prime beef cattle, a thousand acres and lots of them tractor things."

"Them tractor things?" said Danielle. Scooter was standing by the door howling. "He needs to go out, Will."

"Then let him out, babe," said Will. She let the dog out. "You live here? I wondered what ever happened to you. You had any books out? I don't think I've heard a thing from you in years. I read your last book, at least I think it was the last one, the thing about the Civil War."

"Oh, great," said Lucas, putting his hands over his eyes. "Don't talk about that."

"It read like *Gone with the Wind* would have if Margaret Mitchell had been stoned," said Will. "I didn't know soldiers in the Civil War took drugs."

"Well, anyway," said Lucas, clawing at his collar like it was a pair of hands choking the life out of him, "we've come on a cinematic mission, right, Cody?"

"Sure, Kid."

"Kid?" said Danielle.

"He was once the quick draw champion of Pecos County as a boy," I said.

"I thought you were from the East Coast," said Will, finishing his beer in three gulps and throwing the can on the floor. "Get me another one, babe." She rolled her eyes and went to the little refrigerator in the corner.

"Yeah, well, heh, heh, heh," said Lucas. The air conditioner was on and the trailer was freezing cold, but Will didn't seem to notice. The dog was scratching at the door. "Anyway, Cody and I have come to be in this fine motion picture you got here, just bit parts would be fine, but we want to experience the aura of the Old West."

"Have you seen Sally?" he asked. Danielle brought Will another beer and opened the door for Scooter, who came hopping in and immediately started barking at Lucas. "Shut that dog up or I'll put him in the blender." Danielle let the dog back out and muttered under her breath about how mean Will was.

"Sally?" asked Lucas, going for his collar again.

"Yeah, you remember," said Will. "That lady you used to live with, the movie star?" Lucas snapped his fingers and raised his hand in the air like God.

"Oh, that Sally," he said. "I told you about her, Cody."

"Sure did, Kid."

"I want to see your quick draw," said Danielle.

"I bet you do," said Will sourly.

"So how about it?" said Lucas. "We just want to remember this picture here in our home county by being extras in some of these magnificent scenes."

"You hard up for dough?" asked Will, lighting another Winston.

"Aw, hell no," said Lucas, and he laughed like an old mongrel dog. "We don't want money. We just want to get the texture of this movie. Maybe I might even do a magazine piece for *Esquire* or something." That seemed to impress Will. He stood and goofed with his balls again and belched and shrugged.

"Well, that's probably a good idea," he said. He reached out and grabbed Danielle and pulled her to him, and she pouted like a little girl but she still looked like she wanted to put Will on like an overcoat. It made me want to hold Betty. "Go on over to wardrobe and tell them I said you can be in the mountain men scene. They're going to do that first, in a week or so. You can play dress up and pretend all you want. But no pay."

"Fair enough," said Lucas, standing. "Where is it?" Will told us and we went back outside where it was getting hot. Scooter was sitting on the steps and when we came out, Lucas stepped on him. The dog jumped up and bit him on the leg.

"Heh, heh," said Lucas, "fine little dog you have there." Then under his breath he said something about a "goddamn rat." They went back inside and he said, "Gypsies. Trust me."

"I always trusted you, Kid." Lucas smiled and adjusted his cowboy hat to the sharp sun.

"I know," he said. "I never understood that, Jake, but it's a good quality."

Wardrobe was at a huge double-wide trailer half a mile away, not far from the fort, and we went there and Lucas told some tall thin man with short hair we were to be in the mountain man scene because Will McKelsey had said so.

"No, no, no," the man said. "You have to grow your beards out a tad boys. Now we'll start next Thursday. Don't you boys shave one little whisker until then." He pulled out a tape measure and went to touching me and I stiffened up and was thinking about punching him.

"It's okay, Admiral," said Lucas. "Standard procedure."

"Admiral?" the man said.

"You've heard of Bull Halsey?" asked Lucas.

"I thought he was dead," the man said, swishing around us and writing things down on a small pad.

"He is," said Lucas. "That's good that you knew that. This is his nephew, uh, Wilmer Halsey. Got your sea legs back yet, sir?"

"From hell's heart I stab at thee," I said. It was something I'd heard in that Gregory Peck movie about the whale, and I wasn't sure why he'd told that to a whale, but it pleased Lucas enormous, though the wardrobe man just shook his head and shrugged. He measured Lucas.

"Come get your rags on Wednesday afternoon at two," he said.

"Rags?" asked Lucas.

"You are mountain men," sighed the wardrobe man. "You won't be wearing cutaways and ascots." He snorted and sat down on a small plastic chair. "I once worked with Dustin Hoffman on Broadway. Now I'm here."

"Congratulations," I said. Lucas pulled me out the door, and I realized then it was probably the wrong thing to say. We hung around there most of the day and then got home just in time for Wool to chew me out for being late to help with supper.

It was Friday night, so a bunch of the cowboys and me, Lucas and Betty headed down to Hector's.

"Mr. Owens was by today to get some of Missy's stuff," said Betty. She, Lucas and I were in the Jeep.

"It's awful," said Lucas, and he meant it. The three of us had become pals, and Lucas treated her decent like he did me, though not always.

"It's awful," repeated Betty. "And them always wanting children and not ever able to have any. It must be terrible always to want children and never able to have any." It was quiet for a spell. "Well, shit, Betty, you've made a fool of yourself."

"It's okay," I said. Lucas said something, facing away. We'd talked about it before, me and Lucas, about our lines dying out with us, about nobody having our names. You could tell yourself cold in the head that it didn't make a bit of difference, but your heart would tell you back that it hurt, that men and women could make babies and that if you didn't, you'd wasted something God gave you to use.

On Sunday morning, just after Wool and I'd cleaned up and put the dishes away, we heard the buzzer. It was a loud, obnoxious thing Mr. Owens had installed to get us all together in the den of the house. Most of the boys were up, but a few, like Tree and Whizzer Pippin, had got blind drunk the night before and had to struggle out, just their jeans on, looking sick and weak. As soon as I got into the room, I knew it was something bad.

Chuck had a brother named Lewis, who lived in Wichita Falls. He wasn't in the cattle business. In fact, he was a preacher. He'd come by every once in a while and we'd make fun of him without his knowing. He was probably twenty years older than Chuck, tall and wiry, and he stood by the big fireplace looking almost as bad as Tree. Lucas appeared from somewhere and we looked at one another and he just shook his head.

It was Missy Owens. She had died during the night. Reverend Owens told us about how she had gone home to God, how she had died with Chuck holding her to his chest, that Chuck was in right bad shape, but one of the first things he thought of was to tell us.

Most of us weren't close either to Chuck or Missy. Chuck was the boss and Missy in the past few months had stopped even coming outside. But he could have said it was our sister who had died, because several of those cowboys sniffed and rubbed their eyes. I felt real awful about it, that pretty blue-eyed lady gone. It was like she was ours, there at Owensville, and then turned to sand and through our fingers before we could say "Wait, don't leave us!" Reverend Owens, touched by how much we cared, decided to preach, and Lucas and I sneaked out down the hall, through his study and into the yard overlooking the slope and the creek and the cottonwoods.

"Jake, life is so wretchedly short," he said, looking east.

"I thought you said life was worthless."

"I've said a lot of things," he said. "Let's go for a walk." We walked real slow down the slope to the creek. It was a clouding day, I remember, warm but getting cool with rain moving in. Some of the boys were dressed for church, and they were milling around outside. I guess the reverend had quit preaching. I'd never been much of a churchgoer but I believed because I was scared not to.

"You believe she's gone to heaven?" I asked. We sat on the edge of the creek and looked at the water.

"I believe she's there," he said, pointing at the water. A wind came up in our faces. "And here." He held his hand up in the wind just like it was Missy and he was touching her face. "And here." He picked up a handful of dirt and let it slip between his fat old fingers.

We all went to the funeral on Tuesday. It was at a small church in Goree, which is up in Knox County, a plain white church with a steeple and a small graveyard. When we got there, the box was down front and open and most of the boys went by to pay their respects, but Lucas sat in the back, wouldn't go, and so I stayed with him. Anyway, I could see her from there, looking like ivory or stone, beautiful except for those blue eyes that would never open again.

The inside of the church was cool and dark, with clouded windows and a tinny-sounding organ playing sad songs. It was near about full, Chuck having lots of friends. You could hear sniffles every once in a while, coming through the silence like bird's wings. For some reason, I thought of Fieldstone when we were sitting there, though I tried not to. But strange to say, thinking of Fieldstone gave me some comfort, because I'd done something with myself instead of sitting around rotting. And I wasn't through yet.

The service was very short and then, like a dream, we were all standing out in the small graveyard with Missy in that box, under a blue tent which flapped with the breeze. Chuck was with a woman I took to be his sister, though I'd never seen her, and he was okay until the minister finished speaking and he knew it was over and she was gone. Then he began to cry, head down in his lap, and I couldn't take it, and neither could Lucas, so we walked away.

There was a pasture across the road, and since the others were hanging around, we walked over there and looked out at the field that was turning bright green.

"I'm not afraid of dying," Lucas said after a long time. "I'm afraid of being loved. I've always been afraid of being loved." I didn't know what to say so I didn't say anything, but I stood close to him and we leaned on a barbed wire fence and stared at the field, the wind in our faces. "I used to think that everybody you loved left you. It wasn't me, it was just fate or whatever. They left you or they died, so you tried not to love anybody or let them love you." He was completely dry eyed, but I felt real funny, happy but scared of something I couldn't name. He stood up straight and looked at me and I stood up and smiled and was about to say something silly to get him to smile, too. "Jake, you're the best friend I ever had in my life."

I wish now I'd said something, but I couldn't think of a thing, and maybe he didn't want me to say anything. I could have said, "I won't leave you, Kid," but he knew that, and I knew he couldn't leave me. I'd left Belle, and my wife Betty had left me, and there were plenty of leavings in both our lives, but now we lived in Texas and we were cowboys of a kind together. I just nodded and it was enough. We went back across the road and got into the car, J.T.'s car, and went back to the ranch, back home.

Betty was too broke up to go to the funeral, so I went down to the Big House when we got back. All the boys had to get back to work. Missy's death wouldn't stop the work. Betty was sitting in the big kitchen sipping on a glass of sherry. She loved to drink sherry. I just let myself in.

"Howsa goddamn funeral?" she asked. She was drunk. I knew she was hurting awful bad. Missy had been almost like a sister or a daughter to her and Betty had worked for them for many years. "Jesus, I hate funerals." I knew what she was saying but the words were all wrong.

"It was real nice," I said. "You been drinking all afternoon?"

"Yeah, you want one?" she said, her eyes looking at me but not quite able to land anywhere. She picked up the nearly empty bottle from the stove. "This stuff tastes like shit." It's funny, but I felt strong there, stronger than I had in years maybe. I felt like everything was going right in my life and that somehow Missy dying was part of it. That sounds terrible but it was true.

"No thanks," I said. I took the rest of the bottle and poured it down the drain.

"Why'n the hell you do that?" she asked.

"Because I love you," I said.

She had got sober long before the sun started to soften in the west, and we sat on the back steps and watched the light go out while she cried and hiccupped and went to sleep in my arms.

BECAUSE OUR BEARDS WERE still thin, they put fake beards on me and Lucas when we showed up for our mountain man outfits. First they put glue all over your face and then stuck this piece of white fur there. I thought it was awful silly, but Lucas was all happy and full of pep.

"Hey, diddle-de dee!" he yelled. "An actor's life for me!"

"I thought you said they were all gypsies," I said. touching my new beard. We already had on our costumes, hot, heavy fake buckskin with fringe and big floppy hats. The best thing, though, was the Hawken rifles we'd get to hold. They sure looked real.

"When I wish your opinions, I shall solicit them," said Lucas, looking at his beard in a mirror in the trailer where the wardrobe guy was hopping around saying, "Yes, yes," for some reason.

"Please report to the set," the man said. "They're shooting all day. They told me to tell you that. Are you somebody?" He was staring at me.

"Have you ever heard of Edmund Purdom?" asked Lucas, clapping his arm on my shoulder. The man hadn't, and I hadn't, so we left confused, which was the general state of things around Lucas Kraft.

The day was hot as hell and with the cloth that looked like buckskin, I was worried I'd pass out, but Lucas was having more fun playacting than anything we'd done since we escaped from Fieldstone.

We found our way to the set. The director was a man named Arkovitch or something and spoke with a heavy accent. We were supposed to be mountain men having a big get-together down here, even though there weren't any mountains. I wanted to ask about that, but I thought maybe they'd paint some in later or something. Besides, I didn't really give a damn.

What I gave a damn about was Loretta Michelle. Lately it had become like an obsession with me, and I couldn't shake it, like having a bad cold or something. Instead of quitting looking for her like I should, I was spending all my money calling all over Texas to social agencies, leaving messages, hoping something would turn up. I remember I was standing there wondering if she could be in New Mexico when the assistant director Lucas knew herded us all up, about thirty of us mountain men, and explained what we were supposed to be doing.

"Okay, you've gotten together to let off steam after a big season of trapping," he said. "You are firing your guns and drinking and yelling and carousing." He went on to explain it in detail, putting each one of us in a certain place and telling us where to go.

When he got to me, I said, "This sounds like a scene from that TV serial I saw, *Centennial*. Is that where you all got the idea?"

"Yeah, and the next scene is from *Psycho*," he said, kind of mean like. Lucas was standing near me and he started stabbing the air and going "Eeeek, eeeek, eeeek," sort of like singing.

"What you doing there, Kid?" I asked.

"Polishing my technique, you rookie," he said.

Finally we were ready for the cameras to start making pictures of us. The scene was supposed to go on for about three minutes, the director said, at which time a group of Indians would come riding into camp, leading the captive woman and her daughter, when everything would stop. All we had to do then was hold our positions while a couple of real actors spoke some lines.

Me and Lucas both had jugs filled with water that was supposed to be whiskey, but what I really wanted to do was fire my gun. They were all ready. All we had to do was cock them and shoot. I was standing there thinking about what it would have been like to live in those days when the director yelled something and everybody started screaming and falling around, so I did, too.

Lucas was next to me, drinking water and slobbering it all over his beard, drinking water and then spitting it out like a whale blowing, drinking water and growling and yelling. He set his jug down and pointed his gun at the sky, cocked it and shot it. White smoke drifted up.

"Wheee! Do it, Kid!" I yelled, but everybody was yelling loud as they could, and I'm not sure he heard me. I decided it was time to shoot off my gun, so I set my jug between my feet and pointed it straight at the sun and said, "Take this, you son of a bitch," and fired it. I immediately decided I wanted to buy me a gun, a real gun. It made me feel something in my blood.

We were laughing and whooping and hollering so much I didn't hardly notice the Indians come up. In fact, I don't think I wanted them to come up, and I almost believed I was a real mountain man. But Lucas noticed and the first thing he did was drop his jug on my foot.

"Be careful, you stupid jerk," I said, but he looked like he was staring at the face of God on Mt. Sinai. I looked up and knew why. She looked older than I remembered, but a lot younger than she must have been. She was sitting sidesaddle on a pinto pony, being led by a tall Indian wearing only a little floppy bathing suit. Behind her on another pony was a young girl, maybe ten or so, with long blonde pigtails.

I had taken to thinking we were all really drunk and rowdy, so it came as a surprise to me when we all got quiet just like we'd been told.

I wasn't close enough to hear what the actors were saying to the Indian, but I could hear Lucas Kraft.

"Lord have mercy," he said. "Those savages will harm her and the girl." He took two steps toward them, but I grabbed his arm and wouldn't let go and he was mad as hell at me, but then he calmed down and the director yelled something else and everybody started relaxing. "Come on." He started moving through the other mountain men, who were sitting down and waiting, since we'd been told we'd probably have to do it all two or three times. I was sweating through my clothes, and sweating felt good, but I felt awful stupid with all that stuff on and I was glad none of my old friends from when I'd worked steel could see me.

"Don't bother her," I said.

"I'm not, you stupid cracker," he said. "I just want to get closer to her." I stayed by his side and we came over to where she was sitting and talking to the director in a couple of cloth folding chairs. Up close, she looked maybe a few years older, but still really good. We stood off to one side and looked at her and one time Lucas cleared his throat but he didn't say anything, and we then went back to our places and did the whole thing three more times before we quit for the day. We had to leave our Hawken rifles and outfits there in the wardrobe trailer, and by then Lucas was all moody and mad again.

"I told you this was a bad idea," I said as I drove us back toward the ranch in a Jeep. "Kid, you shouldn't orta go looking for how things used to be. You know what you'll be bound to find. It never changes much.

"Spare me your folk wisdom," he said. He sat gloomy for a spell and then started to laugh real low in his throat. I started to ask, but I wasn't sure I wanted to know, but after that, he was planning something in his head and he was back in a good mood again.

The next day, we had to do a big scene with Sally Crandall begging the Indians to spare their lives, her and the young girl. The Indian village was as pretty a thing as you'll ever see, with teepees spread out a long ways and small campfires, Indian children playing and dogs loping along. A lot of the Indians, we heard, were Navajos and Apaches and such they'd brought in, as well as some that lived down on the Hubbard Creek Reservation.

Turns out that the Indians had brought Sally and the girl to the mountain men's campout hoping to trade them for liquor, but they couldn't get enough, so they left them guarded by fighting chiefs while they got drunk from trading pelts. We had to do a little scene in our outfits, and then we were through and Sally had her scene. Lucas and I hung around, holding our Hawken rifles and watching them set up.

We'd already been in a little trouble that morning because Lucas had been whistling some tune from a musical called *South Pacific* during our scene and they had to do it over and the director fussed at him, at least I think he did. I could barely understand his English. Sally was pacing back and forth, saying her lines over and over, and by that time Lucas and I were near as we dared.

"She doesn't know it's me," Lucas said.

"I don't hardly know it's you," I said. When he didn't smart off, I knew he was thinking about something that was probably a bad idea, but I just decided to stay with him. It was the only thing you could do with Lucas sometimes.

The director yelled action. Sally was standing there in her long dress, looking hot and wore out and pretty, the girl huddled behind her. The Indian chief was supposed to have got drunk and was threatening her with a knife. He really did seem drunk, and that was the first time I guess I realized what acting meant.

"You can do what you wish with me, but promise me you will not harm the girl," Sally said.

"Pretty girl," the Indian grunted, pointing his knife blade at Sally's neck.

"That bastard," whispered Lucas.

"I am not afraid," Sally said dramatic-like. "God gave me courage to face this trial and you cannot make me afraid." The Indian grabbed Sally by the hair and pulled her to him. Lucas was hopping up and down and I was going to tell him something when he took off running toward them, fast as his short legs would scurry, holding his rifle over his head. I went with him.

"God?" grunted the Indian, and then he turned when he saw us coming.

"Hold it right there, Hiawatha," said Lucas, leveling his rifle at the chief. The Indian backed up two steps and looked at the director, puzzled. Sally Crandall stared at us without seeming to know who Lucas was or what was going on. "Come on, ma'am, young lady. They may flay this flesh but they shall never harm you in my care."

And before anybody could say a word, the four of us were running off down a gulley, followed at some distance by the director and the Indian and a camera man.

"Did they change the freaking script?" asked the young girl. She was about twelve, and blonde, just like what Loretta Michelle should look like.

"Who the hell are you?" asked Sally. "There's not a rescue scene here, is there?" She kept looking at Lucas oddly. We finally stopped at the edge of a small woods, Sally and the girl real upset by then. Lucas turned away from her and pulled off his beard and then whirled around.

"Hi, babe," he said.

"You know this asshole?" the girl asked. Sally Crandall stared at him for a moment, eyes narrowing, then growing big.

"My sweet Jesus," she said. "Lucas?" She backed up from him.

"You were wonderful, Sally," Lucas said.

"It is you," she said. She looked up for the director and a couple of strong-looking men who were getting close to us. She ran toward them and Lucas stood there grinning without his beard.

"It's all right, everyone," said Lucas. "She is my wife."

"Arrest him!" said Sally Crandall. "Arrest both of them." And that's how, on a mild spring afternoon, Lucas

Kraft and Jake Baker came to find themselves in the Harkin County Jail.

Sally had gone stomping off long before the sheriff had gotten there on the set, while we were being cornered by these two strong men with *Shadow of the Wind* T-shirts. The shirts had pictures of Sally and, in the background, Indians and a handsome cavalryman.

They charged us with trespassing, and I wasn't too happy about it, and I kept thinking I should have known better, that if I was such a good friend to Lucas, I'd have kept him out of trouble, not followed him into it.

If I was worried about being in jail, Lucas loved it better than anything. They took us to Harkin and put us in the jail, which was an old-fashioned thing, me in one cell and Lucas right next door. On the other side of me was a drunk who was yelling about his wife being a bitch and on the other side of Lucas was a colored dwarf who was banging his head on the bars and singing "I'm Just a Love Machine." I felt trapped. Lucas felt like a million bucks.

"Have you ever felt more alive in your ancient life?" Lucas asked walking up and down in the cell and inhaling like he was on a picnic in the mountains.

"Kid, you got us thrown in jail," I said.

"Loree's a bitch," the drunk next to me said suddenly as loud as he could. He slid down to the floor and babbled in a language I'd never heard.

"I know," said Lucas. "Ain't it grand?" The colored dwarf asked Lucas for something real soft and Lucas leaned down to hear him, whereupon the dwarf reached up through the bars and grabbed Lucas about the neck and began to choke him.

"Aaaggh," Lucas said, dropping to his knees. He was trying to break away, but the dwarf had strong fingers,

216

looked like to me, so I yelled for the deputy. He came back, yelled at the dwarf, who let go, and Lucas fell down into the middle of the cell, laughing like he was crazy.

"Kid, this is going to reflect bad on you," I said. Lucas coughed a couple of times while the deputy went back out, and the dwarf went back to singing about he was a love machine, and the drunk next to me said something real bad about Loree. I hoped it wasn't true, not because I cared for some woman I'd never met, but because I've always had a soft spot for German shepherds.

"No man alive ever brought in Kid Kraft until today, and when I get out, they'll never get me again," Lucas said.

"Who you?" asked the colored dwarf.

"What do you care, you vermin?" asked Lucas. "Why should I speak to someone who just tried to assault me?"

"Aw shit, it weren't nothing, man, just something to do," the little guy said.

"He's Kid Kraft," I said. "You never heard of him? You never heard of the Kraft Gang? You one stupid midget."

"I'm a goddamn dwarf," he said. He reached out into Lucas's cell and the Kid came scurrying over toward me.

"That son of Hades is trying again to lay hands upon my person," said Lucas.

"Say what?" said the dwarf.

"He's trying to keep from killing you," I said, serious as I could. "He's got hisself fourteen notches on his gun."

"Say what?" said the dwarf. "Who he killed?"

"Just today he killed three Indians who was holding a woman and her little girl hostage," I said. "It was awful. They come at him with their bows all drawn back, ready to fill him up like a pincushion." The drunk had stopped yelling at Loree and was hanging on the bars listening to me. "But the Kid wasn't near his Hawken rifle, so he rolled over to it down a gulley, arrows flying all around, and he got his rifle and picked off the first one and then used his pistol to get the other two before they could notch up another arrow."

"I'll be durned," said the drunk.

"Tell them about the thirty braves who chased me," said Lucas, nodding and hopping up and down, grinning like a bear.

"Well, soon as Kid Kraft got them Indians spent," I said, "thirty braves come up over the horizon on their ponies, war whooping to beat the band, and Lucas told me to follow him, and we went running into this arroyo, him, me, the lady and the little girl."

"Who the hell are you?" asked the dwarf.

"I'm his sidekick," I said.

"Did he get kilt?" slobbered the drunk, eyes red and watery.

"Piss off, honkey," said the dwarf to the drunk, but the drunk couldn't hear him.

"Anyway, we spun down there, and Kid Kraft said all us had to jump off this big cliff to get away, and we did, landing right in the river, and we got away and saved the lives of the woman and the little girl."

The drunk started clapping and the dwarf was laughing and pointing at Lucas, who didn't take it too kindly.

"Sir, do you aver that our tale is fable?" said Lucas.

"It's just bullshit," he said, eyes hard as lead. "You two old assholes ain't never done nothing like that in your whole life." That was all Lucas could take and he went over and spit on the dwarf, who went into a rage and started screaming and howling and rolling around on the floor.

"I believe it," said the drunk. "Kid Kraft." He said the

words like they were magic, like he was meeting somebody important.

Lucas was real down when Chuck Owens showed up an
hour later, bailed us out and took us back to the ranch.
Chuck had sent somebody up to get our Jeep and he
didn't seem too upset about it all.

I admired Chuck Owens real smart. He looked like a
movie star more than anybody over where they were
making the movie. I just felt bad every time I saw him,
thinking as I did about Missy. When we got home, Lucas
poured himself a drink, locked the door to his little room
on the end of the Long House and started typing. I
helped Wool with supper and once in a while I'd go down
and stand outside Lucas's door and listen and hear him
laughing and cussing and once it sounded like he was
crying.

Wool and I finished washing the dishes. He seemed to
think more of me now that I was a hardened criminal,
and after we finished, I had to tell all the boys in the den
just what had happened to us that day. They thought it
was awful funny, especially J.T., who kept sitting up
straight in his chair, holding his sides and laughing without a word.

I'd finished my story and they were drifting around,
some reading magazines, watching the TV, when Wool
came over and dropped a small piece of paper in my lap.

"What's this?" I asked.

"Some stupid asshole called here for you today," he
said. I looked at the piece of paper and on it was the
name Shelley Hood.

"What did she want?" I asked, trying to recollect who
she might be.

"Something about that girl," he said. He was holding
his pipe between his teeth and it was hard to understand

219

him. "Said she'd talked to you from over Wichita Falls about where she might be. Said call her tonight. That's the number."

"Well, I'll be," I said. There was a phone in the kitchen, and since nobody was there now, I decided to go in. If you called long distance, you had to pay for it when the bills came in, but if it was about Betty's girl, I'd pay for it. I sat down on this tall stool and dialed the number and it rang four times before Shelley Hood answered. I told her who I was.

"Yes, Mr. Baker," she said. "We had not been able to track down the girl through our agency, but I happened to see a name in the *Dallas Morning News*."

"Loretta Michelle Buckley?" I asked.

"Sure was," she said. I wanted to see Betty, but she'd already gone home. She'd given me her in-town address and told me to come by sometimes, but I'd not done it yet.

"Great," I said.

She said, "I'm not sure how great it was, Mr. Baker. This person was in the police news."

"I've been in that myself," I said. I could have bit my tongue off for saying it, but I was excited and carried away and Miss Hood ignored that. "What was it for?"

"Prostitution," she said. I felt sick and sad and weak.

"Oh no," I whispered.

"It could be somebody different," she said.

"Did it say how old she was?" I asked.

"Sixteen."

"Uh huh."

"Do you want her address?" I got a piece of note paper and a pencil and wrote it down.

"I'm mighty obliged to you," I said.

220

"I'm sorry it had to be like this," she said. "Maybe it's all a mistake."

"I expect it was," I said.

I told her goodbye and folded up the paper and put it in my billfold. I felt real bad for Betty and wanted to see her, so I went down outside Lucas's study and he was still typing. I told Wool where I was going and he nodded.

"Anything wrong?" he asked.

"No," I said, "but thanks for asking."

"Shit," he said, looking down.

The night was full of stars and driving the Jeep was fun. I could see the land stretching out on both sides along the dirt road that leads down to Owensville, and I remembered that day when me and Lucas came into Harkin County without much more than the shirts on our backs. When they'd buried Missy Owens, the preacher had told how when we died we took nothing from this world with us. Well, everybody knows you don't take nothing with you. What gets folks all worried is thinking of dying and not having had nothing to begin with. And I don't mean a big car or a boat, though some folks would mean those things. I mean love, children, the respect of people you care for, those kinds of things. I think that's what I was looking for and maybe Lucas was, too. I knew I wouldn't find it back in Georgia. Out here, a man lived or died by his wits and hands back in the olden days, and I liked thinking on that. He had to stay one step ahead of whatever was chasing him, and I'd been doing that since Belle had put me into Fieldstone.

I knew Betty's address by heart. It was 301 Foster Street, which was a quiet area on the other side of Harkin. I pulled up out front and turned off the Jeep. It was so different here than in the Long House, living with all those cowboys. This was a neighborhood where families lived, where they were also, I reckon, trying to stay one step ahead.

Betty's house was small and tidy. From the glow of a streetlight, I could see neat rows of flowers and shrubs around the house, deep grass and a walkway going up to the small front porch. I felt something turn over in my heart standing there. It was loneliness, I guess, but more than that, remembrances of my other Betty and how it felt to be married, to be of and for one another in everything. Unless it's some kind of dying agony, there's nothing worse in this world than being alone.

I walked up to the front door and rang the bell. There was no answer so I rang it again.

"Just a goddamn minute!" a voice yelled. It was a profanity and said meanly, but it was like all the music I'd ever heard to me. She opened the front door and it stopped on the end of a night latch, and when she saw it was me she closed the door, undid the latch and let me in.

"Howdy," I said.

"You were on the news," she said, grinning. "I'm glad you came to see me. Come on in the den. You want a cold beer?" I sure did, and nothing ever tasted better than that beer. Seems like me and Lucas had been on the local news, and then it had made it to the news in Dallas, and finally she'd heard it on that all-news cable TV channel.

"Well, I'll swanny," I said. It made me feel good to be such a famous criminal, but I was thinking mostly on Loretta Michelle and I thought for a spell I was going to tell Betty about her, but then I realized I couldn't. We drank our beers and she cuddled up next to me on the couch. She was wearing this old, loose brown house dress and I felt tired and happy.

"Spend the night with me," she said. "I got to be there

at 6, so we could go back together. I got me some Johnny Mathis records."

"Who's that?" I asked.

"You never heard of Johnny Mathis?" She got up and put one on and I liked it, slow and sweet, and she took my hand and cut the lights out. She had a small closed-in back yard, and from the moon it looked just as neat as the front, and I stared at it as we danced. She snuggled up tight to me, and I was happy and sad and sure that life was something you never quite found no matter how long you looked for it.

I'd like to know where to send a check to Johnny Mathis, because he put us both in the mood, and I decided I would spend the night. Her bedroom was cool, and a new breeze lifted the curtain as we undressed and then lay face to face.

"You must have made one hell of a mountain man," she said. I thought for a spell of telling her about her daughter, but in the end I didn't, and we just loved one another with the breeze running over us until we fell asleep tangled up and a whole lot in love.

THE NEXT DAY, JUST AFTER breakfast, Chuck came up to the Long House and told us they'd dropped all charges. It made me feel right good, but Lucas was all blue about it and set about making plans again for meeting up with Sally Crandall.

"You're going to get us throwed in prison for the rest of our days, Kid," I said.

"How, you rube?" he asked. We were sitting outside in Scout's chair and another alongside it. "She dropped the charges. Don't you understand what that means? Deep down, in her heart of hearts, she wants to see me again."

"Why don't you just call up and ask if you can come by and apologize?" I suggested.

"Are you going senile on me, Jake?" he said, sitting up and throwing his arms up over his head. "One doesn't just apologize to her imperial worship. She would make you grovel even more. Hell, before we left, we would be out there polishing her car and offering to run to town and buy groceries for her. No, no, my boy. These things have to be done with a proper eye for the great meshing of the world's gears."

"Okay," I said. "But I don't want to go back to prison, Kid."

"I don't blame you," he said. "One night's hard time is enough to melt the spine of any real man."

"Piss off," I said, a little mean with him. He gulped and stared at me and nodded. When I let him have it back, he always buckled. I wasn't mad at him, but I just wanted him to calm himself down. But trying to get Kid Kraft to calm himself was as likely as asking the creek down the hill to run the other way.

"Sorry," he said. "Anyway, using your superior detective skills and a secreted spyglass, we will watch her trailer until she alone inhabits it. Then you and I will go, hat in hand, for the mock apology, at which time I will conquer her, you will leave and at the assigned hour retrieve me from my dalliance with bliss."

"Huh?"

"Never mind, Jake, my boy, never mind. Just stay with me." He reached inside his shirt and pulled out a small pair of binoculars. I had no idea where he got them. I know it sounds awful odd, but I just nodded and knew I'd go along with him again. Maybe it was the adventure as much as it was trying to keep Lucas out of trouble. I don't rightly know.

"Speaking of me being a detective, I found out something about Loretta Michelle," I said, and I told him and he groaned and glared at me.

"That is not our girl," he said. "You, of course, are wrong, Jake. Don't worry. Our girl is lovely and tall and strong and when she smiles the sun rises in Texas."

"I reckon you're right," I said, looking down over the creek.

"I'm always right," said Lucas Kraft.

We got in the Jeep and drove up as close to the movie site as we could without being seen. I figured they'd throw us out if they spotted us. We crept like Indians around a small woods and stopped under a big spreading cottonwood from where we could see the trailers where people stayed during the day.

We spent most of the day there, not seeing anybody come or go, except a couple of old men and somebody who looked like a hippie, and by late in the day Lucas was hopping mad and we were both tired, hungry and thirsty.

"Kid, we've got to get out of here," I said. "She's not here."

"The wench has deceived me," he said.

We drove back to the ranch, but after supper he wanted me to drive him down to the Holiday Inn in Abilene, which was where the stars were staying at night.

"I'm too tired," I said. "I want to sleep."

"Did Wellington sleep at the Battle of Waterloo?" boomed Lucas, standing in the kitchen with me and Wool. "Did Holmes sleep when Moriarty was at large? Did Beowulf sleep when Grendel was lowering about the countryside?"

"What in the fuck is that honkey talking about?" asked Wool.

"He's just running on about getting his way," I said.

"Your mouth is as foul as your heart," Lucas said to Wool, who busted out laughing. "I need to get to Abilene to see my former wife, and Mr. Baker here is refusing to be my chauffeur."

"Aw shit," said Wool. "I'll drive you. I want to go to

Abilene and have a drink tonight anyway. Jake, you can sleep on the way down."

And that's just about what happened. I sat in the middle and fell into a dead sleep, leaning on Lucas, while Wool drove and Lucas yelled at him about driving bad and Wool laughed and cussed at Lucas. We were a regular Three Stooges. I woke up five miles this side of Abilene feeling much better, and I realized then that Lucas was dead asleep and leaning on me. It was lucky Wool was wide awake and sucking on his corncob pipe.

"You know where the Holiday Inn is?" I asked. He laughed and didn't say anything, which I took to mean yes. Between Lucas and Wool I'd learned to do a lot of interpreting. I elbowed Lucas just as we pulled up into the parking lot. He snorted and said something about Christmas, so I shook him real good and he woke up.

"Aha, we have arrived," he said, rubbing the sleep out of his face. "Now we must take up surveillance."

"What that mean?" asked Wool, looking at me.

"What that mean?" I asked Lucas.

"Jake, quit emulating the speech patterns of this man," said Lucas. "You've begun to aspirate your contractions. No pretty sight." I looked at Wool and he shrugged and so did I.

"I'm going into the lounge and get me a couple or six drinks," said Wool. "You are driving me home." He poked me in the chest. "And if I ain't working good in the morning, you start breakfast without me."

Me and Lucas slowly walked around the parking lot, trying not to look suspicious. We were standing in front of a balcony whispering about Sally when a door opened above us and, as God is my witness, Sally Crandall came out and stood and looked up at the stars. Lucas and I saw her and he hustled me under the balcony where she couldn't see us.

"Victory is within our grasp," he whispered. We went down along in front of the rooms and then slowly up the stairs. I had a bad feeling about it.

We came up the stairs and she was standing there, leaning on the balcony, wearing a long dressing gown, hair tied back. A breeze came up and the smell of soap and perfume came down toward us. It was a wonderful smell.

"Let me handle this," Lucas whispered.

To my surprise I whispered, "No, you let me handle this." He stopped and stared at me only for a second and then nodded. I didn't know what I'd say, and I wasn't much of a speaker, but from experience I knew it was bound to be better than what he would say. We came right up to her and could see she was holding a drink in her hand. The smell of soap was stronger and in the dim light from the parking lot, we could tell she had removed her makeup and looked a lot older, but somehow prettier.

"Ma'am?" I said, clearing my throat. She turned slowly and looked at us.

"I was wondering when you would come," she said, not seeming surprised or mad. "I'm sorry about jail."

"Hi, baby," said Lucas, peeking out from behind me.

"I'm not your baby," she said, but her voice was tired and still not mad.

"I'm Jake Baker," I said. "I'm Lucas's best friend. We came out here together from Georgia. This is real exciting for me. I never met a movie star before." She took my hand and shook it. "I've got an awful lot of pleasure from what you've done." It must have been the right thing to say because she looked truly moved and invited us into her room for a drink.

We sat on one bed and she sat on another and inside in the lamplight, her age was showing, but I was an old man, and she looked pretty as anything to me. She poured us a whiskey into plastic cups and we sat there sipping.

"Hugh said you were living with a race car driver," Lucas said, after the quietness got sort of heavy.

"I've kicked him out," she said. "You married, Lucas?"

"No, I'm not," he said. "But I'm writing, baby. It's the best thing I've ever done."

"Are you telling me the truth?" she asked. I thought she was going to cry. "I thought you said you'd never write again. What happened?"

"I took a trip and lost some baggage along the way," he said. I never in a million years would have thought things were going to happen like this. They were talking just like they were still married, never had been apart, and Lucas wasn't acting the fool. I think I knew then he still loved her.

"Well, this movie . . ." she said, but she stopped and looked into her drink.

"I miss having my Hawken rifle," I said to nobody in particular. "I would have made a good mountain man, even if this ain't where they had mountain men."

"I'm sure you would have," Sally Crandall said. "And you." She looked at Lucas and laughed and shook her head. "You looked so stupid in that outfit that after they took you off I just sat down and started laughing. It reminded me of that costume party we went to over at Jack Nicholson's house."

"What did you go as?" I asked. Lucas grinned and shrugged.

"He went as a moose, with big antlers . . ."

". . . and she went as a hunter, with a red-checkered jacket and a thirty-thirty," said Lucas. "It was unloaded, wasn't it, baby?" She laughed but didn't say anything.

"I've got me this colored friend who's down in the bar," I said. "I think I'll go down there and see if he's got beat up yet." I stood up and nobody asked me to stay.

"I'll catch you in a while," said Lucas. When I walked out the door, I could hear her telling him about how awful the movie was and that her career was over. I didn't want to hear anymore, so I eased the door shut and walked out on the balcony, feeling the burn of the bourbon in my belly. The sky was full of stars and down in the parking lot, some woman was screaming at her husband and trying to pry a bottle from his hand. I remembered seeing that happen back in Jersey years ago and I expect it'll be happening long after me and Lucas are under the green grass in our long sleep.

They called it the Golden Star Lounge, and a band was in there playing rock and roll real loud. The room was so smoky you could barely see across it. I went in and stood, looking around. A cocktail waitress wearing a cowboy vest, boots and a little frilly dress that covered up nothing but what I wanted to see came up.

"Howdy," she said. "Looking for somebody?"

"A colored feller with gray hair and a red shirt," I said. Her face fell a little bit.

"Oh, him," she said. Lord, I thought, what has he done? "Over there." She pointed back in a corner and I saw him through the smoke, pounding a glass on the table in rhythm to the music. I made my way through the crowd. Wool was sitting there, eyes looking bright and almost crossed.

"Jakie baby!" he yelled when he saw me. Then he stood up and hugged me, and I pushed him down. A man wearing a big diamond pinkie ring was sitting at the next table with a large woman whose face seemed to have been made up of plaster and makeup. The man looked at me real suspicious.

"Would you quit that," I said to Wool. He didn't mind and just grinned and started banging his glass again.

"Lucas get the broad?" he asked.

"They missed one another," I said.

"Awww, ain't that sweet," he said. "Honkey love's such a pretty sight."

"You shut up or I'll bust your lip," I said, and I meant it. I'd about had it with him. He looked mean at me but let it pass. The music was so loud my head hurt, but all of a sudden it stopped and the band went on break. The waitress brought me a drink and another one for Wool, who looked like he'd calmed down.

"You got a light?" the Plaster Woman asked, leaning right up in my face. Pinkie Ring had gone somewhere. "I don't smoke," I said. She almost snarled at me and then got up and wobbled to the next table. "I think you're right about honkeys." Wool laughed.

"Jake, I want to ask you something," he said, seeming serious all of a sudden. "You scared of dying?"

"No," I said. That was the truth. Once, when I was in my thirties, I was scared to death about dying, and every time I had a cold I'd get ready for heaven or hell, but it never came. Any time death came for me, I'd be ready, though lately it would be a pity because I'd been so happy with Betty. But I felt awful about Loretta Michelle, too.

"I'm scared of it," said Wool, then he started to cry and stopped. "I don't want to die, Jake. Tell me I ain't gonna die."

"How come you thinking about dying?" I asked. "That don't sound like you, Wool."

"Look," he said, reaching across the table and grabbing my arm, "if I die before you, promise me one thing. Don't let them bury me in a suit. I want to be buried nekkid." He was drunk.

"How come?"

"It just come into my head," he said. "Promise me."

"I promise." He looked like the weight of this old world had been took off his shoulders.

"Awright!" he yelled. "Bring on the women!"

"Wool, a waitress didn't look happy when I told her I was looking for you," I said. "What did you do?"

"Aw, I just bit her on the tit when she leaned over," he said, like it was nothing. "She don't got no sense of fun a tall."

I didn't have another drink, because Wool was throwing them back so fast he was getting numb drunk. I didn't want to have to carry him back to the Jeep, and I probably couldn't have anyway, so I paid the bill and got him out in the parking lot where he was hooting and hollering and carrying on about how strong he was and did anybody want to try him out.

"Come on, Wool," I said. "You don't want to get us into a tussle."

"I might like a piece of you, you little pissant," he said. I was holding him up and heading toward the balcony up where Lucas and Sally Crandall were.

"You're a drunk nigger," I said, trying not to fall.

"You right about that," he said, then he hooted again and started saying how he could beat the shit out of any man in Texas. His knees had started to go weak on him, but just as he started to fall, there was a loud racket upstairs and we both stopped and the sound as much as me propped Wool up.

233

We looked at one another and listened again and there was the sound of glass breaking and yelling up there.

"I'm sho glad they love one another like you said," Wool said. "Elsewise they'd be done killed one another." He laughed and I took him to the Jeep and put him in the back seat, and he sat there for a second and then just fell over like a rock. There wasn't a sound from upstairs for a minute, but by the time I'd climbed the stairs, the yelling and breaking glass had started again.

I was wondering if I should open the door and go in when it opened and Lucas came tumbling out against the rail. A vodka bottle came right after him and whizzed over the rail and broke down in the parking lot below. Lucas looked up at me.

"Hi, Jake," he said. "How's it going?"

"You stupid son of a bitch!" yelled Sally Crandall. She was standing in the doorway breathing hard, looking pretty, I thought.

"What's going on?" I asked stupidy. "I thought you two missed one another."

"Missed . . ." she started, but she couldn't finish it and just said, "Oooooo," stomped her foot and slammed the door so hard I thought the window would fall out of the room. I helped Lucas to his feet.

"Just in the nick of time, my good fellow," said Lucas. "A few more moments and that woman would have split my skull. Let's depart this foul nest." We walked toward the stairs and I could tell he had been drinking a lot, just like Wool, but he managed to get down the stairs all right.

"What in the name of tarnation happened?" I asked as we climbed into the Jeep.

"That Negro has rigor mortis," said Lucas thoughtfully, looking down on Wool, who was snoring right peaceful.

"He's numb drunk," I said. "What happened to you and Sally?" I pulled out of the driveway and wandered around for a time until I found the right road north while Lucas seemed to be humming and thinking.

"We still disagree on a few things," he said. "She threw me out because I said she was the one who left me. She said I left her."

"Did you?"

"Sure." I turned and looked at him and he was nodding like a school kid who'd just answered a test question right.

"Then how come you said it was her fault?"

"I suppose it has something to do with maintaining what little dignity I have left," he said.

"Lying ain't no way to have dignity," I said. "If you had any left, maybe it's just flown away now." He sighed heavy and didn't say anything for a while.

"I have a character flaw," he said. "We are all afflicted, Jake, my boy, with character flaws. Yours is that you are too uncritical, too easygoing for your own good."

"What's yours?"

"Mine is that I am scared of life and now that it's nearly over, I want to embrace it but I don't know how," he said. "I keep thinking if I could just see my mother she could tell me something to make me understand. She was always good at that."

"You ain't gonna see your mama," I said soft as I could so as not to rile him. "You want answers, you got to start figuring them out for yourself. You got to tell Sally it was your fault and then she'll forgive you. You got to get forgiveness sometimes before you get love." Thinking back now, it sounded sort of high-blown and silly, but then, under the stars in that Jeep, it was real and true.

Lucas started to say something and stopped. We had passed through Stamford and were heading north on 277, out of Jones into Harkin County. Lucas started again, but all of a sudden, Wool rose up out of the back seat and reached up and grabbed Lucas around the neck and started wrestling with him and growling like a dog.

"Aaagh," Lucas said, trying to push Wool off. "The fiend is killing me!" Wool was laughing and slapping on Lucas, who was clawing back. I managed to get the Jeep off the side of the road, and I grabbed on to Wool.

"Let him go, Wool," I said, and I stood and grabbed at him.

"I'm the strongest man in Texas!" Wool yelled. Lucas was making funny noises. "I'm the strongest man in the United States!" Finally, seeing no other way, I straddled Lucas, pushed Wool back a little and slapped the everloving shit out of him. He sat back, rubbing his cheek. A car went past, slowed down and then turned left.

"Summon the law," Lucas squeaked. "This is attempted murder. He'll spend the rest of his days behind bars." I was fixing to dress down Wool when he went out like a light again, head down into the seat. Lucas looked at Wool.

"He's just drunk and thinking he's more than a cook," I said. "Leave him be." I pulled back on the road.

"Yeah," muttered Lucas.

We got home and Lucas and I unloaded Wool and walked him up to the Long House. It was only twelve or so, but I'd never been so tired in my life. In ten minutes, all three of us were in bed, and two minutes after that, I fell asleep.

We managed to get through breakfast the next morning, though Wool was cussing under his breath the whole time and looking mean at me. I hadn't drunk so much so

236

I felt all right. I tried to take it easy, but all I could think about was Betty's daughter. I'd stop and take a break and see her in my mind, smiling and pure, and then I'd think on a girl with her name being arrested for being a whore. The only thing was to find out if she was the same one.

Lucas had his own problems. He didn't come for breakfast and I found him in his underwear sitting in front of the typewriter, staring at it, not typing.

"Morning, Kid," I said. He looked up at me real slow.

"If I don't get her back, I'll die," he said, and then he wouldn't say anything else. It was then that I decided what I'd have to do in the next few days. First, I was going to Dallas to find that girl who'd been arrested. Then I was going to try and talk to Sally Crandall. They were probably both fool's missions, but if I didn't try, I knew I'd be hating myself for a long spell to come.

I walked down that morning to Chuck's house and Betty was out back sweeping off the walkway that led through some hedges down toward the creek. Since Missy had died, Chuck had more and more been wandering around, so she didn't have to cook. She looked for things to do because she was like that.

"Hi," she said and smiled when I got close enough. We kissed and I held her up to me. "What did you do last night? I heard they dropped all the charges against you and Lucas."

"I went to see Lucas get the shit beat out of him by Sally Crandall one more time," I said. "They can't seem to get along. We went down to her motel in Abilene. I thought things were going to go well."

"Did you meet her again?"

"Yeah, without her makeup and all," I said.

"Was she pretty?" Betty asked.

"With a lot of makeup and some fancy clothes, she'd be half as pretty as you." Well, she kissed me again and then I did something stupid. You never know when a dumb idea'll come upon you, so you ought to be ready because dumb ideas can really mess up your life. I wasn't ready for it. I just wanted to make Betty happy. "I got me a lead on Loretta Michelle."

Her face was up close to mine and she bit on her lower lip and nibbled it a spell and her eyes filled with tears.

"You telling me the truth?" Already I had that sick feeling, wondering why I'd said anything, what I'd do next.

"Yeah," I said, "but it could be nothing." I could straighten her out, bring her home maybe.

"Where?" I wasn't ready for that.

"I'm not sure. Look, I'll let you know if I can run her down, okay?"

"Can I go?"

"Not this time. I can't explain now."

"I trust you," she said. By this time, neither one of us could hold back what we were feeling, and Chuck being gone, we availed ourselves of the guest bedroom upstairs. It took me a lot longer than I thought, but Betty was patient with me. I'd forgot how it felt to make love in the morning. Seems like it has more to do with love than lust but I could be wrong.

Lucas slept most of the day and when he woke up, he was in a foul mood. During the day, I'd done something I'd never done but once before. I went into his study and read some of the book he was writing. This was the first sentence:

"Light rose over the Sierra Nevadas, and the first shadows of the two men were long and sharp as they sat up in their bedrolls." That sounded nice, so I sat there and read on. Lots of it was history, but mostly it was about these trappers who had been living in the mountains for years, having come from back East, looking for something more than how they lived. I felt a tingle all up and down my arms, but I wasn't sure why.

Whizzer Pippin's leg was healing and that evening he, Tree and I played rummy, which I won. Lucas sat in a heavy chair and watched the movie of *From Here to Eternity*, all the while making nasty comments about the man, whose name escapes me, who wrote the book.

While I lay in bed that night, I made up my mind to go to Dallas the next morning. There wasn't a thing to be gained by waiting.

WE STOPPED FOR BREAKFAST, Lucas and me, in a little town called Throckmorton on 380, which I was driving over to Jacksboro. From there, we'd swing down 199 to Fort Worth and then over to Dallas. Lucas was mad because the restaurant, called The Wagon Wheel, had run out of eggs.

"How in the name of all that's sacred can you have run out of eggs?" Lucas asked.

"Because the manager's a dumbass," said the waitress. She was tall and skinny and her teeth made her upper lip stick out like a mule's. She looked tired.

"Well, that's a good reason," I said. She took our orders and went away.

"That woman is straight out of a Dorothea Lange photograph," Lucas mused.

"Huh?"

"Never mind, my boy," he said. "What shall we do when we find our darling girl there in the evil city where our president was slain?"

"I be dog," I said. "I'd plumb forgot we went to see where he got shot. That seems like so long ago."

"Everything was long ago," Lucas said, just like that was a secret that I should keep. I nodded.

"Now, I'm not saying that it's the same girl," I said. "I hope to God it ain't. That would kill Betty to find out the girl's gone bad. There ain't hardly a thing worse than finding out somebody you love's gone wrong." Lucas was looking out the window humming something I didn't catch. He didn't seem to be hearing me. It was already a fine day. Wool had been real irritated when I told him Lucas and I wanted to eat on the road because we wanted something different, but lately Wool had been irritated about everything.

"Oh, there are worse things," Lucas said. "The world is filled with unspeakable horrors, my friend."

"It ain't that bad, Kid," I said.

"Well, Dr. Baker, I think I may be going soft in the head, because I have half a mind to believe that myself," he smiled. "Lately it has occurred to me that your nitwit optimism may in fact be the proper course of conduct. Perhaps man is not redeemable, but I am thinking now that redemption is not so important as I always thought."

The waitress brought us the wrong orders and Lucas shrugged and ate. It was good anyway. We didn't say much, but by the time, using a map, we found Blaine Street in Dallas, it was afternoon and both of us were hot and tired. The street was in a neighborhood of tenant houses and run-down apartments, and dirty kids were playing in the streets. Some of the street numbers were missing, but hers wasn't. It was a messy place, with a car on blocks out front and a dirt yard. There must have been ten or twenty beer cans in the yard, trailing up to the front door.

We got out and walked toward the house. I felt my mouth go dry, felt dumb for some reason. I'd never felt like this going to see Sally Crandall. That was one thing, this was something else.

I knocked on the door a couple of times and we waited.

"This place carries disease," said Lucas, holding his hairy hand over his face. I knocked again and the door opened a crack and a young man who hadn't shaved in a few days looked out, squinting against the sun. Inside it was dark and an air conditioner was going.

"Yeah?" he asked.

"We are looking for Loretta Michelle Buckley," I said.

"You cops?" he asked. He stepped back and lit a cigarette. He was wearing only blue jean cutoffs and looked real sleazy.

"No, indeed," said Lucas. He folded his hand and leaned forward on the balls of his feet. "We are emissaries from the girl's family, come to ascertain her status."

"Is he talking English?" the man asked me.

"No, he ain't, " I said. "Sometimes he goes back into his native language. Is she . . ." I stopped. The door opened back and a girl was standing there behind him, or at least what was left of a girl. She was wearing a loose halter top that barely hid her sagging breasts and running shorts. Her hair was blonde but oily and stringy and her skin looked like a fish looks after it's been on the bank a spell. She had a bandage on the inside of her left arm.

"What you want?" she asked. She got a cigarette from the man, who shrugged and went back inside the cool house somewhere.

"I'm a friend of Loretta Michelle's," I said. "Her mama wants to know . . ."

"My mama?" she said. She pushed the hair out of her face but it fell right back. She blew smoke out toward me. "I ain't got no mama." She turned and walked back inside and I followed her into this filthy little room where she sat down on a mattress. A TV set was on to some game show and the place was ankle deep in trash. I looked for somewhere to sit, but it seemed better to stand.

"You're Loretta Michelle?" I asked. "Somebody saw your name in the paper."

"Well, whoopee, some asshole can read," she said. "Sit down . . . what's your name, old man?"

"Jake, Jake Baker." I sat down where I stood, having to kick some candy bar wrappers out of the way. The room smelled bad.

"So what's this shit about my mama?" she asked. The boy brought them each a Pepsi and they opened them and drank like they hadn't been near water in weeks.

"Your papa was Buddy Buckley," I said. She stopped drinking and stared at me. "But he got killed when you lived up in Jacksboro. You moved in then with your aunt down near Zephyr. She's a hard woman."

"She's a bitch," she said. I felt a chill go up my back. Until then, I didn't really think it was her, but it was her, she'd said so now, and I felt sick. Lucas didn't sit down.

"Then it's you," I said, my voice kind of choking. "I know your mother."

"Christ almighty," said Lucas.

"My mama ran off with another man," she said,

"Your daddy tell you that?" I asked. "He must of, because that ain't true. What really happened was your daddy just up and stole you. Your mama's been looking

244

for you for years, but she's not got any money and couldn't find you."

"Who are you, fucking Sherlock Holmes?" she asked. The boy started laughing, real high and hard, and she looked at him and laughed, but her laughing was almost like crying.

"I'm a friend of your mama's," I said. "She's a good woman who's worried about you. She wanted to be there for you, but your daddy up and stole you and it was like she didn't have a daughter."

"She still don't," Loretta Michelle said. She lit a cigarette.

"Are you truly a whore?" Lucas asked. It sounded real weird, the kind of thing you don't ask and when you do sounds like it wasn't really said after you hear it.

"You got twenty dollars?" she said, looking at Lucas like he was a chair. She smiled and her teeth were bad and I felt something in my body I didn't like, my bones all spongy and my head ringing. I stood up and started walking out. "Hey, what about it? Both of you for thirty."

"We just made a mistake," I said. "We was looking for somebody else."

"You looking for somebody who's dead," she said. Lucas followed me outside, where it had got all cloudy and rainy feeling. I felt sad and I just got in and drove for a spell until I found the right road back home. We stopped and ate but we didn't say much.

"What you think I ought to tell Betty?" I asked Lucas when we were almost home.

"They say the truth shall set you free," said Lucas. "I don't know who said that, but I've always thought it was fraudulent advice."

"I keep thinking I ought to of tried and saved her

somehow," I said. "I could have kidnapped her and brought her home to Betty or something."

"Those things only happen in dreams," said Lucas. "She is only lovely in your dreams, Jake. People are what they are by God and climate and heritage and genes and all the other mysteries no man can change. She is a wretch, but she doesn't have to be one to Betty." I looked at him. The sun was going down. It hadn't rained and it felt like it would, but it would be a soft rain, a good-feeling thing to come on you like a breath.

"I reckon you're right," I said.

"Have you ever known me to be wrong?" I looked at him and grinned. "Answer that, you vile rube, and I'll pummel you into jelly."

After supper, I got a Jeep and drove over to Betty's house. By then it was raining, coming straight down. I felt tired in my bones.

I knocked on the door and she looked through the little hole, saw it was me, threw the door back and said, "Did you find out anything about her?"

"Let me in," I said. We went into the den. She got me and her both a beer. The windows in the den were open and we could hear the rain and it sounded almost like the beach. It had been years since I'd seen a beach and all of a sudden I had a powerful strong urge to be at one. She put on a Johnny Mathis record, but I didn't feel much like love.

"Now," she said, sitting close to me on the sofa and pulling her feet up under herself. "Tell me what you know." I took a long pull on the drink and let the fire ease down into my belly. I thought about it. Lucas was right.

"Well," I said, "it was even better than we had thought. She's, far as I can figure, uh, well, it's like this, don't you see. After she left her aunt down there near Zephyr, she moved to Dallas. Now, when she was there, she went to a, uh, let's see, it was this church they said, a big church, and they took her in and gave her shelter and some good clothes. That woman down there'd give her bad clothes. So she lived there with some other kids who didn't have parents."

"But she's not there any more?"

"No," I said, "but it's good what happened to her. You'll be happy." She smiled.

"Tell me."

"She was living there, doing work for the church and such," I said. "I talked to this preacher there and he said, well, he said this, 'There never was a prettier girl I ever seen than Loretta Michelle Buckley.' That's what he said."

"No shit," said Betty.

"No . . . well, that's the truth," I said. "He said she had blonde hair, just like you thought and blue eyes and the thing she lived to do was help people, make them happy."

"Oh my Lord," said Betty. Her eyes were getting wet. Johnny Mathis was singing and the rain was still coming straight down.

"Well, seems like this couple from, uh, France were staying there in Dallas," I said. "The man was a count or something and he and his lady went to this church while they was in town and that's where they met your girl. This preacher feller said this count was one of the richest men in France. Well, they just fell in love with Loretta Michelle, just like everybody fell in love with her."

"I just knew it," Betty said. The tears were slowly wandering across her cheeks.

247

"And so they made adoption papers, got it all legal and they went back to France," I said. "This preacher said she looked just like a princess, which I reckon is what she'll be now. A princess from Texas. Now that's a thing." Betty buried her face in my shoulder and just sobbed and sobbed and I didn't know if I'd go to hell for lying or to heaven for making her feel so good.

We had another beer or two and we tried to make love but I couldn't do anything and it made me feel awful bad, but it wasn't the first time it had happened. I got dressed and ready to go back home. It was still early and I wanted to spend the night at the Long House.

"Tell me how they said she looked when she left for France," said Betty. We were standing in the living room holding each other.

"She was dressed in this blue dress that matched her eyes," I said. "And when she left that church, she cried but she was happier than any girl's ever been about anything in this world. If she'd known her real mama, they'd both be proud of one another."

"My baby a princess," Betty said. "Can you fancy that?"

All the way home, I felt bad because I never did like lying. Lucas could tell stories because he was sort of like a professional liar, being a writer, but I always figured, like Lucas said, the truth will make you free. But I didn't want to tell nobody the truth about Loretta Michelle. I didn't even want to tell myself, and by the time I pulled up in front of the Long House, I half wondered if maybe she had gone off to France to live with a count.

When I came in the front door, Wool and Chuck were standing there, along with a couple of men, Whizzer Pippin, Tree, Tom and a few others. They were staring at me funny.

"Something wrong?" I asked.

"Jake, it's Lucas," said Chuck.

"Shit," Wool said sadly.

"What's wrong?" I finally asked. He was dead. That was the only thing went through my mind, that Lucas Kraft, old Kid Kraft, had just dropped dead there in the Long House yelling about something or another, and I already had that sick hollow feeling inside.

"He's run away," said Chuck.

"Run away?" I squeaked. "What's the big deal about that? He's done run away five times since we been here."

"He left this," said Chuck. Whizzer Pippin, who was still a little gimpy from the broken leg, hobbled over and handed me a crumpled-up piece of paper covered with Lucas's fat handwriting. I sat down in one of the big chairs not far from the TV and read this:

Dear Jake, Old Pal,

    I guess the one thing I've always been good at is losing friends. I've run off nearly everybody I ever cared for, including you. I'm a fool. I'm heading back east. I guess I just wasn't meant to die in a range war after all. I hope you find it in your heart to forgive me, and tell Sally the same thing if you don't mind.

                            Lucas

    P.S. I'll probably die while revisiting where our beloved president was slain or perhaps in that flophouse where we stayed when first we attained this bountiful land.

I had read it out loud and Whizzer kept calling God's name like he wanted him in the room with us.

"He's probably up at the cottonwoods," I said, still staring at the piece of paper.

"I called the bus station in Harkin," said Chuck. "He damn sure did get a bus ticket to Dallas."

"I'm going after him," I said. "He can't make it without a manager."

"Where?" asked Chuck Owens. Well, he had me there, but I was getting this idea and I had to think quick.

"I'm going first thing in the morning, heading east back on I-20," I said. "I'll go honk around in Dallas. I'll catch up with him."

"You too old," said Wool. I stood up and walked over to where he was sitting and slapped the shit out of him. He jumped up and swung at me with his big old fist and caught me on the side of the head, and I saw all sorts of swirling stars in front of me and then we went down wrestling on the floor and they had to pull us apart. Before we were very far apart, Wool was chuckling deep down in his throat like he could and I started laughing too like a silly little girl, and then everybody was laughing just like it was funniest thing they ever saw.

"Am I too old?" I asked Wool.

"Naw, you too stupid," he said, and we all laughed again. I know it doesn't make any sense, but that's what we did.

"I need that old station wagon," I said to Chuck. He was still holding onto my arm but he let it go when it was obvious me and Wool weren't going to fight any more. It was a big old green thing they used to drive in the fields and it was always covered in dust and looked brownish. Everybody called it the Turd, which is a word I never liked for some reason.

"Sure," said Chuck.

"And I need Betty to go with me," I said. "Can you spare her for a spell?" Tree went "Woo woo woo" and everybody laughed and Chuck said sure. That night, I schemed so much that I kept dozing off and then waking up, looking at Lucas's bed, missing his familiar snoring, missing him more than I thought I would. There's no accounting for why you like somebody. I'd heard that before and I believed it, but with me and Lucas it was true all right.

I had to go look for him because I loved him.

I got up the next morning before dawn and helped Wool before I got some stuff together in my laundry bag and got ready to leave.

"Write if you get work," Wool said, and we shook hands.

"I'll be back," I said, but he'd turned around and turned up the radio playing Judas Priest (I was starting to get to know these groups) and he didn't hear me. The station wagon was full of gas and I drove over to Betty's and knocked on her door. She cracked the door and when she saw me she smiled and yawned and let me in.

"What are you doing here?" she asked. She was wearing an ugly housecoat and her hair was up in rollers and she was wearing bedroom slippers that looked like old flowers. I told her and she slumped to the couch.

"You want me to what?" she said. "I got to get to work."

"No you don't," I said. "I talked to Chuck. He said you could come with me."

"Why don't you call the cops?" she said. "You want some coffee?" We went into the kitchen and she put some water on, burned her finger accidentally and yelled "shit" so loud I jumped.

"I can't call the cops because Lucas is a free man to ruin his life if he wants to," I said.

"Then how can you get him back?" she asked.

"I'll just get him," I said. "I don't know. I'll worry about that later. Hurry up and get dressed. We got to pick up Sally Crandall." She stared at me and then laughed as she was pouring the water into our cups.

"I thought you said we were going to pick up Sally Crandall," she said.

"That's right." She stared at me and poured until the cup ran over and spilled along the top of the counter. She looked down and yelled "shit" again and cleaned it up with a paper towel.

"Have you called her?" she asked. "Sally Crandall. A movie actress. Oh God, I look like a witch."

"We got to get over there right now before she goes to the set," I said.

"I thought you said she hated Lucas," said Betty, who was doing some kind of face exercises that made her look awful silly.

"She loves him," I said. "People can't help loving him. It's like a sickness."

"Nobody's got it worse than you," she said.

"Get dressed." She did, and before we were halfway to Holiday Inn in Abilene she was fidgeting like crazy and cussing a blue streak.

"Couldn't you get anything better than this?" she asked. "It's like riding in a goddamn wheelbarrow."

"I'm lucky to have it at all," I said. "And Chuck gave me money." Just before I'd left, he'd pressed it into my hand, five hundred bucks, and I felt real touched. Chuck Owens was a good man who was trying to dig his way out of Missy's being dead.

"It's white trash," she said. "No movie star's gonna get in this piece of shit."

"Trust me," I said.

"I trust you," she said, reaching out and touching me on the arm. "And I think I love you, too." Love's a funny thing, and sometimes all kinds of things hide out pretending to be love, but she was right, we loved one another, and it was the truth and you can't have opinions about the truth.

I drove right to the Holiday Inn and parked under the balcony up where Sally Crandall's room was. We walked up there, Betty doing those face exercises again.

"Quit that," I said. "You acting like there's something in your mouth trying to get out." She slapped me on the arm and giggled like a girl. We stood outside Sally Crandall's door. It was going to be a real hot day with no wind and I was already sweating and before I knocked I thought, Lord, this is another fool's mission. I didn't know where Lucas was, didn't know if I could trace him or anything. I just knew I had to do something. I knocked. There wasn't a sound from inside so I knocked again.

"Who is it?" a thin sort of voice called from behind the door.

"Miss Crandall, it's Jake Baker, Lucas's friend," I said. Betty had stepped to the left and was looking in the window's reflection doing her face exercises when the curtain came back and she was staring at Sally Crandall, making her face move around a couple of more times before stopping.

The door opened a crack. She was still in her bedclothes and looked her age.

"What do you want?" she asked.

"I love your movies," Betty said like she was all out of breath. Sally looked at Betty like she was from another planet.

"It's Lucas," I said. "He's run away." Sally's face twisted

up and she sagged against the door frame.

"Good God," she said. "Oh. Come in." We came in. The room was all messy with beer cans and bottles and newspapers and magazines and clothes all over the floor, not like you'd think a movie star would live. She sat on the edge of one bed and we sat on the other.

"He left a note saying he was heading toward Dallas," I said."

"He's done this before," she said. "But the fool is starting to get old." She shook her head. "Damn his soul to hell. What is it about him that makes me care?

"Beats the shit out of me," Betty said, and I gave her a mean look and she backed off.

"What are you going to do?" Sally said.

"He's my friend and I'm going to get him back. If it's a dumb thing to do, then it's a dumb thing to do. I reckoned you'd like to help me go get him."

"You'd do that for him, wouldn't you?" she said. "Wait. Don't answer that. I know you'd do it. He hasn't changed one little bit. Oh Lord, that man. What is it about him that makes us turn into slathering idiots around him? I've been away from him for years and ever since he showed up in that stupid little mountain man outfit he's all I could think of. And this movie . . ." She picked up what I guessed was the script and threw it on the floor. "It's a joke."

"We want you to come with us to find him," I said. She looked at me and then smiled big. Tears came into her eyes but stayed there. She chewed on her lower lip for a second. Betty got up and sat beside her and held her hand.

"Honey, he needs Jake to look out after him," Betty said. "You come with us and the three of us will find him."

"I'm supposed to be on set at two," she said, but she said it like she was talking to herself. She looked up to her left and caught her reflection in the mirror and got up and went and stood looking at herself real close, and though her expression didn't change, tears came out of her left eye and went down her cheek. She snapped around. "Go get me some toast and coffee and orange juice and I'll shower and be ready in twenty minutes. I'm going."

I whooped like an idiot and Betty hugged her. I went out and got the food at the restaurant and it took nearly forever because the waitress at the counter was new and didn't know what to do next. When I got back to the room, Sally Crandall had put on her makeup and smelled like soap and looked pretty and sexy in her blue jeans.

"What should I bring?" she asked. "How long will it take?"

"I don't have no idea," I admitted. Betty had brought a whole suitcase full of stuff. "Bring a lot, I reckon. You sure you want to do this?" She looked happy and tore into the toast and drank the orange juice and sipped at the coffee. She smiled.

"Yeah," she said. "I want to do this."

"You going to call the movie people and tell them?" I asked. She got a pencil and piece of paper from her purse. She wrote a note and then handed it to me to read. It said this: "Hugh, I've gone to help find Lucas. He's in some kind of trouble. You take care of things for me. I'll call you when I find out something." She signed it S.C.

"That'll do it," she said. She found a small roll of Scotch tape and taped the note to the TV screen. "Let's get out of here before I start thinking about things." Sally put on dark glasses and I carried her bag down and put it in the back of the Turd with my bag and Betty's.

I drove off on I-20, heading east toward Fort Worth.

"What makes you think you can find him just by driving east?" Sally asked.

"He can find him," said Betty, turning. Betty and me sat in front, Sally in the back. "He set out to find my long-lost daughter and found her. She's a princess now living in France." I glanced in the rear-view mirror at Sally, who was trying to look like she believed Betty.

"I see," she said. "Oh God, that man." She shook her head.

"Can I ask you something?" asked Betty.

"Sure," said Sally Crandall. She lit a long cigarette and threw the match out the window. The station wagon didn't have air conditioning and it was hot.

"Didn't you make that movie with Peter Lawford where you were in the, uh, bed with him?" asked Betty. I glanced at Sally who smiled and looked out the window.

"Poor Peter," she said. "He's dead, you know. Yeah, I did that."

"What did he kiss like?" Betty asked.

"Oh, he was a gentleman," Sally said. "He was so gentle and tender. His eyes always danced with mischief but he was tender as a boy. I think I loved him a little."

"I always wondered when actors were in bed if they really . . ."

". . . God no," said Sally. I looked over at Betty, who looked a little disappointed and I reckon Sally saw it, too. "Well, I didn't have anything on up top and he held me against him, if that's what you mean." Betty sighed and nodded, her eyes gone all dreamy.

"He was just always what I thought a man should be in my dreams," said Betty.

"Yeah, and they usually turn out looking like Lucas Kraft," said Sally Crandall. "God help us all."

Well, we drove the whole damn day, all the way to Dallas, a little past it in, fact, stopping only for food and for the girls to use the john. A woman on the road means you got to stop a lot. Once we got settled and ate, I left them at the motel and drove back down to the place where Kennedy got shot.

It was about seven and the traffic was dying and I found a place to park right easy and walked around. The sun was going down and a wind had come up and I half thought Lucas would pop up and tell me it was all a joke. I walked around for a spell and then went up to that wall where Lucas had pretended to shoot from. If I had to drive all the way back to Branton, I'd find Lucas. I knew that. I came up the hill, awful tired and sweaty, and I saw it before I got there, a small piece of paper taped to the wall. When I got to it, I pulled it off, held it up to the fading light and read this: "Jake, I believe I am being pursued by thugs. You must help me. I'm here in Dallas. Lucas."

"I'm a son of a bitch," I said. Something was screwy. This was almost like he knew I'd come after him and then come to this spot. The more I stood there, the less it made sense at all.

I decided to drive over to the flophouse where we stayed when we were in Dallas that first time months ago. The streetlights were on now and I found the flophouse a couple of blocks over and went into the lobby. It looked like it was more rundown than it had been. A wino was standing in the corner peeing on the wall and a woman was right beside him looking bored and tired. They had a small bulletin board just before you went upstairs and there was only one piece of paper on it, put down with seven or eight thumbtacks. I walked over to it and read this: "Jake. They're after me. You got to help me. I'm here in Dallas. He's looking for me. Lucas."

Now it had gone from being weird to ridiculous. He was leading me around by the nose. I took the note off the board and put it in my pocket with the other one and drove back over to the motel. Betty and Sally were in the room eating on a bucket of chicken and talking like they were old friends. I threw the notes on the bed between them, got a drumstick and fell exhausted on the other bed. We'd only got one room, and all I could think about (and it's awful to admit this, but it's true) was if I might get a peek at Sally Crandall's boobs. I figured if she'd let Peter Lawford lay with her, maybe she'd flash me.

"What in the hell does this mean?" Sally asked. "Where'd you get these?"

"He's here?" asked Betty. I told the story and they looked odd about it all just like I did.

"How did he know you'd look in those places?" asked Sally. She had on shorts and she sat on the bed with her legs crossed and I felt weak and sort of like I was going to laugh real loud.

"I'm calling Chuck," I said. So I did, and as soon as Chuck answered the phone he started talking.

"Jake, he called here," said Chuck. "From Dallas. He's in Dallas."

"I know," I said. "So are we. I found some notes he left."

"You know?" said Chuck. "I'll be dog. He was all excited when I told him you'd already left looking for him. You know what he said when I told him you were coming after him?"

"What?"

"He said, 'Oh goody,'" said Chuck. I laughed like a maniac.

"Well, where in the hell is he?" I asked.

"He said he was sleeping in the street near a phone booth and you should call this phone booth. Here's the number." He gave it to me. "He wouldn't tell me where it was, said it was dangerous, which didn't make any sense to me."

"None of this makes any sense to me, either," I said. "Thanks."

I told the girls what had happened and Sally wanted me to call the number right away because she wanted him back. But I just wanted to make one thing sure before I did anything. I called the phone company and told them I was Smith from the Fort Worth business office and needed an address on a number. I gave them the number Lucas had given Chuck.

"Just a second, Mr. Smith," a nice woman said. "Yes. That's a number from the Hilton." I put the phone down and started grinning and couldn't stop. Then I looked at Sally Crandall and she was wanting me to tell her something. I thought about it for a second. I wasn't sure if it was the right thing or not.

"It's in the worst part of town," I said. "I hope he's all right."

IT WAS A FEEBLE EXCUSE, but I told Sally Crandall and Betty that I wanted to go down to the bar and get a drink before I called Lucas. But I acted sort of upset and they let me get away with it, even though Sally wanted me to call right away.

Well, that old son of a bitch.

I went down to the lobby and got a pay phone, dropped the coin in and dialed the number I'd got from Chuck. It rang once and then this voice, sounding feeble said, "Hello?"

"Lucas?" I said. "It's Jake."

"Oh, thank God you found me," he said. "I've been afraid somebody would mug me here. Jake, I'm destitute, old pal. You must come retrieve me. I'm at . . ." He gave some address but I wasn't listening to that. I was listening to the TV in the background. I let him finish and was quiet for a second. "Jake, tell me you're coming to rescue me."

"I may not be man enough to rescue nobody from the Hilton," I said. He laughed a short little laugh and went blustery, saying he wasn't in a hotel, that he was standing by a damn phone booth and there was a huge black guy coming toward him.

"Then it must be the porter," I said. He got quiet. "I traced the number you gave Chuck to the Hilton, Lucas. But thanks for telling me, old buddy, just what an asshole you are."

"But you came after me!" said Lucas, happy for no good reason. "You came after me to get me back."

"Yeah, and so did Betty Silver and Sally Crandall," I said. He gasped.

"The Playgirl of the Western World is with you?" he asked.

"If you mean Sally, yes, and she's been real worried about you," I said. "Now I'd be surprised if she even talks to you ever again. Or me neither."

"Are you with them now?" he asked like he was flinching and expecting me to hit him.

"We're in a motel here in Dallas," I said. "They're in a room and I'm in the lobby. They don't know yet what a worm you are."

"Are you going to tell them what a worm I am?" he asked.

"I told them," I said, "that you were at a phone booth in the worst section of town. Then I told them I was coming down here for a drink. I did it to keep them from knowing what a son of a bitch you are."

"I'm not a son of a bitch," he said like a little boy. "I'm just insecure. I just need people to keep telling me they love me."

"I don't love you," I said. "You knew I'd come after you, didn't you?"

"Hope springs eternal," he said, and I could almost hear him shrug.

"You real smart," I said. "I think I'll tell the girls you decided to become a queer."

"Whoa," he said. "Now you've gone to meddling." I didn't see much point in talking about it much more, but I didn't see any sense in hurting Sally Crandall, either.

"Okay, look, you stupid jerk," I said, "I'm going to do this for Sally and no other reason. Get yourself looking wore out and messed up and we'll meet you at a phone booth in a bad section of town. You got one staked out already?"

"This is all so humiliating," he said.

"You just a crazy old cowboy," I said. He told me about a phone booth he'd seen on the way to Loretta Michelle's house and I wasn't crazy about going near there at all. But I figured we'd just go by, pluck him up and head on back toward Harkin County. I didn't ask where he got money to stay at the Hilton.

"Okay, we'll be there in an hour," I said. He gave me the address and I figured I could find it, since it was right next to a Kentucky Fried Chicken. "You better hope you can stop doing this kind of crap."

"One can always hope," he said, and I told him I'd call him back from the room in a couple of minutes. I walked back up to the room.

When I came in, Sally and Betty jumped up and started talking at once, asking me why it took so long, where was my drink and when was I going to call to see if Lucas was all right. I should have tried to act some way like excited or scared or even mad, but all I felt was tired and old.

I dialed the number and Lucas breathed "yes" into the phone and I asked him was he all right. Sally was at my

263

shoulder and she'd started to cry and wanted to talk to him. I gave her the phone.

"Hi, baby," she said. "You all right" They did? Oh my God, they did? Which hand? Are your fingers all right? Which thumb? That bastard. Have you eaten? Nothing all day? Oh, precious, we'll come after you. Just stay where you are. Here's Jake back." She handed me the phone.

"You okay, pal?" I asked.

"She is a fool for love," Lucas said happily.

"Well, try to hold up," I said. "Give me the address."

I went by the desk and paid and the clerk looked at me and the girls and grinned, and I grinned back at him and made a muscle and Betty hit me in the kidney real hard.

"You wish," she said when we got in the car. "Let's get the hell out of here."

Well, like I said, we were on the other side of Dallas and of course I got lost for a while, but Dallas is like any other city I'd ever been in, no difference much, and after stopping a couple of times to get directions, I came down a street called Bonney Drive and there was the Kentucky Fried Chicken, just like Lucas said, and outside of it was a phone booth, except they don't have phone booths any more and it was one of those stand-up things where you phone.

I pulled up to it in the parking lot of the KFC. Nobody was near the phone. I got out and looked around. It was nearly ten P.M. but it was hot and dry feeling, not at all like Georgia where the water hangs in the air with the lightning bugs.

"Where is he?" asked Sally Crandall. She and Betty got out. I said son of a bitch to myself, wondering what was going on. I told him I'd be there in an hour and it had been an hour and five minutes. Getting lost was something I'd figured into the schedule. But there was no Lucas.

I was looking across the lot toward the KFC when I heard Sally make this kind of mewling cry and I walked over to where she was standing near the phone.

"Blood," was all she could say. She pointed down. I got down on my hands and knees and it was blood all right, a splatter fresh enough so it was still wet in the middle of the drops. Betty got down beside me.

"Is it blood?" she asked.

"Yeah," I said. I reckon I should have been worried. The area was rough and run down. But I was just mad. Lucas must have been jerking us around again. Do it once, do it again and see if he can get Sally Crandall to moan over him some more.

"Son of a bitch," I finally said and stood back up and looked around.

"What do you think's happened to him?" Sally asked, her voice shaking. I wanted to tell her what I thought, that Lucas was hiding out in a Marriott somewhere waiting for me to find him. But if he was, by God, he'd never have me as a friend again.

"Don't get too upset," I said. "This could be from a nosebleed or maybe he cut his hand or something."

"But he'd be here, wouldn't he?" asked Betty.

"I don't know," I said, so tired I couldn't hardly stand up. "I just don't know." It was then I saw the man coming toward us, just out of the side of my eye. He was a big guy with something of a beard and his hands were in his pants pockets. "Get in the car." Betty grabbed my arm. "Get in the car and lock it. Now!" They moved and so did the man, coming up on me quicker.

"Give me five dollars," the man said before he got to me. I could tell by his voice he was drunk.

"I'm busted, pal," I said.

"Bullshit," he said real slow. He took his right hand out of his pocket and flashed a straight razor at me. I put both of my arms up and when he came at me, I kicked him in the balls. He dropped the razor and fell into a heap, gasping and groaning and holding himself. For good measure and to prove he'd better not fool with me any more, I stomped his hand when he took it off his aching privates. I got the razor and folded it up and put it in my back pocket and got in the car.

"Jesus H. Christ," Betty said. "That was neat as shit."

"Get me out of here," cried Sally Crandall. I drove two blocks and there on the corner, looking like I reckon heaven would look, was a Days Inn. It was there because right across the street was some big plant where I reckon bigwigs came to visit.

"We'll look for him in the morning," I said. "I'm almost too tired to hold my head up."

"Shouldn't we call the police?" asked Sally, nervous as a cat.

"Not yet," I said. "I got me a gut feeling he's all right." Well, I had no such a thing, but I wanted to sleep more than I wanted to find old Kid Kraft.

I got us a room. Betty and Sally fretted a little about Lucas, going back and forth in sad, cluttered sentences about what a fool he was and how much he needed tending; I think both of them needed him right smart, which was no shock to me. Sally got up and went in the bathroom, and I didn't think much of it at first. I was standing at the mirror in the room rubbing my eyes when I saw the bathroom door was open a crack and Sally Crandall was before that mirror looking at herself, with her top off and no bra on. but instead of what I'd dreamed, a movie star's high breasts, they sagged bad, even worse than Betty's, with not much shape at all, and I felt sad, like I was peeking in on something painful. So I slid off my pants and shirt and got in bed with Betty and fell into a sleep that didn't have any dreams, at least none to speak of.

In the morning, we got a quick breakfast at the cafeteria and Sally Crandall looked pretty and lively again and Betty was cussing like a sailor because she said the coffee was bitter. It tasted all right to me.

I drove us back down to the phone booth, but there was nothing different and the blood stains now looked like nothing special. It was then, standing there, that I had my first thought something might be wrong and one of those flashes of ideas that seem to come from nowhere.

Lucas knew me too good, I suspect. He knew just what'd I'd do at every turn. He probably knew, then, that I'd go to the only place in the neighborhood we'd ever been: Loretta Michelle Buckley's house. One time when we'd ridden our horses up the creek to the campsite, Lucas had told me about symmetry, how things can seem to dovetail together if you look at them right. Only this wasn't right at all, at least not to me. If he was there, it would mean he thought . . . hell, I was dreaming. Maybe I should call the police.

I didn't. I drove until I found Loretta's house and went past it two blocks and parked on the street. A chihuahua hopped up off a falling-in front porch and started yapping at us, and in the street some Mexican-looking kid was hitting the pavement with what looked like an axe handle. Great neighborhood.

"What in the hell are you stopping here for?" asked Betty.

"I'm just going to ask around, see if anybody's seen him," I lied.

"That's bullshit," she said. "Me and Sally might get raped sitting here alone, right Sally?" I stood there trying to think when Sally pulled a nickel-plated .38 out of her purse.

"Not without getting five holes first," she said.

"Son of a bitch," said Betty. "Let me see that thing." So while they were talking back and forth over the seat, I moved straight back down the street until I was standing in front of Loretta Michelle's house, feeling weird about it all — that's the only way I can describe it.

The house looked the same except somebody had left a pile of stomped-out cigarette butts by the front stoop. I went on up and knocked on the door and a woman's voice yelled, "Piss off."

"I need some help," I yelled back.

"Who don't," she said. Figuring I had nothing to lose, I just went on inside. The house was still dark and I went into the living room, or that's what it once was, and she was lying there on a dirty mattress completely naked, her legs apart, and she was smiling and smoking a cigarette.

"Well, well, it's you again," she said, and she blew smoke out her nose. "Change your mind? I need some bread, man. Come on for a ride." She reached down and touched herself and it was all I could do to keep from gagging. I love women but this was not sex; it was a fearful sadness is what it was.

"I lost my friend," I said. "He was waiting for me last night at the phone booth up by the fried chicken place, but when I got there last night he was gone and blood was there. If he was hurt, where'd he go?"

"No bread?"

"Put some clothes on and I'll give you twenty bucks," I said. She told me I was kinky but she did it. The boy who'd been there before didn't seem to be around. I gave her twenty bucks. "Now where might he be?" I half expected Lucas to pop out and come rolling into the room.

"Might've took him over to the clinic," she said. "I go there and get myself checked over once in a while, you know what I mean."

"Where is it?"

"Man, I don't know streets," she said. "I don't got me a car, you dig? I can take you there. Put me in your car and once I see it all, I can tell you how to get there. I been drove all over this damn town."

She stood at a mirror on the mantel and brushed her hair and then went in the bathroom. I raised the shades and picked up some of the trash and clothes and straightened up as best I could. She came out in a minute smelling like toothpaste and perfume. She had tied her hair back with a rubber band. With the sun coming in the windows she looked pasty and wild, but I almost thought there was some sort of spark about her, almost out, but there.

"Thanks for cleaning up," she said. "I was going to do it today." I just stared at her and she started laughing, and her laugh was like a big-tooth file on a metal bucket. "Come on. I'll show you the clinic. You paid for it already." We went outside.

"Can't you just stand here and point me?" I asked. I felt real funny about her getting into the car.

"You think I'm a fucking bird dog?" she asked. We started walking down the sidewalk. I felt all panicky and out of control.

"Your name's Wanda," I choked. "There's ladies in the car with me know your mama. Not real well but well enough to know your name. I don't want 'em knowing where you are. You don't want that either, do you?

"Fuck no," she said, and when she said it she sounded just like Betty. We went down the sidewalk and when we were about a hundred feet from the Turd, there was a muffled thud and something seemed to fly off the top of the car. I thought some kid was throwing rocks at the car so I looked over into the yard and the chihuahua came out and snorted at me a few times. "Them things all ought to be put to sleep."

I got to the car and the windows were down and smoke was sort of lolling out the windows. I thought Sally Crandall had lit a cigarette. Sally was still in the back, Betty in the front and they were both pale as ghosts.

"What's going on in there?" I asked.

"I just shot a hole in the roof," Betty said like she was just irritated by it. Sally Crandall just shook her head and didn't seem to be able to say a thing.

"Where's the gun?" I asked. Sally held it up and then put it back in her purse.

"Jesus," I said. "Okay. This is Wanda. She's going to show us the clinic. If he ain't there, I'm calling the cops." Loretta looked at Betty and I felt like I was going to throw up, but neither one seemed to think anything of it. Loretta got in the back seat with Sally and I started driving.

"Just drive around the block a spell and it'll come to me," said Loretta. She looked over at Sally — I could see it in the rear-view mirror — and then snapped her fingers. "I know you."

"She's Sally Crandall, honey," said Betty. "She's a big movie star."

"No, that ain't it," she said. "I thought she was that girl does the weather on channel 10. Except now I see you, you're too old."

"Goddamn," said Sally, rolling her eyes. Loretta didn't seem to mind.

"What do you do, honey?" Betty asked.

"Tell me where to go, tell me where to go," I started jabbering, trying to keep them from talking.

"Oh," said Loretta. "Go right here." I turned right into a worse neighborhood than the one we'd been in. "Or maybe it was left."

"Goddamn," said Sally Crandall.

"No, it was right, it was right," said Loretta, bouncing up and down on the seat. "I'm sure it was right."

"So what do you do?" asked Betty again.

"Tell me where to go," I almost yelled.

"I'm talking to her," said Betty, mad.

"And I'm trying to find my friend!" That time I did yell. Everything was quiet for a minute and I hoped that would end it.

"Whore," said Loretta, and I felt my heart sink down into my shoes. "That's me, the whore with the heart of gold."

"You picked up a whore?" Betty asked, turning to me. Then she turned back to Loretta. It was weird, let me tell you, and a little sick. "Are you really a whore?"

"What is this?" asked Loretta. "You wanna scratch and sniff or what? Yeah, I'm a whore."

Betty leaned over the seat and out of the corner of my eye I could see she was grinning.

"What's it like?" she asked. "You ever get sore?"

"Tell me where to go!" I yelled.

"Go to hell," said Loretta, and then she said, "Oops, turn left again right here." I had to cut across three lanes of traffic in front of a sports car and the driver sat on his horn and yelled something at me.

"You drive like shit," said Betty, holding on to the back of the front seat.

"I get everything," sighed Loretta. She looked out the window and shook her head. "Christ, I get everything." I could see Sally Crandall moving away from Loretta to the other side of the car. "But I ain't got nothing now. The clinic takes care of me."

"How many do you do . . . er, a day? asked Betty.

"Tell me where to go," I cried.

"Depends . . . hey!" yelled Loretta. "Here it is!"

I pulled up into the parking lot of a small brick building where a few old men were milling around and a young Mexican kid was falling down drunk or on drugs, hanging off the grillwork on the tiny front porch.

"This is it?" asked Sally

"Something, ain't it?" said Loretta. She got out with me and we went toward the door. Betty and Sally waited in the car. "You sure are antsy. Sure I can't do something for you to calm you down?" I glared at her real heavy. "No, I guess not."

We went inside and it was a zoo. I never saw a room so crammed with people. We went up to this window where a woman in a nurse uniform and smoking a long unfiltered cigarette was staring blankly.

"Get a number!" she bawled. She squinted her eyes at us.

"Oh, hey, Loretta," she said.

"Hi, Mimi," said Loretta.

A tall old man came up toward us, dragging one leg, holding one eye shut.

"I need penguins," he said.

"Bud, get away from me, for Christ's sake!" yelled Mimi, and the old man went off. He reminded me of something from Fieldstone.

"This is my friend," said Loretta touching me on the sleeve. "He's looking for his friend got beat up looks like over by the Kentucky Fried Chicken."

"What's his name?" she asked. She held a notebook up to the light, which was awful dim, and tried to read it.

"Lucas Kraft," I said. The cigarette hung out of her mouth, and smoke made her squint even more as it drifted up over her head. Bud came back by and asked us if we'd seen his harpoon, and I told him I thought it was in the parking lot and he snapped his fingers and went out the door.

"Nope," said Mimi. "But we did bring in one guy. Looks like a bear." My heart went to clattering.

"What's his name?" I asked.

"Uh . . ." she said, looking at the list again. "Let's see, that was William S. Hart." My legs went all rubbery.

"Where is he?" I asked.

"Through the doors, big room on the left," Mimi said, exhaling a cloud with the words. "Loretta, you show him. And you better take him on. Can only stay here two nights max." A man and a woman over in a corner of the room were screaming at each other about the clap. She said he gave it to her, he said she gave it to him. We went through the doors.

On the left just past the doors was a big room lined with beds. Some people were snoring, others were groaning and one man with nothing on but undershorts was standing on his bed in the corner with his hand over his heart saying the Pledge of Allegiance to the flag. We walked along the beds until I saw him propped up on pillows reading a copy of *Woman's Day*.

273

"Howdy, Kid," I said. He dropped the magazine and I could see he'd been hit in the face. It was bandaged up and small scratches were everywhere. His arm was all wrapped up in gauze, his right arm.

"Jake!" he yelled. He got out of bed, flinched and hugged me and glared at Loretta, eyes all beetled up. "Thank God you found me. I thought I was destined to die in this foul nest of ninnies."

"William S. Hart?"

"Never use your real name when you check in," he said. He was wearing his own clothes and he looked terrible. His beard was stubbly and black.

"Hey, remember me?" asked Loretta.

"Is Betty . . ." started Lucas, but I grabbed his arm and took him off a couple of beds and told him about Betty not knowing, and about Sally Crandall being in the car.

"Heloise and Abelard!" he said. "Pyramus and Thisbe! Marc Antony and Cleopatra!"

"Laurel and Hardy," said an old man who was sitting on his bed next to us.

"Don't listen to that man," said Lucas. "His wit, if not his disease, is terminal." He got his things and we headed toward the door.

"Did you pay some guy to beat you up?" I asked. He was limping pretty badly.

"God no," he almost whined. "I was standing there reciting all I could remember from *The Collected Works of Edgar A. Guest* when these two ruffians approached and assaulted me. The next thing I knew, they were bringing me here. I was broke and they took me for a street person. Indignity hath no name."

"What's he talking about?" asked Loretta.

"Nothing," I said. We went by Mimi's window and

Lucas owed nearly a hundred bucks, so I paid it from the money Chuck gave me and we went outside.

"Lordy mercy!" yelled Lucas when we got out. "They have exploded the sun. Its brightness would pluck the eyes from the fiercest warrior."

"I'm a night person myself," said Loretta. We got near the car and the door flew open and Sally Crandall came running over and Lucas starting groaning just before she got there.

"Sweet Jesus," said Sally. "What did they do to my baby?"

"Your baby got his ass kicked," I said. Lucas opened one eye wide and glared at me.

"You inelegant swine," he said. Sally helped him into the back seat. So naturally Loretta got in the front with me and Betty. It had gone from weird to downright awful. I pulled back out and headed in the direction we'd come, hoping nobody would say much. I told what had happened to Lucas and then I made up a few things, and then he made up a few things, I'm sure, making it worse. But I believed him. It was his luck to get beat up.

"So what do you do?" Loretta asked Betty.

"I keep house and cook for one of the richest men in Harkin County," she said proudly.

"Do tell," said Loretta. "Do tell." I found her house and I was sweating like a hog by the time we got there. Loretta got out. "Take care of yourself," she said to Betty.

"You, too, honey," said Betty. "You'll live longer if you keep your knees together a little more often."

"Right," said Loretta. I gave her another twenty and she took it and folded it once and put it in her pocket. "Thanks, man. It's been weird."

All the way back to the ranch, Lucas moaned and Sally Crandall shushed him and held him in her arms and talked baby talk to him, and I could tell Betty thought it was sweet but it sort of made me ill. All I could see as I drove into the sun that afternoon was Betty and Loretta sitting beside one another talking about something no mother should ever say to a daughter. Lucas knew who Loretta was and at least he had kept his mouth shut.

By the time we got home, Sally Crandall and Lucas were all over one another like lovebirds and I didn't have the heart to tell anybody at the ranch just what had happened. They all treated me like a damn hero, which made me feel even worse.

Sally called her manager, Hugh, who was yelling at her, but Sally didn't seem to mind, and then I took Sally back down to her room at the Holiday Inn after she had put Lucas to bed and told him she'd be there in the morning and then they could talk about things.

"You're a good man, Jake," she said as we got to the motel.

"No, I ain't," I said. "I'm a fool."

"You're just tired." I helped her take her bags upstairs to her room and then she kissed me on the cheek and it was the first time I'd ever been kissed by a movie star, if you don't count the time I was licked by Rin Tin Tin when he was selling dog food at a store when I lived in New Jersey.

I drove home real slow and stopped and got a bottle of bourbon. I told Wool I was too wore out to help him with supper and he let me get away with it again, though he cussed at me. I went outside just as the moon was coming up and all the warm stars you ever saw in the heavens and sat in Scout's chair and listened to the creek mumbling down the slope.

I just drank out of the bottle, little sips. Chuck had taken Betty home and she kissed me and called me her hero, but I didn't feel like anybody's hero. I felt like going out to the road and hitchhiking back to Georgia. Lucas had been conked out most of the afternoon, so I was surprised when the door opened behind me letting out a little light and Lucas, too. He pulled one of the white metal lawn chairs up beside me, and without saying anything I handed him the bottle and he bubbled it once and handed it back to me.

We sat like that until the moon was up above us good and you could see Texas like it was daylight.

"Why'n the hell did you do that?" I said. He rubbed his chin and leaned forward.

"I have wasted my life," he said. A bird sang down in the cottonwoods somewhere. "My God, Jake, listen to that. He's part of all this. Can you imagine being a part of all this, of fitting in? I've never fit in. I make people like me with games and stories."

"Aw hell," I said.

"I was just feeling like I was getting out on the edge of things again," he said.

"You don't need to do things like that," I said. "Folks like a person for what he is, not what he does."

"My glib friend, what I am is as loveless as a snake," he said. "Sometimes people love what they wish you were instead of what you are. And if you can appear to be that wish, then you shall be loved."

The bird went to singing again and since I couldn't think of a thing to say, I just sat there and listened to the bird and sipped from the bottle and felt the night coming around us. And it sounds like a story somebody made up, but I swear, the bad feelings, the bitterness and sadness just came off me sitting there like a snake coming out of its skin.

"What in the hell do you know, Kid?" I said when the bird had stopped its song. "Sometimes you talk one hell of a lot better than you think and you think one hell of a lot better than you act. You think you can keep Sally Crandall's love by pretending you're somebody else?"

"Hah," he said.

"And you think you can get away with this kind of crap for the rest of your life?"

"Nah." He laughed a little bit and then I did and we swapped the bottle one more time. I was feeling pretty good but tired to the bones.

"Say something smart," I said. He stood up and walked out a little to the crest of the slope just before it goes down toward the creek. He cleared his throat.

> Old age hath yet his honor and his toil.
> Death closes all; but something ere the end,
> Some work of noble note, may yet be done,
> Not unbecoming men that strove with Gods.
> The lights begin to twinkle from the rocks;
> The long day wanes; the slow moon climbs; the
> deep
> Moans round with many voices. Come, my
> friends.
> 'T is not too late to seek a newer world.

He was still as a shadow there and I got up and went out to him and we looked up into the stars.

"What was that, Kid?" I asked.

"Something my mother taught me," he said. "She told me always to remember it because it would be a comfort to me when I got old."

"And is it?" He rubbed his face where the bandages still covered his cuts.

"It surely is," he said, but it was so soft I could barely hear it over the birds, which had once again gone to singing against the moon.

SALLY CRANDALL GOT OUR JOBS back working on
Shadow of the Wind, but this time we were cowboys, not
mountain men. Lucas couldn't have been happier, but
Betty started getting a mite put out with me because I was
gone up there so much while she had to keep house for
Chuck.

And it was about this time that me and Lucas met Old
Buffalo and he nearly got us killed. Well, maybe that's an
exaggeration, but not much of one. At the time, I
thought I was just getting too old for that kind of crap
and in truth all three of us were, because Old Buffalo was
as old as me.

Old Buffalo was a Sioux Indian they'd hired as sort of
an adviser for the movie. His face was so wrinkled it
looked like the bottom of a tennis shoe and he never
smiled, just like you always heard about Indians being,
but it wasn't because he didn't feel happy but because he
was preparing to live with the Great Spirit.

281

The place they made the movie was really busy now. The fort was all built up and there was the Indian village and a white person's town they'd built just to one side of it.

Lucas and Sally Crandall looked like somebody had loosely sewed them together. They went everywhere and she gave him goo-goo eyes and fussed after him like he was this big old hairy, ugly child and he loved it, just loved it. It seemed double funny to me that she treated him like that because every day, whether we were in a scene or not, we wore our cowboy outfits, with heavy chaps and six guns and neckerchiefs and hats. It was by then early June and hot as the hinges of hell, as they say, so I sweated through the clothes and so did Lucas but Sally Crandall didn't care.

I never thought the movie was going to be all that great a thing, but from the complaining going on and the folks there making fun of it, I was pretty sure it was some sort of jackleg operation now, even though they'd spent one whale of a lot of money on it. Lucas and me were on the payroll and I got $150 a week for doing next to nothing. I gave $30 to Wool just to keep him from cussing me. I'd of given some to Betty if it would of eased her mind.

It wasn't that Betty still didn't love me. We'd set up this thing that we'd spend every Wednesday night together at her place, and we still did, touching all those good-feeling places and laughing and sometimes getting a little drunk, but you could tell she thought next to nothing of me hanging around with the folks on the movie set, a lot of whom were women. Now I know what I look like and I know no woman short of middle age would think twice about me, but Betty was convinced some pretty young thing was going to steal old Jake Baker from her, and I had a hard time arguing it because I wanted to believe it

282

and every time she said it, I could almost hope it was true.

One time I called Belle, and her husband answered and Belle was gone and I talked to him a spell and he sounded like he always did, like somebody'd put a plunger on his ear and sucked his brains out. I told him to tell Belle I was okay and he said "Far out," which I reckon meant he would. It was always hard to tell with that boy.

But I was telling about Old Buffalo. That poor old Indian didn't have an idea he'd mess up my life. Well, he didn't really do it but he led to it. He was tall and kind of deaf and wore his hair in two long braids. The assistant director would meet with Old Buffalo about twice a week and ask him about what Indians would do, to read over the script and see if it was right. Old Buffalo would put on his glasses and run his finger under the words and then grunt a few sentences.

I wasn't hanging around him, but Lucas had taken to doing that, so I saw him a good deal. It was on a cool rainy day that I went off from the crowd and was looking around the fort. I was just walking by myself, trying to put things together. I never was much for planning my life like some folks say they do. Insurance salesmen have a thing called family planning and I reckon that's good, but I just lived usually. But now I was doing some thinking.

Here's what I was thinking about: marrying Betty, moving into her house, about God and if I'd go to heaven or hell, about my family stretching back, all dead now, about Texas and how passing strange it was to end up here as a play cowboy.

I walked around that fort in the mist twice trying to make some sense, but nothing came to me, and when I got back to the trailer where Old Buffalo was staying, Lucas was all excited and hopping up and down. When I came in the door, he grabbed me by the arms.

"Jake, we are going to have visions," he said.

"That's good," I said, not knowing what he was talking about but trying to be pleasant. Old Buffalo was sitting in an old chair straight as a rifle and looking sort of like a dog on a chain, not unhappy but not really happy either.

"Tomorrow at dawn, we are going out and we will see things no man has ever seen," said Lucas.

"I said we would try," said Old Buffalo. "I don't know if white men can have visions. I am doing this only because I liked your books. I have had three visions in my life. In one, I became the crow and flew over my ancestral lands. In the second I was only shapes and became all shapes, but the third was the best. I became Father Buffalo and was shot and eaten and my skin was used for all good things."

"That's nice," I said, not knowing what to think.

"Oh, great," said Lucas, shaking his head at what I'd said.

That was as long a speech as Old Buffalo ever made around me. After that, it was two or three words at best. That night, Lucas told everybody in the Long House me and him were going to see visions with an old Indian, and they hooted and hollered something awful and I felt kind of dumb.

"You better have a vision of working in this goddamn kitchen," said Wool as we cleaned up. He turned up the radio station when the Fat Boys came on and danced around and howled something awful. The men laughed about it but then went to talking cattle and rain and feed and horses and such, the things they always talked about at night.

I don't know why, but I had this feeling everything we were doing was something out of the past, that it wouldn't last much longer than we would. That made me feel excited and sad and happy and all kinds of things at the same time. I thought about how I'd lived all over the East Coast and never seen even half of my country. But I'd seen enough in the past year to cheer me up.

"Lord," said Lucas as he fell asleep. "A vision."

"A vision," I said back to him a few seconds later, but he was already dreaming.

The next day was sunny and hot. We weren't working, them having no need that day for cowboys. We picked up Old Buffalo and drove out in the country on Chuck's property, just miles from anything. Old Buffalo had told us to bring a shovel and some matches and an axe, which sounded awful barbaric to me, but we brought them.

"Walk for mile," said Old Buffalo.

"A mile," said Lucas, his voice full of disbelief. We set off and before we'd gone far, we were wringing wet, but if I'd known what was to come I wouldn't of gone at all. We struggled through that prairie pasture until we came to a spot on a slope with a good view of the land around us and Old Buffalo said, "Here."

"Wood," said Old Buffalo.

"Wood," said Lucas. I sort of felt like they were saying wedding vows, but I kept my mouth shut and me and Lucas found a small woods a few hundred yards away and picked up armloads of dry wood. When we got back, Old Buffalo had set up this dome tent he'd brought in his backpack and was out there in front of it digging a hole in the soft dirt, doing right good for an old Indian.

"Fire," said Old Buffalo, pointing at a spot about ten yards from the little tent.

"Fire," Lucas said, looking at me and nodding like it meant something. So we got this fire going while he kept on digging this hole like a crazy man.

"Big rocks," said Old Buffalo. For him, that was a whole sermon, and at least Lucas didn't repeat it. We had to scout around a long spell for big rocks but we found four or five and lugged them back. By this time, I was almost faint for water and shade.

"I think I'm going back to the car, Kid," I said. "You tell me what your vision was." He grabbed me by the arm.

"You insolent cracker," he hissed. "You can't do that. It would be an insult to the entire Sioux nation. It could provoke outbreaks of hostilities anew. You must accompany me on this vision quest." He was just lathered in sweat and his hair was standing up all over his head.

"Okay," I said, not knowing if he was lying or not. We got back with the rocks and dropped them, and by then Old Buffalo had made this huge hole. That man had arms like steam shovels. It was just plain amazing.

So he finally got out and took the rocks and put them in the fire and let them set for a long spell while none of us said nothing. I kept eyeing the old canteen he had on his belt, but I didn't ask for any because I didn't want him to get offended. Later I saw it wasn't intended for drinking anyhow. Using a leather thong of sorts he'd brought, Old Buffalo got those hot rocks out of the fire and took them in that tent. Then he motioned for us to come in.

"Underwear," he said, and he stripped down to his old shorts. Lucas nodded and did it, too, but I just couldn't until Old Buffalo took my arm and shook it hard and put his old tennis shoe face right up in mine and said "underwear" again. So I did it, and God help me if us three old codgers weren't sitting in that sweltering tent in our skivvies. Old Buffalo commenced to chanting something in

Indian and then he takes the canteen and pours the whole thing over the hot rocks and the steam that comes up fills the tent.

"Mene, mene tekel upharsin," chanted Lucas.

"I didn't know you spoke Indian, Kid," I said. Hell, I thought it was Indian. He later told me it was in the Bible. Anyway, he opened one eye and glared at me and then closed it back. The heat was something unbearable. We were all coughing and gagging and going "whew" all the time, even Old Buffalo, whose chant was like, "Nnn-nnaaahhh nana, hay ya hay ya, whew," at least that's how it sounded to me.

So we all chanted for a spell. I didn't know nothing else, so I did "There was a young girl from Nantucket" and some other dirty poems I'd learned that had that same rhythm as their songs. Neither one of them seemed to mind. Finally none of us could take another second of it, and Old Buffalo had poured out all the water on the hot rocks, and we just sort of fell out of the tent into the sun.

"Hole," said Old Buffalo.

"Hole," said Lucas. So we all got down in the big hole and laid there in the cool dirt, which did feel awful good, the sun right in our eyes. Nothing happened for a long spell and I wondered what would happen if somebody found us there. Three old queers lying in a hole out in the pasture in their skivvies. I've done a lot of strange things, but that was the cake-taker, so to speak.

We laid there all day until the sun was going down and I was getting all feverish and sick. I thought I might die, but that didn't bother me too awful much. A preacher told me when I was not more than thirty that death was a natural part of living, and I called him a bad name. But now I see what he meant. Either the world dies, or you do, and if you leave somebody you love, you don't want the world to pass away.

But I didn't die. What I did was have a vision. I guess I went to sleep, but I felt of a sudden like I was rising up from that hole and flying, and I mean like a jet, flying back east, and I could see Dallas down there and then Louisiana, and I went over my home town up there and could see the cemetery and then over Mississippi, the rest of it, and Alabama, and I could see the motel where me and Lucas had stayed for a few hours and I landed on my feet like Superman outside my old house in Branton, and Betty, the old Betty, was there, smiling at me and holding her arms out, and when I went to grab her, she just misted away and I was crying for her to come back, crying and crying.

That was when I felt somebody slap me. It was Old Buffalo. When I came awake, I thought I'd died and was in heaven because all I could see were bright stars over me. I sat up and thought I was on a cloud but it was the dirt of the hole. Lucas was there, too.

"Am I dead?" I asked.

"You had a vision, brother," said Old Buffalo. It was dark, but the moon was up full, and in that light his face looked like an old gulley, washed and ruined. But now he was grinning like nothing I ever saw.

"I had this dream," I said. I told them about it.

"And so did a vision appear before me," said Lucas. "I was visited by the spirit of Red Cloud who told me that from now on I was to tell nothing but the truth."

"Ai-yiee!" said Old Buffalo. We got dressed and walked back down to the Jeep, and I felt weak and a little sick.

If I'd of known all the grief that day lying in that hole would cause me, I never would have gone up there.

When we got home, we had, of course, missed supper and Wool lit into me for not being there to help him.

"You dumb honkies up there with that Indian while I'm here in this kitchen like some goddamn slave," he said. "I guess being movie actors ain't enough for you."

"Your food tastes like it was made in the Buster Brown shoe leather factory," said Lucas.

"Say what?" said Wool. We were standing in the kitchen where Wool had just finished with the dishes and was wearing his white apron and the air was full of steam.

"I simply stated that you cannot cook," said Lucas. "I should think that even to one with your obviously failed palate that should be obvious."

"Say what?" said Wool, getting mad. He put his hands on his hips. Whizzer Pippin walked in and when he saw Lucas and Wool almost at one another, he grinned in that lopsided way of his and just waited for something to happen.

"I am now a truth sayer," said Lucas. "I have had a vision and the spirit of Red Cloud told me to tell only the truth, and you are an awful cook, though you have a few other qualities which mitigate your culinary perversities."

"What he say?" asked Wool, looking at me. He was clenching and unclenching his hands.

"He's just been laying out in the sun too long," I said. "Don't pay him no mind."

"I'm gone slap a knot upside his ugly old head," said Wool. Whizzer Pippin laughed and stamped his foot.

"I slap one upside your head, too," Wool said to Whizzer. Well, that was about all it took. Things had been quiet there for a long spell and Whizzer and Wool took to arguing real loud, and in a minute Tree and J.D. and about seven or eight others came in and just like an order was given, everybody fell into fighting. The others heard it and in a few seconds, there were twelve men kicking and slapping and swinging.

I grabbed Lucas and we went down to his little study to sit things out. It gradually slowed down and then somebody laughed and I peeked in about half an hour later and they were sitting around drinking tequila, Wool and Whizzer next to each other. Stuff was broke everywhere and Wool had a colander on his head and was drinking from the neck of the bottle.

I went back down to Lucas.

"They've calmed down," I said. "You shouldn't have said that about Wool. He does the best he can. You shouldn't make fun of somebody who's doing the best he can."

"I was not making fun," he said. "I was merely telling the truth. My vision is to tell the truth at all costs. The truth is all that really matters in this life."

"I don't hold with that," I said, but I couldn't think of anything else smart to say.

While we were sitting there, Lucas was getting all these typed pages together and stacking them and flipping through them. He said he was through with his new book and was going to send it to his agent.

"What happens to them two old boys out there in the mountains trapping?" I asked.

"Nothing that anyone will care about," he shrugged.

"Can I read it?"

"Certainly not," he said, and I went to bed and didn't press it. Most everybody stayed up late and got drunk, including Wool, who slept right through breakfast, which I did by myself, which seemed only fair. While I was cleaning up, I noticed Lucas going out for his walk. I wished later he hadn't of done it.

It was a gray morning, hot and gray. I walked down the slope to see my girl. I said me and Betty hadn't been too happy with one another, but when I saw her on the back steps, there was no accounting for the fact she was mad as a hen.

"Get away from me you son of a bitch!" she yelled. She was holding a broom and held in front of her like she thought I was going to grab her.

"What's wrong, baby?" I asked.

"Don't you baby me, you lying bastard," she said. She started shaking and her hair came out of place. It started to rain. She stepped on the back porch, which was screened in.

"I'm getting wet," I said.

"Suit me if you drowned," she said, still shaking.

"What have I done?" I asked.

"What have . . ." she started, but she quit, shook her head and then started crying. The rain came on down hard. I was standing there dripping, wondering what in the hell had gone wrong. "She was right there next to me in the car. Oh, my God, my baby." There was a rocking chair there that had been Missy Owens's, and Betty plopped down in it and cried. I stepped toward the door but she sort of growled and cried at me and I just stood there in the rain.

"Who was?" It was a stupid thing to say, but I didn't know any better.

"My little girl," she said almost in a whisper. "My poor little girl. You son of a bitch. You said she was a princess." I felt suddenly so full of anger I could barely open my mouth.

"Who said that?" I asked.

"Your friend Lucas, that's who, you two-faced son of a

bitch," she said. "Get away from me." I wanted to kill him.

"Why'd he tell you that?" I asked.

"He said he was holding in a lie for you and he was now only telling the truth," she said, sobbing. "He's a good man and you are a . . . a . . . get away from me. Just get away!" I stood there and the rain came real hard and I got soaked before I walked up that slope, feeling my age, wanting to cry and scream. Lucas was in his study.

"I am going to kill you," I said. He stood up and backed against the wall. I looked around for something to kill him with. A couple of days before, Wool had made a German chocolate cake and Lucas had been eating a piece and had a fork on a plate. I picked up the fork and went to kill him.

"I am cleaning myself of the falsehoods within me," he said, holding up his fat hands.

"You about to cross the Jordan, you son of a bitch," I said. He backed away from me and I held up the fork and came for him.

"The truth is always the best way," said Lucas.

"Wolves," I said. "Me and Whizzer's taking you up to the cottonwoods and let the wolves eat your ugly body up."

"I'm scared of wolves," Lucas said. "My aunt used to read me stories about wolves."

I jumped at him and he fell over a chair and scrambled up just as I took a good swipe at him. My fork hit the bottom of the chair and bent up double. That was when it all hit me. Something about seeing that bent-up fork and thinking of Betty made everything blow up in me. I came over the chair and we fell sideways into his desk and the pages from his book went flying everywhere. I grabbed his collar and began banging his head on the floor and that was the last thing I remembered until Wool had me around the neck and was hauling me away.

A couple of the boys got Lucas and took him to the bunk area to look at him, and I broke away from Wool and walked down to the creek, thinking I'd move out that night and head back east for Georgia. I'd had just about all a man could take of Lucas Kraft.

I walked and walked. The rain came on down and I was drenched but I didn't care, and if I got pneumonia maybe it didn't matter. I felt like an old man, and old men are supposed to die, to get ready to die, to think about dying all the time. But I'd put it off for so long that the thought now just sort of filled me up with disgust.

When I got back, I found that Lucas had packed most of his things and had Wool drive him down to Abilene to Sally Crandall's motel room. He was gone. I was glad. I was still thinking about killing him.

That evening, I felt sour and even Wool stayed out of my way. It was something bad growing in me and I started thinking about doing something to hurt Lucas. I went and sat outside in Scout's old chair and thought on it. I looked down the hill and wondered if I'd ever get to hold Betty again, and it hurt me inside so bad I could hardly think on it.

That's when I got the idea. It's hard for me to say how much I was hurting then. Unless that makes sense, nobody would know how blind mad I was toward Lucas. But I got the idea anyway and I planned to carry it out.

The next morning was clear and hot and I drove myself up to where they were filming and got on my cowboy outfit. Lucas was already dressed the first time I saw him, sitting over to one side with Sally Crandall. When he saw me coming toward them, he jumped up and put his hands on his guns like he would draw, and my madness went out for just a second, but I thought of Betty and it came back.

"Leave him alone," Sally Crandall said softly. She was still grateful I'd found the old jerk, I reckon. "He told me what happened. You shouldn't have lied to Betty, and you know it."

Lucas stood there with his hands on his guns trying hard to smile but never quite making it.

"Ask him where he was when I called from that motel in Dallas," I said. Lucas made this sort of strangled noise.

"I'm having another vision!" he said and he fell to his knees.

"He says he's only speaking the truth now," I said mild as I could. "Ask him where he was when I said he was on a bad side of town by that phone booth." Lucas laid out flat on the ground in front of us. A wind had come up and Sally Crandall's hair lifted a little on the breeze.

"I see the spirit of Crazy Horse," chanted Lucas lying flat on the ground. A couple of men dressed up like Indians wandered by and looked down at Lucas, then at one another and shook their heads. "He is saying to speak no more of things past."

"Where were you?" asked Sally Crandall to Lucas, sounding sort of puzzled.

Lucas's voice went all airy and choked up and he said, "I am the spirit of Crazy Horse and I command you never to speak of things past as long as the grass is green and . . ." Sally Crandall poked him in the ribs with the toe of her boot.

"Where were you?" she asked. Lucas sat up and glared at me.

"You vengeful tinhorn," he said down low. He looked up at Sally Crandall and smiled sort of sick. "Sweetie, you won't think ill of poor old Lucas, will you?"

"Where?" she asked. She was getting mad now and I felt real good, God help me.

"Tell her," I said.

"Okay, okay," he said, standing up and dusting off his pants. "I was at the Hilton, but as God is my witness, it was one of their budget rooms." Sally stared at him for a second, then at me.

"The goddamn Hilton?" she yelled. Another Indian came by and stopped when she yelled, but then he went on. "You mean you made up . . ."

Sally started backing up and shaking her head.

"What kind of man are you?" she asked. "What makes you do things like this? My God, what am I doing?" She turned away from Lucas. "I'm about to blow it again. Get your things out of my room by tonight and get out of my life, you bastard." I started grinning like a bobcat and couldn't stop. Lucas fumbled around trying to find something to say, but she just stomped off and left us there looking at each other.

"I reckon you do need another vision, Kid," I said.

"Don't call me that," he said. He took off his cowboy hat and threw it on the ground and sat down next to it. The assistant director called for us all and we went for our scenes, but Lucas looked limp and we just walked through them for about an hour. I turned in my costume and went home, not saying another word to Lucas.

There was to be a break of a week and then we'd finish with three days shooting of the scene when Sally and her girl are rescued from the Indians. When I got back, driving down the still-muddy road to Owensville, I felt sort of sad but not angry any more, just sad for everything.

All the men were out working. Wool was sitting in a chair watching a soap opera and calling the actors bastards and bitches and stuff and laughing like a maniac. I went on down to Lucas's study and closed the door. Wool had told me Lucas had taken everything with him. But he'd left one thing. The pages were still all over the floor where they'd fallen the night before.

I sat in his chair and looked out the window. It was summer, the hot season, the growing season, but I felt like something was dying in me, and maybe I was dying myself. I don't know. I only knew I felt awful. I sat there for a long time looking at those pages on the floor. I couldn't stand it, so I got down and started putting them in order. I got most of it done and sat back down in the chair and looked at the title page.

It said, "*Blue Skies*, A Novel by Lucas Kraft." I flipped the page and it said this: "This book is for Jake Baker."

I went out and laid on the slope overlooking the creek and asked God to give me a vision about things. I asked him if I was to die soon, and I got this feeling I wouldn't and that made me happy. The clouds drifted over me real slow, boiling up for some thundershowers, and I looked for shapes in them but didn't see much.

I reckon what I felt most was peaceful. And I wanted to think about how I could pull things all back together. It hurt so bad not to be loved that I wanted to get it back.

THE NEXT MORNING, just as I was finishing with the breakfast dishes, Betty came up to the Long House. I was feeling okay, and when I saw her standing there in the kitchen, I felt my knees get sort of weak. She wasn't pretty but there was something about her that made me love her just the same.

We stared at each other for a minute across the room and Wool left to go watch some game show. For the longest time we looked at one another and then she came over to me and put her arms around me and we kissed and just stood there holding one another.

"I'm so sorry," she said, whispering.

"I'm sorry," I repeated. "I just didn't want to hurt you about who Loretta was, that's all."

"I know," she said. "Let's walk down to the garden." So that's what we did, arm in arm, down to the big vegetable garden Chuck kept behind the house. Even though it was only June, things were growing green and tall because Chuck watered it every evening at dusk. He'd stayed busy since Missy had died but it was sad to watch him alone, and we all kept hoping he'd meet some new woman to comfort him. I can speak well for a woman's comfort, even at my age.

There were a couple of lawn chairs right in front of the garden in a shady arbor where we would often sit at night and watch the stars. We sat down and she held my hand.

"She'd of turned out right if you'd a been around to teach her," I said. "It's not a bit your fault."

"Oh hell, who knows how anything's going to turn out?" she sighed. "She might've turned out a whore even if she'd stayed with me." That word "whore" really gave me a start, hearing her say it about her own daughter, but it was true. "But I laid awake most of last night thinking, sweetheart, and I want you to take me over there to see her."

"Lord, Betty, I don't think that's too good of an idea," I said. "She lives a pretty hard life. I didn't tell you because . . ."

"I know why you didn't tell me" she said. "Jake, you are an old asshole, but you're my asshole." I kind of flinched because I still didn't hold with that kind of talk from a woman, but I knew she meant well, so I let it pass. "I just want to sit down with her and talk, not for long. But I can't just let her sit over there and not know she's got a mama she can come home to."

"I told her about you."

She said, "That don't matter. It's not the same telling and seeing. You and Lucas can take me back over and just wait in the car. I can handle it."

That was when I had to tell her about Lucas, about what I'd done. She put her face in her hands and kept saying "Lord, Lord" while I told her. I didn't know where Lucas was but I was a little worried about him.

"I caused all this mess by not loving you like I ought to," she said. One tear came out her right eye and wandered down her cheek. "I think you ought to go whip that Indian's ass."

"Wasn't his fault," I said. "He was just trying to get us to see the truth about things instead of how we think they might be."

"Sometimes the truth about things is enough to make you puke," she said.

"That's true," I said.

"Look, sweetie, you find your buddy and bring him over here and we'll settle it all up and go find my baby, okay?"

"I don't know," I said. "He probably don't never want to see me again. We had a good fight and I beat his head on the floor. He'd moved in with Sally Crandall and now she's thrown him out. No telling where he might be."

"Then we'll just have to go see Sally and get her to help us find Lucas."

"Ain't we been down this road one time before?" I asked.

"This time it's for me, Jakey," she said. And she leaned on my shoulder and we sat that way until we began to touch one another and kiss, and before you could say jackrabbit we were upstairs in the guest bedroom, having left a trail of clothes all across the room. When I was a young man, I was a good lover, and I'm not just bragging because any number of young ladies told me that. But when you get older, it's not so easy, so it was a surprise to me that I did so good that day. In fact, I probably never did better in my whole life, and when we got through, Betty was panting like a winded hound and I wanted to

299

howl and climb out on the roof and beat my chest like Tarzan. I've heard preachers say God invented sex only for creating younguns, but I can't help but think the Almighty knew something about love and pleasure, too, which sure makes me think more of him.

We got dressed and drove up to the movie set where nothing much was happening. I found the trailer where Sally stayed and the door was locked and nobody came when I banged on it, so I went over to her friend Hugh's trailer. He opened the door with a beer in his hand. He looked miserable. He had on some old stained khaki pants out of which his drawers had climbed, and his face was bloated, his eyes red and puffy.

"Howdy, Hugh," I said. He stared at me and Betty.

"Come on in," he said. We climbed in and the place was a mess but we sat down on this sofa and he closed the door. At least the air conditioner worked. "You all want a beer?"

"No thanks," I said. "We're just looking for Sally. She got a few days off before the last scenes of the rescue?"

"That's right," he said. "She flew out to the coast for a few days until then. You need her for something? Don't tell me it's about Lucas. God, the word's all over this place. It's going to be in the fan magazines and I heard there's a reporter for *People* magazine snooping around here."

"I'll be damned," said Betty. "The real *People* magazine? I read that at the beauty parlor." Hugh looked at her like he was seeing something from Mars.

"Anyway, she's gone and I don't really know where Lucas went," he sighed. "It looked like for a time they were back to where they were years ago, all lovebirds and it was a thing to see, but then they had this big fight. But I guess you know about that. Sally told me you and Lucas hated one another and that now she hated both of you. I never saw her so miserable in her life."

"We don't hate one another," I said. "There's just been a lot of confusion about things."

"You think this reporter might know Porter Wagoner?" asked Betty. Hugh stared at her again and just shook his head and sprayed beer drops from his droopy mustache.

"Well, we're obliged," I said, and we got up and left. There was something about Hugh and the movie that seemed alike to me, a sense that nothing mattered. At first, everybody thought the movie was a fine thing, but now it was like some bad joke that kept getting told over and over.

We drove down toward Abilene to see if Lucas might be at Sally Crandall's room at the Holiday Inn. For a long spell, Betty was quiet, but finally she talked to me.

"I can't imagine being a whore," she said. "Just doing it for money, I mean without any love nor nothing. God-damn, that would be terrible. She could at least clean house or anything. But to let strangers get inside a her body and . . ." She sort of shuddered and I felt so bad I couldn't think of anything to say, and it was like that all the way to Abilene.

I parked under the balcony of her room and me and Betty went up there and banged on the door, but nobody was around. The curtain was pulled open and unless he was in the john, he wasn't in there, so we went down to the bar and looked around there, but no Lucas.

We drove around crazy all during the day, stopping to eat a hamburger, but I didn't have a clue where he might be. Maybe he'd flown out to the coast with Sally Crandall. Maybe they'd made up, but I reckoned there wasn't a bat's chance in hell of that. Finally, with the sun easing down over west Texas, I stopped at a liquor store on the outskirts of Abilene and bought a bottle before we headed back north. Abilene, I heard tell from Chuck, was where John Wesley Hardin had killed three men back in the 1800s, but they'd not had liquor until 1978, not for seventy-five years. I don't hold with a town not having liquor myself. It's a comfort, though it's a bad thing, too. But nothing's bad except in the hands of the wrong folks.

Halfway back to Harkin County, I took a slug from the neck of the bottle, bubbled it good twice and so did Betty. She could drink — Lord could she drink — and so we enjoyed the warm feeling and drove slow as winter syrup.

"I know where he is," I blurted out. Now this sounds peculiar, but it was like somebody's else's voice inside me saying it.

"If you know where he is, why in the hell have we been wandering all over creation?" asked Betty.

"It just come to me," I said, and I took another drink and drove up toward our vision pit. I got lost one time and by the time I got turned around, it was nearing dark, only a few streaks of light in the west. "Wool is going to barbecue me for missing supper again."

"He's an old son of a bitch," said Betty, and that was true, but he was still my friend. I parked on the side of the road. There was no car around, but Lucas couldn't drive anyway. We got out and took the bottle, climbed through the barbed wire fence and walked up to the top of the slope where Old Buffalo had dug that pit. It was the kind of evening you'd like to bottle and take out once in a while to sniff. The air was warm and fresh and smelled like dirt and trees and other good things. I liked Betty walking beside me. She walked with those fine strong legs. I liked watching how her body moved under her clothes.

"Lucas!" I yelled when we were about forty feet from the hole. There wasn't an answer. I yelled his name again.

"Oh, great," came this faint, sort of disgusted voice. I looked at Betty and grinned and we went on up to the hole and kneeled down and looked in, and there he was, lying on his back, naked as God made him, fat and wooly.

"Howdy, Kid," I said. Betty looked down at him and started sort of snickering, and Lucas groaned when he saw her and put his hand over his privates.

"You have invaded my death chamber, you rube," he said. His voice was weak and far-away sounding. His clothes were neatly folded on the edge of the hole. "I have come here to be swept up into the loving arms of God and now you have ruined it. Isn't it enough that you hate the very blood that courses through my veins? Are you and that woman no longer blood enemies?"

"Don't call me that woman, you old fart," said Betty.

"We're back together, no thanks to you," I said.

"Nothing that has transpired on this earth is any thanks to me," he said. "I am merely an idle king with neither sons nor daughters nor friends to carry my name upon the winds. And now I am come home to the bosom of my God."

"I didn't think you believed in God," I said.

"Sssshhh!" he said. "You are burning bridges I have nearly mended, you dumb cracker. I believe in something now. You have to believe in something. I thought it was truth I believed in, but truth is fragile, Jake, dust on the wings of a monarch. You can only believe in one thing. Hope. Without that, this rotten sphere is drear and void, old friend. The next road, the next adventure. I thought I had run out of adventures until I met you."

"Well, I reckon it's a good thing you got put in Fieldstone," I said. He sat up, still holding his privates. Betty didn't turn away and I didn't mind because somehow it was like looking at something that didn't have sexual parts. It was just old Kid Kraft.

"Give us a draught from your bottle," he said, and I gave it to him and he took a big drink. "I came to Fieldstone on my own. Another custom lie from Lucas Kraft. I was hoping to find out enough to write a novel on nursing homes. And then I ran into you, Jake. You are quite a character."

"Come on and get dressed," I said. "Let's go home. In the morning, me and Betty are going over so she can meet her daughter proper and I want you to come." He laid back down in the hole. It was all but dark now.

"How dull it is to pause, to make an end," he said.

"Get up," I said, but he didn't move. I looked at Betty and she couldn't say a thing. I thought about what would make Lucas get up, something sort of mystical, like a Bible verse, and it came to me. There was something holy about that place Old Buffalo had taken us. I don't know how, but it was, and one word came into my head.

"Goodbye," said Lucas.

"Arise," I said, and I held my arms out over the hole. "Arise, Lucas Kraft, and be whole." I probably never said a better sentence in my life and it sure sounded good up there. He sat up again and reached out for me and I grabbed his hand and pulled him up. Betty turned away because his little dinger was swinging between his fat legs, pitiful and shrunk up and she did have a bit of modesty.

"I . . ." he said as he was dressing. "I'm sorry. I'm sorry for both of you. I'm learning a lot, but it's certainly too late for redemption. You can't lead a horse to water."

"Aw hell, you're the horse's ass," said Betty, and then the three of us, in total dark, walked back down to the car, passing the bottle and holding each other up.

It was a wonder I got home at all that night, drunk as I was, but I did, and when we came down the long road to the ranch, Chuck and a woman were sitting out on the porch drinking and laughing and it made me feel so good I felt like hollering, so I did when I drove by.

"What in the hell did you do that for?" asked Betty, who'd jumped from being scared.

"I was just happy," I said. She laughed and then Lucas tried to holler but it was a kind of screech and I nearly wrecked I was laughing so hard. Wool was leaning in the doorway of the Long House smoking his corncob pipe and looking around at the sky. I got out and still felt happy and drunk.

"Lookey there," I said as we all fell out, "there's Wool, the best colored cook in Harkin County."

"Eat a big one, Jake," said Wool without taking the pipe out of his mouth. Well, that was the funniest thing I could imagine, and I fell down laughing and so did Lucas, and Betty just plopped down on her big bottom and handed me the bottle back. "You all drunk."

"I recommend it heartily, you culinary cretin," said Lucas. He took the bottle from me and held it up toward Wool, who sat with us and took a long pull. Before long, Whizzer Pippin and Tree were helping me and Lucas to bed. I didn't remember what had happened before that. I just remember Wool dancing around the room acting like he was playing a guitar and screeching some rock and roll song.

"Where's Betty?" I managed to say.

"Took her down to Chuck's," said Whizzer, leaning over me. "She's all right, Jake." The last thing I heard was a deep laugh from Whizzer and the voice of Kid Kraft calling somebody a bad name.

We were going to go to Dallas the next morning, but we were all sick and it rained anyway. Lucas and I sat in the den and stared at the walls the whole day, feeling like the dead. Betty stayed down at the Big House doing the same thing.

The next day, the sun was back out and we all felt well again, so we packed us a lunch and Betty drove us over toward Throckmorton on 380, which is the way you go. We went in Betty's old car, a Volare that coughed and spit sometimes, but it held us all, me and her in the front, Lucas in the back reading out loud from some tabloid he'd bought when we stopped to buy Cokes.

"Woman bears child of abominable snowman," read Lucas.

"I don't know what in the hell I'll say to her," said Betty. She looked tired and scared of seeing Loretta Michelle, but eager, too. "You think she'll hate me? I mean, shit, it wasn't me who left her, it was that asshole I married who stole her away from me."

"Siamese twin gets other twin pregnant," said Lucas.

"I don't think it's going to be so bad," I said. "Just keep easy and don't do nothing dumb. Just talk to her and see what she wants to do. I mean, you couldn't hardly support her, could you?"

"Not me alone," she said, and she reached out and touched my hand and I felt scared as if I'd just fallen back behind the Nazi lines like in the Big War. "But I don't know what I'll say. Sometimes it's like a dream. There I was sitting beside her and didn't even know it."

"I wish she had been a princess," I said.

"I'm not a princess, neither, you old son of a bitch," said Betty, and I smiled and she went back to driving.

"German shepherd possessed by the devil," said Lucas.

We went the same way we'd gone last time, through Newcastle, Graham, then to Jacksboro. Betty wanted to drive around and see her old stomping grounds, but I talked her out of it, so we shot off down 199, which led you through Agnes and Azie into Fort Worth. I've said that Loretta Michelle lived in Dallas and I think that's right, but frankly I'm not too sure, because it's all really one big town stretching out for miles and miles. Downtown Dallas is like a city, but after that, it's just suburbs and buildings forever, not like something you'd ever expect to see out in Texas.

I remembered how to get to Loretta Michelle's using this freeway, and though I got us lost one time for about ten minutes, soon we were right in front of that clinic where we'd found Lucas, and from there I directed Betty to her daughter's house without much trouble. She parked the Volare and turned it off.

"I'm afraid," Betty said. She was still holding on to the steering wheel and her hands were shaking. "She probably don't want to hear nothing from me. I'm just some old lady to her." I didn't move. We had the windows down and it was getting hot. The only sound was a lawn mower off somewhere and Lucas turning pages in the back seat.

"You worrying too much," I said.

"I remember the day she was borned," said Betty. "I was scared then, too, scared I was going to hurt so much and die, but then I was crying and she just sort of slipped out and I heard her crying and it was so pretty."

"Lose all your cellulite in fifteen seconds," Lucas said. We got out of the car. The grass in front of the house, what little there was, had grown up and it was full of beer cans and cigarette butts.

"What if she's not home?" said Betty as we got near the front door.

"She works at night," said Lucas, and Betty turned and glared at him, but she was too worried to hold it for long. I glared at Lucas, too, and he tried to smile like he was sorry, but it was a kind of snarl. Poor old Lucas. I knocked on the door.

Nothing happened for a long time, but then it opened a crack and she was standing there in cutoff blue jeans and a man's T-shirt, the kind with the arms scooped out. Her hair was tangled and she was sleepy-eyed and fumbling to light a cigarette.

"Yeah?" she said, and then she recognized me. "Jesus, man, why don't you just move in, huh? What is it this time?" She let the door swing back on its hinges and went into the living room and sat on a mattress on the floor. I went in first, then Betty, holding onto my arm, and then Lucas.

"You looking better than you did last time," she said to Lucas.

"I am positively elated by your sympathy," Lucas said, turning away to look out the window. I sat down on the floor and Betty sat beside me, still holding my arm.

"So what's up?" she said.

"Loretta, this is . . ." I started, but she interrupted me.

"Is that my name now?" she said, blowing smoke through her nose. "Oh, wow."

"Watch your mouth," Betty blurted, and then she put her hand on her mouth like it would stop any more words.

"What's it to you, bitch?" Loretta asked.

"Don't talk to your mama that way," I said. Betty held on to me tighter and started crying and Loretta just stared at us for a minute and then threw the butt from her cigarette, still burning, into an old aquarium that was no longer bubbling and was full of trash. It landed with a hiss.

"Is this bullshit or what?" asked Loretta. "What you said, that's bullshit, right?"

"No," said Betty. "I'm your mama." Loretta looked down and nodded and then looked at Betty and then started shaking, first at her neck and then her shoulders and then her whole body was shaking, and she was looking down in her lap.

"I believe I just saw a rodent in your driveway," said Lucas.

"My mama," said Loretta, still shaking all over, and she took a long drag off the cigarette she'd just lit. Betty was crying and howling like a baby and she reached out toward her girl, but Loretta didn't move a muscle toward her and Betty pulled her hand back. "Long time, no see, right?"

"I didn't know where you was," said Betty. "Or I'd of come for you, I swear to God, baby, I would have. But I didn't know where you was. And look at you, baby, oh Lord God, just look at you here in this old house in this mess."

"You old whore," said Loretta. Betty sat up real straight.

"What did you say?" she hissed.

"Daddy told me about how you'd up and left him, whoring all over Jack County," said Loretta.

Betty stopped crying all of a sudden and jumped over toward Loretta and quick as a cat slapped the fool out of her, knocking her cigarette across the room. I got up and

walked over and stomped it out while Loretta was holding her face and Betty was shaking mad.

"That's a goddamn lie!" yelled Betty. Lucas walked out
of the room and onto the porch. "I was faithful and he
was the one running around. You ever asked anybody in
Jack County who done what? Hell no you ain't, or you'd
know the truth."

"Why would my own daddy lie to me?" she asked, now
crying a little and her nose running. I would have left,
but I felt like I ought to be there for Betty.

"Because he was weak," said Betty, her voice calming
down some. She grabbed Loretta by her thin, wasted
shoulders. "Sweetie, there's things you ought to know
about your daddy. But I won't spoil your memories if you
won't spoil mine. I just don't want us to . . . I just think
we should . . ."

They were both crying then and I went out on the
porch and sat with Lucas in the shade. A skinny dog
loped by and glared at us but didn't bark and then a car
went by, but there weren't many other sounds.

"They're talking," I said. Lucas was quiet for a spell.

"I can't live without her," he said real soft.

"Sally?"

"Yeah. I can't live without her and she can't live with
me."

"I'm sorry about what I did, Kid."

"It was all my fault," he said. "Everything that's ever
gone wrong in my life was my fault. Nothing sticks to me,
Jake. I can't seem to keep anything in my life for more
than a few months. Except you." He turned his great
body and looked at me. "Except you. Why is it that you
and I have managed to stay together when I have made a
shambles of all else in my life? I don't understand what
quality of yours enables you to stay with me."

"Hell, me neither," I said. "Maybe I don't like getting bored."

"Oh, well, I'm not boring," said Lucas.

"That's true."

"But I must get her back this one last time, Jake. This time, she will stick with me, too."

I was going to tell him I thought he'd be better off looking for another lady when there was a scream from inside and the sound of glass breaking. I got up and went back in just as Betty was grabbing Loretta by the arm and trying to drag her out.

"I said no!" yelled Loretta.

"Jake, tell her she's coming home with me!" said Betty, sort of frantic. Loretta broke away and huddled in a corner, picked up an old Pepsi bottle and threw it toward us. It hit the wall but didn't break. Pepsi bottles are hard to break.

"I'm not coming, I can't come," whined Loretta. "Don't you understand? This is what I am, you old bitch, this is what I am."

"You can change," pleaded Betty. She was crying again, heaving and not in good shape. This was turning out to be a worse idea than I'd thought.

"Bullshit," said Loretta.

"You still underage, you slut, I can take you with me!" screamed Betty.

"And I'll stay as long as you got me locked up!" yelled Loretta. "Then I'll be right back over here." She sat up and shivered but calmed down a little. "You might of been my mother one time, but you ain't no more. Can't you understand that? Can't you understand you're just some old woman to me?"

Betty turned to me and I held her and she cried and cried and I glared at Loretta, but it didn't do a lick of good. She was lost to Betty and there was nothing I could do about it. Loretta lit a cigarette and sat back down on her mattress on the floor. Betty then fumbled around in her pocketbook and got a pencil and a little piece of paper and wrote something on it and turned and handed it to Loretta.

"This is my phone numbers," she said. "One at home, one where I work. If you ever need anything, call me." Loretta looked at the numbers like she couldn't understand them, then she nodded, folded up the paper and put it on the mantel.

"I will," said Loretta real soft. "Look, I uh . . . I'm sorry things didn't happen right for us. Don't get too stressed out, lady. Life's just a bitch anyway, right?" Loretta tried to smile but it wouldn't stay.

"Depends on who loves you," said Betty. She walked over and hugged Loretta once and turned back to me and I held onto her and we went outside where Lucas was still sitting.

"Let's get the hell out of here," Betty sniffed. We stopped by a restaurant, but nobody was much hungry, so before we got out of Fort Worth we stopped and got a bottle. I drove and Lucas and Betty got drunk.

They talked for a long time, but I was hardly listening. I was watching the plains start to unroll around us, and I thought about all my old cowboy heroes, Johnny Mack Brown, Hoot Gibson, William S. Hart, Lash LaRue, even Roy Rogers, though I thought a real cowboy shouldn't ever sing. I thought about Hopalong Cassidy and John Wayne, who was my biggest hero of all. It was so awful to watch the Duke shrivel up and die of that cancer. Cowboys shouldn't ever die and neither should heroes of any sort. But they do, they always do, and I knew one day I'd die right along with them. I wondered if there was a spot in heaven just for cowboys. What a wonder that would be, all of them roping and shooting and riding better than anybody ever did on this earth.

I was thinking of cowboy heaven most all the way home and so missed out on much of what Lucas and Betty were saying. By the time we crossed the Harkin County line, they were both oiled up pretty good and Lucas was saying he was going to get back Sally Crandall and then the four of us would build our own ranch.

"How are you going to get her back, Kid?" I asked. He thought about it for a spell. Betty burped real big, which I thought was bad, but Lucas didn't notice.

"Love," he said. "Or kidnapping. One of those."

"Here's to kidnapping," said Betty, her words all slurred together.

"Here's to love," I said real soft, but I don't think either one of them heard me.

I DON'T KNOW WHY GOD'S let me live so long and
see so many things. When I was a boy I thought old folks
were all real smart on account of having lived through so
much, but that's not so. The only good thought that's ever
occurred to me is that one man makes his own life and
can be happy in this world if he can once in a while
bleach the anger out of his bones.

The week after we took Betty to see her daughter was
pretty quiet. Me and Lucas would go out in the warm
evenings just when the stars were rising with the moon
and sit and talk, mostly about Sally Crandall. He wanted
her back so bad he couldn't hardly stand it, and I knew it
was my fault she dropped him again.

Sometimes he'd seem normal and then sometimes he'd
seem like himself. I asked him how he'd get Sally back
this time.

"You are talking to an award-winner," he said in that
big round voice of his. I was sitting in Scout's chair and

Lucas was beside me. It was the night before they started shooting the rescue scenes, and we had to be there at eight to get back in our cowboy outfits. I was already a little sad about not being able to wear mine any more after the movie.

"What does that have to do with anything?" I asked.

"Nothing, you ninny," he said. "But sometimes I throw in that fact to dazzle people with my accomplishments."

"Speaking of that, I saw where you finished your book," I said. He turned and stared at me.

"You saw that thing, huh?" he said. "Well, more's the pity. Just something else that'll never be published. My career is like Banquo's ghost, just hanging around waiting for the next gust of wind to cast it into the aether."

"I bet you could get a lot of money for it," I said.

"Of course I could get a lot of money for it, you back-woods hick," he said. "I want to know how not to get money for it. That's the trick. I'm tired of being a whore."

"Then give it away," I said. "If you give it away, it's not whoring. It's love." He stared at me for a long time and then started laughing real soft. "What are you laughing about?"

"Jake, you are of a different time," he said. "I could almost start believing in things if I hung around with you long enough."

"I thought you already had," I said.

"Maybe I have." He looked up into the stars. It was a cool night, a front having gone through, and millions of stars spread out across the plains to the north. Maybe I'd never seen a night like it in my life.

The next morning, while the bacon was frying and the coffee was perking and the radio blasting, Wool wanted to show me how to do some new dance step he'd learned.

"I've got to get finished and go up to the movie," I said.

He said, "Fuck that, boy. We are talking here about my music." He came over and grabbed me by the hand and started jerking all over and dragging me with him while we listened to some loud rock and roll. "It's bad!"

"Wool, you're breaking my arm," I said. About that time, Tree and J.D. and Whizzer Pippin and a few other cowboys came in and started laughing and whistling at us.

"Sure your name ain't Bojangles?" asked Whizzer, and Wool gave him the finger, let me go and danced over to flip the dozens of pieces of bacon he had frying. Wool might have been a mite weird, but he could cook more and have it all done on time than any man I ever saw.

"Sure your name ain't asshole?" yelled Wool over the music. They all laughed, even Whizzer, because Wool was our friend. Wool and Tree were the only two black folks in the Long House. There weren't many black folks around there for some reason I never understood. Not too many black cowboys. But we all got on together good and whenever somebody said nigger or honkey, it didn't mean nothing.

We were standing there watching Wool dance when Lucas came out from the shower area, looking dandy, like he had a million bucks in his pocket, grinning from ear to ear and whistling.

"Smell him," said Whizzer, elbowing J.D. and pointing at Lucas. "Smells like a Tijuana whorehouse on Saturday night."

"Very original," said Lucas. "Quite original. Ever think of writing that down and becoming rich?" Tree giggled and stretched. J.D., who was always a good sport laughed, too and shrugged.

317

"You look like somebody who needs an introduction," I said.

"Then give me one, Jake, me boy," said Lucas. He pulled himself up a little, which didn't do much good. I cleared my throat.

"Gentlemen, I'd like you to meet one of the bravest hombres in the Old West," I said. "This here's Kid Kraft, the legendary cowboy who has saved ranches in range wars, loved women, fought fights for justice all over this here land. He's saved the honor of women and made this a safer place to live. Some man, that Kid Kraft."

Wool, who had stopped dancing, busted out laughing and the others snickered, but I don't think Lucas heard a one of them. He was staring straight ahead, chin out, just like he believed every word I'd said.

By the time we got to the wardrobe trailer and got in our cowboy outfits, the sun was up good, but the heat had broke and it was as pleasant a day as you'll ever find in Texas in June, a light breeze coming down from the north and the wind smelling of the land.

"Sally, my darling Sally," Lucas said as we walked along, our spurs jingling. "You're my Yellow Rose of Texas." He hummed and sang and clapped his hands together. I don't think I ever saw him happier.

We had to be in the Indian village by nine, and we were on time, milling around there with Indians and cowboys and cavalry folks and such. Old Buffalo was squatting beside a teepee drinking a can of Diet Sprite. We stopped to say hello before the shooting started.

"Howdy, Old Buffalo, how's it going?" I asked.

"Visions are a pestilence," said Lucas, but he was still happy.

"Drink," said Old Buffalo, holding up the sweating can.

"Drink?" said Lucas.

"Don't start that again, " I said.

"Come," said Old Buffalo. We jingled after him and went inside one of the teepees where we surprised a man and a woman who had her shirt off.

"Whoops," said Lucas. We backed out and went to the next teepee and sat down. Old Buffalo had an orange nylon backpack in there and he took out a large bottle of Old Grand Dad.

"Kid, I don't think you ought to be tangling with that bottle," I said. "If you want to get Sally back, you can't do it drunk."

"My capacity for drink is boundless," said Lucas. It was hot as hell in there, so I suggested we take the bottle and go down to a grove of cottonwoods that grew along a stream not far from the fort. We still had about forty minutes before they needed us. We walked down there, Old Buffalo looking around real funny, like he expected the cavalry to come get him.

We got down to the creek and sat in the shade and Old Buffalo held the bottle out in front of him and mumbled a few sentences in Indian that I couldn't understand. He gave the bottle to Lucas and he held it out in front of him and said, *"Veni, Vidi, Vici,"* which he explained to me was Latin. He passed the bottle to me, and I held it out in front of me and started singing "Happy Trails to You," but Lucas and Old Buffalo started yelling at me, so I stopped and we had us a few bubbles of the bourbon.

"What have you learned?" Old Buffalo said, looking into the water of the creek.

"That drinking on hot days will make you puke," I said.

"He isn't talking to you, Jake," said Lucas, gritting his teeth. "It was my vision. I have learned . . ." Lucas squinted his eyes, took another drink and stared at the water with Old Buffalo. I looked down into it, too, but all I saw were some minnows. "I have learned that man is redeemable. I have learned that love is all that ever makes you feel really right. I have learned that if I ever again go looking for my heart's desire, then I don't have to look farther than my own back yard, because if it's not there, I never lost it to begin with."

"That's pretty, kid," I said.

"It's from *The Wizard of Oz*, you illiterate cowhand," sighed Lucas.

"Good," said Old Buffalo.

"Quit calling me names or I'll break this bottle on your head," I said. Lucas nodded.

"I'm sorry," he said. I didn't want any more, but Lucas and Old Buffalo kept drinking until the bottle was empty. When we walked back up the hill, they were both wobbling and laughing and Old Buffalo was talking a blue streak, saying how he had to get back up to Dakota because he was a civil engineer working on a dam project, and that was a real shock. I figured he really lived in a teepee, but I was awful stupid about a lot of things still.

We separated and I went to the set and got my first glimpse in a while of Sally Crandall. She was huddled over to one side with a man who was slim as a mink and whose hair was black and looked like it had been molded from plastic. He had three gold chains showing on his chest and a sweater was tied by the arms around his neck like there was somebody behind him trying to strangle him. I don't know why he had the sweater. It was cooler than before, but still in the low eighties.

Sally was looking around her just like Old Buffalo was, like she expected Indians to get her. I laughed out loud when I thought that, because in *Shadow of the Wind*, the Indians already had her and her little girl. The girl was

sitting on a box eating a Baby Ruth and drinking a Dr
Pepper. Off to one side, the cavalry was milling about on
their horses, with the star in front looking like he didn't
know a thing about horses. I looked around for Lucas but
didn't see him.

I wished Betty had come with me, but Chuck and his
new lady were having a house party and she had to stay
home and cook. She was mad as a wet hen.

All of a sudden, Indians were everywhere. A campfire
in the middle of the village was lit and the breeze blew
the smoke high up into the blue sky. It wouldn't have
been too hard to pretend it really was pioneer times. Sally
Crandall looked up and saw me and whispered something to the guy with the chains and then came over to
talk to me. I pulled my guns up and tried to stand up
straight. Lord, that woman was still pretty, but her face
was kind of tormented, and when she stopped at me, she
took my arm and only said three words: "Where is he?"

"He's here," I said. "Sally, I was wrong to tell you what
I did. He didn't mean nothing by it. He's just felt like for
a long time that didn't nobody love him. He just wanted
to make sure and to have himself another adventure. Last
few years, old Lucas ain't had enough adventures and he
was afraid he'd die without doing a few things."

"He's goddamn sure made up for that," she said,
straining her neck and looking around. "Why isn't he
with you, Jake? The shoot begins in five minutes." She
leaned close to me and I thought she was going to kiss me
and I felt just like John Wayne.

"You've been drinking," she said. "Oh my dear sweet
Jesus."

"It was that Indian," I said, and I'll have to admit it
sounded awful lame. She was standing there staring at
me when the assistant director yelled for places.

"Sweet Jesus," she repeated, and she turned and walked off. I went toward our marks and looked around for Lucas but didn't see him. The way the story went, they told us, was that the cavalry and a bunch of cowboys finally find the Indian village where Sally Crandall and her daughter are being held. There's a big fight and then the Captain comes riding up, jumps off his horse while all the Indians are taking to the hills and Sally and her daughter run up and hug the Captain. All us cowboys had to do was run around shooting. Our guns had blanks and we'd tested them out before. I sure got a kick out of shooting the durned things. So it was just pretend cowboy stuff, just like when I was a boy. I was told I was to count to ten and then go down on one knee and then play-act like I was dead. Some of the other cowboys lived.

Still no Lucas. Sally Crandall and the little blonde girl who was supposed to be her daughter were over by a teepee getting some last-minute makeup by a guy who was tall and walked like a wet spaghetti noodle.

I got my place and looked over to the crowd who were watching a ways back and, sure as I'm living, there was Betty, whistling through her teeth and yelling and waving at me. I figured I had a couple of minutes so I walked quick back that way until she could hear me.

"What are you doing here?" I yelled.

"Got finished cleaning up," she yelled back. A woman next to her asked Betty something, but Betty shook her head and said out loud, "He ain't nobody."

She was wearing jeans and a Western shirt and had her hair all loose and on her shoulders and looked real pretty.

"I got to go," I said. I winked at her and she grinned, but when I turned, I felt this awful, hollow feeling because Lucas was still gone. I was a bit woozy from the liquor, but I felt good and by the time I got back to my mark, everybody was in place and the director, who was sitting in this chair to one side, was standing and looking around. I counted five different cameras, including one from a small crane at the end of the village right beside the Airstream trailer of the makeup man. I looked to my left and saw Hugh, Sally Crandall's manager, smoking a cigarette and rubbing his face. But no Lucas.

I drew my gun. I wondered if there were any real bullets. That wouldn't be such a bad way to go, trying to save Sally Crandall from the Indians. But deep down I knew there wouldn't be. Still no Lucas.

"Ready . . ." said the director. "And . . . action!" Everybody started yelling and moving about and shooting and I did, too, aiming at a hairdresser on the side and shooting him right in the heart. I was having such a good time, shooting all over the place and such that I plumb forgot to count to ten and fall, so I shot four more times into the general mess of folks and screamed at the top of my lungs. It felt good.

I went down on one knee. The assistant director who was working with the cowboys yelled out "Good" when he saw me go down. I dropped my gun and grabbed my chest and stuck my tongue out and shook like a dog out of water and then laid down facing the chief's teepee where I could see the Captain save Sally Crandall. The assistant director, who was of all things a British feller, yelled good again when he saw how I fell. Maybe I could get a career as a movie star.

I saw mostly legs and stuff. Further down the way, the cavalry guys and Indians were fighting hand-to-hand and falling by the wayside. I knew we were to fight about three or four minutes before the Captain rode up on his horse, so I was surprised when I caught sight of the horse out of the corner of my eye. In fact, I had to roll over to avoid getting tromped on.

It was then I saw the rider of the horse and I sat right up and stared.

"Lie down, for God's sake!" yelled the assistant director. "You're dead!" But though I heard him, I stared long enough to see what I was afraid I'd seen. It was Lucas on that big horse and he was moving drunk all over the saddle. I jumped up while the assistant director was screaming "No! No!" and went off after him. He made sort of a circle through the camp before going to the chief's teepee, so I caught up with him for a minute and he saw it was me.

"Jake!" he yelled. "I'm a hero!" I was going to yell back to get off that damned horse, but he kicked the horse and headed toward the teepee. By now, people were falling away, staring at him, and the actors, I mean the real ones, were just quitting and the director was yelling something I couldn't catch. I was about half drunk and out of breath. My chest hurt and I thought I was going to have myself a heart attack right there.

But I didn't. I was about thirty yards away. Sally Crandall and the girl were standing with the chief outside the teepee. She had a look of absolute horror on her face, but it passed and there was something else, almost a smile.

"Kid!" I yelled. "Kid!" I remember thinking that when this was all over I was going to chew him out good. He was almost to Sally Crandall when the girl and the Indian chief ran out of the way, but Sally Crandall stayed fixed on her spot. Lucas passed her, stopped, almost falling off the horse, and came back toward her, fast.

I wish I could describe the look on Sally Crandall's face. It was pain and fear and love and maybe hope of some sort. I don't know. I was yelling "Kid!" as loud as I could, and the director was yelling. Back up behind us, some of the cowboys hadn't heard and they went right on shooting and yelling. The cavalry suddenly came clomping up from the rear but stopped short and looked around.

"Kid!" I yelled, but he didn't hear me. He came toward Sally as fast as he could. She held her arms up toward him and he threw his hat off high in the air and started leaning down like he was going to try and pick her up. When he got about twenty feet from her, he slipped and fell off the horse. I said "Oh, no," which was all I could think of. I started walking toward him as fast as I could but my knees felt like sponge and the faster I went, it seemed like I was getting deeper in the earth.

Sally Crandall ran to him and knelt down. By then others were coming, a doctor I'd seen around giving people shots, a few others. I finally got to him and my heart was in my throat. Sally had managed to pull his head up in her lap and she was getting blood all over her gingham dress.

"You poor fool," she said over and over. I got there just as the doctor did, and she screamed at him to get away and he backed up just like the others there did.

"Oh my God, Lucas, what have you done?" I said as I knelt down. Blood was coming out of his ears and from the corners of his mouth and his neck was turned at a funny angle.

"Easy, baby," said Sally Crandall.

"That which we are, we are," he whispered, blood on every word. "One equal temper of heroic hearts . . ." Then he choked and coughed up blood.

"Sweet Jesus, let him go easy," said Sally Crandall. She was crying and so was I, and so were a couple of people around us. Lucas looked up and closed his eyes and then opened them again.

"I can't remember the rest of it," he said. "Some death-bed speech." Then he closed his eyes again and I got his hand, his hairy old hand, and held it with both of mine. He opened his eyes one more time. "Did we win?"

"You damn right we won, Kid," I said, "and you were the hero." He tried to say something else, but he coughed again and closed his eyes once more.

"I love you," said Sally Crandall. "Goddamnit, I love you."

"I love you, too, Kid," I said, and I thought I felt him squeeze my hand, but I wasn't sure. I was watching him, thinking a million things when I realized his chest had stopped rising and falling, just quit like that, and a cold chill ran all over my body and all of a sudden I quit crying.

"Let me . . ." said the doctor, and he got in between us and put a stethescope on Lucas's chest, but there wasn't a thing to listen to and we all knew it. "He's gone."

"Bullshit," I said, and until later I wasn't sure I knew what I meant, since I knew he was dead. But Sally knew, too, and she hugged him one time and kissed him on the forehead and set him down in the dust and I helped her up.

The man with the slick hair and the chains was beside her and he touched her sleeve but she jerked it away. We stopped and she stared at him and he nodded and walked off. The little blonde girl who played Sally Crandall's daughter was sitting down shivering and crying, a man holding her and patting her on the head and saying, "There, there."

Sally and I walked through the village and people were talking, asking what happened, but neither of us said a thing. We passed Old Buffalo, who was sitting flat on his bottom near a teepee, and I told him Lucas was dead and he started singing this funny, high-pitched Indian song.

Just as we got to the end of the village area, I could see Betty walking fast toward us, her eyes full of questions.

"Dead," I said, and she busted out crying so awful that Sally started again and the two of them went with me to my Jeep and we sat there in the sunshine for a minute until we'd calmed down. A siren sounded far away and then it was closer.

"That crazy damn fool," said Sally Crandall.

"Yeah," I said, and I found myself starting to smile.

"You're being unrespectful," sniffed Betty. "You shouldn't ought to smile when somebody dies."

"Yeah," I repeated, but I couldn't stop. I could almost see old Lucas heading into heaven in his chaps and spurs and six guns and God taking one look and saying, "Well now, cowboy, you've come to a good end. Come on in and rest."

We sat there a spell, not talking, and then Sally got up and headed back toward the village just as the ambulance, neither siren nor light on, pulled back out carrying Lucas. She stopped and looked over her shoulder at me.

"I'll call you," she said. "I've got to be alone now."

"I know," I said. And that's just about how things ended. Betty and I went home and sat for a while before I called the funeral home in Harkin where they'd taken him. They had checked in the courthouse for a will and had found one. They couldn't say what it held, only that it asked that Lucas be cremated and his ashes strewn on the creek down the slope where the cottonwoods grew out at the ranch.

"I be dog," I said. When I told Betty and Chuck, they were surprised, too. One by one, the cowboys came in, and word got around. Betty had to go on home and Chuck had to entertain his guest. I sat outside in the cool plains air and thought about Lucas, about the first time I'd seen him at Fieldstone, about my own family grave-yard back there in Mississippi, about the house I'd built in Georgia. I didn't have much left and Lucas dying left a big hole in my heart I didn't think I could fill.

I sat there all through supper and Wool didn't come get me. I was still sitting there when he came out, still wearing his apron, wet from dishwashing, and sat down in old Scout's chair. He brought a bottle and handed it to me.

"Being alone's one hell of a thing," he said. "Seems like I been alone my whole life sometimes. But it's like this, Jake, don't nobody you love ever die." He looked up at the sky where there were already stars popping out here and there. "I imagine Old Lucas's somewhere out there pissing off angels."

I laughed and took a drink and he took one, too, and one by one, they came out there with me, Tree, Tom, J.D., Whizzer Pippin and seven or eight others, and we talked about Lucas and laughed and drank, and talked some more about the ranch, about cattle and such. And I didn't feel alone anymore, and since that evening out there, I never have.

Two days later, we had services for Lucas. The press was all over town, all over the movie set, but Chuck wouldn't let none of them down to Owensville. The funeral director brought a small box with Lucas's ashes. I was chosen to give a talk since he was my best friend. Betty was beside me, dressed nice and looking pretty. Sally Crandall wore dark glasses, but I could tell she'd been crying, there with Hugh. The man with the chains and the hair was gone. And all the cowboys were turned out, dressed nice, hair combed and acting respectful.

The funeral home man handed me the box and it was heavy and I felt odd. We kind of huddled on the bank of the creek. It was a pretty day, the sky high and blue, a cowboy's kind of day.

"Well, these here are the remains of my pal, Kid Kraft," I said. "There was people knew him longer than me, but maybe nobody knew him better. Lucas was awful strange at times. He always said I was his manager, but what he needed was somebody to hold his hand, just like he was a child afraid of the dark. Well, you don't need to be afraid of nothing anymore, pal." It was sad and I sniffed but I didn't cry. "He loved this land, the creek and the cottonwoods, the big sky and the history. All he wanted was to do something important before he died. I reckon he did that, at least he did with me. Let's make old Lucas part of this land forever."

A wind had come up and I had trouble getting the top off the box, so the funeral director helped me. I walked down to the edge of the creek and stood there and reached my hand in the box. I grabbed a handful of ashes and threw them on the water, but a few blew back on me.

"So long, Kid," I said, and behind me Betty and Sally Crandall were crying bad, and a few of the men were sniffing. I emptied out the box and hit it on the bottom and Lucas went off down the creek, heading for somewhere new.

We went back up to the Long House and had a party, which seemed the only thing to do, and we all got happy drunk except Sally Crandall. She hugged me and left, heading back to the shooting. I never went back and I never saw her again. So far, *Shadow of the Wind*'s not been released, either, though sometimes you read rumors about it in the local papers.

A week after we put Lucas in the creek, they called me from the courthouse and told me that Lucas had left his estate to me.

"What is it?" I asked. A man at the courthouse shuffled some papers and grunted once or twice.

"Well, according to his lawyer in Atlanta, it amounts, in cash and land, to about $300,000." I nodded and then something funny happened. I started to laugh, first like a kind of giggle and then loud, like an old jackass braying. That son of a bitch was rich all the time, and here he was, working for $40 a week in Texas. I think the man at the courthouse thought I was crazy, but I didn't care.

I got the address of the lawyer and sent him Lucas's book. He sent it to Lucas's publisher and they say they're going to print it. They said they'd send me another $75,000. But I told them no thanks. That would have been whoring, like Lucas said.

Me and Betty went to talk to Chuck and I told him I wanted to buy that land up there by the cottonwoods on the creek and put me a little house up there. We sat there in the living room and I thought about Missy Owens and how we'd lost her, and how we'd lost Lucas and Loretta Michelle, too. But I'd found my new Betty, and Chuck was happier than a kid to sell us that piece of land.

In October, just when it was cooling off with winds from the northern plains, me and Betty got married at the Baptist Church there in Harkin. They set to work right away building our house, but I did most of the work myself until I got me a dizzy spell and had to give it up. By the time of the first snow, Mr. and Mrs. Jake Baker were sitting by the fireplace in their home. I'd like to say I used the money to practical ends, but I bought Betty a Mercedes-Benz automobile.

Like I say, it's a peaceful satisfaction here on this creek in the edge of the prairie. I don't reckon I would have ever got here without the Kid, and if he never was all that happy, I'm making up for both of us. That's why I wanted to tell about me and him, because to lots of folks, he was just this dumpy little guy who was a fool without the sense God gave turnips. But he was more than that, and I know, because I was there.

Kid Kraft was my hero.

Philip Lee Williams lives in Athens, Georgia, with his wife, Linda, and son, Brandon.